LITTLE SISTER SONG

WYNTER WILD 1

SARA CREASY

Little Sister Song
by Sara Creasy
www.saracreasy.com
© 2019 Sara Creasy

ISBN: 9781092673259

Dedication

For my mother
whose support in all things
has never wavered

The Wynter Wild Series

books2read.com/saracreasy

1 Little Sister Song
2 Out of Tune
3 Rhythm and Rhyme
4 Lost Melodies
5 Distorted
6 Natural Harmonics
7 Duet
8 Minor Key
9 Broken Strings
10 The Beat Goes On
11 Echoes
Twelve Days of Jessemas

The Fairn Boys Series

Waiting For Her
The Feast That Wasn't

Sign up

to my newsletter for updates and a free story:
saracreasy.com

Something Wonderful

Wynter leaned her guitar against the piano and stacked her sheet music neatly inside the bench.

I have something wonderful to tell you.

Joy's voice still echoed in her ears.

All our prayers answered!

Her sister had whispered the words that afternoon when she and Wynter were alone for a few moments. Wynter never prayed for anything these days and knew nothing about Joy's prayers. She couldn't imagine what the *something wonderful* might be.

With the music part of the program over, people shuffled into a large circle on the temple floor for a Reflections and Intentions session. Wynter took advantage of the few seconds of disorganization to slip out through a side door, unnoticed. On this last day of the winter solstice celebrations, the temple had been warm with the heat of dozens of bodies swaying and singing. Outside, the night air was cold on Wynter's bare legs. She wore shorts and sandals, as she did every day in the desert.

She ran across the compound toward the boundary fence. What *wonderful* thing was so important and urgent it must be said in secret in the middle of the night?

Or was Joy trying to get her alone for some other reason? Wynter was in trouble all the time and sometimes she didn't even know why. Was she heading for a scolding or worse? She *had* spilled the laundry detergent last week. And she'd forgotten to set out the sun tea earlier today, but she was fairly sure no one had found out yet.

Wynter slowed her pace, trepidation mounting, as she walked the length of the ten-foot chain-link fence that divided the compound into two. She passed the familiar rip in the bottom of the fence. How many times had she snuck out of bed and crawled through that hole to spend time in her sanctuary? Perhaps as many as one hundred times. What if Joy had found out about that? What might the punishment be for doing a forbidden thing *one hundred* times?

The moon, almost a full disc in the clear sky, watched her critically. Wynter dragged her feet. In the distance, Joy stood huddled against the perimeter fence near the old crooked gate. It used to be the main gate to the ashram but was rarely used anymore. There were fancy new double gates on the other side of the compound, for the public to use.

"Ten o'clock! I told you to be here by ten!" Joy hissed when Wynter reached her. She shook Wynter by the arm. "And I told you to wear a sweater."

Had she said that? Wynter couldn't remember. She often had trouble remembering things. Her brain felt fuzzy and mixed up much of the time. Joy wore a sweater and a long skirt, and had a tote bag over her shoulder.

"I don't have a sweater."

"You should've found one. Never mind." Joy pulled her to the gate and produced a key for the padlock. Her voice turned breathy and bright as she said, "You'll never guess what's happened. Miriam is flying in from Thailand tonight."

Wynter's breath caught. "Momma's coming home?"

"Isn't it exciting? We're going to surprise her at the airport. I told you it was something wonderful."

Joy sounded more nervous than excited. Wynter could hardly believe her ears. She hadn't seen or heard from Momma in five years — she was doing important work for the Light in Thailand.

"Help me here," Joy said. They hauled open the gate, its edge dragging a quarter-circle scar in the dry dirt. "We'll drive to Tucson and catch the bus to Los Angeles."

"Do you know the way to Tucson?"

"I've printed off a map. You can direct me." Joy handed Wynter a folded-up piece of paper from her bag, and Wynter opened it to reveal a jumble of crisscrossing yellow lines and green blobs and tiny words.

"I don't understand this."

"You're fourteen years old! You can read a map."

"Is Momma coming to live with us here?"

"Maybe, maybe not. We'll ask her. Wait here. I'll drive the truck out, and then you lock up behind us, okay? Then jump in the truck."

As Joy hurried toward the three-sided shelter housing one of the old trucks, Wynter clutched the gate and stared at the dirt road beyond. She had never set foot outside the ashram, had never imagined leaving even when the Australian boys would tell her stories about the outside. This unexpectedly imminent freedom felt surreal.

Behind her, the truck engine turned over a few times before spluttering to life. Joy steered the truck slowly through the gate and stopped on the other side. Wynter pushed the gate back into place, slipping out at the last moment before pulling it closed. With fumbling fingers she snapped the padlock shut. She looked back through the diamond shapes of the fence, across the vast compound, the flat expanse of dirt and scrub, the farm to the left and a cluster of prefab buildings beyond that, a few with lights on. And to the right, the two-story homestead where she lived with its courtyard of packed earth, and the nearby warehouse and office. In the distance, the lanterns of the temple garden shimmered.

Wynter turned away from the fence. She was standing on the *outside*. Standing in the world for the first time, facing the darkness.

A slender white arm beckoned her from the truck window. Wynter drew in a lungful of cold air that cleared her mind. The ground tugged at her feet, a new sensation after a lifetime of feeling so inconsequential she might float away. She ran to the truck, climbed inside, and leaned out to pull the door to.

"Did you lock the gate properly?"

"I think so."

"You *think* so?"

"Yes. Yes, I did."

"Put the key in the glove compartment and find the flashlight." Joy put the truck in gear and set off. "You need to direct me to I-10, toward Benson. I've never been this way except that time Althea drove me to Bisbee."

"Can we go through Bisbee?" Wynter asked. Joy had loved the four days she spent in Bisbee.

"Look at the map, idiot! It's all the way south. We're going to the bus station in Tucson."

Wynter studied the map, printed out on scrap paper from the office — the reverse had a long list on it, probably part of a customer database. The map itself was very confusing. As she tried to make sense of it, they traveled parallel to the fence, passing the farm and outbuildings. In the farthest corner of the compound was the abandoned storage shed, Wynter's sanctuary for the last year-and-a-half. Had she been braver, she'd have asked Joy to let her retrieve a few things from there, just in case they never came back. The little radio, at the very least. Surely Miriam would let her keep that. But months of holding on to so many secrets and lies kept her mouth shut.

Joy hunched over the wheel, eyes darting across the road. Her husband Sean had taught her to drive, but only within the compound.

"Why didn't you ask Sean to drive us to Tucson?" Wynter said.

"He's much too busy tonight. Did anyone see you leave?"

"No."

The flashlight picked out landmarks on the map. Circled on the left, next to I-10, was the bus station. A neatly drawn X on the right edge marked the location of the ashram. It looked to be in the middle of nowhere. Wynter focused on the path between the red X and the circle.

After several tense minutes, Joy stopped at a T-intersection with no signposts.

"Which way to I-10?"

"I don't know. What road are we on? Which way are we traveling?"

Joy snatched the map to study it, looking as confused as Wynter felt.

"I think we're here." Joy jabbed at the map. "So it's right, then we merge with this road, and then left into Touchstone Pass."

Joy set off again. Wynter's stomach churned. This bleak road was the real world, dark and dangerous, and already they were lost.

"Is that a railroad?" Joy said, glancing left. "We have to cross the railroad and head west."

They kept parallel to the tracks and reached a crossing. They passed a church and a lone store.

"Is this the town? Where are the houses?" Joy muttered.

A car approached from the opposite direction, the first sign of life they'd seen outside. Its headlights flashed repeatedly as it passed them.

"Why did they do that?" Wynter said.

"Headlights." Joy fiddled with levers on the steering wheel until she found the switch. "I don't know why they did that. None of their business."

"They were being helpful."

"No. There's no one to help us. Are we going the right way?"

"Yes." Wynter wasn't sure but she didn't want to antagonize her sister further.

A few miles farther, a huge bridge loomed over them. They rounded a bend and found themselves on a wide road, three-lanes in each direction dotted with the lights of fast-moving vehicles. Rocks and dirt rose up on either side.

Another sign flashed by and Wynter sang out, triumphantly, "Tucson, fifty-nine miles!"

A car pulled out sharply and overtook them. Joy gave a cry of alarm. When a second car did the same, Wynter figured perhaps Joy was driving too slowly. She kept quiet about it and fixed her eyes dead ahead, on the dark uneven shapes of a distant mountain range. They drove under another concrete bridge. The minutes and miles trickled past, marked by streaks of poles and wires.

Whenever Wynter tried to speak, Joy told her to shut up so she could concentrate.

As they approached the city, the world became increasingly bright and crowded. People were scarce at this time of night, but cars of all shapes and sizes were parked on the sides of roads. There were closely packed houses, huge stores with labels on them, a maze of roads leading off in every direction, and street signs and overhead signs. Signs everywhere. No one could ever be lost out here when everything was labeled.

Wynter directed Joy off the interstate and onto Congress Street.

"Turn there!" Wynter said, as Joy drove on. "The bus station was back there, down that street on the right."

"I can't park there. They'll know we took the bus if they find the truck parked right outside."

"Why does it matter if they know?"

Joy shook her head sharply, like she was trying to jog her thoughts loose. "That's not what I meant. It's a surprise, remember? We'll park nearby."

A dead weight settled on Wynter's chest. "Were you not supposed to take the truck?"

"You're right, I wasn't supposed to. They don't know about us leaving to meet Miriam. I didn't want anyone to spoil the surprise. We need to hurry. We can't miss that bus."

"We could just drive all the way to LA, couldn't we?"

"It's five hundred miles, Wynter! I can't drive that far."

"You could show me how to. We'll take turns."

Joy fell silent to negotiate a left-hand turn into a side street. She turned left again and pulled onto the side of the road.

"Come on. It's only a short walk back from here."

Joy grabbed her bag, leaving the keys in the ignition to prove they had only borrowed the truck, not stolen it. They went back around the corner, crossed the main street, and walked down a quiet dark road leading to the bus terminal — a squat building with a ramp all the way along the front and big blue doors.

Joy hurried up the ramp. Wynter paused at the bottom, breathless with anticipation, to drink in the view — the moon, the trees with crooked trunks, the street lamps in the parking lot, the tall square buildings across the street with dozens and dozens of windows.

The *freedom*.

Running parallel to the building was the elevated freeway they'd just left, and beyond it a mountain peak with a big white "A" on the side.

"Joy, look! On the outside they even label the mountains."

"Hurry up!" Joy hissed from above.

Wynter ran up the ramp and followed her sister in, and across the open room with rows of gray metal chairs, a ticket counter along the wall, and a row of lettered doors to the bus bays out the back. A board listed all the buses departing that day. Wynter found Los Angeles on the list and her excitement built.

Joy produced a wad of folded bills from her bag as she made her way to the ticket counter.

"Where does all that money come from?"

"I collected it from the office before we left."

Collected?

"You mean you stole it?"

"Miriam will pay them back. It's only two hundred dollars." That sounded like a lot to Wynter. "Wait here."

She nudged Wynter toward a big, brightly lit cupboard that had already caught her attention. Wynter pushed her face up against the glass doors. The cupboard was filled with rows and columns of food, each with a tiny square sticker — A1, B5, C3...

E4 was a candy bar called Snickers. Xay asked her once if you could get Snickers in America, and Wynter said she'd never seen one. She'd never seen any of these snacks before. She pressed buttons on the machine, hoping to get something to eat, *anything*, but nothing fell out.

Across the room, Joy's voice was getting louder as she talked with the ticket seller. Whatever they were arguing about, it seemed to work out in the end. Joy gave the woman behind the counter a lot of cash, and the woman handed Joy some pieces of paper.

"Why were you fighting with that woman?" Wynter said as Joy joined her.

"She wouldn't help me."

"But you bought the tickets?"

Joy nodded and gave one ticket to Wynter. Wynter read it all over, carefully, especially the words *Los Angeles*.

They barely made it aboard in time. The driver raised an eyebrow when Joy said they had no luggage, but was otherwise uninterested. He announced it was an eleven-hour ride to Los Angeles, with several stops along the way.

As they hit the highway, Wynter watched the desert race past. The rumbling bus, heavy and solid, kept her connected to this world. The interior lights were out and she was supposed to be sleeping. Sleep was impossible. Joy dozed all the way to Phoenix. The driver said they could get off for one hour, but Joy wouldn't let Wynter move from her seat. Then they were back on the road.

Joy made Wynter duck her head so she could work on her hair.

"Can't let people see you like this. All these knots and beads... What a mess."

Wynter snuck sidelong looks out the window. The first glow of dawn light was creeping up over the horizon. "Will we go to Disneyland? They have miles and miles of beaches in Los Angeles. We could surf! We might meet a dolphin."

Wynter's mind played through all the things Xay and Roman had told her about life on the outside. The boys were from Australia but knew lots about America from watching TV. What should she do first? Eat a doughnut? Ride a bike? Buy a t-shirt from a store? Hit a bong? She wasn't sure what that last one meant, but the boys used to talk enthusiastically about it.

They might not have time to do anything if Momma wanted to get straight back to the ashram. Still, she hoped to live on the outside at least for a while.

"Where will we live? Can we go to Nevada?"

Joy became evasive and dismissive, and stopped talking altogether. Wynter didn't want to go back to the ashram, but if Momma was there it might be okay. Things had only gotten really bad after she left for Thailand. Momma would help her behave so she stopped getting into trouble all the time. Or maybe they'd all go to Thailand. Joy had talked endlessly about going to Thailand, always hoping she would be summoned there. The summons never came, but now Momma was coming to *them*. There would be plenty of time to do all the things the boys had talked about.

It felt odd to be thinking about Momma with a sense of hope.
She hadn't dared do that in years.

For hours, Joy worked on Wynter's hair, untying and untwisting
it strand by strand. She combed her fingers through the matted
locks, picking out sand grains and tiny beads with her fingernails,
trying to tame those muddy blonde tangles into something
"respectable". Eventually she gave up, unhappy with the results
although Wynter's hair hadn't felt this clean in as long as she could
remember. In Joy's lap was a pile of beads, string, rubber bands,
and a good deal of knotted hair. Joy balled up the lot and dropped
it into a little pocket attached to the seat in front of her. She tied
Wynter's hair into a simple ponytail.

"No more talking," she said, when Wynter started up with her
questions again. "Listen, for a change. Out here, you can't talk
about the Light. You won't fit in. Don't tell anyone about the
things you did at the ashram — not the good things or the bad.
Don't tell anyone how naughty you were or they won't want you."

"Momma won't want me?"

"*No one* will want you."

Wynter didn't care if no one *else* wanted her, as long as Momma
did. "So we're going to live on the outside? Are we leaving the
Light?"

"I told you to *listen*. You never listen, Wynter. That's why you
can't hear the universe speak. That's why you're always in trouble.
You've always been too much trouble. Listen to me now. You keep
quiet about the Light. Everyone out here lives in darkness and they
won't understand. Everything will work out for you *if* you're good.
Please, please, please be good."

Wynter promised she would be good.

"Get some sleep. There's still a long way to go."

But sleep wouldn't come. Wynter pressed her forehead against the
window as stretches of brown dirt and disfigured bushes drifted past,
and the shadowy shapes of distant mountain ranges. Endless miles of
it, unchanging, until she began to feel the entire world was the same
as the view she'd seen from behind the ashram fence all her life.

They crossed into California, slowing to go under a stone
archway topped with a bell and a big WELCOME sign. Wynter
craned her neck to watch the sun rise.

They left the highway and drove into a town.

"Blythe," Wynter read off a sign, white lettering on a green background. "*Bonny and blithe and good and gay.* You used to say that to
me, because I was born on a Sunday."

"And *were* you good?" Joy muttered.

They got off the bus for a restroom break. Wynter asked the driver, "Did we go through Nevada?" She knew Nevada lay between Arizona and California.

"Nevada's just north of here, missy. We don't go through Nevada."

She was disappointed. Xay was in Nevada — at least, that was where he and his mother Ember were headed when they left the ashram last summer.

Joy led Wynter off the bus, scolding her for talking to the driver. Wynter was hungry. Joy said they'd buy food in Los Angeles.

When they set off again, the driver switched on music — a rock station. Wynter recognized some of the songs. She smiled and realized Xay had been right, after all. She didn't need their secret radio in the shed. There were a billion radios out here and music on the airwaves wherever you went.

No Trouble

Wynter dozed on the bus, woken intermittently by the gnawing in her stomach. They arrived in Los Angeles at noon.

Joy glanced around the busy station as if she expected someone to be waiting for them. But no one noticed them — a young woman and a teenager dressed for summer in the mild Californian winter were hardly out of place.

"How will we get to the airport?" Wynter said.

Joy chewed her lip. She guided Wynter to sit on a bench, one of many arranged in long forward-facing rows like chairs in a prayer meeting. While Joy fiddled with something in her bag, Wynter watched the people, fascinated by their clothes and their conversations. Some sprawled motionless on the benches, like they'd been that way for days. Others sat amid their luggage looking anxious or sad or bored. Still others seemed to know exactly where they were going, even if it was only to the restroom or the water fountain.

Joy gave Wynter another bus ticket. "Our journey isn't over."

The bus ticket was for Seattle.

"But we have to get to the airport."

"Miriam isn't here, Wynter. She's in Thailand. There's no plane. She's not coming. Haven't you figured that out yet?"

Wynter had *not* figured it out. Despite Joy's evasiveness, it hadn't occurred to Wynter that she'd invent such a huge lie.

"Why do you think we had to sneak away?" Joy went on, like it was Wynter's fault for being too stupid to realize the truth. "We had to leave the ashram because you don't belong there. I know how scared you are of the outside and I needed you to come right away, without a fuss. That's why I said what I said."

Wynter had never considered leaving the ashram, but she *wasn't* scared of the outside. Xay and Roman had made the outside seem incredible and they'd lived out here longer than Wynter had been alive. It was *Joy* who was scared.

"Can we go to Thailand?" Wynter whispered. "Do we have enough money?"

"Of course we're not going to Thailand. We're going to Seattle."

Seattle was all the way up north, about as far from the ashram as it was possible to be. That alone was a good reason to go. But...

"Why Seattle?"

"The only person I know on the outside is my father. Miriam told me, years ago, that he'd moved to Seattle." Joy flipped over the map Wynter had used earlier. "See? I found his name with an address in Everett, which is near Seattle."

The list of names wasn't from a customer database after all. It was a directory listing — names, addresses, phone numbers. All the names started with F.

"Are we allowed to go to him? You told me he's an apostate."

"Who's going to stop us?" Joy snapped. "Harry is family, and on the outside that means something special. He has to help. I haven't seen him since..." Joy's brow quivered. "I mean, I was just a little girl. But there's no one else." She drew Wynter to her feet. "That ticket seller in Tucson told me I only had enough money for one ticket all the way to Seattle. You'll go ahead of me. I'll follow when I get more money."

Wynter couldn't take it in. "I can't go by myself. Harry's not *my* father. What if he sends me back before you get there? Can't we go to Nevada?"

"Stop talking about Nevada!"

"There's a Light office in Las Vegas. Didn't Ember go there? Ember knows us!"

"Ember isn't in the Light anymore. Why would she help us? She's bad news. You're going to Seattle. I'll call Harry and explain."

Joy dragged her to a payphone, one of several in a row on the wall and covered in a bewildering array of stickers and numbers. She smoothed out the piece of paper on the metal shelf, lifted the receiver, and pushed coins into the slot.

"Read the number to me," Joy said, her hand shaking as she looked over her shoulder like she still expected someone to recognize them.

Wynter peered at the list. There were at least two dozen names, all of them similar but with different initials, like Joy had printed off an entire screen of search results. Fair, Fairn, Farn, Fearn, Fern, Furne...

"Which one?"

"H Fairn, near the top."

She read off the number and Joy dialed. After five rings, someone answered. Wynter could just make out the male voice on the other end of the line — a mumbled query followed by a harsh, confused bark.

Joy hung up, looking more lost than ever. "We can't... we can't go there. That's not a good place."

"But you didn't even ask if he remembers you!"

"There's something wrong with him." Joy staggered back to a seat, arms wrapped around herself. "Miriam was right. She's always right about everything."

Wynter watched Joy fold up in despair. She understood that feeling because Joy had just made her feel it, too, by raising her hopes for a reunion, making her believe Momma wanted her when Momma hadn't even left Thailand and knew nothing about their trip to the west coast in the middle of the night.

Wynter looked at the list again. "Who's C Fairn?" She pointed to the name above Harry's, the only other Fairn on the list.

"Never mind. I made a mistake. I should've known. Two tickets to Seattle was more than we could afford — the universe couldn't have been clearer. I shouldn't have bought those tickets in Tucson."

Wynter clutched the ticket to her chest.

"We have to go home. I'm so sorry. I made a mistake." Joy started to cry. "Give it to me. Maybe they'll let me exchange it for two tickets back to Tucson."

Wynter stepped back sharply as Joy reached for the ticket. "Who's C Fairn?"

Joy pressed her face into her hands for a moment. "It must be Caleb. Harry and Miriam's son."

"You have a brother? Will he remember you?"

"I suppose so. He was nine when I left."

"Call him!"

Joy looked over at the phone as though she was afraid of it. "What if he says no?" she whispered.

Then they truly had nowhere to go but back to the ashram. And they were not allowed to leave the ashram without permission. Joy would pay with extra shifts in the laundry and lengthy Reflections sessions, with people screaming at her until she broke. Wynter would pay in a different way. Cold terror knotted her stomach.

She stared at the ticket in her hand. Neat lines of print swam before her eyes. "The universe wants me to go to Seattle. I'm sure of it. I have a ticket and an address. I have everything I need. I'm going to Seattle. Caleb will help me."

"*No one* on the outside will help us!"

"Someone flashed their lights to tell us to switch on our headlights. The very first person we saw on the outside, and they helped us. Caleb will help." Wynter was going to Seattle, whether Caleb wanted her or not. She was not going back to the ashram. She was going to travel more highways and eat those snacks and find Xay.

Joy blinked at her surroundings, searching for something.

Looking for a sign from the universe.

Wynter looked around, too. Colors, lights, words and numbers were everywhere. Roped-off lanes led to the bay doors, each marked with a big white letter on a stand.

"Look! It says here I'm supposed to board with Group C." She thrust her ticket under Joy's nose and pointed excitedly at the lanes. "C for Caleb! Even the door has a white C on it." Her sister tended to ascribe significance to anything white.

"Oh, Wynter, the universe doesn't speak to *you.*" Joy spoke with pity rather than spite. She was right, though. Wynter had never heard the universe speak and until this moment had never pretended otherwise.

"Out here, I think I can hear the universe properly for the first time," Wynter said, panic rising because they only had minutes until the bus to Seattle departed. "You said I didn't belong in the Light. Maybe that's because I'm meant to be here, in darkness, where the universe can get through to me."

Joy was listening, but she didn't look convinced.

Wynter couldn't resist making more connections. "That big white A on the mountain – I showed it to you. Doesn't A mean the start of something?" She injected uncertainty into her voice, enough to motivate Joy to elaborate.

"Alpha – a new beginning," Joy murmured.

"The starting point of my journey, labeled for me. And then... and then... We stopped in Blythe, and it made me think of the poem about Sunday's Child – that's me! A on the mountain, B for Blythe..." Her words tumbled out. "It's the universe mapping out my path. And now the door labeled C for Caleb, the next step on my path."

Was she getting through? Joy's gaze had turned inward.

"Don't take me back," she pleaded. "I'm supposed to go to Seattle."

Joy came to her decision. "You'll always walk in darkness, and I've accepted that even if Miriam never could. Yes, you belong out here."

Wynter gasped with relief.

Joy bought her a sandwich and stuffed a few bills into the paper bag the food had come in. She tore a strip off the top of the piece of paper, the part with Caleb's details, and gave it to Wynter.

"You'll go to Seattle and take a taxi to that address. You'll tell Caleb who you are. Tell him your name is Wynter Wild."

Wild?

"Is that my name?"

"That was Miriam's second name before she came into the Light. You'll tell Caleb your name, and mine. Only him, understand? Listen carefully to me." Joy's voice hardened as Wynter's attention waned from tiredness and overload. "Don't talk to anyone else. Stay away from the cops. Stay away from Social Services. Don't you go into the house until you're sure it's him. Ask his name to be sure. *Caleb Henry Fairn.* He has dark hair and blue eyes, like me. Don't trust anyone else."

Wynter nodded, filing away each piece of information. Excitement mingled with terror, making the blood pound in her head. She could so easily get lost in this new world. Joy was her only guide, and Joy was staying behind.

"What about you? Are you going back to the Light?"

"I'll follow when I get more money. I promise. I'll be right there to help you, darling, like I've always been." She hugged Wynter. "Sometimes I'm not sure of the best way to help. This time, I believe the universe wants me to listen to you. I can't think here, in this dark place."

Wynter didn't feel like Joy had always been there to help her. They hardly ever saw each other at the ashram. There were plenty of times she *wished* Joy had helped, but no one had.

"Remember everything I told you on the bus. You don't belong in the Light, but if you behave yourself you'll fit into this world. You have to be *no trouble* for Caleb, understand? No trouble at all."

She sent Wynter toward Bay C. Wynter handed her ticket to the driver, a garrulous older woman who was too busy talking to the family ahead of her to take any notice of Wynter. Perhaps she thought Wynter belonged with them. Wynter went straight to the back of the bus so the driver wouldn't talk to her.

Exhaustion took over, yet she still couldn't sleep. Lulled by the rocking of the bus, hypnotized by the shapes of the hills and the emerald trees, her mind fell blank. She travelled north through the night and at each stop the air grew colder. The bus was blessedly warm.

By Thursday morning, more than a day after leaving Tucson, the bus crossed into Oregon. A few hours later it departed the station in Portland and started on the last leg to Seattle.

To Caleb.

Hot Chocolate

The clock at the bus station in Seattle said 4:30PM. Wynter had been traveling for almost forty hours with little sleep and nothing but the sandwich to eat.

She stumbled out of the bus and found her way to the taxi rank. She waited in line, shivering, until she reached the front, and got into the back seat of the taxi as she'd seen other people do. She showed the address to the driver.

He eyed her suspiciously. "You got money?"

She gave him a quick peek at the cash in the paper bag, and he seemed satisfied. She'd counted it several times on the bus. She had nine dollar bills.

The taxi pulled out into busy traffic. The meter ticked over, even when they were stopped at lights. Five dollars, six... How far away was Caleb's house? Nine dollars. Ten. She clutched the paper bag. She couldn't pay. She should give the driver what she had and ask him to stop. Joy hadn't covered this situation in her instructions. She curled up and refused to think about it.

The taxi stopped and Wynter woke from a doze. It was dark now.

"Here we are, young lady. $17.50."

She handed the driver the crumpled paper bag and got out while he counted the cash. They were in a long, quiet street lined with bare trees. The air was still, with a cold dampness she'd never breathed before. The single-story house before her stood in a row of similar-sized houses, each a different shape. A driveway led to a wide metal door, a bike was chained on the porch, and the street light revealed a neatly cut lawn. Wynter checked the address on the slip of paper, though she'd memorized it hours ago, and checked the number on the gate.

She went through the gate and started up the driveway.

"Hey!" The driver had gotten out and was calling over the roof of the taxi. "You're $8.50 short."

Wynter ignored him. She turned down a narrow path cut through the front yard, climbed two steps to the porch, and knocked on the door. Surely Caleb would give the driver his money.

A boy opened the door. He was only a little older than her — definitely not Caleb, who was supposed to be older than Joy. This boy was tall with dark scruffy curls and blue eyes, and had a pen in his hand. He looked at her very oddly, like he'd never seen a human being before in his life.

"Is Caleb Henry Fairn here?"

"He's not home yet." The boy's curious expression deepened.

"Thank you. I'll wait for him."

She sat on the porch, facing the street. She expected the boy to close the door. Instead, he stepped out.

"Uh, who are you?"

"I'm waiting for Caleb."

The taxi driver was marching up the driveway. "She owes me $8.50. You go in and tell your parents. Go on."

"They're not home," the boy told him. He moved in front of Wynter. "Are you supposed to be here?"

"Yes."

"You sure about that?"

"Joy sent me."

He was suddenly very interested. "*Joy?* Where is she?"

Wynter wasn't sure she should say more. "When will Caleb be home? I can only talk to Caleb."

"I'm his brother, Jesse. You can talk to me."

So, now there were *two* brothers Joy had never mentioned.

"Only Caleb," she said. "Only Caleb."

Jesse shook his head and took a phone from his back pocket. The driver tried to ask for his money again. Jesse waved him into silence and called someone.

"There's a girl on the porch," Jesse said into the phone. "A kid. She's in sandals and shorts and she showed up in a taxi. She says *Joy* sent her. And the taxi driver wants $8.50." He listened for a moment, never taking his eyes off Wynter, before ending the call. "Caleb's on his way. He works at the base, not far from here. Come inside and wait." To the driver he called out, "I'll get your money. Gimme a second."

He went in, hesitating in the doorway, waiting for Wynter to follow. She wasn't supposed to go inside any house without Caleb. This might be a trick. Maybe it wasn't Caleb on the phone. Maybe this wasn't Caleb's brother.

She didn't move. Jesse gave up, went inside and returned moments later with a ten-dollar bill for the driver, who didn't ask if he wanted change and didn't give him any.

"He owes you one dollar fifty!" Wynter cried as the driver returned to his car.

"Don't worry about it."

Wynter didn't worry about it. She was too relieved to see the taxi leave.

"You look cold," Jesse said.

She was freezing. January nights in Tucson were cold, but not wet like this. It was an interesting sensation. Jesse disappeared inside again and brought out a blanket. He draped it around her shoulders and sat beside her on the porch step.

"You gonna tell me your name now?"

Just her name — no harm in that. "Wynter."

"Like the season?"

"Yes. With a Y."

"Wynter. That's a cool name. And Joy sent you. Joy Fairn?"

In the Light, Joy's second name was not Fairn. But if Harry Fairn was Joy's father, and Caleb Fairn her brother, then Jesse would think Joy's name was Fairn. Wynter gave a tight nod.

"Joy is my big sister, y'know," Jesse said. "Where is she now?"

Wynter sucked on her lips and said nothing. She shivered under the blanket.

"If you won't come inside, I'll get you a hot drink, okay?"

In a few minutes he was back with a dark, sickly-sweet smelling drink in a mug. She sipped it. The sugar hit her brain like a sledge-hammer.

"Oh, it's good," she said.

"I know, right?" He grinned and she found herself shyly returning the smile.

She sipped again. Warmth slid down to her belly.

Now he frowned. "You've never had hot chocolate before?"

"No."

He scrutinized her. "You've come up from Arizona, haven't you."

She tensed under the blanket. How did he know that? She put

down the mug and pulled the edges of the blanket closer around her.

Jesse didn't ask any more questions. He stood up and leaned against the porch pillar, looking out at the street, and sometimes staring down at her. At last a black truck pulled up in the driveway and its headlights flicked off.

"That's Caleb." Jesse pushed himself off the pillar to stand straight.

A man got out of the truck. In the dark Wynter couldn't see his face. He was even taller than Jesse, solidly built, and he wore a dark coat and pants and black boots. He strode purposefully across the yard toward them, nodding a greeting to Jesse.

"She says her name's Wynter," Jesse said, adding "with a Y," like it was very important.

The blanket slipped away as Wynter struggled to her feet, her legs stiff with cold. Backlit by the streetlight, Caleb's face was in shadow. His hair was dark like Jesse's, but cut short and neat. He loomed over her. For an instant she felt it was all a mistake. She wasn't supposed to be here. Maybe she *wasn't* here. Maybe she'd never left Arizona and this was all a dream.

No, this was real. She'd *make* it real. She resisted the impulse to take a step back. She stood her ground.

Then Caleb smiled at her — a tense, confused smile, but she recognized it. Recognized him, somehow.

"Wynter. Nice to meet you. I'm Caleb Fairn." He stuck out his hand, very formally. She shook it — she'd never shaken an adult's hand before. His hand was huge and warm. "You're ice cold."

"She wouldn't come inside," Jesse said, scooping up the discarded blanket.

"Let's go in."

Caleb ushered them both through the front door. The small entry hall was lit with a single lamp that left the corners in darkness. To the right, an archway led to a room with a big table. Books and papers were spread over the table, where Jesse must've been working, and a board game was set up at one end. On the other side of the hall was a tiny kitchen overlooking a living room. Wynter had read old novels about families who lived in houses, but had never been inside a family home before. She stared at everything.

"Sit," Caleb said.

Wynter chose a large armchair in the living room and perched on the edge of the seat.

"Find Wynter some warm clothes," Caleb told his brother. "A sweater, some socks."

Jesse disappeared into the back of the house. Caleb sat on the couch and leaned forward, his brow drawn low. He had very blue eyes that captured her gaze.

"Where's Joy?"

"She's in Los Angeles. She only had enough money to buy one ticket to Seattle."

"Where were you before LA?"

"Arizona."

"The ashram?"

Wynter nodded. Her throat tightened in anticipation of questions about the ashram, which she wasn't supposed to talk about.

"I'm Joy's brother," Caleb said. "I'd like to help her."

"I know. I mean, I didn't know. She just told me. She said you would help."

"I will help her in any way I can." His brow furrowed. "We haven't seen her since we were little kids. Is our mother... is Miriam in Arizona?"

"She's in Thailand."

"*Thailand?*"

"It's a country in southeast Asia, east of India and north of Austral—"

"Yeah, hun, I know where Thailand is." He patted her knee, a touch so brief she didn't have time to shrink away. "Can you tell me why Joy took you with her when she left?"

"She's my sister, too. My half-sister."

Caleb drew in his breath. Behind him, Jesse stopped in his tracks before composing himself and coming forward with the clothes he'd fetched. Wynter took off her sandals and pulled the thick gray socks onto her dirty feet. Caleb helped her draw on the oversized sweater. When her frozen fingers fumbled with the zipper, he did it for her.

"Miriam Wild is your mother?" Caleb said, looking at her very carefully. His steady gaze anchored her in this world.

She was *here*. She existed.

"My name is Wynter Wild," she whispered.

Jesse stood behind the couch, clicking his pen.

"How old are you?" Caleb said.

"Fourteen."

"Who's your dad?"

"His name's Malcolm. They were married for a while."

"When's Miriam due back from Thailand?"

"I don't think... I don't know. She went about five years ago and I think she lives there now."

"You haven't seen her since?"

Wynter shook her head, chewing on her lip as Caleb rubbed his hand over his eyes, hiding his reaction. Then he closed his hands over hers. They were so warm, and hers so cold, it felt like her hands were buried under hot desert sand.

"Okay. Does Joy have a phone? Any way to contact her?"

"No. I left her at the bus station in LA. She said she'd follow me soon."

"Does she have any money?"

Wynter shook her head hopelessly. Her desire to come to Seattle and leave Joy behind now seemed selfish and reckless. Would Caleb blame her for abandoning her sister? His sister. *Their* sister. She processed the implications. Caleb was her half-brother and so was Jesse. She was connected to two people on the outside. For her whole life she'd believed there was no one.

"The universe told me to come," she said.

Jesse stopped clicking his pen. "What does *that* mean?"

"We saw a big white A on a mountain in Tucson, and we stopped in Blythe, from the poem, which is B. And then C on my ticket, the door to Caleb. I read the signs and told Joy we were on the right path, that we shouldn't go back to the ashram."

Jesse got that look on his face again, like she wasn't a real person. *Click-click, click-click,* went his pen. Wynter turned back to Caleb. Maybe she didn't exist for Jesse, but she had to make Caleb believe in her.

"Joy's on her way. She'll explain everything, I promise."

A rash promise. It might even be a lie. At the ashram, it never mattered if she told truths or lies. No one cared. Mostly she would say nothing at all and let them reach their own conclusions.

"How did Joy know where I live?" As Caleb spoke, he reached over the back of the couch and snatched the pen out of Jesse's hand, making Wynter jump. Caleb clicked the nib in and handed the pen back, and Jesse stuck it in his pocket with a rueful look.

"She found your name on the computer," Wynter stammered, unnerved by his sudden movement and the way Jesse accepted the rebuke without comment. Jesse was about Xay's age, and she couldn't imagine Xay submitting like that. "She called Harry Fairn first, but... I don't know. She called him and hung up."

A strange, fleeting expression crossed Caleb's face. "That's our dad, up in Everett. I'll call him. Jesse, heat some soup. Make toast or something."

Jesse went into the kitchen and Wynter was alone for a moment as Caleb walked away, tapping his phone. From his side of the conversation she knew he was talking to Harry.

"...No, listen to me, dammit, that was Joy calling from LA. Did she say *anything*? Did she say where she was staying?"

Wynter crept forward to watch Caleb pacing the front room, his free hand rubbing his forehead in frustration. She could've told him Harry knew nothing. Joy hadn't spoken a single word. Something in Harry's voice had made her hang up immediately.

In the kitchen, Jesse had a pot on the stove and a can of soup in his hand. He clipped the can into a machine on the corner of the bench and it whirred, turning the can around.

"What is that?"

Jesse gave a sharp laugh of disbelief. "A can opener."

He extracted the can and pulled the lid off a magnet in the machine. Wynter had used a can opener every day of her life since she was about seven years old, but never one like this. She looked at the machine carefully, trying not to be too obvious, wondering how it worked. Jesse emptied the soup into the pot and busied himself stirring it.

She heard Caleb making another call, barking orders like he was used to being obeyed. As his tone grew ever more insistent, the tension made her nervous. Jesse offered her an apologetic look.

"I called the bus station in LA," Caleb said, coming into the kitchen. "Persuaded one of their security guys to take a look around for Joy, but they didn't see her, or remember seeing her."

"She was there. *We* were there," Wynter said, fearing he didn't believe her story. "I left yesterday afternoon. Maybe she went somewhere. She still had some money left. Or, maybe she went to Disneyland."

"Does she have eighty dollars?" Jesse said. "Cuz that's what it costs."

"Oh. Someone told me it was free."

Jesse laughed again, earning himself a severe look from Caleb. Jesse had an easy smile that reminded her of Xay, and it was Xay who'd told her about Disneyland. *As an American-born citizen, free entry into Disneyland is my constitutional right!* he'd say, making fun of Roman who was born in Australia, though they were both raised there and considered it home.

"Where do you think she might've gone?" Caleb said, taking a seat on the far side of the counter.

"She doesn't know anyone. There's no one to help, except..."

Caleb's eyebrow went up and he waited for her to continue.

"Except the Light," Wynter finished. "But we've *left* the Light. She wanted us to live on the outside."

"I'll call the Light office in LA tomorrow morning. You sit here and eat. Then you can have a bath, if you like. Warm you up." Caleb patted the tall stool next to him. He shrugged off his coat. Underneath he wore a dark shirt with US COAST GUARD embroidered in white over one pocket, and FAIRN over the other.

Even her own brother was labeled.

While the soup heated and Jesse made toast, Caleb asked her to recount her trip from Tucson. Not knowing what was important, Wynter tried to recall every detail of the bus ride. She talked about the scenery and how it turned thick and green the further north she traveled. She described the bus's velvety blue seats and named a dozen songs she'd heard on the radio, probably in the wrong order. She explained how the taxi driver got upset when she couldn't pay. It was okay to tell him all this, because it was nothing to do with the Light. She must remember not to talk about the Light.

Jesse served out the soup and toast. It smelled so good. She had to eat slowly because the soup was very hot and the buttered toast scratched her throat, though it was all delicious. Caleb told Jesse to print off the bus schedule between Los Angeles and Seattle. Jesse looked like he wanted to stay in the kitchen, in case he missed anything, but he did what he was told.

"When did you last have something to eat?" Caleb asked her.

"I had a sandwich in LA. It's okay, I don't eat much."

He frowned at that. Maybe she wasn't supposed to say it, but she needed him to understand she'd be no trouble.

"Can I stay here until Joy comes?" Wynter said.

"Where else would you go?"

Was he ready to send her away already? Wynter didn't want to leave, but she wouldn't stay where she wasn't welcome. She struggled to think of a plan.

"If you lend me $17.50, I could take a taxi back to the bus station and wait for Joy. She'll explain everything much better. They have these long wire benches you can sleep on." She'd like a blanket, too, but asking for one might be pushing her luck.

"You're not going back to the bus station. Jesse and me will do that."

She realized she'd misunderstood his query. She heard Roman's admonishment: *It was a rhetorical question, Wynnie. Don't be so literal all the time.* She was in the habit of being literal, of telling the simple truth in the hope it would keep her out of trouble. Wasn't always easy when you were holding secrets and when no one believed you anyway.

"If Joy shows up," Caleb went on, "we'll bring her home."

Home. She wanted *home.* She was prepared to fight for it.

"If she doesn't come, I don't want to go back to Arizona."

"Will you tell me why you left?" Caleb spoke in a gentle way that no adult had every used with her before. But now he was asking about the Light.

What should she say? She felt compelled to answer, somehow knowing it was safe, but she heeded Joy's warning.

She said, "Joy married someone she didn't much like." That seemed like the safest answer. People married and divorced all the time. Like Momma, and like plenty of other people at the ashram. "Are you going to send me back?"

"You can stay here for now, if you want to. You're our sister, too."

Her body felt weighed down, anchored to this world and this house by the connection he'd spoken aloud. She looked into his honest eyes in a face etched with concern and confusion.

"Thank you, I will stay."

Someone New

Caleb showed Wynter the bathroom and she confronted the tub — two sets of faucets and a shower head, a rail, a curtain, bottles and towels and a mat on the floor. Her vision blurred. It was all very confusing and she didn't want to do anything wrong.

"I don't know how to use that."

"Nothing to it." Caleb twisted in the plug, turned on the water, checked the temperature, and squeezed something from a bottle that foamed the water. "That one over there is shampoo. For your hair."

"I know what shampoo is." She fingered her hair self-consciously, knowing it was filthy despite Joy's best efforts earlier. She couldn't remember the last time she'd used shampoo.

Caleb fetched a folded gray towel from the cupboard in the corner, along with a new toothbrush and a washcloth. "Put that robe on when you're done. I'll find some PJs. You want to take off your bracelet first?"

Wynter touched the braided bracelet on her left wrist. "No, I never take it off."

When he was gone, she undressed and sank into the water, cocooned in heat and steam. Everything was so shiny — the blue patterned tiles, the white basin, the silver faucets. How could she ever make herself clean enough to live here?

The water rose higher. Caleb's footsteps approached on the other side of the door, which was slightly ajar.

He rapped on the door and called, "Turn the water off, hun. You're gonna overflow the tub."

She sat up in alarm, sloshing a great wave of water and suds over the edge. She reached for the faucets. One was stiff. She tried the other, turning it the wrong way so the water gushed even faster.

"Help me...?" she cried, though she was mortified about making a mess. Everything in Caleb's house that she'd so far seen was meticulously tidy. Everything except Jesse's work on the table.

Caleb came in and turned off the faucets. The water level was only an inch below the top of the tub.

"We have pressure showers at the ashram," she said, feeling the need to explain her mistake, though he didn't look angry.

"I've used those, when I'm camping."

He frowned, glancing at her shoulders as she hunched over in the water, the bubbles keeping her decent. She rubbed her shoulder, wondering what was wrong.

Caleb drew the shower curtain across the tub and spoke from behind it, moving toward the door. "When you're done, you can eat more if you're still hungry. I've made up the bed in Indio's room, just opposite. You can sleep there."

"India?"

"*Indio*. Our brother — Joy's twin. You didn't know she had a twin?"

She poked her head around the curtain. "How many more of you are there?"

He grinned. In a burst of emotion, she felt she would do anything, whatever it took, to make him smile like that every day from this moment on.

"Just the three of us. Indio's at Portland State, a couple hours from here."

"Oh! My bus stopped in Portland. It's not a state."

He gave a little chuckle, but not making fun of her like Jesse had. "Portland State is a university. Jesse's in college, too, just down the road. He's packed his schedule, hoping to graduate in three years."

"So, he's smart?"

"Very smart. He'll tell you so. Indio... he has your hair color, or a bit lighter, and hazel eyes like you."

No one had ever described her eyes as hazel. Was that a color or a shape or something else?

"Can I go to a real school?"

"Didn't you go to school at the ashram?"

"We had a classroom. I don't think it was much like a real school." Xay had mentioned school in Australia — not very often because he'd hated it.

Caleb looked troubled for a moment. "Wynter, you're only fourteen. When Joy comes, there will be legal stuff we have to sort out. But everything will be okay."

He left and she finished her bath. She brushed her teeth and combed out her damp hair with her fingers. It was certainly clean now, but more matted than before she washed it and she gave up trying to smooth it out. Her face in the mirror looked different already – flushed and soft from the steam. Her eyes shone like the tiles. She didn't look like herself. And that was fine. In this new world, she would be someone new. The dark pieces were left behind.

As for Xay – he wasn't a dark piece. She wanted to find him, but how? He and his mother had most likely returned to Australia. He'd always talked about living near the beach again. He'd explained to her how time in Australia was upside-down and back-to-front, which meant it was daytime right now, and summer. He was surfing.

Across the hall, the door to Indio's room was open. She went in to find a t-shirt and pajama pants on the bed, folded neatly on the dark gray quilt. They smelled of unfamiliar soap, like the towel and robe. Everything was too big. She rolled up the ankle cuffs and pulled the drawstring tight to hold the pants up. The bedroom was small with just a bed, a low bookcase, and a desk. Inside the built-in closet was a chest of drawers. A few clothes remained on the rack. Caleb and Jesse were real to her now, but Indio was nebulous. And Joy was from another world altogether.

Exhausted, she lay on the bed, intending to rest for a moment before going out to ask for more food. She'd never slept in such a tiny room, at least not one with a bed. At the ashram the living spaces were large and open, to let the Light in. There were small dark rooms there, too, and they were invariably bad places. This room didn't feel like a bad place. When she pressed her face into the pillow, it even smelled right. This room reminded her of the shed in the corner of the compound – her sanctuary, the one place she was always welcome.

Wynter awoke to the feel of a hand on her shoulder.

"Joy?"

"It's me." *Caleb.* "Get back into bed. You'll get cold."

It took a moment to get her bearings. She was on the floor in the corner of the room, wedged between the end of the bed and the closet doors, tangled up in blankets and pillows. She remembered crawling out of bed and making a nest. She couldn't remember why she'd done it.

Caleb helped her replace the bedding. He covered her up and hunkered down. "Just got back from the bus station. Joy wasn't on the evening bus, so we'll try again with the next one."

"How many buses are there?"

"Four every day. So she has lots of chances to catch one." He brushed strands of hair off her face and said, softly, "I didn't even know you existed."

She took his hand in both of hers and held it close, tucked under her chin. "I didn't know about you, either. Once, when I was sick, Joy told me stories about when she was a little girl in a house with a patio, and about piggyback rides in the backyard. She never said your name. She never told me she had three brothers."

"That house was in Montana, where we lived before..." *Before Momma and Joy left.* "I used to give her piggyback rides. She always asked me, not Indio, because I was faster than him. I could tell you so many stories. I remember us getting into trouble for jumping on her bed until the slats cracked. We were pretending we were on the moon."

"She told me about a boy who fell out of a tree and broke his arm, fetching down her doll. Was that you?"

"Yup. Did she tell you why the doll was in the tree in the first place? I was teasing her and threw it up there, and it got stuck."

"Did you get into trouble for that, too?"

"Miriam was more concerned about my broken arm."

"What did they do to you after you cracked the bed slats?"

"I don't remember. Probably got sent outside to rake leaves. No candy for a week. Something like that."

In the half-light she watched his expression turn serious. She realized she was clutching his hand too tightly. He lay his free hand on her shoulder.

"You're trembling." His eyes narrowed. "Wynter, did they hurt you?"

A shiver ran through her. She had to be careful or everything would go wrong. She understood now why Joy had told her not to talk about her life in the Light. If she told Caleb how badly behaved she was, and the way they punished her, he might think she was too much trouble to keep.

No, she belonged here.

Caleb accepted her silence. He extracted his hand from hers.

"Go to sleep. We'll figure it out."

Responsibility

Caleb had spent most of his life dealing with the unexpected. However things turned out, tonight was going to be a tale for the future grandkids.

He leaned in Jesse's doorway. "Move your books out of the front room before morning, okay?"

Jesse's room was a disaster area. As a kid he'd kept it fairly tidy — kept the floor clear, in any case — to avoid confrontations with Caleb. These days Caleb was less concerned about it as long as Jesse kept the rest of the house tidy. Not that he was going to encourage bad habits by telling Jesse that. Tonight, Jesse had emptied the contents of his closet all over the floor. He was sitting cross-legged in the middle of it, surrounded by files and shoeboxes.

"Look at this." Jesse handed him an old photo.

Three brothers in shorts and t-shirts, a few years before they moved to Seattle. They stood on a riverbank, Caleb and Jesse with fishing nets, Indio holding up a mason jar of murky water.

"Where is that — Lost Creek State Park?"

"I don't know, but look at Indio."

The shape of his chin, his brow... the resemblance was unmistakable. Indio's ratty hair was almost down to his shoulders, so it must be the end of summer. Before school started Caleb and Harry would've wrestled him into the yard to clip off those locks.

"You're right, she looks a lot like him," Caleb said. "Did you doubt her story?"

"No. Just thought maybe you'd want proof."

"I believe her, Jess. Didn't need a photo of Indio to see she belongs with us."

Jesse nodded, satisfied. "Have you told him yet?"

"It's been four hours — thought you probably would've, by now."

"Nope." Jesse grinned. "You haven't spoken with him since Christmas, have you."

Caleb set his jaw. Indio had been home twice in the last year — a few days in the summer for Jesse's high school graduation, and a few days over Christmas. On that occasion, Indio and Caleb had gotten into a vicious argument. Nothing out of the ordinary. They argued a lot.

"You could text him," Jesse said. "Nah, I guess this isn't really textable news. It's okay, I'll call him."

"No. I'll do it." Caleb handed back the photo.

"D'you think she's okay?"

"I don't know. I don't really know the first thing about the Light or what she's been taught."

"Her eyes are all hollowed out and she's so thin."

Caleb nodded agreement. He'd seen the sharp bones of her shoulders in the tub. "Set your alarm early and get to the bus station for the 4:35AM, okay? I'll do it tomorrow night."

"I don't even remember Joy."

"I'm sure she'll remember you."

"That goes without saying. I was a memorable toddler."

"You could come with me when I visit Harry next week. He might have a few stories."

Jesse grunted. "Do I have to?"

"Thought you liked visiting Harry?"

"I like visiting his *dog*."

✿

Caleb's thumb hesitated over Indio's name on the screen. He assigned the blame equally for their strained relationship. He'd spent his life bearing the responsibility for his younger brothers. As kids, it was the three of them against the world and he'd pulled more than his share of the weight. Which was fine — he was the oldest, it was his job. Yes, he'd been harder on Indio because Indio could be irrationally stubborn. Caleb didn't like being defied. It just made his job harder.

By the time Caleb graduated high school, Harry was going through a relatively good patch — same job for three years, drinking only on his days off, staying away from the horses. Caleb enlisted for six years in the Coast Guard and was largely absent for the first four. He should've paid more attention to his gut instinct — those lingering reservations about Harry's ability to cope. It didn't take long for things to fall apart. Much of what had happened in this house, Caleb only learned about later from Jesse.

With Indio established in college in Ohio, Caleb had requested a relatively stationary assignment at the Seattle base. He knew nothing of Indio's life in Ohio — nothing good, anyway. He concentrated on Jesse instead, and to that end threw Harry out of his own home in order to give Jesse a fresh start for his junior year of high school.

When Indio transferred to Portland State before Christmas, Caleb entertained some hope his brother was finally making the effort to reconnect. Hadn't taken long to learn the real reason. It wasn't about being closer to his family. It was about being the front man in his friend's college band — a trivial reason to change colleges mid-year.

"Caleb." Indio answered the phone in a monotone. The jangle of guitars and drums in the background indicated he was probably at rehearsal.

"Hey, d'you have a minute? It's important."

"If this is about Christmas, just forget it."

"It's not."

"Make it quick." Indio sounded like he was ready to hang up.

"Our sister Joy left the ashram in Arizona a couple days ago."

"Wow. Have you seen her?" Indio sounded genuinely interested, although it might just be relief that it was nothing to do with him.

"She ran out of money in LA. Hopefully she'll make it up here soon, but I can't contact her."

"Then how d'you know about it?"

"Well, that's the thing... She *escaped*. I think that's the right word. She escaped with a teenage girl who did make it here. Her name is Wynter Wild — Miriam's daughter."

"Miriam has another daughter?"

"She's fourteen. She just showed up at my door this evening. She..." Caleb's voice went thick with emotion, catching him by surprise. "She kinda looks like you, when you were nine or ten."

"Huh." Silence for a few seconds. "You sure about all this?"

"Yeah. She's our half-sister."

"What's she like?"

"Your coloring — Mom's coloring, I guess. Real pretty, but she's skin and bones. Scared of being sent back. She doesn't seem to know much about... well, about the world. Never tasted hot chocolate."

"That sucks. What's our mother up to these days?"

"She's been in Thailand for a few years, on sabbatical or something. Look, I don't know what will happen with Wynter, but I assume they'll report her missing and Social Services may get involved."

"You're not gonna let them send her back, are you?"

"Not if I can help it. She won't talk about it, but Joy took her away for a reason. When Joy shows up, I guess we figure out a way for her to get custody. Find her a job, whatever's necessary."

"Why not you?"

"A single parent in the military? That's not easy to do, especially without family living locally." In fact, Caleb could be discharged for taking on a child without an acceptable plan in the event he was deployed. "I'd like you to meet her before things get too crazy."

"Okay. I can't make it up there, Caleb. I mean, I want to, but I got Blunderbelly gigs tomorrow and Saturday night."

"You need to find someone to fill in for you. Spend the weekend here."

"Can't do that." His tone was edging toward irritation. "I have a responsibility. You're big on responsibility, right?"

"Sunday, then."

"I don't get up on Sundays. I'll get plenty more chances to see them."

"Yes. Yes, you will. I'd like to hear a little more enthusiasm about doing that sooner rather than later. These are your sisters."

"Bring them here, then. The gig on Saturday's all-ages."

"That's not appropriate for a fourteen-year-old."

Indio chuckled dismissively. "Whatever you say, dude."

Caleb held his temper as the conversation slipped away from him, and the good news — incredible news — morphed into sarcasm and contention.

"There is something I need you to do," Caleb said. "Please pay attention. Joy may take a bus to Seattle in the next couple of days, and it goes through Portland. We need to be checking every bus, either there or here, so we'll spread the load. If you can check Friday and Saturday morning at—" He glanced at the schedule Jesse had printed off. "—at 9:15, we won't have to worry about those buses when they arrive here in the afternoon."

"Whoa, nine in the morning? I'll be sleeping in on Friday cuz my classes don't start until next week. I can't get there by nine."

"Indio, you'll be there at nine."

Indio muttered a curse. "Fine, I'll do Friday, but I have a gig in the evening. I told you already. There's no way I can be up that early on Saturday."

Caleb would take what he could. "Okay, just do Friday morning. You also need to check the 4:20PM on Friday and Saturday." Another curse, but no refusal this time. "If for some reason you don't get a good look at the bus, if you're not sure she isn't on it, you need to let me know so I can check the same bus again when it arrives in Seattle five hours later."

"I get it."

He hated having to lay things out like that, but Indio wasn't inclined to admit to his screw-ups. In this case, Caleb needed to know.

"You'll do it, then?"

"Yes, *sir*. I gotta go."

Nine Guitars

A distant alarm woke Wynter. Still dark outside. She was used to getting up in the dark at this time of year, so she dressed and meticulously made her bed. She wasn't by nature a tidy or well-organized person, and many of the adults at the ashram hadn't particularly cared — the homestead where the kids lived was dirtier and messier than Caleb's house. The upstairs dorm, though, was always spotless because Miss Althea was in charge of it.

She peeked out the door. The house was dark, too, except for the far end of the corridor where one of the two closed doors had a crack of light under it.

She sat on the edge of her bed, waiting.

A few minutes later, Jesse walked past and stopped in her doorway.

"Up already?"

"I heard the alarm."

"That was just for me. I gotta get to the bus station in case Joy's on the 4:35. Did you... did you make your bed?" He stepped in for a closer look, incredulous. "Caleb's gonna give you a medal for that."

Good to hear. She didn't want to fall short of expectations on her first morning.

Jesse was looking at her oddly yet again. "So... why are you just sitting there? I'll make you more toast, if you're hungry."

She was famished, but Jesse was supposed to be getting to the bus station. She shook her head.

"Won't Caleb want to see the bed?" she said.

"Is that what they did at the ashram? Checked your hospital corners every morning?" He chuckled, cutting himself off as her face heated. "Well, there are no bed inspections here, I promise. You don't have to do that. I mean, you can make your bed — that's great. You can make *my* bed or it won't get done. But you don't get graded on it."

Wynter smoothed the quilt defensively.

"Go back to sleep, okay?" Jesse said. "It's not natural to get up at four in the morning."

He walked away and she heard the front door open and close, and the truck driving off.

Wynter managed to fall asleep again. She woke to weak morning light filtering through the drapes and drew them open. Outside, a low fence ran alongside the wall of the house, close to the window, with trees and bushes on the other side blocking the view of the neighboring house. The sky was overcast, the hidden sun lighting up clouds low on the horizon. More often than not, mornings in Arizona had been clear other than during the monsoon season. The sun here in the north was supposed to be kinder, and she was looking forward to seeing it. She remade her bed and took Jesse at his word that she didn't need to wait for Caleb to approve it.

Outside her room, she almost tripped over a tiny girl in bright pink leggings and a blue sweater with mouse ears and whiskers on the front. The little girl looked up at her, startled, and toddled off to the front of the house. Wynter followed to find a woman in the kitchen with Jesse, who was adding powder to a big plastic tumbler of milk.

No sign of Joy, which meant she hadn't been on the bus Jesse checked earlier.

Jesse grinned at Wynter like he'd known her forever. "Morning again. This is Beatrice. Bea. She's Caleb's girlfriend. She's brought over some clothes for you."

Bea smiled and said, "Hi, Wynter. Come see what I've got."

Wynter followed Bea into the living room, aware of Jesse watching her like he might find something else to laugh about. On the couch were plastic bags with clothes spilling out. The child stared round-eyed at Wynter.

"This is Jilly, my little one," Bea said. "Okay, let's take a look. I didn't know what would fit."

Bea sorted through the clothes, talking enthusiastically in a way that required no response, and handed Wynter a few pairs of jeans and tops and skirts. Wynter headed to her room to try them on and passed Caleb in the hallway.

"You okay with this?" he said. "I called Bea last night, thought she could help."

"Is that baby yours?"

"Jilly? No. Bea and I have only been dating a few months."

"Do they live here?"

"No, Wynter. Like I said, we just started dating."

"Why is she helping me?"

"I asked her to."

"I don't think I should take her stuff." She indicated the clothes in her arms.

"Just for today, okay? Bea will take you shopping for your own clothes. I'll give you some money."

"I don't want to go with her."

Caleb opened his mouth to speak, hesitated, and changed what he was going to say. "I'll come too. And I made an appointment for you to see a doctor this afternoon."

"I'm not sick."

"I know. Just a check-up."

"Okay." It wasn't okay, not really. She wanted to stay here, in this house, and wait for Joy.

When she returned to the living room a while later, Bea was bouncing Jilly on her knees and making her giggle. The little girl kept leaning in for kisses. She was a cute thing with rosy cheeks and huge brown eyes. Wynter watched, fascinated. She'd never heard a baby laugh like that before. Never seen a mother cuddling a child like that.

"Oh, look at you!" Bea said when she noticed Wynter in badly fitting jeans and a long-sleeved top. "Here, put this on for when we go out." She handed over a purple zip-up puffy vest. Wynter hated the color, which reminded her of the robes the leadership at the ashram wore, but it felt warm and comfortable.

Caleb walked in with a coffee mug. "I'm coming with you. I've taken a few days' emergency leave from work."

"You've managed to get Caleb to agree to come shopping. Good work!" Bea teased Wynter. "We'll get you a bra, too," she added under her breath.

"What is your job?" Wynter asked Caleb.

"I'm in the USCG — over at the base. A desk job. Pretty much a nine-to-fiver."

Wynter wrinkled her nose. "I don't know what any of that means."

Bea's eyebrows went up and Wynter wondered how much Caleb had told her. She should probably stop displaying her ignorance in front of strangers.

"Caleb's a Coastie," Jesse said from the kitchen, where he was fitting a lid to his milkshake. "He rescues people for a living."

Wynter said, "Is that true?" Jesse's offhand manner made it hard to tell when he was joking.

"I occasionally help rescue people, among other things," Caleb said. "Now I mostly push paper and do a little teaching."

A shiver went through Wynter. She did not like teachers. Maybe Caleb was a different kind of teacher. He seemed too self-controlled to act like the teachers she knew.

"What d'you want for breakfast?" Jesse asked her.

"Toast and soup," Wynter said.

"Soup for breakfast?" Caleb said.

"Sure, why not!" Bea said, giving Caleb a look that made him go into the kitchen to prepare it. He had a little smile on his lips — still, it was odd to see someone telling Caleb what to do instead of the other way around.

Caleb's phone pinged and he checked it. "That's Indio — Joy's not on the bus that just arrived in Portland. Jesse, you need to check the 4:30."

Jesse nodded. "I can do that. I just have an astronomy club meeting today. You ever been to a mall before?" he asked Wynter as he shrugged on his jacket, preparing to leave.

"No, but I know all about them."

"Such as?"

"If your friend distracts the sales assistant, you can put a t-shirt down your shorts or a lighter in your pocket. Or just wear a bracelet right out the door, but peel off the price tag first."

"Uh..." Jesse exchanged a look with Caleb. "All true, I guess."

"I know it's stealing. I know it's wrong. I'm just saying, you can do that at the mall. Shoe stores are no good because they only have one shoe on display."

"Anything else?"

"At night you can skateboard in the parking lot, and on the disabled ramps, until Security throws you out."

"Who told you all that?"

Wynter stopped, realizing her mistake. She wasn't talking about the Light, so that was okay, but Xay and Roman had been her friends in the Light so everything was mixed up. She should probably not mention them.

When she didn't answer, Jesse grinned again, slung a backpack over his shoulder, and said, "I'm outta here."

"Should I go make your bed now?"

Jesse, strapping on a helmet, froze.

"What?" Bea said with a laugh.

"You said it wouldn't get done unless—"

"No, no, no..." Jesse gave Caleb an uneasy look. Caleb glared back at him. "She made hers — really nicely, too — and I made a joke about it. Just a misunderstanding."

Caleb said, "Wynter, you don't ever have to make anyone else's bed, okay? New house rule."

"What about my bed?"

"Well, I don't insist on Jesse making his, so it's up to you."

"I think I will make it. I don't want to make your house untidy."

"Thank you, that's very considerate of you."

Jesse looked like he was going to burst out laughing. Caleb jerked his chin at him, dismissing him, and Jesse opened the front door to leave.

"Have a fun day, Wyn. I'm a thirty-six long, if you wanna pick out a nice suit."

✿

Shopping wasn't fun. It was hard work. The noise, people, and lights were overwhelming. Wynter tried not to let it show because this outing had an air of importance about it, at least from the way Bea was behaving. Caleb followed them around the clothing stores, feigning interest. Wynter was mesmerized by Bea, by how she clucked over her little girl. When Jilly fell over and cried, her mother pulled her close with soft words and kisses. When she threw food on the floor and giggled, Wynter expected to hear a reprimand, but Bea tut-tutted with a smile and called her *silly Jilly* in a sweet voice.

Bea took Jilly into the restroom to clean her up after lunch, leaving Wynter and Caleb alone at the table for a few minutes. Wynter watched them leave. Caleb watched her. She felt herself flush and stared at her hands instead.

"Are all mothers like that?" she said at last.

"Like what?"

"She's always *attending* to her. Noticing her. Hugging and touching. Laughing. Is it really that much fun?"

"It's just love. I don't think she'd say motherhood is always fun, but she's crazy about that little girl. I guess most mothers are like that. Not all."

Not ours.

She risked looking at him. Was the pain in his eyes his own, or pity for her?

He leaned forward. "I was nine years old when Miriam left us. About the same age as you were, when she left you."

A sudden rush of kinship stopped her breath. He held her gaze for a moment. Nothing to say.

Then he sat back and relaxed. "I called Indio last night to tell him about you and Joy. He can't get away this weekend. Hopefully, you can meet him soon."

"Do you have a picture of him at your house?"

"Have some right here."

He set his phone on the table and scrolled quickly through a few photos. When the images stopped moving, the photo showed a guy standing at a microphone, holding a guitar amid a splash of lights.

"Oh, he's a rockstar."

Caleb's eyes crinkled at the corners as he smiled. "Not quite. He's played in a bunch of campus bands. He only just transferred to Portland. Before that he was on the other side of the country."

He swiped the screen. In the next photo, Indio had stepped back from the mic and she could see his features more clearly. He looked as familiar to her as Caleb, his expression somehow both friendlier and more intense. His hair fell around his face in straggly dark blond locks, not at all like Caleb. He wore a black t-shirt with a strange logo, and blue jeans.

"What do you know about rockstars, anyway?" Caleb said.

"I love music. We listened to rock music on a radio that no one else knew about."

"We?"

She bit her lip and stopped, and pretended he hadn't asked. "I love rock music," she said after a moment. "Is that what Indio plays?"

Caleb laughed. "Oh yeah. Do you play an instrument?"

"I played guitar." She pointed to Indio's guitar. "Not like that one. A hollow wooden one."

"Acoustic. That's great. I play, too. Not like Indio, I'm afraid. We have some guitars at home."

"*Some?* How many?"

"Uh, nine, I think, at last count. Mostly his, and he has a few more in Portland."

"I didn't see any in his room."

"They're in the basement. We have a little rehearsal space down there — we call it the jamroom."

"Okay. Show me that."

He grinned. "I will."

She was already standing up to leave. She wanted to see it *now*. A place to make rock music — she had to see that.

"Uh, I don't think we're quite done here. Bea?" Caleb had spotted Bea walking back with Jilly in tow. "Where to next, Bea?"

"I'm taking Wynter to the lingerie department. You can babysit. There's a play zone over there."

Bea handed Jilly to Caleb, who took her gingerly in his arms. Jilly giggled and stuck her fingers in Caleb's nostrils.

✿

The shopping done, they stopped by the house where Bea had left her car — she lived half an hour away and needed to get home with Jilly. Caleb drove Wynter to the local clinic.

"Birthdate?" Caleb asked her as he filled out a form in the waiting area.

"I'm fourteen. I told you already."

"The exact date, though?" He tapped the form with his pen.

"I was born in 1998."

He frowned as he studied her. "Month? Day?"

The Light didn't do birthdays. Xay and Roman thought it was hilarious she didn't know her own birthday. Birthdays were a big deal to them.

"Around March," she said, her best guess given Joy did keep a mental track of it. Joy always seemed to know how old she was, and that number increased after winter solstice each year.

"Let's say March fifteenth," Caleb said with a smile. "Two months until the big day. We'll do something special."

"Like what?"

"Uh, something. Birthdays and Christmas are Jesse's thing."

The doctor's appointment was as bewildering as everything else had been to this point. Caleb sat with Wynter for the first few minutes to explain she'd been living with relatives in Arizona. He didn't lie, but didn't fill in any details.

The doctor was a pleasant young woman who asked questions, after Caleb left the room, that Wynter didn't know how to answer. Wynter didn't know what vaccinations she'd had, if any. She didn't know if her diet was "balanced". When the doctor asked if her periods were regular, she said she'd never had a period. The doctor frowned like that was the wrong answer.

A nurse came to draw vials of blood and to look very carefully through Wynter's hair. She made her take off her jeans and sweater and step on the scales. Removing that much clothing in front of a stranger made Wynter's heart hammer, though she dared not make a fuss about it. Trying on bras with Bea hadn't been nearly so difficult. The nurse took her blood pressure, then made her lie quietly for a few minutes before taking it again. She gave Wynter a little tub for a urine sample. Caleb had told Wynter what to expect, that everything would be okay. She imagined him repeating the words, over and over, to calm herself down.

She sat in the foyer to wait while Caleb spoke in private with the doctor. Flicking through a garish magazine, she admired photos of immaculately furnished rooms in other people's houses that didn't look much like Caleb's house. His house was small and plain and old by comparison.

When Caleb emerged he was tucking a piece of paper into his back pocket and he looked upset. But he smiled when he caught her eye. In the truck, she asked what the doctor had said. She didn't like the idea they were talking about her in secret.

"You need vaccinations — she gave me a schedule. We can start on that next week. And I had to tell her more about your situation. She can see that you're... well, underweight. Neglected, to be blunt. And because you're a minor, that means Social Services will get involved."

Wynter's blood ran cold. Social Services were an evil force on the outside. It was allowable and often necessary to lie to Social Services.

"I'm seeing a lawyer right after I drop you home. We have to find out who your legal guardian is."

"Can I still live with you?"

He threw her a tight smile. "I hope so. And I'll do what I can to find Joy. I called the LA bus station again earlier to see if she's hanging around there — no luck. The Light office in LA is just an answering machine. We may just have to wait for her to show up. She'll show up."

"I know she will."

They got home and sat in silence for a while in the truck.

"If something happened to you in that place," Caleb said at last, "anything at all you want to talk about, you can tell me."

Discomfort radiated off him. And... fear? Wynter didn't want to scare him.

"Nothing happened that I want to talk about," she said.

He squeezed her hand. "You let me know if you change your mind. You belong with my family now. I'll take care of you."

She believed him.

✿

Caleb suggested Wynter unpack her new clothes and watch some TV while he visited the lawyer.

For a couple of hours, she was alone in the house. She changed into new clothes, struggling with the bra until she figured out the straps and hooks. She put pretty bottles of nice-smelling toiletries in the bathroom and reread the instructions on the bottle of conditioner, which Bea had told her to use next time she washed her hair. She folded the rest of the clothes and put them into one of Indio's empty drawers, and used his hangers. She was intruding on his space, taking over. But Caleb had told her to do this, so she did.

She couldn't work out how to turn on the TV and didn't waste too much time with it. Those nine guitars were calling her name. She found the steps to the basement outside Jesse's bedroom, went down, and opened the door at the bottom. Flicking on the light, she discovered a small room with exposed brick walls covered in scraps of carpet.

The *jamroom.*

It was packed with instruments and stools and microphone stands, yet everything was neatly stacked — tidy and clean like the rest of the house.

Something dug into her feet. Cables lay everywhere. Snakes lying in wait. A sense of dread settled in her stomach as she heard the echo of them whistling through the air. No, the cables were taped to the carpet. It was safe.

Walking around the room slowly, she touched nothing. She lingered at the row of guitars in their stands against one wall. One had four thick strings — a bass guitar. Xay had told her about those and how they were tuned. Some of the guitars were acoustic, some colorful electric ones in different shapes like the one Indio had in the photos. There were racks of amps — Xay had told her about those, too. Definitely necessary for rock music. And a drum kit in the corner with a baffling array of drums and cymbals. She had picked apart drum beats while listening to songs on the radio, and now tried to guess which drums made which sounds. She didn't dare grab a drumstick to find out. With her knuckles she tapped a couple of drums and cymbals very gently, disturbing the silence.

The sound faded and she heard only her own breath, an unsteady exhalation. Her head spun with possibilities. She would make rock music here.

✿

When she heard Caleb's truck returning, she went up. It was growing dark. He dropped a file on the table. Lawyers were expensive, she knew that from Roman, whose mother's divorce had "cost big bikkies". Was that why he looked so grim?

"Jesse called to let me know Joy wasn't on this afternoon's bus," he said, "and according to Indio she won't be on the one after that, which gets in later this evening." It was now twenty-four hours since Wynter had arrived in Seattle and they were none the wiser about where Joy might be. "Let's eat, and then I'll show you the jamroom."

"I went down there." She added quickly, "I didn't touch anything." Well, the drums, but barely.

"You can play anything you like."

Did he really mean that? In her experience, the things adults said when they were in a good mood were apt to change on a whim. And she wasn't used to touching things just because they were there. At the ashram, every item she touched was something she was supposed to touch — every kitchen knife, every pencil, every box and bead and packing slip. She played every note on her guitar exactly as instructed, at least when there were others around.

Caleb pulled plastic tubs of food from the refrigerator and heated them in the microwave. He called the food *take-out leftovers* and she pretended to understand what he meant. They ate in the dining room, where Jesse had been studying the day before. Caleb said they rarely ate in here. The table had been cleared, except for the board game.

"Is this checkers?" she asked, eager to show she knew *something* about *something*. The board was familiar but the pieces were all different shapes.

"Chess. Jesse always has a game set up." He examined the board and moved a black horse's head to another square. "Let's see what he thinks of that."

Jesse showed up halfway through the meal. Caleb kept the conversation going, so Wynter didn't have to, with a long-suffering account of his babysitting experience in the play zone. Jesse made fun of Caleb's latest chess move and Caleb gave a knowing smile that made Jesse stare at the board again, like he'd missed something. Jesse talked about the local schools, and the high school all three brothers had attended. He was excited about Wynter going there because of the science and math program.

"I don't think I can do math," Wynter said.

"What grade are you? Ninth?"

"I don't know."

Jesse fetched some of his old math workbooks. He opened his ninth-grade book and asked her to show him what she recognized as he flipped through the handwritten pages. Page after page of numbered calculations and graphs and diagrams. Her face heated and her ears buzzed. He opened his eighth-grade book. She shook her head and refused to look at more than a page or two. She didn't understand anything. Perhaps Xay was right and real school wasn't so great after all.

"What *did* you learn in school?" Jesse said.

"Lots of things. We did two hours in the classroom every morning."

"Two hours of school a day?" Jesse's horrified reaction mystified her. "What did you do in the afternoons?"

"Warehouse."

Caleb had that grim look on his face again, his attention never wavering from her. "What does that mean?"

"We worked in the warehouse. The Light sold all kinds of things. We put together the orders. Made some of the items, too. All kinds of things." She shouldn't be talking like this, but their attitude put her on the defensive.

"How many hours a day?" Caleb said.

"Usually from twelve until nine."

"Nine hours a day. How old are the kids working there?"

Wynter winced at his questions, feeling under pressure. "There are no kids there now. All the kids left a few months ago."

"Except you."

"Yes. They turned half the compound into a retreat — lots of new buildings. Once it opened to the public they didn't want children around. Those families were reassigned to other chapters across the country. Miriam didn't want me sent away, so I stayed."

"How old were you when you started working in the warehouse?"

"About six, I guess. But only for a few hours a day then."

Caleb looked upset again. Jesse looked stunned.

To break the silence, she said, "Can we go down to the jamroom now?"

Heartbeat

Jesse slid behind the drums and played a beat. Caleb watched Wynter eye him curiously, perhaps astonished by the volume. She leaned over and touched the skin of the bass drum, feeling its vibrations. Jesse grinned at her reaction, twirled a drumstick, and crashed a cymbal. Jesse's infectious smile could melt ice. Caleb hoped it would help Wynter relax.

That afternoon, waiting to see his lawyer, Caleb had texted Jesse a brief update — not Indio, because Indio had shown no interest. The old bruises and minor scars, the doc said, could be a sign of abuse or could be normal childhood accidents. The mild sore throat, probably from some lingering infection, wasn't out of the ordinary — they'd get the bloodwork results next week. By Wynter's account her diet had been unvaried though not unhealthy, but clearly she was underfed and needed to put on ten pounds. She wasn't pregnant, thank god.

Wynter hadn't mentioned any abuse but the suspicion of it, and the neglect, were enough to convince the doctor to report her case to Social Services. Caleb was uneasy about that. He and his brothers had spent their childhoods fearing intervention that might remove them from home and separate them. His opinion of the authorities had matured since then, but that didn't mean he wanted to deal with them again.

Wynter's eyes were drawn to the guitars. Caleb stood beside her. "Which one do you like?"

She pointed to an acoustic. "That looks like the one I had."

Jesse made a noise of disbelief. "You played a steel-string? Show me your hand." He reached back from his drum throne to take her left hand, turning it palm-up, and ran his fingers along hers to straighten them. She hunched her shoulders at the touch, as if preparing to draw back, but let Jesse have a closer look. "Look at this, Caleb. Proof's in the calluses."

She twisted her hand free and pointed to a Strat. "This one looks like Indio's in the photo."

"Let's start with what you know," Caleb said, "and I'll show you the electric guitars after."

He handed her the acoustic and indicated a couple of stools in front of the drums. She hopped on one, her feet finding the crossbars, and got comfortable. Softly, she picked an arpeggio and quickly fine-tuned the guitar like a pro. Caleb took another acoustic and sat opposite her. She'd stopped playing once it was in tune.

He said, "Tell me a song you know and we'll play it together."

"I don't know what songs *you* know."

"Try me."

"There were some songs in the old tutorial books I had. I never heard any of them on the radio, though."

"Such as?"

He expected her to say *She'll Be Comin' Round the Mountain* or *Frère Jacques*. He was pleasantly surprised.

"*Here Comes the Sun*? I like that one. I thought about it this morning when I opened the drapes."

He couldn't help smiling. "The Beatles. Great start. You wanna sing it?"

He wanted to know if she could sing. That slight huskiness to her voice would sound gorgeous if she knew how to use it. She shook her head and he didn't press her.

"Okay. Key of A?" he said, and she nodded. "Can you do the intro?" Another nod. "Go ahead. I'll follow your lead."

She fingerpicked the intro with a surety that surprised him again, and he came in with vocals and rhythm, along with Jesse playing drums with a light touch. Her head went up and she stared first at Jesse, then him. If she'd never heard the song before, other than strumming it herself, she'd be unprepared for the music they were making. When Jesse joined the vocals with that sweet harmonization of his, she actually cracked a quick smile. She handled the odd timing without faltering.

The song ended and they sat for a few seconds in silence. She was breathing deeply, her eyes bright with excitement.

"What are those things on your guitar?" she asked after a moment.

"That's the EQ — the equalizer. This is an acoustic-electric, which means I can amp it. The EQ adjusts the tone."

"Show me?"

Caleb plugged in a cable, switched on the amp, and strummed it to show her the new sound.

"I like it," she said with satisfaction. "But it doesn't sound like rock music." Her gaze drifted to the Strat.

Caleb said, "Wanna try it?"

"Yes, please." She hopped off the stool as he fetched the electric guitar. "Is it Indio's? Will he mind?"

"He will not mind." Caleb arranged the strap on her shoulder. His eyes met Jesse's over her head. No, Indio would *not* mind loaning his guitar to a pint-sized musician whose eyes lit up at a drum beat and who just wanted to play rock music.

"It's heavy," she said.

"Sit for now. Just hold it normally. Have you used a pick before?" She nodded and he handed her one.

She played a few chords. "Why is it so quiet?"

"The body's solid, so there's nowhere for the sound to go."

He flicked on the amp behind her stool. She jumped at the popping sound it made.

"Those pickups convert the string vibrations into an electric signal, which the amp amplifies," he said, pointing to each part in turn. "Go for it."

Wynter played a chord, a single strum. The amp blared at her and she jumped again. She tried a basic chord progression, strumming like she was playing folk music. She stopped, shook her head.

"How do you play rock music?"

"It's all in the rhythm." Caleb took back his acoustic-electric. He strummed a simple three-chord progression, then repeated it with an R&B vibe. "Use a lot of barred chords, and half-barred, so you're using your left hand for rhythm as well — see, lift up to mute the strings, to keep it snappy."

Her foot was already tapping. She followed along, a little stiffly at first, but quickly caught on and experimented with the left-hand muting. He tested her, sliding into a new progression. She was watching and listening carefully and within two beats had changed to match him. Impressive.

Jesse picked up the beat, which made her glow with pleasure. Caleb was determined to get a real smile out of her if it took all day.

They got a mid-tempo rock groove going, and she played through the chord progressions with flawless rhythm. He and Jesse exchanged a look to acknowledge that. They were used to tight rhythm — three brothers with the same heartbeat, and now their sister shared it.

"Cue Indio's solo," Jesse called out, and Caleb's heart twinged because he hadn't jammed with Indio in a very long time. He noodled a few bars of melody and they played on.

Jesse cued the last four bars with a fill — Caleb recognized it but would Wynter know what it meant? Her head tilted toward the drums — she had heard and understood. She was a natural musician, already in sync with this little band. They ended the song together.

"Good teamwork, Wynter." Jesse gave Caleb a meaningful look, as impressed with her as Caleb was.

"You said you had a radio at the ashram?" Caleb asked her.

"Yes. We... I listened to it for hours out in a storage shed at night. I tried to remember everything, and to work out the songs in my head, and on the guitar when I had the chance."

"You have a good foundation. We'll make a rockstar out of you in no time," he teased, strumming through a random progression out of habit.

"What's that chord you just played?" She repeated the sequence.

"That's..." He took a moment to figure it out. "C minor six."

"But this is a major sixth."

"It's a minor third, and the sixth added. You know some theory, then? Can you read music?"

"Yes. I had a classical guitar book, and a piano teacher for a while."

"You didn't mention the piano earlier."

"I didn't like it as much."

He laughed. "Okay. No pianos here, so you're safe." She copied his smile, but slowly, like she was out of practice. "Look, if you have musical questions you should ask Indio. I'm not great with the theory." He couldn't wait to tell Indio she was a musician. That feeling was short-lived as he recalled the tenor of his most recent conversation with his brother. Indio might not care.

No, that was crazy. Music was Indio's life. He would care.

"Why didn't you like the piano?" Jesse said. "I always wanted to learn to play piano."

Wynter hunched over the guitar. "I wasn't very good at it, and sometimes there was no one else to play at the prayer meetings so

I had to do it even though I was gonna screw it up." She sucked her lips in, like she regretted talking too much.

"Did that make them mad?" Jesse was pushing for more, desperate to know exactly what had happened to her.

Wynter sat very still and said nothing.

"You can tell us," Jesse said. "You can tell us anything."

The atmosphere of discovery and camaraderie drained from the room. Caleb was as keen as Jesse for information, but Jesse couldn't see her face right now, couldn't see the way her eyes went blank as she retreated into herself.

Before Caleb could think of the words to rescue her, she spoke.

"Sometimes, anything you say is wrong, so you say nothing and you get in trouble anyway."

Jesse persisted out of sheer frustration. And because he was being Jesse. "What does that mean — *get in trouble?* What did they do when you were in trouble? The doctor said you had old bruises. Did they do that, or did you fall over playing soccer or something?"

She ignored him and turned an earnest look on Caleb. "I won't cause any trouble, I promise. You won't even know I'm here."

Jesse opened his mouth to say more. Caleb silenced him with a look, and for several seconds they were locked in a struggle as Wynter glanced from one to the other, growing increasingly anxious.

Jesse backed down.

Caleb searched for a way to recover the situation. "D'you want to see real live rock music, Wynter? We'll drive down to Portland tomorrow night and see Indio's band."

Her demeanor changed in a flash. She sat up, her expression brightening. "Can I? Am I allowed to?"

"I just said we're going, so we're going." His previous objections seemed irrelevant, now he'd heard her play. She'd love the live experience, and it was a valid excuse to force Indio to make the effort to meet her. "Jesse, when we're done here, text your brother and let him know."

"Awesome!" Jesse bounced on his seat. "Wynter, give me some bands and we'll play another."

She reeled off a string of bands and musicians from the current decade, and then from back before she was born — Oasis, Nirvana, Guns n' Roses — and further still to the 'seventies with Dire Straits, Journey, Led Zeppelin, and the Stones...

"Classic rock fan, huh?" Caleb remarked.

She and Indio would get along just fine.

They spent a few minutes working out the chords before launching into another song — it was clear Wynter shared Indio's seemingly magical ability to play by ear, or even from memory, whereas Caleb had always needed to write down and rehearse his parts. To round out the sound, he swapped his guitar for the bass, his preferred instrument. Jesse took over the vocals entirely, dutifully censoring himself on any curse words. They had fun with another round of improvisation. They played *Here Comes the Sun* again, and again, until Wynter was completely satisfied with it, and now her smile was as easy and natural as Jesse's.

Girl Scout Cookies

Jesse had entered an alternate universe.

Ever since he'd read that paper on parallel universes, he imagined each moment in his timeline as a fork in the tree of his life. Every incident or decision created a new branching line of possibilities. Those moments were easy to see in retrospect. Only rarely did the universe offer the chance to witness them in real time. Answering the door on Thursday evening had been one of those moments — but instead of crossing to a different branch, he'd climbed a whole different tree.

He'd thought she was selling Girl Scout cookies. In that moment, his brain couldn't come up with any other explanation for a teenage girl to be on his doorstep — despite the fact she wasn't in uniform. In fact, she was in summer clothing on a freezing night, no Thin Mints in sight. But *Girl Scout cookies* was the only way to make sense of it.

The misinterpretation had lasted about five seconds, long enough for her to ask for Caleb Henry Fairn. And that had made about as much sense as the cookies thing. So now he was sitting in a new tree, the one where he had a half-sister — this strange creature from another world, a creature he'd dragged into *this* world with her first taste of hot chocolate.

Wynter was the alien who'd crash-landed on his porch, a raw bundle of untapped potential, ill-equipped to live among humankind. Twenty-four hours later, Jesse had already made an extensive mental list of the things he needed to show her ASAP in order to ground her in reality and begin the long process of getting her acquainted with this world. If Caleb was her rescuer, he would be her mentor.

The universe didn't come to a standstill just because it had sent

an alien/sister into his life. On Friday, his last free day before the
new semester began, he went out with his friends, including the
girl who considered herself his girlfriend, and for a few hours
things were normal again. They watched a very silly horror movie
— not his choice, but it was nice when Natalie burrowed her face
into his chest during the scary parts. They all ate at a cheap
Vietnamese diner in the University District. He made fun of those
among the group who thought the movie was good, and they made
fun of him for complaining, not for the first time, about the B he'd
received for a paper last semester — entirely the fault of the professor, who'd failed to fully appreciate his subtle yet admittedly
controversial approach to the topic. They went to a club for an
hour. He made out with Natalie outside her dorm room and she
wouldn't let him in even though her roommate was away for the
weekend.

On Saturday morning he brewed the coffee and emptied the
dishwasher so Caleb wouldn't have to bug him about it, and did
an hour's study before Caleb got up — for the second time, as he'd
gone to the bus station in the wee hours to check for Joy. Jesse
asked about his visit to the lawyer.

"Washington isn't her home state," Caleb explained, "but until
Arizona reports her missing, Social Services here will make an
initial placement decision. They prefer to place kids with family,
so she can live with Joy."

"Permanently?"

"No, an emergency placement pending a custody hearing. The
court will notify Miriam, if they can find her. If she suddenly
decides to step up, she could dispute custody from Arizona."

Not what Jesse wanted to hear. "Then Wynter would end up
back at the ashram."

"That's the worst-case scenario. I'm hoping Joy brings some
paperwork with her, or everything's going to take longer. The important thing is that we need Social Services on our side."

It was starting to sound complicated. It should be simple.
Wynter was their sister and needed a home. Case closed. But it
wasn't that simple.

Then there was her health — physical and emotional. She hadn't
been fed properly, that much was clear. More than that they could
only guess. Jesse had heard horror stories about cults, of course,
although he knew little about the Light, and like any cult the Light
didn't consider itself to be one. When he looked them up online,

the Arizona ashram seventy miles east of Tucson was described as a "communal residence and temple headquarters for devotees". The website touted the brand-new retreat on the property where you could pay fifteen hundred dollars for a weekend of "spiritual awakening and replenishment".

"What if they hurt her?" Jesse said. "Did the doctor examine her for... you know, for sexual abuse?"

"Not specifically. And I don't want to put her through that for no reason. Let's back off from the questions, okay? Be gentle with her, and maybe she'll talk."

Jesse wasn't one to *back off* from the questions. Asking questions was the only way to make sense of the world. *Ubi dubium, ibi libertas.* Where there is doubt, there is freedom. Jesse lived in a state of doubt — the only honest way to live. Doubt everything, question everything. Wynter had fading bruises on her body and was ten pounds underweight. Jesse wanted to know *why*. He spent every free moment on his phone or computer finding out as much as he could about the Light. He'd never bothered before. He'd turned three years old that summer Miriam and Joy left and had no memories of either of them. Never felt the loss or the desire to know what happened to them. Now he had a reason to find out.

Meanwhile, his primary concern was helping Wynter navigate this new world she found so fascinating. Every time she touched something in the house — from the TV remote to the doorbell to the bread bin — he recognized it as a signal she didn't know what it was and explained it for her, taking care not to be patronizing. He teased her gently and even managed to make her giggle as she watched a bag of popcorn expand in the microwave. Popcorn for breakfast had never been permissible in this household, but it was for educational purposes.

After breakfast, she found him in his room at the computer. He figured she'd have questions but she showed little interest.

"You've used a computer before?"

"A bit. They had them in the warehouse for spreadsheets and bookkeeping."

"Did you go online?"

"No. But some computers were online. That's how Joy printed out the map and the page from the phone directory."

"Well, let me know if you want a tour of the internet."

"How long will that take?"

"The rest of our lives."

"What do you use it for?"

"You can find out anything you want. Ninety percent of it is rubbish, so you have to learn how to figure out what's true."

"Like the Light."

That caught his attention. He'd been wondering how seriously Wynter had taken it.

"How much of the Light do you think is true?" He felt daring for delving into it, knowing Caleb would disapprove of him questioning another's religious beliefs.

She pursed her lips like she knew she wasn't supposed to speak badly of it. "They said it was all true."

"But what do *you* think?"

Now she looked troubled. "Is there a way to tell?" she said at last.

Wow. He loved that she asked that question. *How do you know what's true?* – the entire basis of modern science.

"Religion's a tricky thing," he said, settling for an answer Caleb might approve of. "I think it comes down to your worldview – whether you believe something's true because of strict standards of evidence, or because it *feels* right. Head versus heart."

"What's my worldview?"

"You're gonna have to figure that out for yourself."

"Are you head or heart?"

"Head, all the way."

She thought about that. "I could try both, and see."

"Good idea. Put it on the back burner. Plenty of time."

She looked at his screen. "Is that the internet?"

"Yep. I'm just chatting with friends – they want me to fill in for a gig next week. The internet's great for keeping up with things. World events, new music, friends on social media." He could see he'd lost her. "Never mind about all that for now. Saturday morning is for grocery shopping. Caleb gets beer and jeans and household stuff from the Exchange, but for food we go to the regular store. You ready to go?"

He'd cancelled laser tag with Marcus so he could come along, even though he and Caleb usually alternated weeks and it wasn't his turn. Caleb handed him the keys. He'd taken Jesse's driving instruction seriously, sending him to a driver education course at fifteen and encouraging him to drive as much as possible for the practice.

At the store, it took Wynter ages to walk down the first aisle because she stopped to look at everything. Caleb left her there with

Jesse and went off to start filling the cart.

"Why are there so many kinds of bread?" she asked Jesse.

"They're different brands and different flours. White, whole-wheat, grain, buckwheat, rye, sourdough. We get bread from the bakery around the corner so don't worry about it."

She eyed packets of factory-made cakes and cookies.

"You wanna buy those?" he said when she picked up a box of cookies. He and Caleb didn't have a sweet tooth but they were happy to feed her anything at this point, just to put some weight on her.

She smiled shyly, shook her head and put it back.

"You can have anything you want," Jesse assured her. "This stuff is crap, to be honest. And that one has palm oil, which we don't buy because of the orangutans. We'll get something fresh at the bakery."

At the end of the aisle she stared at the two-dozen kinds of milk in the refrigerator. Jesse grabbed a gallon of their usual. The ridiculousness of modern grocery excess hit him again as they started down the next aisle — cereals.

"Okay, what d'you like for breakfast?"

"I liked Caleb's pancakes."

"He only makes those on special occasions. Usually we eat cereal or oatmeal."

She pointed to a box with colored loops on it. "That one?"

"God, that stuff is dreadful." He grinned and took it off the shelf, along with two more cereals with much less sugar.

Caleb found them, the cart half full, and Jesse dumped the cereal and milk into it. Caleb was trying not to roll his eyes at Wynter's choice.

"What do you like to eat?" Caleb asked her. "We're not cooks, I'm afraid, but we can give it a try."

"If you don't cook, what do you eat?" Wynter said, confused.

"We just grab takeout, like what we had last night. Bea's been spoiling us on Sundays lately — she usually comes over with Jilly and makes a casserole. So, what about today? We'll eat early before we head down to Indio's gig."

"What are you used to?" Jesse asked.

"Rice or tortillas and bits."

"Bits of what?"

"Just whatever there was. Vegetables, beans, chicken." She chewed her lip. "I know how to cook that, but you won't like it. It doesn't taste like takeout. It doesn't taste of anything much."

"You like steak?" Caleb said. "We could barbecue."

She nodded, looking uncertain. Jesse figured she'd never had steak and didn't want to admit it.

"Why don't the two of you get some salad stuff and I'll get the steak."

Caleb handed off the cart to Jesse, who took Wynter to the other side of the store. They wandered through the produce section. Jesse dumped salad ingredients into the cart while she walked slowly past six kinds of potato, nine kinds of lettuce, a huge rack of fresh herbs...

"What's this?" She held up a string bag.

"Tangerines."

She sniffed them. "Are they good?"

"Very good."

He ripped a small hole in the bag and handed her one. She inspected it, and he wondered if she knew what to do with it. He took it back and peeled it.

"Is this allowed?"

"I'll buy the bag anyway. Eat."

She broke it open and pushed one entire half into her mouth, chewing and screwing up her face at the tartness. Then she swallowed, nodding enthusiastically.

"Are they expensive?"

"Don't worry about it. I made eighty dollars last month on YouTube." At her puzzled look, he added, "I'll show you when we get home. Another wonder of the internet."

While he picked out tomatoes, she wandered off to something that had caught her eye in the corner. When he looked up, she was standing at the wall of nut and coffee dispensers. She twisted the knob on one of the dispensers and stuck her hand underneath the flow, letting the nuts spill into the trough below.

"Whoa!" He rushed over to stop her. "We don't need those. Don't touch stuff without asking me, okay?"

At her shocked expression, Jesse realized his voice had come out harder than he'd intended. Caleb was approaching and Jesse knew exactly what was going to happen. Sure enough, Caleb tore a plastic bag off the roll and handed it to Jesse, raising his eyebrow in a sort of sympathetic scold. Yep, they were going to have to buy a pound of pistachios scraped out of the trough.

"Are those expensive, too?" Wynter said. "I'll pay for them."

"With what?" Jesse scooped the nuts into the bag. He was more annoyed with himself, for not paying attention, than with her. Still, ten dollars' worth of pistachios wasn't the way he'd have chosen to spend the household budget.

"I'll make some money on YouTube," Wynter said with an air of desperation.

"Uh, sure, okay." It had taken Jesse four years to build up a following that barely covered his gas money. Currently he was riding around on his dirt bike, which Natalie hated, because he couldn't afford to renew the tags on his car until Rob paid him for last week's gig.

Wynter wasn't happy with Jesse's response, perhaps picking up on the sarcasm.

"We love pistachios," Caleb assured her. "We'll add them to the rest of that popcorn with some M&Ms. Instant trail mix."

Now she looked a lot happier, although the odds were vanishingly small she knew what trail mix was. Or M&Ms.

Caleb poured a pound of coffee beans into another bag, with Jesse directing him to a new fair-trade brand — "because of slave labor," he told Wynter. He had so much to tell her. He might have to write an instruction manual.

They went to the self-checkout, which he thought would impress her. She didn't know enough about grocery shopping to understand it was cool. Still, she was interested in how it worked, especially when their tangerines set off the indignant Voice because the bag was underweight. The total came to almost one hundred dollars, which wasn't unexpected considering they'd bought pistachios and steak — still, it was more than usual.

Wynter was staring at the screen. "That's my birthday," she said. "Ninety-eight dollars. I was born in 1998."

"What about the thirty-two cents?" Jesse pointed out.

"And those pistachios were $9.80 a pound," she said, ignoring his perfectly reasonable question. "That's why I touched them."

"So what?"

"When you see repeating numbers, it means something, doesn't it?"

Jesse grabbed a bag of M&Ms from the rack behind him, scanned it and dropped it in the grocery bag. "Now we're at $99.71. What does that mean?"

"I don't know. What does it mean?" she asked in all seriousness.

"Nothing, Wyn. It means nothing at all." At her look of dismay, he added, "What did you think it meant?"

"I thought it meant I belong here."

"Belong where? In a Safeway?"

"Just... here," she said, deflated. "With you."

Caleb swiped his card to pay, and said, "I already told you that you belong here."

"Sometimes the universe has other plans. It sends messages if you listen. It puts up roadblocks if you're on the wrong path."

She sounded very unsure of herself — that, at least, was progress. The less firmly entrenched her superstitions were, the better. In any case, before he could begin her education Jesse was going to have to knock those dumb ideas out of her.

Caleb handed him ten dollars for the bakery while he took the groceries back to the truck. Wynter deferred to Jesse in choosing bread and bagels and a few other things. On the way back to the parking lot, they passed a small used bookstore — one of Jesse's favorite hangouts. He grabbed Wynter's hand.

"Come inside with me. I'll get you something."

"I thought you could find out anything on the internet?"

"Sometimes it's nice to hold a book in your hands."

While she waited by a table of books at the front, he found what he wanted in the Reference section.

"Something to help with your worldview," Jesse said as they returned to the truck, where Caleb was finishing up a phone call. Jesse flashed the cover at Caleb before handing her the book.

She settled in the back seat to look at it.

"A *Brief History of Time*," she read off the cover — the illustrated hardback edition, in pretty good shape. Jesse was pleased with the find. She flicked through the pages. "Looks complicated. Will I understand it?"

"It's written for anyone to understand. And I can help you with it."

"Will I learn about coffee slaves and orangutans?"

"Not in this book. This book starts at the beginning of time."

"Is it about religion?" she asked dubiously.

"The opposite of religion." Jesse backed out and started for home.

Caleb grinned. "You're kinda coloring her perspective, aren't you?"

"Because my perspective is the correct one." Jesse threw Wynter a look over his shoulder. "You can ask someone else for the other side of things, but not Caleb. Unfortunately, he knows nothing about physics *or* metaphysics."

That surprised her, as if she thought Caleb surely knew everything about everything.

"It all goes over my head," Caleb said.

"Don't let his modesty fool you," Jesse told Wynter. "Mediocre high school student and took him four years to get an associate degree, but our Caleb is a smart cookie."

"How d'you know?"

"I've never beaten him at chess."

At home, Wynter put the book aside to help unpack the groceries.

"I talked to Social Services," Caleb said. "A woman, Tina, is coming over at 3:30." Jesse could tell he'd been trying to find the right moment to tell her.

Wynter stuttered to a halt, a box of cereal in her hand. "Why?"

"Tina's your caseworker. She helps to decide where you'll live and who'll take care of you."

"I thought Joy would take care of me. Or you."

Caleb leaned back against the counter with a look Jesse had rarely seen on his face – the look he occasionally got when life dealt a blow he wasn't sure he could deflect. Only Indio's or Harry's worst shenanigans brought on that expression. "It's not up to me. I'm not your guardian."

"Who is?"

"I presume it's Miriam."

"Will they send me to Thailand?"

"Would you want to go there?"

"She doesn't want me. She's never written or called me in all these years, and even before that..." Wynter looked terrified. "Where will I live?"

"My lawyer believes when Joy shows up with proof of your identity, the court will place you with her. It's called an emergency placement."

"Joy doesn't have a job," Jesse said. "Why would the court let her have Wynter?"

Caleb's brow creased. "I'll help her find a job."

"She's very good with numbers," Wynter said. "She kept the books in the warehouse. She can get a job as a bookkeeper."

"That's a possibility. Tina will explain what's happening and ask some questions."

"Do I have to tell her the truth?"

Caleb and Jesse exchanged a look.

"It's good to always tell the truth," Caleb said slowly.

"It's okay to lie to Social Services."

"Who told you that?"

"Everyone knows that." She looked at Jesse. "Or is that a problem with my worldview?"

Jesse didn't know what to say.

"In this family, we tell the truth," Caleb said. "Is there something you don't want Social Services to know?"

Wynter shifted uncomfortably. "What do I say so they won't send me away?"

"They'll do what's best for you." Caleb turned back to the groceries to hide his expression. "Tell the truth, so Tina will have all the necessary information to make the best decision."

So typical of Caleb to side with the authorities, even though he didn't believe they always made the best decisions any more than Jesse did.

"We'll have lunch and then let's tidy the place up," Caleb said, forcing brightness into his tone. "First impressions count. I'll clear up outside and then I have to get to the dojo. I'll check the bus station as well. Wynter, you and Jesse give the bathroom a once-over. And maybe try that conditioner Bea got you?"

Type One

Wynter knelt over the tub. "Does my hair matter that much?"

"In my experience," Jesse said as he poured warm water over her head and worked the conditioner in, "social workers fall into one of two extreme types. The first type finds fault in everything from a smudge on your shirt to a speck of mold in the shower. The second type wouldn't blink at a black eye on a twelve-year-old as long as his obviously inebriated father swears the stupid kid walked into a door."

"Did you?"

"Did I what?"

"Walk into a door."

"Not me. Indio. And no, of course he didn't." Jesse scrubbed harder. "My point is, your hair is a problem if this Tina is the first type, because she's gonna think we're not taking good care of you."

His fingers stopped suddenly and he leaned in.

"Is something wrong?"

"No. Just checking for... uh... never mind."

"For lice? The nurse already did that. Wait! What are you...?" She slid out of the way as he poured a pitcher of water on her head.

"Hold still! I'm rinsing it."

"You have to wait two minutes," Wynter retorted. "It says on the label."

"That's bullcrap."

"Didn't you read the instructions?"

"They write that to make you think it's doing something *so* amazing, it takes two whole minutes."

She narrowed her eyes at him, wet strands of hair plastered to her face. "Are you sure?"

"Pretty sure."

She would have to trust him. She let him rinse her hair and dry it roughly with a towel. He tugged a comb through it.

"Much better, huh?" he said, stepping back to admire his work.

Wynter ran her fingers through her hair. It had never felt so soft. It didn't feel *right*, though. It didn't feel like her.

"I have to braid it," she said.

"Can't help you there."

"I think the social worker will be more impressed if I braid it." Wynter had only one hair tie — the same one Joy had left her with on the bus. As they talked, she made a single fat French braid down the back of her head. "Why did Social Services come to your house?"

Jesse's expression clouded. "They came a few times over the years, when a neighbor or teacher reported something. Harry wasn't the greatest parent, in case you hadn't picked up on that. But the last thing we wanted was to be taken into care. So we put on our happy faces and told lies."

"But Caleb told me not to lie to them."

"You got nothing to lie about, right? Tell that woman you want to stay here until Joy comes, and then live with Joy — either here or someplace nearby if that's what Joy wants. Tell her you don't want to go back to Arizona because your mom isn't even there."

"She'll let me stay, won't she? We made the house look great."

"We did! And I'm gonna tidy my room right now, and make my bed for the first time ever. If I can figure out how."

By the time Caleb left for the dojo, where he taught a karate class, the house was immaculate. It had been tidy and clean beforehand, by Wynter's standards, but now it was perfect. Jesse even put away the half-finished chess game.

"How will you remember where all the pieces go for next time?"

"It's chess. Of course we'll remember."

That made no sense. Wynter let it drop.

"Hungry?" he asked her, and she nodded with a guilty feeling because it wasn't really time to eat. "We'll have a snack."

"Are we allowed?"

He stopped halfway to the kitchen to stare back at her. "Yes, Wyn, we are allowed." He opened the pantry door. "You can eat anything you want, any time you want, okay? You don't have to ask. Ever."

He toasted Pop-Tarts, which turned out to be the oddest food item she'd ever seen or eaten. She made it through one, after which he found her some crackers.

"Do you know how to play?" he asked, waiting for his fourth and fifth Pop-Tarts to pop.

"Chess? No."

"I mean do you know how to play... anything?"

"I play guitar and piano."

"No. Just *playing*. Did you ever play games? Barbie dolls and jump ropes — anything like that?"

"Some friends had these metal clockwork toys that you wound up. We would make them fight in an arena."

"That sounds awesome! Retro, but awesome. What else?"

"Nothing else."

"Okay. I'm gonna show you something."

Jesse took her into his bedroom, switched on his laptop, and spent half an hour showing her the gaming videos he'd made online. They made even less sense than chess.

"I get why my hair was important, but why is *this* important?"

"I'm checking to see if you might be interested in playing games like this."

Wynter tried her best to pay attention, standing beside him while he sat at his desk.

"I have no clue what's going on," she said after viewing what Jesse called a "narration" of a "run-through" of a "level" of a "first-person shooter" game.

"Don't worry, we can start with something simpler." He twisted to face her. "It's pretty exciting, though, right?"

"It's so confusing. All those little symbols and dials and numbers — how do you keep your eye on all of those at once?"

"Takes practice. I'll teach you."

"You should probably teach me math first."

"I'll teach you both. I'm gonna teach you *everything*. First things first — I'll set up an email account for you. When you start school, you'll need email to talk to your friends and send them stuff."

"Can't I call them on the phone?"

"Sure, but everyone has an email address."

Everyone. Xay had an email address, and Wynter had once memorized it.

"Can I send an email to anyone I want?" she said.

"Absolutely. Well, there are safety concerns..." He gave her a thorough look. "You can email anyone you already know, okay?"

"Okay."

"Do you know anyone?" He was poking fun again.

"I know you."

"And I have an email address! We're off to a good start." Jesse typed and clicked at his laptop. "Ready to go. What username would you like?"

"I don't know what that is."

"It can be anything. Best not to use your real name. I'm drumheadgamerboy, same as my video channel."

"Can I be... guitarheadgamergirl?"

"Uh, that doesn't really... You're not a gamer girl, although I'll be doing my best to turn you into one. And guitarhead doesn't mean anything. So that's not a logical choice."

"You said it could be anything."

"Yes, I did. You can be guitarheadgamergirl if you really want. This is your identity that you're showing to the world. So think carefully."

Wynter thought carefully. This was rather more complicated than Jesse had initially made it seem.

Finally, she said, "I don't *have* an identity in this world."

"Sure you do. What words would you use to describe yourself?"

"Short."

Jesse laughed and tweaked her hip. "You'll grow. I don't mean physical descriptions. Who are you?"

"I'm your little sister." It felt very good to say that.

"Who do you want to be?"

"A little sister who plays music with you."

"I like where this is going. Little sister guitar player. Little sister music maker..."

"Little sister song."

"Okay, let's see if it's available — littlesistersong." He typed it in. "Your password is columbiacity, where we live. Lower case, all one word. Don't tell anyone."

"But you know it."

"I've already forgotten. You should change it, anyway. Okay, done. You now have an email address." He slid the laptop in front of her. "Do you know how to send an email?"

"I did it once before."

"Send me one."

She started a new message, typed in his address, and wrote, *Thank you for my new identity* in the subject line. In the body of the email she wrote:

    Let's read the worldview book you gave me.

Her heart raced. She grabbed the mouse and clicked the send button as fast as she could.

"Your hands are shaking," Jesse said.

"I'm okay."

He gave her a strange look before turning the laptop toward him and logging into his account. He showed her the unread email at the top of his inbox.

"Send me one," she said. "I want to get my first ever email."

He did so, and she switched to her account to read it.

> *Re. Thank you for my new identity*
>
> *I'll read with you for one hour if you play a video game with me for one hour first.*
>
> *J*
>
> XOXO

"I did say I'm gonna turn you into a gamer girl," he said.

"What are those X's and O's?"

"Those are hugs and kisses. How can you not know that?" He said it kindly, but she felt her face heating at yet another reminder of how little she knew. "That's just what kids put at the end of messages sometimes, to their friends or their mom or... y'know, their sisters, I guess, although I never emailed a sister before so I'm not sure."

"Would you put those in an email to Indio or Caleb?"

"God, no. That would be weird. Indio and me are good buddies, though. We text, more than email." Jesse pulled out his phone and clicked Indio's name from the message app. He held the screen in front of her face and she read aloud from one of the bubbles:

> Stop polluting my playlist with your crappy EDM. I'd rather fuck a frog than listen to another—

Jesse snatched back his phone. "Whoa, okay, that's not appropriate. Sorry." He gave her a sheepish look. "We share playlists from a music streaming site. At the club last night I heard some awesome beats — he's not so impressed. Anyway, we'll get you a phone and then we can talk or text any time."

"But we live in the same house."

"I mean when you're at school or... wherever."

Wynter didn't know what *wherever* meant. She was going to live in this house with Joy, wasn't she?

"I want to send an email to someone else," she said.

"Do you know the address?"

"I think so, if I remember it."

"I'll go set up our video game on the TV."

After he left, she started a new email. Xay had a complicated username with lots of numbers and she wasn't sure if she got it right. She wrote *Where are you?* in the subject line, and *This is Wynter* in the body of the email. As she signed it with XOXO, her hand started shaking again. She clicked *Send* and sat back, satisfied.

Almost at once, a new email appeared in her inbox. Her initial thrill was quickly dampened when she read the subject line.

Address not found.

Wynter tried again, searching her memory for the correct number sequence. Xay had made her memorize it so she could log into his account, because she had occasional access to an online computer and he did not. That was a year ago. More than a year. In another world.

After several more tries, each one returned with the same blunt response, she gave up — for now, anyway. Maybe the correct address would come to her.

Would Xay write back, even if she managed to get through to him? If he thought she was still in the Light, he might think it was a trick. He would've gotten on with his life, wouldn't he? He didn't want or need her making things difficult. And she was being greedy. She'd known Caleb and Jesse for two days and already felt like she belonged with them. She was going to meet Indio, and soon Joy would be here.

She shut down the browser and went to join Jesse in the living room.

✿

Wynter had never held or seen a gaming controller in her life. She was terrible at the video game. Frustrated by her mistakes, Jesse took frequent deep breaths to keep himself calm as he talked her through the buttons and explained the options.

"I'm not a patient person," he admitted after she got herself killed yet again in a particularly disastrous manner. "I'm gonna try harder. I'm not used to slowing down for people."

He did try harder, cheering on her little victories and offering encouraging words when she failed at the simplest tasks. When their hour was up, she was glad it was over because he seemed quite stressed.

"Do I have to learn how to do this in order to fit in? To survive?"

"Absolutely! Not *this*, necessarily, but something like this. You're gonna need something to talk about with the friends you make at school. Some of them might want to talk about repeating numbers and other messages from the universe, but pretty soon you're not gonna believe in that stuff anymore, so you'll need something else. Did you watch TV at the ashram?"

"No."

"Ever been to a movie theater?"

"No."

"How about books?"

"Someone had a little library of really old novels. I liked those."

"Awesome. We'll watch some TV tomorrow. And you already know about music, although none of your friends will've heard of Status Quo, to be honest. I've only heard of them because Indio's weird like that. Anyway, the social stuff is just as important as the worldview stuff. We'll find something that suits you perfectly." Jesse packed away the gaming equipment. "This was a learning experience for me, too. I might get work tutoring high school kids this semester, so I need to practice being calm and patient."

"You can practice on me. I'm gonna need help with everything."

"You'll be my guinea pig. I think you're the youngest person I know."

"Don't you have lots of friends? I saw your inbox — it's very full."

"My friends are all a bit older than me. My friend Marcus has a brother in high school — that's about it."

"What about Bea's little girl?"

"Jilly doesn't have a personality yet. I wouldn't say you could get to *know* someone until they're older."

"I thought she had a personality."

"I mean she's not rational. She can't even talk."

"Am I rational?"

"I'm sure you are, because we share DNA. If you're not, don't worry about it. I'm gonna make you rational. We'll start by reading Hawking."

They sat on the living room floor and looked at the book. Jesse didn't start at the beginning. He flicked the pages back and forth in some sort of order that made sense to him. Wynter didn't know why he thought she'd understand it — she didn't — but his enthusiasm kept it interesting. Jesse sounded confident about these strange tales, and Caleb said Jesse was smart, and she trusted Caleb. Still, doubt niggled at the back of her mind.

"I've never heard of gravity waves or exploding stars," she said. "Is it all true?"

"It's absolutely true. It's the reason the universe hangs together."

"But why does this stuff matter to us? We're such a tiny part of it and we can never visit those places."

"Knowledge is good for its own sake, Wyn. Doesn't have to be practical. In any case, every single thing that happens, or has ever happened, or will ever happen, comes down to the physics in this book. Isn't that right, Caleb?"

Caleb had come home as they were finishing up, and was getting together the food for their barbecue on the kitchen counter. He smiled without answering or looking up.

"He does at least listen when I go on about it, until I hit his limit," Jesse said, as if Caleb wasn't there. "Indio, on the other hand, pretends this stuff isn't important. It's *mega* important. If you have questions, just ask me."

"I do have a question," Wynter said. "What's a guinea pig?"

✿

Wynter did not like the look of the social worker. Tina had frizzy gray hair tied in a ponytail and she bustled around as if she owned the house. Her smile for Wynter was friendly enough, but every time she talked to Caleb or looked at Jesse, her face turned into a blank mask.

It became clear to Wynter that Caleb had already explained a lot over the phone, and he repeated more than once that their twenty-two-year-old sister Joy was going to arrive soon to take care of Wynter. Caleb was very pleasant to Tina. Under it, he was anxious. Wynter didn't like the way Tina made him behave. She gave him some paperwork and said she would explain everything to Wynter.

Caleb sat next to Wynter on the couch and Tina took the armchair opposite. Jesse hung back in the corner directing dark looks to the back of Tina's head. After a while, his fingertips began drumming a beat on the wall behind him.

Sitting shoulder-to-shoulder with Caleb, Wynter tried to take it in as Tina said she'd been unable to extract Miriam's contact details from the Light, or her current location. She would keep trying. She talked on and on. Guardianship, temporary custody, foster homes, the family court system, wards of state, and plenty of other things Wynter didn't understand.

Her ears were ringing and spots danced before her eyes.

"Jesse!" Caleb snapped, making Wynter jump. Jesse stopped his drum beat.

"I'd like to talk to Wynter alone," Tina said.

Wynter had zoned out of the conversation and didn't know why

Tina said that. Caleb patted her hand and stood up. He gave a curt sign to Jesse and the two of them went out to the front yard.

"Well, Wynter, what an adventure you've had," Tina said. "This must be quite a change for you. How are you coping?"

How *was* she coping? The lights and sounds and crowds in the mall and grocery store filled her head. She felt uneasy in those places, except that Caleb had been right there and she felt safe with him, and Jesse was so good at explaining everything — from cookies to guinea pigs to quantum singularities. Was she coping? What did coping feel like?

Tina waited for an answer.

Wynter wasn't going to lie, despite a lifetime of conditioning by the Light to do just that. She already trusted Caleb more than anyone at the ashram, except perhaps Joy, and Joy wasn't here. She'd tell the truth. But she wouldn't talk about the Light.

"Everything is different. I like it," she said. And she did. The confusion, the choices, the new things — she liked it because it had nothing to do with the Light.

"And Caleb? Is he taking good care of you?"

"Yes. This house is very clean. His girlfriend took me shopping for clothes."

"Oh, he didn't mention a girlfriend. Does she live here?"

"No."

"So, she visited?"

"Yesterday morning."

"Did she stay the night?"

"I don't think so. She was just here when I woke up."

"And what about Jesse? What's he like?"

"He showed me a book to fix my worldview. We watched videos in his room. He told me about—"

"In his bedroom?" Tina's eyes widened a fraction. "What videos?"

"Shooting and blowing things up. He told me about all the different kinds of bread when he drove us to the grocery store earlier."

"*He* drove? How old is he?"

"Eighteen. Can I stay here?"

"We'll see. Show me your room."

She led Tina down the hallway to Indio's room. Her clothes were all put away and she'd made the bed and straightened the drapes perfectly. According to the magazine in the doctor's waiting room, girls were supposed to have teddy bears and fluffy rugs and tiny string lights in their rooms. This room, with its gray quilt, no rug, and a poster on the wall of a skull wearing headphones, looked like a boy's room.

Tina poked her head briefly around the door. Then she indicated the room opposite. "Do you all share this bathroom?"

Wynter nodded, wondering what could possibly be the problem with that. She used to share a bathroom with twenty other people. Tina examined the inside of the bathroom door and fiddled with the handle.

"There's no lock on the door." She sounded disapproving.

"Why does it need a lock?" The bathrooms at the ashram didn't have locks. Only the offices and warehouse and store rooms and closets had locks — on the outside.

"A lock is so someone doesn't come in while you're taking a shower or a bath."

"Caleb knocked first."

"He knocked and then came in?"

Wynter was confused about where this was leading. "I couldn't turn off the faucets. I didn't realize the water was rising and I made it slosh over the edge. By accident. He helped me turn them off."

"While you were in the tub?"

"Yes, but..." Her stomach sank at the look on Tina's face. "I needed help," she finished lamely.

Tina's eyebrow went up. Then she put on a bright smile. A fake smile. "Have you met your other brother yet?"

"We're driving down to Portland later."

"Portland?" She frowned again. It seemed every single answer Wynter gave was wrong. "Out of state?"

"It's not that far."

"Mmm. His name is Indio Fairn, right? Born September 1990?"

"That's his name. I don't know his birthdate."

"I'm going outside to have a quick chat with Caleb." She handed Wynter a card. "You call me, any time, if you have a problem or a question, or if ever you don't feel safe."

"Why would I not feel safe?" She really did not like this woman.

Tina was already on her way out. Wynter followed, hesitating in the living room as Jesse came back inside.

"What did she ask you?" he said.

"She asked me about Indio's birthdate."

"What?"

"She thinks there should be a lock on the bathroom door, and I think she thinks you're too young to drive me around."

"Yeah, she was a type one, for sure."

"Did she tell Caleb I can stay?"

"Not yet."

"You made your bed for nothing. She didn't even check the rooms at the back."

Jesse sat next to her on the couch as Caleb had, offering tacit support. Five minutes later they heard Tina's car drive off. Caleb came inside.

"Did she believe you?" Jesse said.

"Believe you about what?" Wynter said, feeling numb.

"She wasn't happy to let you stay," Caleb said. "There's no proof, you see, that you're our sister."

"But we have the same mother."

"I know, hun, but Tina needs more than your say-so. We can do a DNA test, which takes time and costs a lot of money. When Joy comes, let's hope she has your birth certificate. The thing is, you're a runaway, by Tina's definition, but the place you came from doesn't want you back. She wanted to take you to a youth shelter tonight." He waved down Jesse, who had drawn breath to protest. "I showed her Jesse's photo of the three of us from a few years back. Convinced her you look like Indio, which you do. She's going to discuss your case with her colleagues, but for now you can stay."

"How long is *for now?*" Jesse said.

But all Caleb said was, "Let's enjoy our weekend and we'll figure it all out on Monday."

"She asked Wynter about Indio," Jesse said. Some sort of signal passed between her brothers. "He doesn't even live here. What does it matter?"

"Does she know Indio?" Wynter asked.

Caleb drew a deep breath. "No, I don't think so. Never mind about that. Jesse, you've got twelve minutes to get to the bus station and meet the 4:30. I'll start dinner so we can leave for Portland on time. Tina's not happy about us driving out of state, and I imagine she'd be even unhappier to know we're going to a college gig, so how about we keep that part to ourselves."

"You said not to lie," Wynter pointed out.

"Yeah." Caleb tilted an eyebrow. "No secrets or lies in this house. Let's call this a privacy issue. Privacy is just fine."

Rockstar

Joy wasn't on the afternoon bus. Wynter felt hope slipping away.
Tina hadn't been impressed with Caleb's house, or with Jesse, or
even with Indio in another state. If Joy didn't hurry up, Wynter
might be sent away. Or worse — she might be sent back.

They put on sweaters and went outside in the twilight to
barbecue the steaks. Her brothers' faces echoed her worries,
though they were making an effort to act happy. Caleb's mood
improved with Jesse's jokes. Wynter managed to smile when she
should. She found herself looking around for signs, though she
kept quiet about it so Jesse didn't make fun of her again. If only
the universe would send a message that Joy was coming, she could
stop worrying about Social Services. She'd had a good day, other
than the bouncing emails and Tina showing up. She'd learned so
much already. She was filling up with all the new things she was
experiencing.

She could hardly get the food down, tasty as it was. The steak
was rich, with a metallic tang she quite liked, but her stomach was
in knots and after a few mouthfuls she stopped eating. Caleb and
Jesse ate like they hadn't had a meal in a week. Then again, she
didn't know how much food men were supposed to eat.

They set out for Portland, with Caleb driving this time. Jesse
provided a running commentary on the landmarks they passed.
She recognized some of the place names.

"This is the same highway I traveled," she said. "If Joy's on her
way right now, we might pass her bus going in the other direction."

"Indio checked the last bus out of Portland a couple hours ago,"
Caleb said. "Don't worry, hun, she'll show up."

But would she show up in time? Wynter didn't want to spend
even one night in some other house that Tina found for her.

When they entered the college hall, music was playing over the
PA. People milled around, dancing and drinking sodas. At the back

of the darkened stage was a drum kit, and at the front stood a row of microphones. Caleb held her hand tightly as they pushed through the crowd. This was as overwhelming as the mall had been, but somehow easier because it was dark, muting the sensations. All she had to do was cling to Caleb's hand and let him lead the way.

Caleb took her to a spot halfway down the hall, to one side.

"Not too close to the speakers," he said, and nodded toward the front. "There he is."

Wynter stood on tiptoes to fully see the stage, which was still in near-darkness. Some people had walked on. One went behind the drum kit and played a flourish. Three guys with guitars took their places at the mics and one of them, she couldn't tell which, yelled a greeting at the crowd, which cheered in response, and introduced the band as Blunderbelly.

The spotlights hit the stage in a sudden burst, and people cheered again. The screams of a group of girls rose above the noise, and the music started.

Indio stood in the center, in ordinary jeans, t-shirt, and boots, but he looked anything but ordinary. Lit up, larger than life, he filled her vision. His band played hard rock with driving riffs that made the audience near the stage jump and pound their arms to the beat. The music pulsed through Wynter's body and pushed the air from her lungs in gasps of excitement. She loved it. She loved Indio's voice and the emotion he put into the vocals. He was trapped behind the mic but the songs soared. She recognized some of them — Jesse had explained the band played a mix of originals and covers, and then he'd explained what those words meant.

Indio's voice was a more melodic and versatile version of Caleb's rawness, punctuated with hard-rock growls that rattled her bones. She stared at him, barely noticing the other three players on stage. Her throat ached, tight with emotion. She wanted to do that, make that music. She'd already had a taste of it and she wanted more.

Most of all, she wished Xay were here with her.

Jesse bounced off to join the mayhem near the stage. Wynter backed up against Caleb, just close enough to maintain physical contact, which helped her feel safe and stopped her getting jostled around as the audience turned increasingly wild.

As the fourth song ended, Indio noticed Jesse at the front and leaned over the edge of the stage to high-five him.

"You okay?" Caleb's lips were right on her ear, the only way to make himself heard.

She'd fallen so deep into the music and lights, it took her a moment to register the words. Unwilling to break the spell, she struggled even to nod her head.

The band played a few more songs, and it was all over. Another band came on. Caleb drew Wynter away, to the door at the back, checking his phone.

"Let's wait for Jesse, and we'll meet Indio at the side door."

Jesse bounded outside to join them a few minutes later, his eyes bright, sweat on his skin in the cold air. "Hey, you liked it?"

She nodded enthusiastically. "My ears hurt."

"Awesome!"

They headed to the side exit. Muffled music from inside boomed into the night. Among the people leaving the building, she recognized the Blunderbelly bass player, carrying a case. Indio followed him out, saw them waiting a few yards away, and called over his bandmate to hand him his guitar.

Indio walked across the gravel toward them. Wynter was reminded of that moment two days and a lifetime ago, when Caleb approached her for the first time. She'd first seen Caleb in silence and darkness, and now seen Indio in noise and light. Unlike Caleb's commanding, authoritative presence, Indio radiated a gentler vibe. He looked briefly at his brothers, then his focus went to Wynter. He walked right up to her.

"Hey, Wynter."

"Hey," she mimicked shyly.

He placed his hands on her upper arms in a greeting that felt halfway between a hug and a handshake. He was flushed and sweaty, like Jesse, heat radiating off him.

"Jesse tells me you play."

"She's incredible," Jesse said.

Indio nodded and smiled at her, thoughtfully. Wynter was surprised by Jesse's endorsement. *Incredible*? Was he teasing? For once he sounded deadly serious.

"You coming home with us?" Jesse said.

"Yeah. Don't have class until Tuesday afternoon. I'll fetch my bag."

He released Wynter. She tingled from the contact. Must be because he was a rockstar. Xay talked about rockstars like they were gods. Indio went to fetch his bag from a van in the parking lot.

"I didn't know he was coming back with us," Wynter said.

"He didn't give me a firm answer before," Jesse said. "Didn't want to get anyone's hopes up." He was looking at Caleb as he spoke, and Wynter sensed the tension between them.

Did Indio not come home much?

The Fairn Boys

Indio met up with his family at the Silverado. He didn't like going home, and despite Jesse's pleading that had guilted him into packing a bag, he hadn't known until he laid eyes on Wynter whether or not he would.

Thursday night he'd learned he had another sister. *Great. Whatever.* Following Caleb's phone call, Jesse had sent fifty texts about her — her weird questions, her charming naïvety, the effect she was going to have on his life. Jesse was a kid, still living at home, and didn't know the first thing about life. He'd texted a screed about "climbing a whole new tree" and thought he was being profound. He'd made fun of the Light's beliefs, as far as he could determine them, and about Wynter's "harmful" superstitions, yet didn't have one word to say about how a child might be affected by her mother walking out on her.

Indio could tell him a few things about that, except that he thought about his mother as little as possible and his twin sister even less. A second sister meant nothing when the first meant so little. He barely even remembered Joy.

Then, after his gig on Friday night, he'd found Jesse's voicemail.

She's got talent, bro. Not like me. Like you.

That piqued his interest.

It jolted free a few memories, too, stuff from *before* that he hadn't thought about in years. Joy singing Mariah Carey on the morning walk to elementary school in Missoula, Montana — it had seemed a long walk, with Caleb in charge hurrying them along as they were both prone to dawdle, though it was probably only half a mile. Accompanying Joy on the ukulele for a performance at the kindergarten concert. They sang *Octopus's Garden* — the song choice was definitely hers — and by the last verse she had tears rolling down her cheeks because Miriam's front-row reserved seat was still empty.

Miriam made it up to her. After taking them all to Harry's place in Anaconda that summer, she left forever a week or so later with Joy. Only Joy.

Indio had walked up to Wynter and knew this wasn't nothing. This was something. Probably helped that she looked nothing like Joy. He did recognize her, though. Caleb said she looked like him and it was sort of true. But there was something else. He felt like he'd been punched in the gut by an unshakable truth. She *belonged* with them.

Which was all the crazier because he'd spent years convincing himself he didn't belong with his family. Other than the music, what did he have in common with his brothers? He and Jesse were pals but he didn't understand the way his younger brother's brain worked. Their social circles were completely different, too. Jesse had once drawn him a Venn diagram to illustrate this fact. And Caleb — he understood Caleb just fine. Life was so much easier when he stayed out of Caleb's way.

Jesse rode shotgun so Indio and Wynter could sit in the back for the ride home. *Blood is thicker...* For all the words Jesse had sent, he hadn't sent a picture. Indio tried not to stare. In the end it didn't matter because she spent much of the first hour staring at him, so they gave up avoiding each other and just enjoyed it. It didn't feel awkward. Her eyes still shone from the excitement of the gig.

He talked about music with her. She'd heard of half the bands he mentioned from the last five decades. She told him what songs she loved, and why — the bass in this one, the beat in that one, the breakdown, the vocal tone, or just the sheer energy of it. He could tell she understood musical structure from the way she talked about the songs, even if she didn't always know the correct terminology.

Caleb had the radio on quietly. Jesse turned it up when a favorite song came on during a lull in the conversation, and he belted it out using the dashboard as his drum kit.

"Will you play with us in the jamroom?" Wynter asked Indio.

"*Us?* You guys already have a band?" Indio teased.

"We do!" Jesse said. "We are now the Fairn Boys plus Girl."

"Fairn Boys?" Wynter queried.

"The Fairn Boys was founded right after we moved to Seattle," Jesse explained. "I'd been drumming for about a year — I was in fourth grade and already awesome. We played grunge back then, of course, inspired by our new location. Soundgarden, Pearl Jam, Mudhoney. Not Caleb's scene at all but he was game. Indio persuaded him to switch to bass."

Those were good times. Music was a great way to avoid conversation, for starters, and as a bonus it was a great way to avoid Harry. Their father never joined them, though he had the talent, but nor did he complain about the noise. They wrote their own songs and honed their musical style into a melodic riff-based rock with judicious use of harmonies to make the most of three different voices.

"We made demo tapes," Jesse said. "Just for fun."

"I need to hear that," Wynter said earnestly.

Jesse took a CD from the glove compartment and slotted it in. This one was from the last time they'd all jammed together — the summer after Indio's freshman year when he was home from Ohio.

Wynter settled back to listen. Indio did most of the vocals — his voice suited these particular songs — but despite being center-stage with various high school and college bands over the years he didn't aspire to be a lead singer. He was pretty sure Jesse should be in that role, but no one could keep Jesse away from the drums.

He stole a look at Wynter. She was leaning back in the seat, her eyes unfocused as she listened. After a while, she closed her eyes and a half-smile formed on her lips. Her fingers tapped the beat.

Near Seattle they stopped for gas. Caleb got out to fill the tank.

Jesse turned around in his seat. "Someone from Social Services came by today."

Indio sensed Wynter's mood drop at once. "On the weekend?" he said.

"She wasn't keen on letting Wynter stay with us."

"Why not? She can have my room. I'm never gonna need it — Wynter, you can paint it pink." He was joking. Neither Jesse or Wynter looked happy.

Jesse said, "She can live with Joy, if Joy shows up, but not with Caleb."

"Why not?"

"A teenage girl living with two guys she only just met? Not gonna happen."

Indio stared out the window, into the night. "Fucking social workers."

"She knew who you were," Wynter said. She'd silently watched their conversation, sitting cross-legged on the seat. "Why did she know?"

Indio drew a deep breath, in and out. "I had some dealings with them a while back."

"He spent four months in juvie." Trust Jesse to lay it all out.

"What's juvie?"

"It's like prison for kids," Jesse said.

Wynter's expression didn't change, which surprised Indio. Maybe she had no yardstick to measure it by. Hell, maybe she didn't know what prison was.

She turned to him. "What law did you break?"

Okay, so she knew what prison was.

"Just silly teenage boy stuff. Fighting."

"Second-degree assault," Jesse clarified.

Indio was mortified that Wynter's opinion of him might be diminished by the revelation. Well, she would've found out sooner or later.

"What's assault?" Wynter asked.

Now that was something no one had ever asked him. Jesse gave a little shrug that said, *She really doesn't know anything about anything.*

"It means I hurt a kid. Put him in the hospital."

"He did the world a favor," Jesse said. "Of course, violence is *never* the answer." He used his mock-Caleb voice that even Wynter recognized, and she smiled.

"Caleb made us learn karate," Indio told Wynter. "He always said: Now you can win any fight so you take responsibility for walking away before you hurt someone. That was a fight I should've walked away from — but, y'know, it's not so easy to do in the moment."

"Caleb was deployed overseas at the time," Jesse added. "His powerful influence only reaches so far."

"Yeah, I was a little tired of Caleb's influence by then."

"But Caleb's wonderful," Wynter said spontaneously. "Isn't he?" She had Jesse's directness. Unlike Jesse, she didn't know when her questions made someone uncomfortable. Jesse knew and asked anyway to watch you squirm.

Now was probably not the best time to make a joke about his little brother's name for the rift in the family — the Mariana Trench. Instead, he said, carefully, "That's the general consensus, so I won't *disagree* with you."

Wynter saw right through him. "How could you not think he's wonderful?"

Regret and resentment dragged the breath from Indio's body.

He still blamed Caleb for every last childhood battle. Still resisted coming back to Washington. He'd split himself off from this family at the first opportunity and spent every day trying to justify it.

He reached over and touched Wynter's arm. "He's my brother. We'll work it out."

They sat in silence until Caleb got back in the truck. He sensed the change in the atmosphere. "What's up?"

"Indio's talking in double negatives," Jesse said. "We gotta get him home, down to the basement, knock some sense into him before he makes a lyric out of that nonsense."

Indio ate the last of his post-midnight snack — four pieces of raisin toast — and put the plate in the sink.

"Is the bathroom free?" he called out in the direction of the hallway. He'd been desperate for a shower three hours ago and the situation hadn't improved.

"Did you forget the *no yelling* rule?" Jesse said. "That's, like, number three on the list. He won't answer. You gotta go down there and speak at a normal volume."

Indio was well acquainted with the rules, of course. "What if the house was on fire?" he mused.

Caleb walked in from the back and dumped a sleeping bag and pillow on the couch. "If you only yelled for genuine emergencies," he said, "I'd know it was a genuine emergency when you yelled."

"Guys!" Jesse was playing back a message on the answering machine next to the kettle. "It's Joy."

> ... hope Wynter arrived safely. I've made a mess of things but everything will work out. Next week someone will be driving me to Seattle. Please take care of her, Caleb. Of course you will. I know you will, like you always took care of us. I'll see you soon.

Caleb spanned his hand over his face and exhaled. "Okay, that's good. That's great news. I'll turn around the bed in Wynter's room so we can fit another one in there. Jesse, maybe you can ask on campus or at the clubs about jobs? Cashier or waitress or something? Just to get her started. I'll ask around at work. On Monday I'll call the school to see about enrolling Wynter—"

"What about that woman from Social Services?" Jesse said.

"What about her? Go to the hardware store tomorrow and get a bolt lock for the bathroom door. Fixed."

Indio wasn't so sure a bolt lock was going to fix anything. He opened his mouth to point out all the ways it could go wrong, and thought better of it.

"Did you have a question for me?" Caleb asked him. The impatience in his tone indicated he was a lot more worried than he looked.

"Shower — is it free?"

"Yes. Wynter's already gone to bed."

Indio took a quick shower and flopped on the couch. Caleb had decided that 2AM was a good time to rinse dishes and noisily load the dishwasher. Given the living room and kitchen were open-plan, that meant another five minutes or so before he could think about sleep.

When Caleb closed the hallway door, Indio held his breath.

"Regardless of whether Joy gets custody," Caleb said, "Tina wants me and Jesse to get background checks. You, too, so you can visit."

Indio knew exactly where this was heading and braced himself for the onslaught. Conversations with Caleb were like a survival course — clear those obstacles one by one and hope it didn't go off the rails before reaching the finish line.

Caleb leaned on the back of the couch, looming over him. "You could've applied to get your juvenile records sealed two years after you got out of detention. I personally handed you the forms in Ohio at the time. It didn't get done, and now this woman Tina is already on to you."

"Did you see those forms? There's about a million of them and they have to be sent to two million different places. Certified copies, too. It costs money."

"Jesse offered to help you with it when you came to Washington that summer, and to get your ass to the County Court to schedule a hearing. You did nothing."

"I would've had to come back here in the middle of the semester for the hearing—"

"How can I make you understand how important this is? Not just because of the background check you're about to fail. This will follow you for the rest of your life. Employers, landlords, credit and insurance companies — that's life, Indio. That's adult life. You need to fix this, wipe that slate clean, so you can survive."

Indio threw an arm across his eyes to block it all out. Everything Caleb said was true, of course. Indio hadn't filed the paperwork, but the reason wasn't procrastination or the ridiculous complexity of the process or even the filing fees and the cost of certified copies. He hadn't done it because he *hadn't* in fact been eligible to get his records sealed thanks to a more recent misdemeanor conviction that neither Caleb or Jesse knew about.

That was just over two years ago, which meant he was now eligible to apply again. He could get his juvenile record sealed, but he'd still fail the background check because of the other charge. No way to wipe *that* slate clean.

Still, the juvenile conviction was a violent felony and he really should deal with it.

"You're right. I'll get it done," he said, surprising Caleb. "I'm gonna need copies of my records, though. I threw all that crap out when I moved to Portland."

"Go visit Harry tomorrow. He has a fat folder with your name on it."

Okay, that wasn't part of the plan.

"I just saw him at Christmas. Twice in two weeks? Not gonna happen."

He locked eyes with his brother in a familiar battle of wills. To his surprise, Caleb caved.

"Fine. I'm seeing him on Tuesday. I'll get the reports. I'll print off the forms, too, and mail the lot to you."

"Awesome." Indio grabbed the chance to change the subject. "Does Wynter have problems — emotional stuff, brainwashing, from growing up in that place?"

"She won't talk about it, which in itself is worrying."

"Maybe if a woman talked to her? You can be pretty intimidating. You still seeing that girl — Bea?" Indio had met Bea at Christmas. She seemed like the ultimate in marriage material, not that he knew much about that. A bit fragile, but stable, kind, and loving. Three things Indio rarely found together in the girls he hung out with.

"Yes. She's pretty great. And how's your love life?"

"Same as ever," he muttered.

"I'm not gonna tell you not to make the most of your college years, but take care, okay?"

"Not gonna go there with you." Indio didn't bother masking his irritation.

"Can we go to your grades, then? You never told me if you passed the fall semester at Ohio."

"I skipped out on my finals. You know that. What was the point in sitting for classes that Portland wouldn't credit?"

"So you're now repeating two entire semesters."

"I transferred a few third-year credits. But yes, that's what I'm doing." Indio waited for another tongue-lashing.

Caleb had already moved to the next thing on his mind. "You realize the only way Joy could get a ride from LA to Seattle is by going to the Light for help."

"Yeah. Well, that shit's addictive. My first memories are that tiny rental in Billings — you and me camped on the living room floor for two years and Joy slept in Mom's bed. Remember that place? The endless procession of women passing through for crystal healings and yoga, and in between sessions they'd take turns feeding and rocking Jesse like he was a kitten you could just pass around. She kept having kids but the Light always won her attention in the end."

"Let's hope Joy has different priorities. I'm out with Bea tomorrow. You could go to the Light office downtown and inquire about Joy."

"They have an office here?"

"International District, just east of I-5. Took Jesse a while to track it down — it's not explicitly associated with the Light. More of a New Age store and yoga center."

"Even if she sets out tomorrow, she won't be here until Monday."

"Ask if anyone knows what's going on. Someone there may have a cell number for whoever is driving her."

"How about you check on that? You're going out anyway."

Caleb's jaw twitched. "Fine. I'll do it." He left at last.

Indio probably should go visit that office, do his part. Truth was, it was hard to muster the enthusiasm when every instinct resisted acknowledging Miriam and Joy at all. And that was monumentally unfair to Joy, of course, but Joy wasn't here. It was Caleb he had to deal with.

He cast his mind back to when things went wrong between them. Hard to pinpoint the exact time. He did remember when things were good. That summer before he and Joy started school, they were based in Bozeman and Miriam was selling prayer cards and dreamcatchers and Light courses door-to-door along I-90. Sometimes her four kids waited in the car, bored out of their minds. More often they were left home alone for the day, and those had been days of glorious freedom. This was before Caleb felt the need to take charge, when they still considered each other play-mates. The driveway to their apartment complex backed onto the County Detention Center, which even Caleb thought was cool. They'd leave Joy and Jesse, load up their cap guns, and run up and down the fence hunting bad guys.

Indio would've done anything for *that* Caleb. All these years later, he was balking at the "suggestion" he drive ten minutes down the street to check on the twin sister he hadn't seen since he was six years old.

Caleb's presence and Joy's absence in his life were not what he needed to be focusing on right now. He'd focus on Wynter, and for her sake he'd attempt to make it through the weekend without a blowout.

Marriage Material

Caleb drew back his drapes on Sunday morning to the sight of Wynter in the backyard doing some sort of exercise routine. Frost spiked the lawn and she was in her new PJs with bare feet. She went through the forms with slow precision. It wasn't graceful — her gangly limbs formed odd angles — but her concentration was impressive.

He wandered down the hall. The bathroom door was open to reveal Indio washing at the basin. So much for not getting up on Sundays. In the living room, Jesse watched Wynter through the sliding door.

"Look at this. What is it? Tai chi?"

Caleb stood beside him. "Or something like it."

"She looks like a hungover puppy doing slow-motion ballet."

"How about you keep that opinion to yourself."

Jesse grinned. "It's kinda cute, though."

They watched her for a while. A low fog blanketed the lawn, creating an ethereal stage for the performance.

"She doesn't know much about the world," Jesse remarked, "but she has these odd, random skills. She knows her way around a computer, but not the internet. She knows how to wipe down a table — you notice that?"

"So, she can aspire to be a waitress," Caleb said dryly.

"I'm just saying, it gives us clues about what her life was like. I wish she'd talk about it."

"Joy can fill us in. And if Social Services stays involved, they'll probably send her to a counselor."

"She doesn't need a counselor. She's fine!"

"We don't know that. We've known her three days."

"No, she's fine," Jesse insisted. "She's smart and asking all the right questions. She's curious about the world, always looking, looking, looking at everything. I sure hope Joy's not indoctrinated or she'll undo all my good work." He kicked the door frame in frustration before wandering into the kitchen to grab a box of cereal.

Caleb opened the sliding door. "Wynter, come inside. It's freezing out there."

She straightened and stared at him across the garden, in a trance. He beckoned to her, and she snapped out of it.

"Didn't Bea get you some sneakers?" he said as she came inside. He directed her to the kitchen. "Have some breakfast. Good news — Joy left a message last night. She's on her way."

Wynter's face lit up. "When will she get here?"

"Monday, at the earliest."

"Where did you learn that... whatever you were doing out there?" Jesse asked her.

"We did exercises every morning. It was my favorite part of the day."

"What was your least favorite part?"

"School."

"You'll get six hours of school a day from now on," Jesse pointed out.

Wynter's jaw dropped. "Is there that much to learn?"

"It's not nearly enough time. Don't worry, I'll help you out."

Indio came in from the bathroom. Caleb counted to ten, and ten again, as Indio made himself coffee.

"Take a look at the closet doors in your room, will you?" Caleb said. "The hinges need work."

Indio bristled, barely acknowledging him. "Wynter, wanna jam this morning?"

She nodded enthusiastically.

"Jesse can do the home maintenance," Indio said, daring Caleb to contradict him. Caleb would've done the job himself just to avoid a scene in front of Wynter, but it was important to give Indio the chance, now and then. He didn't live here anymore but helping out kept him connected to the family.

Jesse contradicted him instead. "I can't hang doors."

"I'll do it!" Wynter piped up.

To his credit, Indio looked uncomfortable that she'd felt the need to intervene. While Indio had never shown understanding for the parental role Caleb had assumed in childhood, he'd always been compassionate toward Jesse. Good to know that extended to Wynter as well.

"Never mind," Caleb said. "I'll get it done later. You guys enjoy your music. I'm taking Bea out on the bike while her parents are home to take care of Jilly. Back around two."

"Why don't we all go for a ride?" Jesse said. They had motor-cycles, a passion of their father's passed to his sons. "You ever ridden a motorcycle, Wynter?"

She shook her head, munching on her multi-colored cereal.

"We'll leave that for another time," Caleb said. The social worker wouldn't be happy to find out Wynter had been on the back of a motorcycle.

"I have to take a couple of amps over to Rob's," Jesse said. "Can I borrow the Silverado?"

"You need to renew those expired tabs and get your own vehicle running."

"I know. I'm sorting it out Monday after I get paid. So... the truck?"

"Just bring it back with a—"

"A full tank." Jesse rolled his eyes, but good-naturedly. "How's that cereal, Wyn?"

She swallowed and stirred the purple milk in her bowl. "Am I supposed to like it?"

"Just give your honest opinion."

"Not good."

"Jeez, why are you eating it then?"

"Because you bought it and..."

She trailed off as Jesse swooped in and took the bowl away. He tipped the remains into the sink.

"Try this one." He returned the empty bowl and pushed the granola toward her. "You don't have to eat something you don't like."

Unsure what to do, she looked to Caleb for guidance.

"It's okay, you can try something else," Caleb said.

Caleb knew, from that look, she wasn't used to having choices in this matter. She'd been given food, and evidently not much of it, and she'd eaten whatever was put in front of her. He emptied the offending cereal in the trash and put the box in the recycling.

Since becoming a single mom, Bea had been living with her parents in Renton. Caleb picked her up on his Honda V65 Magna — it was older than he was and his buddies in the Coast Guard never let him forget it, or stopped ribbing him for riding a foreign bike. Bea looked gorgeous in jeans and boots, a wool scarf wrapped around her neck and the riding jacket he'd bought for her birthday in November. She pushed her light brown curls into the helmet, hopped on and wrapped her arms around him. They took the 405 north along Lake Washington, then east to Cougar Mountain and up the winding mountain road. The morning was only a few degrees above freezing, the skies overcast, and he loved that she didn't care — or, at least, didn't complain.

"Let's walk to Coal Creek Falls," she said when they arrived at the trailhead and parked the bike. "With all the runoff, this is the best time of year to see it."

He held her hand over tiny bridges and walkways and along the well maintained trail surrounded by gently swaying conifers. They'd started at fourteen hundred feet, and it was downhill much of the way — not too muddy, and the wind dropped as they descended deeper into the forest.

Caleb fell into silence and let Bea talk. Jilly had recently developed a fascination for animal noises and a dislike for wearing socks, and had just learned to say "cookie", which was somehow causing Bea's mother to overfeed her cookies.

Two miles in, they heard running water and the trail narrowed as they approached the waterfall. Bea led him down the wooden stairs so they could admire it close-up — thirty feet high, gushing at full force.

Bea unfolded a picnic blanket from her little backpack, set it on a flat patch of ground on the bank, and they flopped onto it. Caleb rolled onto his back, hands behind his head. All along the trail, an idea had been brewing but this wasn't quite the right time to lay it out. He pulled Bea against him. She put her head on his chest and slipped her hand under his t-shirt. When her hand wandered lower he grabbed it.

She giggled. "There's no one around."

"We passed a dozen people, at least." The waterfall was a popular resting spot, too.

"What's wrong?"

Caleb winced. He wasn't in the habit of holding grudges, but when he thought on the life Wynter had led he couldn't help being angry with their mother. Bea was doing everything she could for her child. Miriam had done less than nothing — she'd done actual damage.

He was in a bad headspace today. Bea preferred his undivided attention when Jilly wasn't around. She deserved it, too. They hadn't been alone together since Christmas.

"Just found out Wynter's years behind in her schooling," he said. "Joy's supposed to show up in the next few days, which will keep her out of foster care for now."

"What about in the long-term?"

"I'm worried the court won't find Joy suitable as a permanent guardian. If she's as clueless about the world as Wynter is, that's gonna be tough."

"Maybe dad can find her a job," Bea said. "He has loads of contacts."

"That would be great. He's a good guy."

She raised up on her elbow. "My parents are crazy about you."

He made a noncommittal sound.

"And they want to meet Harry."

Bea's parents had always been welcoming toward Caleb, effusively so. They saw a future son-in-law and that was more than a little disconcerting. Her dad was ex-military like Harry. There was little else similar about their families. Bea's mother was a pediatric nurse and their lifestyle was comfortably middle-class, while Harry had the brains to move up in the world and had squandered it all. The idea of her parents meeting his father was embarrassing.

"Let's give it a while."

"Why? He seemed fine when I met him at Christmas. Dad can control how much beer he gets. He's good like that, believe me. He has plenty of drunks for friends."

Caleb sighed. "I don't want to push it, Bea. We're just getting started."

"Eight months is *just getting started*?" She gave a little pout and kissed him quickly before getting up. "Let's go off-road."

Bea drew him off the trail and they waded a few yards through ferns and brown leaf litter.

She gave a mischievous grin. "Mind the nettles."

She grabbed his hands and urged him into the trees, out of sight. He got the message and pressed her against a thick-trunked tree to kiss her. She was flushed with excitement. He still had the weight of the world dragging on his heart. Her hands were all over him, sweeping down to his groin, and she broke the kiss to grin at what she found. Before he knew it, she'd unzipped him.

"Jesus, not here," he groaned, breathless.

He was unused to anyone refusing his orders, but Bea was determined and he didn't stop her. She dropped to her knees. Caleb leaned his hand against the tree above her head, praying no one strayed off the path to see them. Tina the social worker would have a field day with this.

On top of everything else, he couldn't shake the feeling Bea was doing it because she wanted something from him. She'd had a shitty time with men, including Jilly's father who was entirely off the scene now but had left some scars. Bea would mold herself into whatever Caleb wanted, whatever any man wanted, and other men had taken advantage of it. He'd always been gentle with her, not his usual MO with people in general, and she'd responded and come out of her shell. It had given her confidence to find a better job, take night classes, repair a rocky relationship with her mother.

And give him a blow job in public. The other things she'd done for herself and for Jilly. This was meant to persuade him to invite Harry to her parents' house, thus taking their relationship to the next level.

Now wasn't the time to complain. He pushed his hand into her hair and watched her looking up at him. She redoubled her efforts, thank god, because he was able to finish quickly. He zipped up.

"Let's get back." He was sweating under his jacket.

She stopped him walking off, wrapping her arms around his waist, and they embraced for a moment. He loved her, he knew that much, but his mind was all over the place at the moment. They walked back to the trail and collected the blanket.

"I have this idea but I don't know how you'll react," he said.

"Let's find out."

Caleb was tempted to lay it all out — his duty to Wynter that pretty much required him to take custody if Joy could not, which meant asking Bea to agree to be her designated long-term guardian should he be deployed. That would satisfy the Coast Guard's regulations for him to become a single parent. He could only hope it was enough to convince a family court judge, too. In a way he'd been a single parent since kicking out Harry when Jesse was sixteen, but he wasn't Jesse's legal guardian and he'd never worried that Jesse wouldn't be okay if he was deployed. Jesse had plenty of friends whose parents kept an eye on him or took him into their homes for weeks at a time.

He knew Bea would balk at the idea of filling a similar role, and rightfully so. He had to test the waters first.

"If the court won't immediately give Joy custody for whatever reason, I was thinking, as a back-up plan, if you moved in..." Bea gave him a sharp look, more in surprise than horror. Caleb pressed on. "If you moved in, I think there's a better chance they'd let Wynter live with me. If we had a woman in the house."

Bea didn't say anything.

"We sort of talked about it at Christmas, didn't we? You talked about it."

Bea stopped and faced him. "Caleb, I talked about *us* getting a place together. A new place, for you and me and Jilly. You didn't want to sell up and abandon Jesse, so you nixed it. Now you're talking about *two* teenagers in the house with us."

"Well, that's my family."

"I'm twenty-three years old. I don't want responsibility for two more kids."

"If she goes into care, she'll be with strangers who don't know her."

He hadn't meant to raise his voice. Bea narrowed her eyes, not liking it. "*You're* practically a stranger to her."

"Doesn't feel that way. She already trusts me. Jesse's amazing with her. It's like she fits right in."

"That's great. It's great for *you*. It's not what I had in mind right now."

He nodded, defeated. He briefly considered manipulating her into it with some noble speech about duty — which would be the truth, and would probably work, too, but it wouldn't change her *feelings* about the matter. He'd spent his childhood manipulating Harry, just to survive, and it had left him with next to no respect for the man. He wouldn't do that to Bea.

His phone pinged and he took it out of his back pocket. "I have to call Wynter's caseworker."

Bea gave a little shrug, unhappy he wasn't focused fully on her when they only had a couple of hours. He moved to the side of the path and returned the call.

"Caleb, thank you for getting back to me so quickly," Tina said in that pleasant, indifferent tone. "This is just to let you know a decision has been made to place Wynter into foster care for the foreseeable future."

Caleb turned away from Bea, pushing his hand through his hair in frustration. He drew a steadying breath. "Can you tell me why?"

"We've been unable to contact her mother. My colleagues and I don't feel your home environment is suitable, especially as we have no proof of a familial relationship. Additionally, it appears she's come out of a volatile situation. All kinds of issues are likely to come up that you don't have the skills to deal with."

"She's my sister. I'll deal with it." Bea rubbed his back as she realized what was happening. "Listen, our sister Joy made contact — she's coming up from Los Angeles just like I told you. She'll be here in the next few days." Caleb had called at the Light office that morning to find it closed, so he had no new information, but he'd put his faith in Joy.

"There will be a hearing tomorrow before a court commissioner — just a formality. We expect our recommendation for emergency placement to be approved. Joy can of course request temporary custody but she'll need to establish the relationship, as well as residency and employment. Once Wynter's resided in Washington for six months, permanent custody will be an option. There will be opportunities down the track."

Caleb knew what that meant. If Social Services took Wynter, they'd have a fight on their hands *down the track* to get her back. But what was the alternative? Hoping for Miriam to come to the rescue? Caleb had spent a lifetime trying not to judge his mother harshly, but his instincts told him she would never have Wynter's best interests at heart.

"The good news," Tina went on, "is that I've found the perfect placement for Wynter. A single woman, a psychologist who has experience with children from difficult situations. She's fostered before so everything's already set up. It'll be just her and Wynter in the home. Very safe and supportive."

"Where does she live?"

"Richland, in Benton County."

"Christ. That's halfway across the state."

"Teenagers are very hard to place, Caleb, and there's a drastic shortage of foster homes. This is a wonderful opportunity for Wynter. Beautiful home. Excellent school district. I think it'll work out very well."

Caleb had rarely felt so powerless. The idea of losing Wynter so soon after meeting her hit him harder than he could have imagined.

"When does she go?"

"I'll pick her up this afternoon. She'll stay overnight in a shelter, and tomorrow I'll drive her to Richland."

"God, please, don't put her in a shelter. Let her stay with me one more night." He felt Tina's hesitation. Hesitation was good — better than an immediate denial. He pounced on it. "I understand everything you've said, Tina. I want to help Joy take care of her, but I understand there's a procedure. Let's work together on this and for Wynter's sake make the transition as simple as possible. A shelter will be incredibly stressful. She'll do better staying the night with me, where she's settled, and I'll be home all day tomorrow with her." Best not to mention that Indio would be, too.

"I'll come for her Monday, then, around five. She can bring whatever she likes."

"She doesn't have anything," he said bitterly.

"I see. Would you like me to talk to her?"

"No, I'll do it."

He rang off. Bea put her arms around him and he gave her a half-hearted hug. His mind was already racing ahead. He had to tell Wynter and his brothers and put a positive spin on it. He had to figure out how to make his home more "suitable", and Bea wasn't about to help with that. He had to pray Joy had the incentive and enthusiasm to do what was necessary to apply for custody.

"I'll take you home," he told Bea, setting off up the path.

Voice

As soon as Caleb and Jesse were gone, Wynter wanted to go down to the jamroom.

"Shower and clothes first," Indio said.

"I had a bath on Thursday."

So, daily bathing apparently wasn't a priority in the Light.

Without blinking, he said, "Shower every morning. That's one of Caleb's house rules I happen to agree with. When I'm up before noon, anyway."

She nodded because, of course, if Caleb said something it was the law. As she stood up to leave the table, she said, "How many house rules are there?"

"Thousands. Millions." At her look of horror, he added, "Sure seems that way sometimes. Why are your PJs wet? Have you been outside?"

"Yes. We did exercises every morning, so I thought I'd keep that up."

"Exercise is good, but not in bare feet when its forty degrees outside, baby."

She did a double-take and he realized it was because of the term of endearment he'd used without thinking. Had anyone in the Light shown her any affection at all?

He said, "You can't be used to this cold, surely?"

"No. I've never been this cold. I don't mind."

"So, winter suits Wynter." They exchanged a little smile at the pun. "Jesse texted me about you, so I know it's spelled with a Y. I've spent my life saying, *Indio, like the country but with an O.*" She acknowledged that with another smile, of sympathy this time. "Why couldn't she give us regular names like Bob and Sue? Or, y'know, Caleb, Joy, Jesse."

Wynter looked away, fiddling with her braided hair, evidently not wanting to talk about, or even hear any mention of, Miriam. Well, that made two of them. The old resentment toward his mother – their mother – surfaced. He pushed it down. He wasn't going to let that ruin their time together.

"Go on," he said. "I'll get the gear ready."

He went downstairs. This basement held bittersweet memories. Harry had bought the house when they moved from Montana, when he was having one of his good runs. Didn't last, of course, and Caleb, at fifteen, had taken over again. After all those years with Harry failing to provide, all Caleb had wanted to do was take care of them. He did so with military precision that suited Jesse. Indio, two years Caleb's junior, had resented it. Not that anything about his life improved after Caleb left to join the Coast Guard.

After his stint in juvie and scraping through his senior year at a different high school, Caleb promised financial support if he went to college – any college. He got a map and picked half a dozen options as far from Washington as possible. Ohio made an offer and Caleb paid up. Indio rewarded his brother's generosity by almost never coming home, which was best for everyone, all things considered.

But this basement – they'd had some good times here. Music was the way he and Caleb communicated because they sure as hell didn't have much success verbally. There had been fights, too. In the end, Jesse had decreed they not talk down here about *anything* but music. Everything else, take it upstairs.

Wynter came down and he talked her through his guitars. He'd acquired them through all manner of schemes, buying them cheap from friends or persuading Harry to pitch in. Harry was persuadable and generous after a few drinks and his sons knew how to take advantage of it. A few more drinks and he was an ugly mother-fucker, so you had to play it just right.

Wynter loved the look of his black Les Paul in particular. He handed it over and turned on the amp. She sat on the stool to tune it.

"It sounds different from that one." She indicated the Strat she'd played with Caleb. "Richer or something. Like a growl."

"It's my favorite. Also the most valuable."

"Why didn't you play it on stage?"

"I don't take anything on stage that cost more than a hundred bucks or so."

"How much was this one?"

"Got it second-hand for about fifteen hundred. Yeah." He

grinned at her reaction. "The one I want is eight grand. One day."

"You could buy a house with that much. Couldn't you?"

Her naïveté about money was something they'd have to fix before someone took advantage of *her*.

"A car, maybe. Just you wait. When I get it, and you hear it, you'll realize it was worth the money."

"How long does it take to earn eight thousand dollars?"

"Flipping burgers, about a year — if you sleep on the street and don't eat."

"What is flipping burgers?"

He laughed, but gently, so she didn't think he was making fun. "You are truly unique, Wynter. It means a short order cook." She was no less confused. "A low-paying job where you do basic cooking in a diner or a burger joint."

His phone rang — the ringtone made her sit up and take notice.

"Why does it sound like that?"

"It's Led Zeppelin."

"Oh! I know four of their songs."

He let the call go to voicemail after checking the name on the screen — a girl he'd met at the campus bookstore. They'd exchanged numbers with a plan to swap old textbooks with each other, but now she wanted to take him to a play, of all things. That was a *date* and he had no intention of responding.

"Which song is your favorite?" he asked Wynter, putting away his phone.

"*Black Dog*. My friend... um, I knew someone... He could sing it exactly like the radio."

"In that case, he's a talented guy. I couldn't do it."

"So, what job will you have when you finish college?"

"Whatever it is graphic designers do."

"What do they do?" Another one of those earnest questions. Jesse called her an alien from another planet but to Indio she seemed more like a changeling, one of the faerie folk, with her huge mossy eyes and twisted otherworldly perceptions.

"They design all kinds of stuff. Anything visual — marketing materials like logos, brochures, websites."

"What's the point of that?"

"That's a good question. To buy an eight-thousand-dollar guitar, maybe?"

"Wouldn't you rather be a rockstar?"

He chuckled. "I'd rather make music, that's true. Okay, what will we play today?"

"The songs you did last night. You did an Aerosmith song."

"*Get the Lead Out*. That's an old one."

"Yes. Show me that one."

He grabbed a guitar and taught her to play the riffs, surprised at how fast she picked it up. She had the *feel* of it even when the notes and fingering weren't quite right, and never skipped a beat regardless of mistakes. He added some licks to spice it up, and sang through a verse or two. The jamming turned to improv, beats and phrases that flowed between them, a give and take of rhythm and melody. He understood now why Jesse had raved about how she was "in sync". Once she had a little more technical experience under her belt, he'd be able to take it in any direction and she'd follow.

"Who taught you to play?" he asked.

"I had books – classical guitar books and a few tutorial books of folk and modern music. They used to just leave me alone to get on with it, sometimes for hours at a time if they forgot about me. For piano there was a teacher."

"Do you sing?"

"I sang in the temple. I preferred arranging songs for the prayer meetings, and I wrote some as well."

"You're a songwriter?"

"No. I mean, yes, I wrote music for the Light, or arranged other people's songs. Stupid stuff. I hated it." She spoke shyly, like she thought she shouldn't be passing judgment.

"I'll bet you have songs in your head you didn't write for the Light," he guessed.

She gave him a secretive smile but didn't answer. He didn't push it. And he didn't ask about singing again. She wasn't quite ready to give up that much.

"Can you show me this song you did last night – I don't know it. This one." She played a riff.

"It's called *Dead End Rodeo*. An original."

"You wrote it?"

"Our lead guitarist Anže Turk wrote the lyrics, and I wrote the music."

"I really liked it."

She played more. He couldn't believe she remembered so much of it. He showed her the rest, and after that another original from the previous night, which she remembered even better and was soon playing along as he sang it for her.

She asked him theory questions, and that led to a primer on the blues, which she knew nothing about except for what she'd absorbed from listening to rock. There was nothing he said that she didn't understand. She soaked up everything he told her. He explained the blues turnaround, and a few minutes after that she was instinctively adding her own interpretations to it, and they jammed for a solid half hour.

Then she stared at her left hand like it didn't belong to her any more.

"My fingers hurt."

"You must be doing it right." He examined her hand. She already had calluses from years of playing. Now her fingertips were red and tender. "Hmm. Maybe we should stop for today."

Jesse was barreling down the stairs. "No way!" he called out. "I came right back so we could jam."

"If we keep going, there will be blood," Indio said. Wynter gasped. "I'm joking. But you have to take care of your hands. Don't overdo it."

"I can keep going for a bit."

Jesse was already at the drum kit, and she looked determined.

"Okay. How about we play some of that Aerosmith again?" Indio said.

Jesse was impressed. "You've been doing Aerosmith?"

"But it's gonna sound better with drums," Indio said.

"Everything sounds better with drums."

✿

The walls vibrated with music thumping from below. The basement door was open and Caleb sat at the top of the steps to listen for a while. Soon, he'd join them and it would be all four of them for the first time. And then, when he could manage to get the words out, he'd have to tell them Wynter couldn't stay.

"I think she's ready for The Who," he heard Jesse say when the song ended.

"C'mon, Jess, she needs to rest her hands," Indio said. "Let's take it down a notch."

Caleb descended the stairs to watch them, staying in the shadows so they weren't disturbed. Indio started playing a different song—Caleb recognized it as a popular female singer's ballad.

"This was on the radio on the drive home last night. You know it, right?" Indio said.

Wynter nodded. "Yes, I like that one."

"Will you sing it?"

"I don't think I know all the words."

Indio took his phone out and looked up the lyrics. He set the phone on a music stand next to Wynter.

Caleb wondered when she was going to back out. She didn't look happy, but he could see she'd developed a level of trust with Indio. Maybe she was going to do it, after all.

"Um, I've never sung it before."

Or maybe not.

"Okay, well... Jesse can sing it. Join in, if you like. And the chords are easy." Indio ran through them. He sounded casual, but Caleb knew he was mentally crossing his fingers. Indio swapped her guitar for an acoustic and settled back into the seat opposite her, also with an acoustic.

They started the intro together, and Jesse sang the first verse. To everyone's surprise, she came in after a few lines with the harmony. Quietly, unsure of herself, her eyes on Jesse. Then the drums kicked in for the chorus, and Jesse sang louder, which encouraged her to sing louder, in unison.

Jesse dropped out halfway through the chorus. She hesitated for a beat when she realized. She kept going into the second verse. Caleb exhaled the breath he'd been holding. His head filled with the sound of her voice. A touch husky, like her speaking voice, but the tone was a pure and beautiful contralto, and every note was sure.

Indio caught her gaze, and she returned to him after each glance at the lyrics. Now the groove was going, her confidence picked up. Caleb leaned in the doorway and basked in it. To some extent she was mimicking the recording, but there was enough of Wynter in there to make it distinctive.

He came into the room and circled around the back of her. Jesse caught his eye and shook his head with a grin to indicate his amazement. Her throaty voice brought a devastating emotion to the song. Indio wore an expression Caleb had never seen on his brother's face before.

The song ended, and Wynter's gaze locked on Indio, hoping for his approval. Indio was looking down, letting the final chord fade out. Caleb felt for him. He didn't think he could speak just now, either.

Indio gave her a nod and a smile and caught Caleb's eye, which made Wynter aware of his presence. She swung around.

"You have a unique voice," Caleb said.

"Is that a good thing?"

"It's beautiful," he reassured her.

She gave him a real smile, her first one just for him. He was surprised his praise was even more important to her than Indio's.

"Hey, Wynter," Jesse said, "Do you know *True Colors? Linger?* How about Dido's *White Flag?*" He was throwing out emotional songs that would highlight her voice, because like the rest of them he needed to hear more.

"It's someone else's turn to sing." She gave Caleb a meaningful look.

"He can't sing *True Colors.*"

"So, let's find one he can sing."

Caleb faced the rack of guitars to avoid answering, and picked up his bass. His movements were mechanical. He was still stunned, overwhelmed, by the discovery of Wynter's voice. And by the news he'd have to deliver soon. He had to say something. She was becoming confused, looking to Indio for reassurance. Caleb didn't think he could handle hearing *True Colors* or some other haunting tune right now.

"Let's keep it upbeat," he said. "*Sweet Home Alabama.* You gotta know that one, right, Wynter?"

"Yes. I mean, I know the basic chords."

"Indio can do the fancy stuff. Just keep that rhythm going."

"We call this one *Sweet Home Anaconda*, where we grew up," Jesse said, and counted them in.

Indio gave Caleb a little chin-jut to tell him to take lead vocals. He obliged, and it was more his style anyway. They played through the song, with Caleb substituting the lyrics for some silly shit they'd made up as children, and between them it ticked over. Even at the worst of times this room had always been their safe place, the only place where the music was all that mattered. For a few minutes at a time, everything else would fade away. Wynter was enjoying herself, and by the second half she was adding a little fingerpicking to her chords to match the radio song playing in her head. Indio looked more relaxed than Caleb had seen him in years. Jesse looked just a little smug, like he'd figured out how to take credit for the afternoon—and he might just be right, given his rule about no fights in the basement.

No fights, only music.

Caleb didn't like delaying the inevitable. He always said what needed to be said, outlined the options so nothing was hidden and no one was tricked. But he couldn't bring himself to tell them the bad news. Not yet.

Every Man's Duty

Indio suggested they drive out to Patty's on Cougar Mountain to eat. He described it as a Western-style diner. When they arrived, the place was already filling up. A woman in her forties with ash-blonde curls and a warm smile approached while they waited in the foyer. She gave the three brothers big hugs.

"Who's this, then?" she said, realizing Wynter was part of their group.

"This is Wynter," Caleb said. "Our little sister."

The woman did a good job hiding her reaction. Clearly, she knew them well, so to have them present a previously unknown sister out of the blue must've surprised her.

"Honored to meet you. I'm Patricia. Come on, then. Special treatment."

She led them toward a booth at the back. The place was lined with dark wood. Saddles and horseshoes and old posters adorned the walls. Each table had a low-hanging lightshade over it.

"Does she know you?" she whispered to Jesse.

"Patricia owns the place, and her father ran it before that. We've been coming here for years."

"You mean, with Harry?"

"Yeah."

Their father was still a mystery to Wynter. They'd barely mentioned him. Something must be wrong there, given Caleb had taken over raising his brothers years ago.

Indio and Caleb went off to chat with an older man in the corner, who sat on a stool surrounded by amps and other equipment on what she realized was a tiny stage.

"How often do you see your dad?" she asked Jesse.

"Every couple of months."

"How far away is Everett?"

"About twenty minutes north of Seattle."

"That doesn't sound very far."

"Twenty minutes and twenty years." Jesse twisted his mouth with a flash of annoyance, the most negative expression she'd seen on his face. It didn't last long. "I get along fine with him, I guess, if I catch him on a dry day. We talk about music."

"He's a musician?"

"Yeah, like Miriam. That's how they met. The story goes, he's back home in Montana on leave with his army buddies. She's singing in the bar and the pianist accompanying her is so bad, Harry gets up, throws the guy off the stage, and takes his place for the night. Pretty soon, she's pregnant and he's stationed in Germany. After his discharge, the two of them played the local music scene around west Montana for a few years. They had the twins, and then they split up right after I was born. After that we only saw Harry a few times a year."

"Were they good?"

"Harry claims they were. I've never seen or heard the evidence. No YouTube back then."

Caleb and Indio returned to the table and menus were passed around. Wynter struggled through it, bewildered by the options. Indio, sitting opposite her, noticed.

"Never been to a restaurant before?"

"Yes, at the mall."

"The food court," Caleb clarified, and Wynter realized it didn't count.

"This is a bit different," Indio said. "What do you like — burgers, chicken wings, ribs?"

"You can eat chicken *ribs?*"

Her brothers laughed and she buried her nose back in the menu. She wasn't sure she liked them laughing at her ignorance, although it seemed a gentle laughter, not mocking.

"Pork ribs," Indio said. "They might be a challenge for your first true dining experience."

"I'll take them." She was determined not to take the easy option. She was in the real world now. She wanted to experience everything.

Indio grinned approvingly. "What about your sides? Baked potato, fries, corn, slaw — see the list there?" He pointed to the boxed list of a dozen items. "You can pick two. And a drink."

She muddled through. Patricia came to take their order, although she wasn't wearing a uniform like the other staff.

"Come to the bar for a beer?" Patricia said to Caleb.

"Sure." Caleb excused himself and went to another room through a large archway, where there was a bar behind a low wall. Wynter knew from the way Patricia had asked the question, and the way he'd answered it, that Patricia wanted to get him alone to ask about her.

"Don't you want a beer, too?" she asked the others.

"I'll skip it tonight," Indio said.

"Not for me. You have to be twenty-one," Jesse said.

"Have you never had a beer, then?"

"I have ways and means," Jesse said slyly. "And Caleb doesn't mind if I have a couple of drinks at home on the weekend."

"That's a bit of a changed attitude for him," Indio told his brother. "When I was your age, he was paranoid I'd turn into an alcoholic."

"Like Harry?" Wynter said.

They both stared at her. Was that something she wasn't supposed to say? She'd picked up enough clues to know that much about Harry. She knew what an alcoholic was. People who joined the Light often came with stories of alcoholism and drug abuse in their previous lives. And there had been booze at the ashram, although there wasn't supposed to be. It was drunk in secret and one of the teachers had it constantly on her breath.

Music started and Wynter realized the man in the corner was there to perform. He had a hollow electric guitar and another man played drums. Not a drum kit like Jesse's, but a strange assortment of boxes that he tapped and scraped with his hands.

Wynter watched and listened. It was a style of music she hadn't heard before — melodic and emotional, but without the rock riffs.

"Do you know him?" she asked Indio. "You were talking to him earlier."

"That's Les Buckaroo."

"Is that his real name?"

"I doubt it."

"What style of music is that?"

"They're playing country and western. What d'you think of it?"

"I can hear some blues in there."

"You're right. It's a bit of blues, a bit of folk."

"D'you like it?" Jesse said.

She shrugged. "It's nice, but... sort of tame. If you can't dance to it, or bang your head to it, then it's no good." She realized that sounded rude. "That might not be true. It's what someone told me."

"He's got a fiddle player coming in for his second set in about an hour," Indio said. "You can dance then."

"Who? Jenny?" Jesse said.

Indio nodded and Jesse looked self-satisfied, and then Indio squirmed awkwardly on his seat. Why were they acting that way?

"I don't dance," she said. She was fairly sure the wild stuff she and Xay and Roman did in the shed, which Roman called *freaking out*, didn't count.

"Spend too much time around Caleb and he's gonna make you learn how," Jesse said, just as Caleb returned to the table with their drinks and sat next to Wynter.

"You taught them to dance?" she asked Caleb.

"Only the country swing," Caleb said. "It's every man's duty to learn the country swing."

"Who taught you?"

"My twelfth-grade girlfriend's parents taught me, and her, in preparation for the prom."

"One of Caleb's necessary life skills," Jesse said. "Along with... let's see, defensive driving, self-defense, how to fire and clean a gun, how to drink and smoke responsibly."

"But you don't smoke," Wynter said.

"Different kind of smoking," Jesse said with a grin.

She wasn't sure what he meant. Beside her, Caleb shifted the pepper and salt shakers around. Why was there so much about the outside that made people uncomfortable? Or was it only because she was there? She was determined to learn everything she could from them and these moments of awkwardness weren't helping. There had been no awkwardness when all four of them were jamming, as Caleb called it. Even the tension between Caleb and Indio had melted. Music held the brothers together as a family. Music could hold *her* to this family, too.

A server brought out their food. They passed around the plates so she got to try everything.

"What's that?" She pointed to a thin strip of crinkled, crispy meat on Jesse's plate.

"Oh my god, you've never seen bacon?" He handed it to her.

It smelled good but looked awful. She held it tentatively to her lips.

"Eat!" Jesse almost shouted the word in his eagerness.

She bit off the end and crushed the piece between her tongue and the roof of her mouth. Salty flavor covered her tongue and her eyes went wide. She couldn't help smiling, both at the taste and at Jesse's expression as he watched her. Then they all laughed, and Wynter devoured the rest of the bacon.

"Can I have this every day?" No one said anything and the laughter died away, so she asked Caleb, "Why didn't you teach them cooking?"

"I admit, that was an oversight," Caleb said. "That's what Patty's is for."

"Indio told me you have thousands of house rules. I should start learning them."

Opposite her, Jesse and Indio both gave Caleb a look and she felt the tension rise. Her heart started to pound. She didn't dare turn to look at Caleb. When he put his hand over hers on the table, she knew why.

"Social Services is putting you in a foster home for a while." Caleb was looking at her now. She stared at her plate. She could hear how he was trying to keep his tone light. "But you can visit, and we'll go through the house rules then."

She slid her hand out from under his and clasped both hands in her lap. "When?"

"Tina's coming over tomorrow afternoon to collect you."

"I don't like Tina."

"Why not?"

"Because she doesn't like you."

"She's trying to do what's best. She's found a woman to be your foster mother. You'll live in Richland."

"Fuck!" Jesse cried.

Wynter jumped at the aggression in his tone. Caleb glared at Jesse, who was entirely unashamed of himself.

"This is just temporary," Caleb said. "When Joy comes, I'll help her apply for custody. I don't know how long it'll take. Until then, you'll be in a good home and we'll still see lots of each other."

"It's two hundred miles away," Jesse pointed out, his face red.

"Two hundred miles?" Wynter whispered. "I don't want to go. Don't I have a say?"

"Tina thinks this is best." Caleb rubbed at the furrows on his forehead, his eyes squeezed shut. She'd thought of him as a tower of calming strength. Now he looked stressed and unsure.

Across the table, Jesse picked paint chips off the wall looking like he was going to cry. Indio just looked at her. Bad things happened all the time at the ashram, a place of constant disappointment that taught her not to bother hoping. Out here, in Caleb's house, and especially in the basement with a guitar in her hands, she'd started hoping again.

Big mistake.

The music started up and now it had a toe-tapping beat and a pretty girl with black hair playing the fiddle. A server cleared away their plates and cheerfully asked how the food was. Indio smiled at her and said it was all just fine.

"Dessert?" The server realized the mood of the table didn't match her own and her face fell.

"Wynter, you want ice cream?" Indio seemed to be the only one capable of speaking.

The server turned her attention to Wynter. "We have chocolate sundae with Oreo crumbles, caramel fudge sundae, choc chip and walnut brownie with vanilla ice cream, banana split with fresh cream — what would you like, honey? Or I can bring out the menu?"

From the way the woman reeled off the desserts, Wynter couldn't tell where one item ended and the next one began.

"One of each," Indio said.

"You're easy to please."

Indio responded with a charming smile that made the server blush as she walked off.

"You can call me on the phone, can't you?" Wynter said. "And Jesse, I can get some of that social media thing."

"Yeah," Jesse mumbled. "It's not that we don't want you. You know that, right?"

Wynter nodded mutely.

Caleb said, "Hun, this woman who'll be taking care of you is a psychologist. That means she's a safe person you can talk to."

"I don't want to talk to anyone," Wynter said in a small voice, which was all she could manage.

"Let's enjoy our evening. Tomorrow we'll make music again, and we'll organize with Tina when we can visit you." His hand was on her arm, very lightly, like he wasn't sure if she'd accept it.

Patricia came over and pulled Caleb up for a dance.

"Watch and learn," Caleb told Wynter.

He and Patricia went to the cleared area in front of the band and danced what Wynter assumed was the country swing, because the music had a swing rhythm. A trickle of happiness returned because Caleb was smiling, totally focused on Patricia as he swung her around and snapped her close and dipped her over his knee. He looked like someone else, moving in a casual yet still controlled way, with a physical energy he normally suppressed. Both dancers were very good, with a fun and natural style.

The desserts arrived, ridiculously huge goblets and dishes of ice cream and syrup. The smell made Wynter queasy. She and Indio and Jesse had a few bites of each before declaring defeat. By the end of it they were all smiling again. She could do this. She could pretend for a few more hours, and so could they.

Caleb returned and held out his hand to her.

"I can't," she said.

"Sure you can. I'll do all the work. Just follow my lead."

He took her to the dance floor. There were more couples dancing now, so she didn't feel conspicuous.

"Don't let go of my hand," he said.

She knew the basic movements from watching Patricia. He took her through a simpler version of that, and pretty soon she got the hang of how to keep her feet moving while he swung her around. She wasn't as elegant as Patricia, and she didn't care. The physicality of it made her happy, like her morning exercises. Anything that wasn't sitting in a classroom or cutting open boxes in the warehouse or hunched for hours over tiny pieces of jewelry making beaded mandalas.

They danced through one song, and the next had a waltz beat. Caleb put his hand on her waist and changed the step. She matched his footwork, moving backwards as he moved forwards.

Slow, slow, quick-quick. Slow, slow, quick-quick.

"This is the two-step," he said, bending his head down to her ear. "You're a natural."

He lifted her hand overhead and made a twirling motion with his other hand. She did a twirl and laughed as he pulled her back in and continued the dance. She felt so safe there in his arms, and every time a thought about the future crept in she pushed it down and let the music wash it out.

The next song picked up the pace and they did another country swing. She noticed Jesse dancing with Patricia. She couldn't see Indio. As Caleb brought her back to the table, Indio was returning to his seat.

"I'll go pay and we should think about leaving," Caleb said.

"I took care of it," Indio said.

Caleb looked surprised, but pleased. "Thanks."

"Can't we stay a bit longer?" Wynter said. She didn't want to go home. Home and bed and tomorrow morning meant they were that much closer to tomorrow afternoon, when she had to go.

Caleb relented. He ordered coffees and they watched Jesse dancing. Patricia was gone and his new partner was a girl his own age wearing tasseled boots — a real dancer, from the look of her. A lot of what she and Jesse were doing didn't look much like the country swing.

The band finished their set. Jesse came back to the table and flopped on the bench. Indio went to talk to the fiddle player.

"Didn't he and Jenny go out once or twice, right before he left for college?" Caleb asked Jesse.

"No, it was the summer after that. He had a thing for her all through his senior year, though. He went to a different school that last year," Jesse explained for Wynter. "She was the year below him and had a boyfriend."

Indio and Jenny seemed at ease as they chatted, like old friends catching up.

Jesse hopped off his seat. "Watch and learn," he said, mimicking Caleb with a wicked grin.

He crossed the diner and put coins in a brightly lit machine in the corner. It played a slow number. Couples returned to the dance floor in each other's arms and swayed. Jesse came to sit down.

Across the room, Indio leaned over to say something in Jenny's ear and she gave a lovely smile, and they went onto the dance floor to join the other couples. They moved very slowly, her smooth black hair swaying against her back. After a while, Indio bowed his head into the crook of Jenny's shoulder and kept it there.

Jesse gave an *I told you so* quirk of his eyebrow.

"Who was that girl in the funny boots?" Wynter asked him.

Jesse shrugged, still flushed from the effort. "She was *hot!* Told her I was a drummer and she asked me to dance. Everyone loves a drummer boy."

Chances

Indio held Jenny and thought about all the chances he'd blown. She'd caught his eye that very first day at the new school, a neatly dressed junior with a violin case, stunning dark eyes and golden skin, sleek hair pulled back in a perfect braid, a shy dimpled smile. She was new to the school, too. He wasted a month working up the courage to talk to her, although he'd never had trouble talking to girls before, only to have Kevin Tsang get there first.

He'd told himself she would've rejected him anyway. By then, the other kids had found out why he'd transferred so he had a bad boy rep he couldn't live down. Sometimes it came in handy – there were girls who thought it was sexy and boys who thought it was cool. And sometimes it was a pain in the ass.

A different song started, with an up-tempo swing beat, and Indio danced with Jenny just as Caleb had with Wynter. He couldn't match Caleb for style but he wasn't too bad. After he graduated high school, when he'd given up on Jenny and couldn't wait to escape to Ohio, he'd instead hung around in Seattle to keep Jesse company. Jesse had turned fifteen and pretty soon it would be just him and Harry in the house for long stretches while Caleb was deployed. In fact, that summer Caleb was on a cutter somewhere off the coast of West Africa. In July he came home on leave and Indio had an even greater incentive to get out quick. Jesse persuaded him to stick around so the three of them could play music for a couple of weeks. They did that, and in between arguing with Harry about how to fix a water heater and how to budget for groceries, Caleb had somehow found time to teach his brothers how to not look like fools when they had a girl in their arms on the dance floor.

So, he could dance. Thanks to Caleb.

Come to think of it, he was only here tonight because Caleb had

had a change of heart about bringing Wynter to Portland, which in turn changed *his* mind about visiting Seattle.

After his first wild year in Ohio, he'd come home in the summer and Jenny was free. They went on two dates and she was exactly as pure and perfect as he remembered. He'd treated her right and she confessed she'd always liked him. And then he'd screwed it all up. Back to college as a sophomore, to the music, to that other sort of girl, the sort who didn't care if you treated them right as long as you made them feel special for a night, or a few nights, however long it took for them to start thinking they *were* special. Then it was time to move on to the next one. He was drinking and doing drugs and flunking and hating himself, although he always found time for music.

"Can we go out the back and talk for a bit?" he said when the dance was over.

Jenny nodded. He passed his family at their booth — Caleb and Jesse were halfway through their coffees. Wynter looked ready to drop into bed. He was proud of himself for paying for the meal. Caleb always paid. Indio was trying to be a man now. He could step up on occasion.

"Give me five minutes?" he said, and Caleb acknowledged his request.

There was a patio out the back, overlooking the mountains. Patricia put tables out here in the warmer months. Tonight they were alone.

Indio leaned against the wall and Jenny pressed up against him, like when they were slow-dancing, and they kissed for the third time ever. She seemed desperate, which wasn't like her at all.

"You should know, I'm seeing someone," she said.

She may as well have punched him in the balls. He set her away from him. She backed up against the wall beside him as he stared at the dark mountains.

He made a joke of it, like he imagined Jesse might. "You could've told me before the dance. In my head we were already an item."

"Yes, I should've. Got caught up in the moment. It was so good to see you again. His name's Stefan. He transferred to the Arts course at U-Dub in the fall."

Indio really didn't want to know, but this was Jenny so he was nice about it. "He's a musician?"

"An actor, a theater major."

He could not picture Jenny with an actor. Weren't actors vain pricks? Jenny deserved someone focused on her, not on himself.

He hated Stefan already. Pretentious name, too.

"Whatever happened to Kevin Tsang?" he said, to change the subject. Kevin wasn't a bad guy but he'd always been highly suspicious of Indio, with good cause, which had made him snappy toward Jenny when she paid Indio any attention.

"He's been accepted to medical school at UCLA."

"Wow. Didn't realize he was a smart one."

"You always made it your business to know as little about him as possible."

Okay, he was done talking about her boyfriends.

"I should've stayed with you, that summer two years ago," he said. "Wish I had."

"So do I." She gave him that sweet smile that had always seemed both innocent and all-knowing.

"Really? I assumed you'd dump me before summer was out."

"Dump you? We weren't really together. Two dates. You were always nice to me, Indio, from the day we met. I know that's the real you, not the crap everyone says. I wish *you* believed it."

"You could make me believe it." He didn't mean it. He didn't need Caleb to tell him not to make a move on an unavailable girl. It might even work, given the way she'd kissed him, and then she'd be tainted by his poor behavior.

"Listen." She turned to him and took his hand. "Next time a girl takes you to an open-air concert on the second date and holds your hand the whole time, don't run off to Mexico and leave her hanging."

"Yeah. Learned my lesson." That trip to Mexico with friends had been planned months earlier. He could've canceled. Instead, he went along, had a meaningless fling with one of the girls in the group, and returned so ashamed of himself that he hightailed it back to Ohio without speaking to Jenny again.

"So, why'd you transfer to Portland?"

He hesitated so long she raised an eyebrow quizzically. "Trying to decide which reason to give you," he said. "I could tell you my best friend from Ohio transferred there and wanted me to sing in his band. Or I could make myself look good and tell you I wanted to be closer to my family."

"Tell me about that second reason," Jenny said, a twinkle in her eye.

"I guess, around October, Jesse asked me to come home for Christmas. I'd skipped three already. I'd just been home for his high school graduation, and things were... a bit rough between me and Caleb. Really bad. I was a mess, to be honest. I didn't want to show up again in that state, so I cleaned up and thought about leaving Ohio for good. Burned so many bridges there, and they were always threatening to throw me out anyway."

"Well, you look great now. Really good."

He gave her an uneasy smile. He wasn't exactly clean and sober but things were a lot better. He was looking forward to the year ahead. He hadn't known, of course, when he moved to Portland, that in a month he'd meet Wynter, or that he'd be given the chance to hope, for twenty minutes anyway, that he had another chance with Jenny.

"Who was that girl with your family?" Jenny said. "I thought from the back she was Jesse's girlfriend but she looks about twelve."

"That's Wynter. She's nearly fifteen and she's our half-sister. We didn't know about her. I just met her yesterday."

"How incredible!" She looked more excited about it than he remembered being when Caleb told him.

"She grew up in a... well, let's call it a commune, in Arizona. They're taking her into foster care tomorrow." A wave of sadness passed through him. He leaned forward, hands on his knees, and drew a few deep breaths. "Sorry. Just having a shitty night. You're right, it is incredible. She's kind of amazing and we really wanted her to stay in Seattle. Caleb's still being a jerk about my lifestyle choices. Stefan's the final straw."

Jenny rubbed his back until he straightened again.

"God, I wish I never went to Mexico. It was a fucking horrible vacation anyway."

"Can't change the past, Indio." She handed him her phone. "Give me your number. No reason we can't stay in touch. I'd love to come to your gig next time I'm in Portland."

She gave him a quick hug and they went back inside.

Indio returned to the booth. "Ready to go? I'll drive."

In the truck, Wynter leaned forward from the back seat and asked him, "Are you gonna date Jenny again?"

"She's with someone else."

"But I thought you liked her."

"Yeah, missed my chance."

"Sorry, bro," Jesse said.

In the rear-view mirror, Indio saw Wynter sit back with a confused look. *Great.* The dancing had put everyone back in a good mood and made the evening bearable, and now he'd given it a sad ending.

Broken Doll

The doorbell rang on Monday morning just as Caleb was preparing to call the Light office in Seattle. He opened the door to a young dark-haired woman, thin and tired, with an anxious expression on her vaguely familiar face.

"Joy!"

"Hello, Caleb."

She tried a smile. He stepped out and put his arm around her to invite her inside.

"Wynter's here," he said, because that must be her main concern. He looked to the street for a car or taxi. Nothing there. "How did you get here?"

The simple question flustered her. "Oh, a friend brought me. Did you get my message?"

"Yes. Thank god you're here. We've got some things to sort out before this afternoon." He didn't want to overload her, but the placement hearing was at two o'clock. With Joy attending, it would no longer be "just a formality". Now they had a real shot at keeping Wynter after all.

"How's Wynter?"

"She's great. She's still asleep."

"Can I see her?"

He led her down the hallway to Indio's room and knocked softly. When there was no reply, he opened the door a crack. Joy peeked inside and looked at their sleeping sister for a moment.

"I won't wake her," she said.

They returned to the front of the house. Caleb put on coffee and Joy perched on a bar stool.

"Do Indio and Jesse live here?"

"Jesse does. He left for campus half an hour ago. Indio's staying over — he went to the store. I'll text them. I bet Jesse can skip a couple of classes. They'll want to see you."

"No, please don't do that. I don't want to disrupt their day."

"They won't think of it that way."

"Let's talk for a bit, you and me."

"Sure. You do remember them?"

"Of course. I was thinking about Jesse on the bus ride from Tucson, when I was working on Wynter's hair. I'm so sorry it was such a mess."

Caleb shook his head to dismiss the concern, bewildered by what she chose to prioritize.

"I used to tie ribbons in Jesse's curls," she said. "He was my little live doll. He even giggled when you pressed his tummy. I remember playing with Indio on that patio at the house in Missoula. Making blanket forts."

"You always had to have a princess tower."

A pained expression crossed her face, like she didn't want to think about those times even though she'd brought it up. For Caleb, they were mostly happy memories — their mom was raising them alone, alternating between neglect and near-competence, and they'd stayed in cheap rental places all over west Montana.

"So, Jesse's in college? I worked out he'd be a high school senior."

"He's in his first year at the University of Washington, studying engineering. Indio's doing design at Portland State. We drove down there Saturday night to see his band, and he came back with us for the weekend."

"How about you?"

"I joined the Coast Guard at eighteen. Figured it'd be a good way to see the world, and it has been." He mentally winced, remembering Joy's view of the world had been confined to a few acres of desert since she was six years old. "Have you seen Harry?"

"No. I called from LA. He sounded... odd."

"Drunk?"

She shrugged. "I didn't get a good vibe. In any case, I couldn't very well send Wynter there, not by herself — she's not his."

"We didn't know about her. We were never told Mom remarried and had another child."

"Well, she wanted a clean break." Joy looked around. "This is a nice house, Caleb. I'm so glad you're all okay."

It wasn't a nice house. It was thirteen hundred square feet of a 1950s fixer-upper that devoured most of Caleb's spare time just to keep the walls from crumbling. Joy, like Wynter, presumably didn't know the difference.

He slid a coffee mug toward her. "Where are you staying?"

"A very nice woman from the Seattle office has given me a room in her house in Magnolia."

"I know you're finding your feet, but it's crucial we sort out a few things. This afternoon we'll attend Wynter's emergency placement hearing, to make sure she's placed with you. In the longer term—"

"Caleb, wait." Joy had gone pale. "I don't think... I thought *you* would take care of her."

"I will. I'll provide for you both. But you need to live with her, as her court-appointed guardian."

"Can't you be her guardian?"

"This hearing has nothing to do with me. It's taking place only because the ashram won't have Wynter back. The court will place her with you for now, and I'll help you get a job so you can apply for custody."

Joy frowned, shivering in an oversized sweater. She wasn't going to present well at the hearing in this state — bewildered and nervous. He needed to be gentle with her, boost her confidence, or she wasn't going to impress the judge.

"You don't understand. I'm in terrible trouble for taking Wynter out of the ashram." She was picking her words carefully.

"Why does that matter? You're safe now. You never need to see those people again."

"It does matter. It matters to me. The followers at the LA office and here in Seattle have been very kind to me, but the leadership in Arizona has already excommunicated me from the temple for what I did." She twisted her hands together in anguish. "Truth is, they're probably secretly glad I took Wynter away — they don't want her there — but still, I broke vows by leaving and went against Miriam's explicit wishes. She's very upset with me. She has a lot of influence."

"Have you spoken with her?"

"No." Joy bit her lip, which made her look like Wynter for a moment. "Someone in LA spoke to her. She's refusing to speak with me. I'm sure... I'm sure she'll come around."

Caleb was rather hoping Miriam didn't come around. He needed her to stay out of it. His heart went out to Joy, though, who was feeling for the first time what the rest of them had already been through — their mother's rejection.

"I feared this would happen," Joy said. "Living out here in darkness, with Harry or with you, I knew I'd pay a price for getting Wynter out of there."

"Why was it so important to get her out? Did they not take proper care of her? She's scared of that place. She's underweight—"

"Oh, she's always been very healthy. Probably just a growth spurt. I was skinny at that age, too."

Caleb was too polite to point out she still was.

"Joy, please tell me — was she mistreated? Were you?"

That pained expression was back and it made Caleb's heart sink.

"She doesn't belong in the Light. They said she has... No, it doesn't matter." Joy fiddled with her mug. She hadn't taken one sip. "You won't understand. You can love her just as she is, can't you? Just as I have, from the day she was born."

"I need to know what happened to her. She was clearly neglected and had almost no schooling. She said she worked for hours a day in a warehouse."

"Oh, that wasn't really work. The kids liked doing that, helping out."

Caleb pushed his hand through his hair, getting nowhere. Joy was brushing it off, yet she'd risked everything to get Wynter out.

"Okay, never mind about that for now. The hearing's at two. I'll call my lawyer to run through the procedure with you."

"I can't do it, Caleb," Joy said despairingly. So different from Wynter, who had faced everything bravely. "You're talking about going to court? I can hardly breathe out here and you want me to convince a judge I can take care of Wynter?"

"If you don't come forward, today, this afternoon, she'll be placed in foster care by default. Her social worker's already set the time to take her away."

Joy was horrified. "Oh! I didn't know that would happen. For how long?"

"As long as it takes for us to get a custody hearing. Even then, Washington doesn't have jurisdiction to award permanent custody for six months. Foster care isn't what Wynter needs. She needs you."

"I can't do it. I'm so sorry. Not today. Not for a while."

Caleb searched for an alternative. "Miriam could recommend me as Wynter's guardian, then. It might be enough to convince Social Services."

"She won't want to get involved with the authorities."

"That's her child! What the fuck is wrong with her?"

Joy blanched. Caleb turned away, admonishing himself for losing control. Joy was a broken doll, incapable of accepting help from anyone but the people who broke her and who would grind her pieces to dust. Yelling at her wouldn't fix anything. He clenched his hands on the counter. This was like dealing with Indio — her manner was very different from her twin's, yet Caleb felt the same frustration as his words rolled off her without effect. What could he do? Joy was in no state to appear in court, even if she wanted to take Wynter. He needed to plan ahead.

"Okay, even if you're not ready right now, you need to start the application process for custody or she's going to get stuck in the system."

Joy gave a quick smile that he knew was intended to placate him. "We can talk about that later, of course."

Later. Caleb would have to accept that for now.

"I know this is difficult for you," he said. "Harder than I can imagine. I know that. They're taking Wynter away today, but you can stay. You can have that room. Please stay."

"No, I couldn't impose." Joy pushed back her seat and he realized she wanted to leave.

"I want to help you." Caleb heard the edge of desperation in his voice. "God, you're our sister. Your family is right here. Not... those people. Just let me know what you need. I'll do anything."

"I'll be fine, Caleb. Give me your cell number and I'll call you later, when I have a phone of my own."

He grabbed a scrap of paper and wrote it down.

"Did you think to bring Wynter's birth certificate with you? I can use it to prove she's my sister, and there's a small chance they'll give me the emergency placement today after all." Joy shook her head. "Can you get it sent to me?"

"I don't think she has a birth certificate."

"Everyone has a birth certificate."

"Miriam used to say she was a child of the Light. Not of this world. She was born at the ashram. I don't think her birth was registered."

Caleb stood back, stunned. "So, she doesn't exist. She could've died in that place and no one would even know she'd lived. I would never have known."

Joy sat in miserable silence.

"There must be a way to register her now. What's her birthdate?"

"We don't do birthdays."

"I need to know, Joy."

"March eighth. She's turning fifteen."

"Middle name?"

"She doesn't have one."

"We all have one."

"Well, she doesn't have one." The hint of defensiveness in Joy's tone was the first sign of strength he'd yet seen.

"What's her father's full name?"

"Malcolm something. I don't really remember him. He and Miriam were only together a few months."

"How about a marriage certificate or divorce papers?"

"It wasn't that sort of marriage. The Light has a spiritual commitment ceremony but it's not a legal thing."

Caleb mentally ran through his options. "If you speak to Miriam, please find out his full name, and his date and place of birth. And tell her I want to talk to her. Not for recriminations — that's over and done. I just need to sort out the legal issues."

"She won't want to speak with you, Caleb. She's left this world behind."

"I'm painfully aware of that."

Joy fidgeted with the strap of her purse. "I'm waiting for the universe to illuminate my path. I know there are things I have to do, to survive out here. I know I have to join the outside world. Do you have my birth certificate and social security number?"

"Not here. Harry will have them."

"I can't see Harry."

"I'll get them for you."

"Thank you."

"Wynter said you were married."

"Yes. I've done a terrible thing by leaving like this."

"Will he come after you?"

"Oh, no, it's not like that. He's not a bad man. I must go. I'll just pop my head around the door again." She indicated the direction of the bedrooms.

Caleb followed her to Wynter's room. Joy sat on the edge of the bed and stroked Wynter's hair until she stirred. Wynter sat up and gripped her sister's arm.

"Here I am, darling," Joy said. "What do you think of your big brothers, then? You were a bit of a surprise to them. I've had a good long talk with Caleb."

"You came just in time!"

Joy gave Caleb a nervous look over her shoulder. "I have to go. I'll visit you later."

Wynter was instantly devastated. "But you have to stay and be my guardian. We'll live here. You can have this bed and we can put a mattress on the floor for me. Can't we, Caleb?"

"I'll talk to you soon." Joy extracted herself from Wynter's grasp.

She couldn't get out of the room fast enough.

Wynter tossed off the covers and got out of bed, unsure whether to follow. The look on her face broke Caleb's heart.

He followed Joy up the hall. "Do you want me to call a taxi?"

"No, thank you. There's a car waiting for me up the street." She stopped at the front door and touched his arm. "Take care of her."

And she was gone.

He turned to see Wynter standing in the hallway. Once again, he was struck by how small and thin she looked, like a gust of wind would blow her away. But she'd turned up on a freezing evening in shorts and sandals and she was still standing.

Then he remembered she was nobody. Didn't exist. He couldn't even fathom why their mother wouldn't register her birth. Miriam had always been eccentric and preoccupied, but this was unforgivable.

"Why wouldn't she stay?"

Caleb went to her, put a hand on her shoulder. "She has some things to sort out. She's staying with someone from the Light."

"But she left the Light."

"She left the ashram. I don't think she's ready to leave the Light. I'll do everything I can to help her, hun. Breaking free — that's got to be her decision."

"I don't understand. I would never go back to them."

"I believe you."

She stared at the front door. "She's not gonna take care of me?"

"She can't do that right now."

"I have to live with that woman in Richland?"

"For now." He made tiny circles with his thumb on her thin shoulder, with no other idea how to offer comfort. "I know this isn't what we wanted. We'll get through it. You're strong enough, Wynter. Maybe Joy isn't, yet. I know you are."

She returned to her room to get dressed. Caleb stood for a long time there in the hallway, leaning against the wall, with nowhere to direct his ire.

He'd convince Joy to step up — even if her sense of duty was lacking, she surely loved Wynter. She'd do the right thing and he'd help her. Still, he felt weighed down by failure, and Wynter's distress magnified his sense of powerlessness.

Indio let himself in through the front door, a grocery bag in his arms, and went into the kitchen. Caleb rapped on Wynter's door.

"Hungry? I'll make pancakes. Indio's back with the bacon."

One Promise

The morning spun by in a blur. While Caleb made some calls in the house, Indio asked Wynter to show him the exercises Jesse had told him about. She went through a routine on the deck, not really knowing if he was enjoying it or simply indulging her. He had studied karate, like his brothers, but not stuck with it in Ohio. He followed her moves and showed her a couple of his own.

After her shower, she found Caleb pulling clothes out of one of the two machines in the utilities room.

"Why do you have two washers?"

"This one's a dryer. I guess you didn't need dryers in Arizona."

Wynter was very familiar with laundry equipment. It never occurred to her there would be an entire machine she'd never heard of. Most of the clothes in the basket were dark blue t-shirts along with more of those collared shirts with his name on them. Caleb picked out a collared shirt and put it on a hanger.

"Gotta hang 'em up while they're hot, so they don't crease."

"Is that your uniform?"

"My work clothes, yeah. I have fancy jackets and pants for important occasions. Find your stuff so you can pack."

He said it with a tense smile, because *packing* her stuff was an essential step toward *leaving*. She ran her hands through the warm clothes and found the jeans Bea had bought her on Friday. They worked in silence for a minute, Caleb hanging his shirts and Wynter folding her clothes.

"Everything will work out," he said at last. "Joy's scared, I imagine, and overwhelmed right now. I'll help her find a job and persuade her to move home, and then she'll be ready to seek custody."

"Why not you? I want you to be my guardian."

"Hun, it's not that simple. Single parents and the military don't mix. If Jesse was a little older, or if Indio lived nearer as a back-up..." He shook his head. "For now, I'm not the right choice to—"

He stopped at Wynter's gasp as she grabbed a dark gray t-shirt from the basket. She'd noticed a half-hidden logo on the shirt. Shaking it out, she held it up and stared at the full image.

"You are! You are the right choice." She blinked away hot tears. The universe didn't speak to her. She *knew* that. But here it was — a message plain as day. The logo was an elaborate design featuring a skull and wrenches and the words, *If you break it, I will come.* But the message wasn't in the words. "Why does it have this shape on it?" She pointed to the cogwheel integrated into the design.

"It's the MK insignia — machinery technician. That's my class shirt from when I graduated A-School in '07. I wear it around the house sometimes."

He took the shirt from her and closed his hand around hers, to stop it shaking.

"It means I belong with you," she stammered.

He watched her closely, trying to understand. "Why does it mean that?"

"I'm supposed to stay. I'm supposed to be *here.*"

"You can't, hun, not right now. You can't." His eyes flashed with that same look of pain she'd seen in the shopping mall, when he'd asked her about Miriam.

Wynter withdrew her hand, staring at the bracelet on her wrist. She could show him, right now, what it meant. Would he understand? Would anyone care that the universe wanted her on a different path from the one *they* were forcing her onto?

Jesse had laughed at her description of the signs that led her to Caleb's door, and at the numbers in the grocery store. He would laugh at this, too.

She couldn't bear the thought that Caleb might laugh at her.

"Doesn't matter. It's nothing," she muttered, grabbing her pile of folded clothes. "Do we have time to play in the jamroom for a bit?"

"Sure. Indio's already down there."

He left his laundry, even though she'd seen at least one more collared shirt in the basket that was going to get creased now.

They jammed for a while, waiting for Jesse. Wynter wouldn't sing but she loved listening to her brothers' voices harmonizing. Her chest was tight with fear at the thought of going to some other house, far away from this safe place. Every time she looked at Caleb, he seemed calm and accepting. She needed to be like that, to cut out the emotion and wait patiently for Joy to change her mind. Indio's expression was a mask and she couldn't tell if he cared one way or the other.

"You can have that." Indio indicated the acoustic-electric guitar she'd been playing.

"I can't take your guitar."

"It's just gonna lie around here doing nothing. Let's find a case for it."

He rummaged around in a metal cabinet and found a soft guitar cover. Wynter followed him upstairs. In his bedroom, he pulled a canvas duffle bag out of his closet.

"Pack your things in here." He sat on the edge of the bed, next to her. "Jesse and I shared this room when Harry lived here — did he tell you? For three years, until Caleb headed off to bootcamp and Jesse took his room. There was a bunk bed here."

"I didn't know Harry lived here."

"This is his house. He bought it when we moved to Seattle. But it always felt like Caleb's house. Caleb wore the pants."

"Didn't everyone wear pants?"

"Just an expression. Harry wasn't much use to anyone, so Caleb took over. Then he left for a few years, deployed all over the country, all over the world. He'd crash on the couch when he was home on leave. When he got assigned to the Seattle base, he kicked Harry out. Can't say I blame him."

"Are kids allowed to kick their parents out?"

"You wouldn't think so." He shrugged. "Caleb had the nerve to do it, but more remarkable is that Harry let it happen. Justified it to himself, somehow, so he could live with it."

"Like Momma."

He gave her a long look, his mouth a hard line. "This sucks. You want to stay — we all want you to stay. I couldn't wait to get out of here. I've been back, I think, three times in three years."

He unzipped the bag and emptied out its random contents on the bed — a hardback notebook, a couple of paperbacks, various receipts and bus tickets, a scrunched-up hand towel and a pair of worn, red leather gloves.

"What are those?"

"Boxing gloves. I did mixed martial arts training for a while. I did wonder what happened to these." He picked up the notebook and flicked through it. The pages were thick and unlined, mostly blank except for pencil sketches on the first few pages. "Do you draw?"

"I never tried."

He dropped the book in her lap. "You can take it — use the blank pages to write down your lyrics."

"What lyrics?"

"Whatever you come up with. Or write a poem, or a story. Maybe do some sketches. Don't tell Jesse. He thinks art's a waste of time. He makes exceptions for the art he personally likes, of course."

"Does that make music a waste of time?"

"Music is mathematics, not art. According to Jesse."

"I think math and physics make him *feel* something — here." She pressed her fist against her lower sternum, the place where pleasure simmered and spiraled when she heard music.

Indio cocked his head. "You could be right. I've been trying to figure him out his whole life. That's the first time something makes sense."

"Maybe I'll learn to feel that way about math and science, too. His worldview book is interesting." She indicated the Hawking on the quilt. "Interesting for my brain, anyway. I don't *feel* it yet."

"Jesse will turn you into his clone, if you let him. Figure out what works for you."

"What works for you?"

"I got only one piece of advice, and it comes from Harry, believe it or not, and while he was under the influence. Make one promise to yourself and keep it. Something that means the world to you, that keeps you true."

"What happens if you break the promise?"

"Well, you feel like crap and then you recommit to it."

"The Light teaches us to keep true, but our true selves are made of light, or pieces of God. Our human parts aren't too important, except to move us closer to God."

"How do you move closer?"

"All sorts of ways. Prayer and fasting and meditation. And you're supposed to have a talisman, something the universe uses to talk to you. Could be a number sequence or an animal or a pattern you keep seeing. I knew a boy who talked about it openly, even though it's supposed to be private — he was convinced his talisman was the gecko. Every time he saw a gecko, he tried to figure out what message the universe was sending. He kept one as a pet. When it died, he said it was a sign he was leaving. Soon after that he was sent away for a while."

"Did you find your talisman?"

"Your talisman finds *you*. I'm still waiting. Don't tell Jesse. He'd call it superstitious, wouldn't he?"

"Definitely."

"I figured out Joy's, though, years ago. It's the color white. She always goes toward white."

"She must get confused — there's a lot of white in the world."

"Was that her favorite color as a child?"

"Don't remember. Don't remember much about her."

Was he upset Joy had visited that morning and not waited for him? Maybe Joy didn't remember much about him, either. She'd certainly never mentioned him, or any of them, to Wynter.

She ran her fingers over the sketchbook cover. "I don't think I can write lyrics. I don't have anything to say."

"Write music, then. I'll email you a PDF of manuscript paper to print off."

"I don't know what that means. I don't know how to print. What's PDF?"

"Someone at school will help out."

"School..." A tremor went through her. "I didn't like doing two hours a day. How am I gonna do six?"

"I felt the same way, baby. You'll figure it out. You're gonna be something different for those kids. Just remember, each of them is something different, too. They're all a bit lost in their own way."

"Was Jesse lost?"

"Well, no."

"I think I'm gonna miss him even more than Caleb."

"Yeah, Jesse knows how to make an impression. A brutally honest impression."

"What does that mean?"

"Just that he's brutally honest. You'll learn to love it. Or tolerate it. You'll still see lots of him. Both of them."

"And you?"

"I'll ride up when I can."

"But you don't like coming home."

"Now I have a reason to."

"To fix those hinges?" she joked, indicating his closet.

Indio chuckled, putting his arms around her in a spontaneous hug. His body was warm and strong and she was reminded of other hugs, from a boy who was otherwise not much like Indio in manner or in looks, except for the straggly light hair, but made her feel just as safe.

"I *will* fix them," Indio said, drawing back. "Just so we're clear, though — I'll be fixing them for you. Not for him."

"I don't think he minds who you're fixing them for, as long as it gets done."

"You've figured us all out pretty quick. I'm gonna try harder. I'm gonna do better with Caleb."

"You have three hours to talk to him on the drive back to Portland."

"Hmm, no, not quite ready for that. I'll take the bus."

He left her to pack.

Now it was getting very close, very real. Wynter took a long time re-folding her clothes and packing them into the bag. She fetched her toothbrush and the nice toiletries Bea had chosen for her. She put Jesse's book on top of everything and zipped up the bag. Then she unzipped it and added Indio's sketchbook. She didn't plan to write lyrics but she wanted to see his drawings.

Jesse came home from class early, soon after lunch. He handed her an old phone of his. "Here, I put you on our family plan so you can call or send messages and photos, and browse the internet."

They sat at the table and he showed her how to use it, going through each step several times. He programmed all their numbers into it.

Tina showed up. She offered no objection to the guitar as it was placed in her trunk. Wynter had hoped she would, so Caleb or Indio would be forced to defend her. As her brothers gathered around the vehicle she wanted to hug them, like Indio had hugged her earlier. She didn't know how to initiate it and she didn't know if they'd like it. Most of all, she didn't want to do it in front of Tina. She found she couldn't even say goodbye.

She got in the car. Tina promised to tell Caleb as soon as she'd organized a visitation schedule.

As Tina backed out of the driveway, Wynter watched her brothers walk into the house — Caleb with his hand on Jesse's shoulder, Indio trailing a few paces behind.

Lovely

"It's a long drive, but we'll be there before bedtime. I've packed snacks and drinks." Tina indicated a grocery bag on the back seat next to Indio's canvas bag. "Your foster mother's name is Rosa. She's a lovely lady and she has a lovely home. Today she enrolled you in the local middle school."

Wynter stared out the window. "What grade?"

"Eighth grade."

"Jesse said I should be in ninth grade."

"I've talked to Rosa and she feels it would be better to wait until September before you start high school."

"Doesn't matter anyway. I can't even do eighth-grade math."

"Rosa will help with your homework. She'll always be around to help you. And to listen to you."

Tina glanced over at Wynter, and back to the road, and to Wynter again, looking increasingly irritated. Wynter wondered what she'd done wrong.

At last Tina said, "That was your brother Indio? The blond one?"

"Yes. He came home with us on Saturday night."

"I'm very unhappy Caleb allowed him to stay in the house."

"It's Indio's home."

"It shows a blatant disregard for my wishes and your safety. Had I known, I'd have collected you yesterday and put you in a youth shelter for the night."

Put. Wynter hated that word. *Put* was for *things*. She hadn't felt like a thing in Caleb's house. Was she a thing to Tina?

"When can I see Caleb again?"

"I'm going to arrange a supervised visit for this weekend. See? Not long to wait."

"Why do I need to be supervised?"

"It's standard procedure, until Caleb has been cleared."

She realized the supervision was for Caleb, not for her. "Cleared of what?"

"He needs to go through a background check for any criminal history."

"And Jesse?"

"Jesse too, if you want unsupervised visits."

And Indio? She was suddenly terrified. Indio assaulted someone and went to jail. He had a criminal history. Tina knew this and was already making a big deal of it. Wynter wouldn't be allowed to see him without Tina being there to *supervise*, ruining everything with her suspicious questions and unspoken accusations.

Wynter closed her eyes and pretended to sleep so she wouldn't have to talk to Tina again.

✿

They turned into the driveway of a majestic two-story house. Every window in the front was lit, and strings of glittering white lights crisscrossed the porch.

Tina switched off the engine. "How lovely. Her Christmas lights are still up. Aren't they pretty?"

The front door opened before Wynter was out of the car, and a woman stepped onto the porch. She was in her fifties, with dark hair cut short, and she wore a brown skirt and jacket on her petite frame. Tina took the bag from the back seat and they approached the house.

"This is Dr Rosamund Meyers," Tina said. "And here's Wynter."

"Hello, Wynter. Call me Rosa."

The woman held out her hand, just like Caleb had that first day. But when Wynter shook it, the hand was cool and thin.

They followed Rosa inside. The entry hall was enormous, with a ceiling that went all the way up to the second story. Large rooms were visible through archways on either side. A wide staircase wound up to a balcony, with doors leading off it. Wynter had never imagined you could have a balcony *inside* a house. But this was only the second house she'd ever been inside.

"Let's go straight to your room, shall we?" Rosa said, after she and Tina had exchanged pleasantries.

They went upstairs. Wynter's new bedroom was three times the size of Indio's. Even the bed was huge. There were two floor-to-ceiling windows in the far wall. A floor lamp and a second lamp on the nightstand illuminated the room with a warm glow.

Tina put the bag on the bed. "How lovely."

Wynter was tired of everything being *lovely*.

"I expect you're exhausted after that drive," Rosa said. "Let's have supper and then you can get to bed. I've arranged for you to start school on Wednesday, so we'll have tomorrow to ourselves, to get everything ready."

Downstairs, Rosa spoke to Tina for a few minutes at the front door while Wynter wandered through the rooms, bewildered by all the *stuff*. Glass-doored bookcases that covered one entire wall. A fireplace, a fancy clock under a glass dome, overstuffed armchairs and tables with carved legs. Rugs and lamps everywhere. Odd, unidentifiable trinkets on the side tables and window sills.

She heard the door close, and then she remembered the guitar in the trunk.

She raced past Rosa and tugged on the front door in a panic. She banged her fists on it.

"Wynter, it's all right. Calm down."

"Don't let her leave. I have something in the trunk. Please!"

Rosa spent precious seconds trying to calm her. The car engine started up. Headlights flashed across the window.

"Open the door!" Wynter screamed.

Rosa unlocked and opened the door and Wynter rushed out, catching her bracelet on the handle. She yanked herself free, snapping the braid, and ran down the driveway just as Tina finished backing the car onto the street. Wynter thumped on the hood and on the windows.

"My guitar!" she yelled through the glass.

Tina got out and opened the trunk. "What a close call. We almost forgot it."

Wynter pulled out the guitar, taking care not to bang the soft case on anything. Tina gave her an apologetic smile, closed the trunk and drove off.

"I won't make noise," Wynter said raggedly, marching back to the house with Rosa on her heels. "I won't disturb you, I promise."

"That's quite all right..."

Wynter made it to her room before her knees went weak. She sank cross-legged to the floor in the corner and shifted a trash basket and a huge bean bag to make room for the guitar.

"Here, you broke your bracelet." Rosa handed her the frayed braid. "Can you tie a knot to fix it?"

Heart pounding, Wynter tossed the bracelet aside and concentrated on what she was doing, leaning the guitar against the desk and pressing the bean bag against it so it wouldn't fall.

"I have some sewing supplies. I'll help you fix it." There was a hopeful note to Rosa's voice, like she thought this would be a perfect bonding activity for them.

Wynter didn't want to bond and she didn't care about the bracelet. She'd woven thousands of them and couldn't recall weaving this particular one. Still, it served a purpose and she should repair it.

"I can do it myself." She retrieved the braid from the carpet, careful not to expose her wrist to Rosa.

"Supper?" Rosa said.

"I want to go to bed."

"Of course. The bathroom is two doors down. I'll leave a snack out in the kitchen, in case you get hungry in the night. Would you like to have a little talk before bed? I'd like to make sure you know what's going on."

"Tina explained."

"We'll talk tomorrow, then."

Wynter pulled out her phone.

"Oh, I do have a house rule, dear. No electronic devices after nine."

The clock on her phone said 9:09PM. If Rosa denied her, she felt she might throw something heavy at the woman. It was an odd feeling. She'd never considered violence against a total stranger before.

She said, very slowly, "I'm going to call my brother."

"Well, just this once, to let him know you've arrived safely. Five minutes, okay? You can talk to him again tomorrow."

Rosa went away at last, her footsteps fading down the hall.

Wynter curled up on her bed and tapped Caleb's name on the screen.

✿

In the morning, Wynter put her bag in the closet, unpacking only enough to find clothes to wear for the day — jeans, t-shirt, sweater. She put Jesse's worldview book and Indio's sketchbook on the nightstand. She fixed her bracelet and slipped it on. As she returned from her shower she heard dishes clinking downstairs in the kitchen.

She took another look around the bedroom, at all the things she hadn't noticed last night. Novels on the bookshelf, stuffed animals on the end of the bed, a desk in the corner and a pretty rug on the floor. The décor was a nice shade of pale blue with white wood. Everything really was *lovely*, like those magazine photos. How many other children without approved guardians had lived in this house, in this room? She preferred Indio's sparse, plain room with its faded drapes and normal sized bed.

She went downstairs. The hallway floors were slate tile, the bannisters dark wood, and the windows tall and arched. Everything was large, neat, and perfect.

Rosa had made waffles, which Wynter had heard of but never seen or eaten. They stuck in her throat.

"I think Tina told you, I'm a psychologist," her new foster mother said. "If something is ever troubling you, you can tell me."

Wynter had no plans to tell Rosa *anything*. She shoved waffles in her mouth.

"Do you have any skirts for school?"

"Bea bought me a denim one."

"No, not denim for school. We'll go shopping this morning for some suitable skirts and collared shirts. You let me know if there's anything else you need. Underwear? Tampons?"

She had never heard of tampons. She said, "I don't need anything else."

Rosa talked on and on and Wynter knew she was trying to put her at ease. After a while she started acting like she *was* at ease, forcing herself to nod and smile, just to make the talking stop.

They went out and bought clothes. Rosa had very specific ideas about what was suitable and Wynter offered no opinions because she had none. She walked out of the mall with bags full of clothes, real leather shoes, and a thick, pale brown coat that Rosa called *camel*.

"We'll stop by the salon and get your hair cut," Rosa said, pulling into a strip mall.

Wynter put her hand possessively on her head. "I don't want to."

"It will make things much easier at school, with the other girls."

Wynter had no idea what she meant by that.

The hairdresser pushed her back at an awkward angle at the basin and washed her hair. Wynter sat still for the cut, except to tilt her head as instructed, ignoring the woman's chit-chat until she gave up asking questions. It was like being at the doctor's office but she didn't have Caleb to debrief with afterward.

"There, you've got a pretty wave now we've taken some weight off and snipped those split ends," the hairdresser said.

Wynter glared at her reflection. What did a pretty wave matter when Rosa had already told her she'd have to tie it up for school?

Rosa drove past the school to show her where the bus stopped. Set back from the fence were several long, low buildings with fields in the distance. Kids in sports uniforms were playing soccer. There was no one else around.

When they got home, Wynter said, "I want to call Caleb again. You said I could."

"Of course. I'll make us sandwiches for lunch."

Wynter went to her room and closed the door. She pressed the button on her phone. Nothing happened. The screen was black. She stared at the thing, her stomach fluttering in dismay.

After a while she admitted defeat and went down to the kitchen.

"My phone's broken."

Rosa examined it. "It's flat, dear."

"I need new batteries."

"We can recharge it. I have a charger right over there." She showed Wynter how to plug the phone in next to the fruit bowl. It came back to life.

But now Wynter had to call Caleb with Rosa right there, listening in.

"Hey, hun, how's things?" Caleb said when he picked up. He sounded completely normal, not tired and upset like last night.

She pressed the phone hard against her ear, as if that would bring him closer. "Where are you?"

"At work. Dropped Indio off at the bus station at seven, so he's back in Portland by now. What've you been doing this morning?"

"I had a haircut. We bought a lunchbox and backpack, a drink bottle, notebooks and pens and sport shoes. So many things. New clothes for school, and a camel coat."

"A *camel* coat?"

"That's what Rosa called it. Maybe it's made from a camel?"

"Huh. Maybe. You're all set, then."

"What am I gonna do about math?"

"You'll be fine."

"I won't, Caleb. I can't do math."

He paused and she sensed him realizing the platitudes wouldn't work. "I'll talk to Jesse about it. He can tutor you long-distance."

"I don't understand how that would work."

"You could email him any problems, and then he'd call and talk you through them."

"Yes. I want to do that." She planned to have daily math problems. Talking to Jesse every day, even about math, would make her feel better.

"You can get together on the phone once or twice a week. We'll set up a regular schedule."

"Oh. Okay." Only time for a few problems, then. Her heart sank.

"D'you need anything? Jesse told me he forgot to give you a phone charger."

"I'm using Rosa's. What are tampons?"

Rosa gave her a sharp look.

"Um." Caleb hesitated again. "Hun, you can ask Rosa about that."

Wynter's heart sank just a little more. Jesse could only spend a bit of time with her, and Caleb wouldn't help her with a difficult word. She felt them slipping away.

No, that was silly. They were always right there at the other end of the phone line. Until 9PM, anyway.

"Hun, I gotta go. I've got a meeting. How about you send a text next time, if you need to talk during the day, and I'll text back with the best time to call. Okay?"

Her throat closed up. "Okay," she whispered.

She rang off and tapped Jesse's name on the contact list before Rosa had the chance to say anything. After two rings it went to voicemail. She ended that call and tapped Indio's name. It went to voicemail, too.

She put the phone down, staring at it like it had betrayed her. "Why did I get voicemail? Why don't they answer?"

"Aren't they in college, the younger two? They're probably sitting in class. They have to turn their phones off. You won't be allowed to call them while you're in class, either."

So that was hours and hours every day when she wouldn't be able to talk to them. And she had to make an appointment to talk to Caleb.

Rosa said, "Now, you asked about tampons. Those are for your period."

"I don't have periods."

"Well, I'll keep a supply of pads and tampons in the bathroom for you, for when you need them. Do you know what periods are?"

"I think so. The older girls made pads from cotton and washed them in the laundry sink." Wynter wrinkled her nose, remembering the sight and the smell, and the confusion because she wasn't really sure what it was all about.

"I'll find you a book about it," Rosa said.

Claiming tiredness, Wynter went upstairs and lay on the bed. She drifted to sleep and woke in a sweat, her heart pounding. Gasping for air.

It was getting dark. She stumbled off the bed, washed her face and went downstairs. She found Rosa in the front room, reading a book.

"There you are. Did you nap? Let's pack your school bag for tomorrow, shall we?"

Afterward, they ate dinner — a tender piece of beef with all kinds of vegetables in the gravy.

"Can you teach me to cook?" Wynter said.

"Of course. That's a very useful skill to have. Who did the cooking at your last home?"

"My brothers don't cook. We had a barbecue, if that counts. We ate takeout." It seemed so long ago. When was the barbecue? Saturday, before they drove to Portland. Three days ago.

"I meant, who cooked at home in Arizona?"

Wynter had never heard it described that way: *home in Arizona.* It didn't sound right.

"Everyone helped in the kitchen. Just rice and bits, we called it. And oatmeal. Sometimes bananas and nuts and chicken or rabbit."

"I see. Well, we'll have fun with our cooking. You seem concerned about school, about math in particular. Do you feel you might be a bit behind?"

"Jesse showed me his old math books. I didn't understand any of it."

"Your teacher will help you. I'll give you my old laptop for your homework. Did you enjoy school in Arizona?"

Wynter shivered and bit her lip. "One of the teachers had a shelf of really old novels. I liked those. The rest was mostly copying out things and reading grammar books."

"Ah, grammar!" Rosa said, like it was a revelation. "You'll be good at English, then. I can tell you're a bright girl. You'll pick it all up quickly. Tell me about your teachers."

"The women took turns minding us in the classroom. We called them teachers. I don't think they taught us much. I've learned more in three days from the worldview book Jesse gave me."

She was saying too much. Joy told her not to talk about the Light, and here she was criticizing the teachers. Her ears were ringing.

"A worldview book? Goodness, what's that?"

"*A Brief History of Time.*"

"Ah, I know that one."

"You've read it?"

"No, dear. Let's have some ice cream."

Rosa asked her more questions over dessert. Wynter was more careful now. She avoided saying anything negative. She said "I don't remember" a lot, and sometimes nothing at all. The awkward interrogation went on a long time, until finally Rosa changed the subject.

"Shall we go over the rules?"

She wasn't surprised to hear that Rosa had rules. Caleb had thousands of rules according to Indio, who had broken quite a few of them and as a result he and Caleb had a strained relationship. Wynter needed to obey Rosa's rules so Caleb wouldn't get the idea she was too much trouble. Rosa's rules revolved around respectful behavior, lights out, curfews, and completing her work before watching TV, all of which she figured Caleb would approve of. Some of the rules she had no idea what Caleb would think – no inappropriate social media, no leaving the house without permission, no loud music.

"No loud music *ever*?"

"No. I work from home three days a week and it's very distracting."

Wynter was pretty sure Caleb was okay with loud music. In any case, she had earbuds for her phone.

Rosa produced what she called a *Behavior Contract* and asked Wynter to sign it.

"I've fostered teens before, and we've found this very useful. Read through it, so you understand what's expected and the consequences if you break the rules."

Wynter's heart thumped in her throat at that word – *consequences*. The contract on the table glared at her, stark white with tiny typed text. The first page was the rules they'd just discussed. She was unable to move her hand to turn the page to discover the consequences. She could hardly believe a grown-up would actually list all the punishments she intended to inflict instead of making them up on the spot.

To delay the awful moment, she got up in a daze and helped Rosa clear the dishes. Seeing her phone on the counter, she grabbed it.

"Is it charged yet?"

"Yes, it only takes a couple of hours."

Wynter switched it on. There were eight text messages — two from Caleb, one from Indio, five from Jesse, sent at various times during the afternoon when she was out. The words blurred before her eyes in a jumble.

> Sorry I missed your call
>
> Call me this evening
>
> How's everything?
>
> Have you seen your new school?
>
> Do you like the shrink?
>
> Let me know how you're doing...

Her ears were ringing as if her brothers were screaming at her. She read through it all again.

"It's past nine, dear. You can call them tomorrow morning."

"But they're waiting for me to call."

"I'll allow you to reply by text. Tell them you'll call tomorrow."

Jesse had shown her how to do that. She hit reply on Caleb's message and started typing. The keyboard was tiny and she kept hitting the wrong letters.

"Here, I'll help." Rosa took the phone from her and spent a few seconds tapping the screen with her thumbs. "There you go. I've written, *Thank you so much for your kind messages. I will call tomorrow immediately after school. Goodnight.* And... sent. I added all three recipients."

Wynter was horrified. "But that message wasn't from me. They'll think I wrote it and I didn't."

"It's perfectly fine. Off to bed for a good night's sleep. I'll put you on the bus for school before I head to my office tomorrow morning. Take that contract with you."

Wynter took the contract and stumbled upstairs. It felt very wrong that her brothers would get a message from her that she hadn't written. *Thank you so much for your kind messages.* She would never have written that.

She pushed the contract under her mattress where she wouldn't accidentally see what it said, and reached for Jesse's book. She noticed the sketchbook was missing.

She ran downstairs.

"Where's that sketchbook? The book with the gray cover?"

Rosa looked up from wiping the counter. "Goodness, I forgot to tell you — we've had such a busy day. I happened to look through it this afternoon and I'm afraid I can't let you have it."

"But that's Indio's book."

"Did you look inside?"

"I never had a chance."

Rosa breathed a little sigh. "I'm sorry, Wynter. The drawings are not suitable. You would find them quite disturbing."

"What does that mean? Those are Indio's drawings and he gave the book to me, to write in."

"Let's not argue about it. Sometimes you will just have to trust my judgment. Bedtime, please."

Wynter returned to her room, unsure what to think. Those sketches were created by Indio's hand, through his eyes, from his mind. How could Rosa decide which parts of Indio's mind Wynter should see? Would she stop Wynter listening to his songs — the music and words from his heart? Caleb hadn't cared. He'd taken her to Indio's gig and played their CD for her.

And now her brothers had been sent a message that wasn't from her mind or her heart or her hands. She didn't know how to figure out if maybe Rosa was right.

She lay in bed, composing in her head the messages she wanted to send. They all turned into the same thing in the end.

Save me, I'm drowning.

The Smallest Effort

Caleb sat in Harry's tiny two-bedroom house in Everett, on the
same kitchen stool he'd sat on two dozen times, next to the same
filth-encrusted sink, the same cracked window pane, the same crate
of empty beer bottles that may or may not make it into the recycling cart on the scheduled collection day. In the corner of the
living room was the old piano from Caleb's childhood, which
Harry had moved to Seattle at great expense while leaving most of
their other furniture behind. Harry was a brilliant player but that
instrument clearly wasn't getting any love — the closed fallboard
was stacked with newspapers, mail, and crushed beer cans.
Crumpled laundry hid the bench entirely.

"I could paint that siding for you, when we get a dry weekend,"
Caleb said, scratching Lexie behind the ears when she trotted over
to greet him. Harry had acquired the border collie a year ago.

"Don't need your help with that, son. I can manage."

In the two years he'd lived here, Harry never had gotten around
to *managing* much of anything. The clapboard house was falling
apart, the window frames had rotted through, and the entire place
was in desperate need of patching and painting.

"At the very least, you need to put a water-repellent coat on it."

Harry waved away the suggestion and reached for his smokes.
"How's the Silverado?"

He always asked that. He loved that truck. Caleb had guilted him
into handing over the title when he moved out. When Caleb threw
him out.

"The truck's running great. Can we talk about Joy?"

"Sure thing. You say that was her calling me last week? How was
I supposed to know? Out of the blue like that. Have you seen her?"

"She showed up yesterday morning. Wouldn't hang around."

"Well, how is she?"

Caleb rubbed his temples, struggling to find a way to talk about what needed to be said. "Uh, I'm not sure. She won't tell me exactly why she left. Miriam moved overseas years ago."

"Miriam's gone, huh," Harry mused. "She's still in that cult though, I'll bet."

"She's working for them in Thailand. Did you know she remarried and had a daughter after she moved to Arizona?"

Harry shrugged, uninterested, as he lit a cigarette. "No idea what she got up to. Never heard from her again, you know that. Loved having babies, that woman. Made her feel fruitful and connected to Mother Earth, she used to say. The pregnancy part of it, I mean. Can't say she was very interested in the babies themselves. Still, I'm surprised she stopped at only one more. Me, I thought two, *total*, was a good number. An environmentally responsible number." He stumbled over the long words, from which Caleb inferred he wasn't entirely sober. "But the twins put an end to that. And Jesse, well, he wasn't my idea. You need to watch out for him. Needs a firm hand, that one."

Nothing could be further from the truth when it came to Jesse, but Caleb wasn't going to argue the point. And a firm hand hadn't exactly worked wonders on Indio.

"He's calmed down a bit now," Harry went on, like he was any kind of authority on his sons, "but he only drops by when he needs something signed. As I recall, the momentous occasion of his conception was a little gift from my dear wife when I got a promotion to senior grounds manager at the school. That kid's always had a few screws loose, eh? Not my idea."

Harry waved his hand dismissively, which the dog took as an invitation to get some attention. Harry stroked her head with a smile that conveyed more affection than he'd ever offered his boys. Caleb propped his elbow on the counter and pressed his fist against his jaw to force himself into silence.

At moments like this, he wondered why he bothered with his father at all.

He pushed the conversation back on track. "Joy left the ashram with Miriam's younger daughter. Her name's Wynter. She was staying with me up until yesterday."

"Where is she now, then?"

"Foster care."

"Hah!" Harry cried with satisfaction. "Karma's a bitch, eh? That's gotta burn."

"What d'you mean?"

"Your mother was always terrified of social workers. They tried to take you away. Did you know that? She used to leave you alone for hours when you were a baby, out singing in bars half the night. They were that close to putting *you* in foster care. Your Grandma and Grandpa found out just in time, took Miriam in, treated her like their own daughter until I got back from Germany. And now her kid's with the authorities. Priceless."

He awaited Caleb's reaction. Caleb wasn't going to take the bait.

"I was hoping you had some way to contact her," Caleb said, "or information on her second husband. Anything at all."

"Told you, I know nothing about it. How about you concentrate on the sister you know instead of Miriam's brat? I want to meet Joy. Can you arrange that? Never did get to see much of her, but I remember everything. Beautiful child, was my Joy, with those big blue eyes and delicate hands. Voice of an angel. And stuck like glue to Indio. Remember the way she followed him around? His little shadow. He was always more interested in playing with you, but they had their moments. I never forgave Miriam for..." Harry stared at the cigarette burning between his fingers. "Well, you know all that."

Caleb did know that. He pitied Harry for his loss, but it was sixteen years ago. Caleb had stepped up while Harry had fallen over almost every day – and was chronically unable to admit or accept that fact.

"I intend to help both of them," Caleb said. "Wynter's in foster care in the Tri-Cities area. She should be with Joy. I'm gonna try and make that happen."

"You'll bring Joy to see me, won't you? Next time you visit. I'm only doing four nightshifts at the marina."

"I'll talk to her about it."

"Why wouldn't she want to meet her dad again?"

Caleb glanced around Harry's decrepit shack. "Maybe you can visit with her at my house."

"*Your* house, is it?" Harry barked a laugh, then let it drop. "Whatever works, son. I'm free most afternoons before work. I got AA meetings on Wednesday morning, Sunday morning, and Monday evening."

"How's that working out for you?" Caleb couldn't resist the jab. Harry hadn't been sober for more than a few days at a time through Caleb's entire life, and he wasn't sober today. Whatever he was getting out of AA, it wasn't sobriety.

"It's only been a few months. Met some nice people and some real dicks and some boring fucks. I gotta say, it's hard listening to a bunch of strangers talking about how much they crave a drink when you're trying to cut back." He chuckled to himself. "I'll give it a few more tries, I guess. There's a very nice lady at the Sunday meeting who's been a big help."

So *that's* what he was getting out of AA.

"Listen, Harry, I need a few things from you. I need Joy's birth certificate and social security number so she can get herself a photo ID. Do you have them?"

"I suppose so. All the paperwork's back there somewhere."

Caleb stood up, which made Harry jump up to stop him.

"Now, wait a minute. If she wants her stuff, she can come get it herself. Give me a chance to catch up with her."

Caleb strode past his father, ignoring his vague protests, and proceeded to the back room. It was piled high with boxes and other junk that he'd made Harry take with him when he moved out. Some of these boxes hadn't been opened since they left Anaconda. Some were even older — things Miriam had left behind in Missoula, which her landlord had put into storage until he'd tracked down Harry to collect them.

Caleb whipped out a pocket knife to open the older boxes while Harry stood in the doorway with his cigarette, nursing his wounded pride at being bested by his eldest son. Not for the first time.

"Don't go expecting any of it to be stored in a neat logical manner," Harry said. "Your mother was a scatterbrain. I lost count of how many times she forgot to pay the utilities bill or locked herself out of the house. This one time — I've probably mentioned it before — she went off to the store with the twins in the double stroller and you riding up on the bar, and she came back without you. I said, *Where's your firstborn, ya mad woman?* She wouldn't admit she forgot you, of course. Wouldn't call the cops. *Oh, he'll find his way home,* she said. They call it free-range parenting these days, eh?"

Caleb had heard the story a dozen times. As always, he remained silent in anticipation of the rest, where Harry had rushed to the rescue and found him sitting in the corner of the store breaking up candy bars to stuff them into his tiny pockets. Today, Harry skipped over the end. He leaned against the door jam, tapping ash into a mug, scowling as if to say, *I dare you to find what you're looking for.*

In the fourth box, Caleb did find what he was looking for — a folder with Joy's name on it, and her birth certificate and social security card inside. Underneath the folder were two thick photo albums from his childhood.

"Hey, I'll take these. Wynter and Joy will want to take a look." That might not be true, but *he* wanted to see and Jesse would certainly be interested.

Harry came into the room to take one and opened it at the last page. "Your first day of high school. Look at you, in your buttoned shirt. You look like a tax accountant. Miriam would've thrown a fit. Indio with the guitar I bought him. That's set him on the road to fame and fortune — mark my words." He turned back a few pages. "Ah, that damn golden retriever you boys adopted. Nothing but trouble, that mutt. Never retrieved a thing. Thank god it ran off."

Caleb glared at his father just long enough to signal he didn't appreciate the comment. He didn't say anything. What was the point, after all these years? Maybe Harry's pickled brain had forgotten what actually happened to the dog. Maybe he thought he was telling the truth. The way he'd said it, though, with that little chuckle of his, it forced you to weigh your next move carefully — challenge the lie and risk a blowout, or shut up and take it.

"Where's Indio's file?" Caleb said. "I need copies of everything so we can get his juvenile record sealed."

"Thought he did that ages ago?"

"Well, he was supposed to." Caleb found the file in a newer box. Too late for Wynter's social worker but it still had to be done.

"It's outrageous, that's what it is, that he has to jump through hoops. He was just a kid. They should've automatically sealed those records when he turned eighteen."

"You take that up with the state of Washington," Caleb muttered, gathering everything together and preparing to leave. "I'll let you know about Joy."

"Don't suppose you got a twenty on you, do you? I need to buy heartworm tablets for Lexie here."

Caleb had a self-imposed rule to never give Harry cash. As he headed for the door, he said, "Give me the name of the medicine. I'll buy it for you."

"That's nice of you. I don't know the name. Anything'll do, I guess. There's a vet clinic a few blocks south of here. Still need the twenty, though. I'm out of dog food and she's chewed through her leash."

"I don't have cash on me, sorry."

"Don't worry about it. No problem at all. I can make it to payday."

"I'll leave the medicine in your mailbox. You want me to take out that recycling?"

Caleb left with the same heaviness in his chest he always felt after a visit with his father. He wanted to help but he wasn't a pushover. He wasn't going to give Harry cash. He wasn't going to take out the recycling or paint the siding without asking first, because it wasn't his job to force help upon Harry. And he wasn't going to allow Harry to influence or impose on his life, or the lives of his siblings, until he got his act together.

He might still get his act together. The odds were miniscule but Caleb had spent four years on a cutter and seen people defy the odds a hundred times. Meanwhile, he visited as often as he could and encouraged Jesse to do the same. He offered help, accepted the rebuttals, and waited patiently for his father to make the smallest effort.

Besides, he had more important considerations now. While Harry plodded on, never changing, Caleb's life had been upended. Last Friday he'd put in for a week's emergency leave, intending to use the time to get Wynter settled and enrolled in school. This morning he'd canceled it. Wynter was gone and Joy had so far refused his help. Tomorrow his life would go back to normal.

Except that nothing was the same.

Strong Enough

At the front office at school, a woman behind a glass wall with a name tag, *Myra*, gave Wynter some forms. They were pre-filled with her details, with asterisks all over them where she had to add missing information. She gave up after five minutes and Myra took the forms back with an impatient frown.

"Rosa will deal with this," Wynter said. "The woman who... my foster..." She couldn't say it. Couldn't say the word *mother*.

"That's fine. Come with me. I'll take you to your class. Your homeroom teacher is Mrs Ling."

As they walked, Myra talked about timetables and hall passes and rules and lunch orders. They arrived at a locker and Wynter put her bag and coat inside.

"What a lovely coat," Myra said. "The other girls will be jealous. Is that wool?"

"It's camel."

"Camel is a color, pet. I think that's wool."

They walked to a classroom door, and Myra knocked and opened it.

"In you come," Myra said.

The teacher had stopped talking to the class, waiting for Wynter to enter. She felt hot all over. Her feet wouldn't move.

Myra made some apologetic comment and shut the door. She took Wynter's arm and directed her away from the door.

"Whatever is the matter? Are you ill?"

Wynter nodded, her head in a fog.

Myra took her to the nurse's office. Wynter lay on a narrow bed and the nurse put a cold washcloth on her forehead and asked questions. The room spun.

"I need to call someone," Wynter said.

"We don't allow phone use during school hours," the nurse said. "Have you been given a rule sheet about electronic devices?"

"I have to call my brother."

"Well, all right. You can use the phone in my office."

"I don't know his number. I have to tap on his name on the screen."

The nurse thought about it and finally said, "As it's your first day, I'll let you fetch your phone. You come right back here to make the call, okay? Here's a hall pass."

Why did she need a pass to walk down a corridor? Wynter went to her locker and grabbed her phone, slipped outside the building and hunkered down against a wall. She called Caleb and almost screamed when he answered.

"Hey, Wynter." He didn't sound annoyed that she'd broken all kinds of rules. No phones during class time, no text message first to arrange a time, and hadn't that message from Rosa said she'd call him *after* school, not during?

"Caleb." She couldn't say more. Just his name.

"Hun, what's up? Aren't you supposed to be at school?"

She took a few deep breaths. "I am at school... Can't go in."

"Why not?"

"I mean, I went in. They gave me forms and a locker. I couldn't go in the classroom."

There was a long pause.

"Caleb? Are you there?"

"Why can't you go in?" he said at last.

"My feet wouldn't move. I don't like... I don't like the classroom."

"What's wrong with it?"

"I don't know. I didn't see inside."

"Then how do you know... You mean, you don't like *classrooms*?"

"Yes."

"This classroom is different. I promise. You'll like it. You'll learn lots. You'll make friends."

Caleb was so far away and his voice sounded odd, tight somehow. She hated that she was stressing him out with her fears. Her pounding heart made it hard to draw breath.

"Wynter, tell me why you don't like classrooms."

"Teachers. I don't like teachers. They were angry all the time. They didn't want to be there, and we didn't want to be there."

"What's your teacher's name at the new school?"

"Mrs Ling."

"Okay. Mrs Ling is different. She wants to be there and she's not angry. She won't hurt you."

Wynter snatched the phone away from her ear and stared at it. Why would he say that? She'd never said the teachers hurt her. How did he know? What else did he know?

"...and you'll do fine, you'll settle in soon," he was saying as she put the phone back to her ear.

"Why are you saying that? Why do you keep saying everything's okay when it's not?"

"I'm so sorry, hun. I know you don't want to be there in Richland, but that's where you have to be. You need to find a way to make it work, to make the best of it. And so do I. Now listen, you're coming to lunch with Jesse and Joy and me on Saturday. We're meeting halfway at a restaurant. Tina just confirmed it this morning. Rosa will drive you down."

His voice calmed her down a bit.

"How long for?"

"A couple hours, I guess."

"Will Tina be there?"

"Yes. We're waiting on the background checks, so until then she has to be there."

"Are they... will they find something bad in the background checks?"

"Of course not."

"What about Indio?"

"Well, she knows about his juvenile record but hopefully it won't count. He was seventeen."

"Oh." Relief swept through her. "But he's not coming on Saturday?"

"No. He won't always be able to make it. He has band and study commitments. You need to hang up and go back to the classroom, okay?"

She'd do what he said. Caleb had never mentioned *consequences* for disobedience but if she didn't behave at school Rosa would find out. Rosa had an entire list of consequences that Wynter hadn't dared look at yet.

"Call me after six and let me know how it went," Caleb said before hanging up.

Wynter walked slowly to her locker. Her phone pinged – a message from Caleb.

You're strong enough.

She found her way to the classroom. If she pushed down those dark pieces from that other classroom, the pieces she'd washed away, she could trust Caleb to know about schools and teachers and classrooms on the outside. She knocked and waited for Mrs Ling to open the door. Her feet moved her into the room.

"Here's our new student," Mrs Ling said. "This is Wynter."

"Like the season?" said a girl in the front row.

"Yes, with a Y — isn't that right? Wynter just moved here from Arizona. Why don't you take a seat there, next to Stacey."

Wynter sat next to Stacey, a plump, freckled girl with pretty brown eyes, and returned her smile mechanically. She would make it through. She would learn new things and make new memories to flood out all the dark pieces that threatened to surface. Mrs Ling kept talking. Wynter concentrated on breathing slowly until her ears stopped ringing.

When the bell went, Mrs Ling asked Wynter to stay behind, and Stacey said she'd wait outside for her. Caleb had said the teacher wouldn't hurt her. She held onto that. Still, she was nervous to be all alone in the room with a teacher.

After the children emptied out, Mrs Ling came over with a few sheets of paper.

"Here you go. This is your timetable. You're down for French and technology systems for your options. Does that sound right?"

Wynter didn't know a word of French and she didn't know what technology systems meant, so she just nodded.

"And here's the homework your teachers assigned for this week. Take a look through it and do whatever you can manage. We'll talk next week about catching up, once you've settled in. Your next class is math in room 409. That's building number four. Stacey will take you there."

Stacey and Wynter walked to room 409.

"Mr Yannis is the math teacher," Stacey said. "He's not too bad. So, you're from Arizona? That's funny, that you're called Wynter, because Arizona is a desert — like, summer all the time, isn't it?"

"It gets cold at night."

"I like your bracelet. You should cover that with your sleeve or they'll make you take it off."

Wynter pulled her left sleeve down over the braided cuff.

"Did you place a lunch order? You have to hand it in before ten or you might not get what you want."

"I have lunch in my locker."

Stacey twittered away until they reached room 409. The teacher had already started and they slipped into an empty desk. Wynter knew she was behind in math and braced herself. After Mr Yannis finished an incomprehensible fifteen-minute talk at the board, he told the class to work on some problems and came over to Wynter.

"Where were you at with math at your last school?"

"I'm not sure."

"Give these problems a try and we'll see."

Wynter stared at equations for the rest of the lesson, clueless, and escaped when the bell rang before Mr Yannis had a chance to talk to her. Stacey caught up with her and they sat together for English and social studies, which for the most part made sense, and then it was lunch time. They went outside to a paved area with benches where half a dozen girls gathered around, interested in the newcomer, and bombarded Wynter with questions.

Where are you from?

What was your last school like?

Do you prefer Katy Perry or Lady Gaga?

The questions came so thick and fast, Wynter could pick and choose which to answer.

What do your parents do?

Do you have brothers and sisters?

"Three older brothers and a sister."

Which school do they go to?

Are your brothers hot?

Wynter thought her brothers were very handsome, so she answered, "Yes."

The girls laughed, their eyes wide, and some clapped their hands over their mouths as if that was the most outrageous thing they'd ever heard.

Do your brothers live in Seattle?

Are they single?

What's it like living in the desert?

As the questions continued, she realized she could make up whatever she liked about her life and they'd never know. It was the perfect way to not talk about the Light, which she wasn't supposed to do, and it might help her make friends. She'd have to be careful, though, and not contradict herself and make mistakes. For now, she fended off as many questions as she could and answered the rest carefully.

Next, she had French in room 114. Stacey had something else so she found her own way there. Wynter arrived a minute late and listened outside the door as the teacher talked in French. Pointless to go inside if she didn't understand what was being said, so she walked away.

The corridors were empty. Wynter heard distant music and followed the sound. Someone was playing violin, very badly, in a room around the corner. She peered through the window in the door. A woman was instructing a boy, making him repeat scales over and over. Not only was he out of tune, he couldn't get his melodic minor sequence right no matter how the teacher tried to explain the different ascending and descending notes. Wynter couldn't bear to listen.

She wandered around until another teacher found her, a younger woman with round cheeks who scolded her for not having a hall pass.

"It's my first day," Wynter said.

"Where are you supposed to be? I'll take you."

"French. But I don't speak any French."

"Why did you choose French, then?"

"I didn't." She supposed Rosa or a random person in the office must have signed her up for French.

The teacher smiled, suddenly sympathetic. "Let's take you to the office and you can change your options. I'm Ms Driscoll."

At the front office, Ms Driscoll explained the problem to Myra, who handed over a printed list.

Woodwork. Spanish. Domestic Science. Music...

"Music." Wynter hoped it wouldn't mean practicing violin scales.

"Excellent choice," said Ms Driscoll. "I'm one of the music teachers, although you won't be in my class. But if you'd like to join the band, just ask me."

"A rock band?"

Ms Driscoll laughed, a light ringing sound. "No, we have a marching band. Do you play an instrument?"

"Guitar and a bit of piano."

"Well, we don't need those for the marching band. You could pick up something else. We're always short of trombone players. For now, let's put you down for music in place of French. I'll take you to Ms Gerald's class."

Wynter sat in Ms Gerald's class and started to feel better about her day.

That evening, Rosa asked her for the signed behavior contract, so Wynter had to fetch it. Before going back downstairs, she glanced at the second page only to discover Rosa was somewhat lacking in imagination when it came to *consequences*. Grounding, removing phone and TV privileges, paying for careless breakages... Had Caleb imposed similar consequences on his brothers when they were younger? Did Jesse still get grounded? Did Jesse still misbehave?

If the worst that could happen to her was losing TV privileges, perhaps living with Rosa wouldn't be so bad. If she could make the girls at school like her, perhaps school wouldn't be so bad. It wasn't for long. Just until Joy found her feet.

✿

Wynter had it all figured out. At school she couldn't talk about the Light because Joy had told her it would prevent her fitting in with the outside world. In any case, she didn't want to relive any of that or get teased about it. Rosa and Caleb thought it was important she make friends. And Jesse, who had vast numbers of friends, thought it was important, too. She quickly developed a way to achieve this, and some of it was even true. She constructed a detailed past based on what she knew of her siblings' childhoods, and added a few details from Xay's idyllic life in Australia as well.

"We lived on a horse ranch in Montana," she told the kids at school, growing more confident with the embellishments once she established that none of them knew much about Montana and couldn't contradict her. "After our parents died on a sunken cruise ship, we lived in an orphanage until Caleb was eighteen. Then he bought a huge old farmhouse with our inheritance for us all to live in." She knew the appeal of being an orphan when it came to storytelling, having read *Jane Eyre* and *Oliver Twist* years ago.

"Do they even have orphanages anymore?" someone asked.

"In Montana they do."

"I thought you were from Arizona," Stacey said.

"We *were* in Arizona for a few weeks before we moved here. We were visiting our grandmother but she died of consumption."

Thus, with the death of her fictional grandmother, she wiped Arizona from her backstory.

"Why don't you live with your brothers and sister now?"

"I do, during vacation time. Last summer we went to California and surfed all day, every day. During the semester I live with my Aunt Rosa so I can go to this school. My brother has a house in Seattle. He's a petty officer first class." She didn't know what that was, but it was absolutely true. The rest, not so much. "He has a wife and a little girl called Jilly. My sister Joy runs a diner on Cougar Mountain. And my other brothers are in a rock band."

"No way! What band?"

"They're just starting out so you won't have heard of them. They're gonna be famous."

She made it through the week and felt she was making good progress. She told her newfound friends she was going to Seattle for the weekend. In fact she was only going as far as the restaurant in Yakima to meet up with Caleb and Joy and Jesse, and Tina had to supervise because they were waiting on their background checks.

What would her family think of her lies? The Light did not generally approve of lying, so Joy would be unhappy about it — although judgment wasn't allowed in the Light, either. In any case, Wynter wasn't in the Light anymore. Jesse would think she was very clever. Caleb? He would be disappointed in her. That was an uncomfortable thought. But there was no reason he'd find out.

✿❀

Mr Yannis quickly discovered Wynter didn't know math and made her sit a seventh-grade test.

"I got forty-five percent," she told Jesse over the phone on Friday evening, in a panic because it seemed all the more awful to have a number on it.

"We'll go through the test when I see you tomorrow, and look at where you went wrong. I can't believe they put you in middle school. You won't graduate high school until you're nineteen!"

"Does that matter?"

"We're gonna do summer school, okay?" he went on, without answering her question.

"We?"

"I'll tutor you in every subject. You'll test out of ninth grade and you can start tenth in September, with kids your own age."

"What if my brain just can't do math?"

"I'm gonna teach your brain to do math."

It was hard to hear him over the background noise at his end. She imagined sitting in the dining room in the little house in Columbia City with Jesse, talking across the table with their books spread out all over it, working on math together every single evening. Or perhaps she'd be doing English homework while he wrote a paper for college. She ached with sadness that she was stuck here in Rosa's house.

"What about the rest? I don't understand what anyone's talking about in the other classes."

"You'll be okay. Math is an easy fix. I'll teach you some strategies to make it through. The rest — the geopolitical and social stuff, that's been filtered through the Light and it's all skewed. You can unlearn it and start to deal in facts."

His determination made her believe.

"And I know you love science, right?" he continued. "The way the physical world works? That's how my brain is wired, too. With my help, you're gonna ace science. Tell me about your music class."

"They're doing theory this semester. It's very easy. One of the teachers wants me to take up trombone and play in the band."

"Have you heard the band play?"

"Yes, they had a lunchtime practice parade today. It was awful. I don't wanna play with them."

"You don't have to."

"I want to play with you."

"When you visit Seattle, we'll do that."

Rosa's footsteps were coming up the stairs.

"When? When am I visiting you?"

"Caleb and Tina are working out a schedule. Does Rosa mind you playing that guitar?"

"I haven't played it yet." She hadn't felt like it. The guitar sat in its case in the corner of her room.

"Play it, Wynter, and write me a little sister song." She heard the smile in his voice on the other end of the line. "Gotta go. Just got to the front of the line at the ticket booth. See you tomorrow."

Rosa knocked on her open door and came in looking very pleased with herself. "Look what I have for you. We've reached the end of the week and you've had such a good start. Here's a little reward."

Wynter had spent the last two days lying to her schoolmates and failing at math. She wasn't inclined to contradict Rosa because in Rosa's hand was Indio's sketchbook. She wanted that book back. Rosa handed it over and Wynter opened it to the first page, which was blank except for writing in the top corner:

Indio Fairn, September 2005

The page was loose, and fell out when she turned it. All the pages were loose.

"What happened?"

"I removed the unsuitable material. You may keep the rest. He's very talented."

"You've ripped up Indio's book." Wynter was horrified, yet her voice came out flat and pained. She didn't dare express her outrage in case Rosa was right and she was wrong about this. And deep down she feared the universe was punishing her for those lies at school. The universe's consequences were real and painful, even if Rosa's weren't.

"There are some lovely illustrations in here." Rosa sat, uninvited, beside her on the bed. "I particularly like this one."

She turned a couple of pages to a heavily shaded pencil drawing of a street by night. Two rows of suburban rooftops stretched into the distance, and the foreground was crowded with intricate details — a trellis on the wall, a garbage can with a crooked lid, a single lit window with a shadowy figure.

"I did a bit of sketching in my younger days," Rosa said. "This is called perspective drawing, which means representing three-dimensional objects in two-dimensions. It's like a technical exercise." She traced her finger along the line of rooftops. "And see how he shaded these areas, and then erased the edges where the moonlight hits? It's quite beautiful. Yes, I think he's very talented. I wonder how old he was when he drew these."

"Fifteen." Wynter showed her the date. "Only two months older than I am now. So why can't I see the other things he drew?"

"We've talked about that. Let's not repeat ourselves. Come down to dinner and you can tell me all about the new friends you've made."

Wynter hadn't made any new friends, unless she counted Stacey who sat by her sometimes. At what point did someone become a friend, anyway? Was Rosa her friend? Rosa took something belonging to her, with no intention of giving it back. That didn't seem like friendly behavior. Wynter could impose a few consequences of her own. Rosa seemed desperate to connect but Wynter didn't want or need her friendship or advice or rules or anything else. Wynter would cut her out.

She looked at Indio's drawing again, drinking in every line and smudge. Was this a street he'd seen with his own eyes? The elevated angle would put him on a rooftop. That didn't seem right. He must've imagined it, like the unfinished dragon roaming across the previous page with its hundreds of scales and glistening teeth. The street looked honest and real but it was a lie, an invented world like the one she'd created for her own past to tell the kids at school.

On one rooftop was a sleek cat, belly pressed to the tiles, face raised to the sky. Wynter smiled because there was so much personality in that simple figure, in its pricked ears, the arch of its back and the kink of its tail. Its eyes glinted in the moonlight.

She turned the page to look at the next sketch.

Setting the Pace

Bea nudged Caleb as they left the ticket booth, nodding toward the line at the concessions stand. Caleb followed her gaze. Jesse was there on a date of his own — a lanky, dark-haired girl with her hand in the back pocket of his jeans. She was whispering in his ear, distracting him so successfully that the guy behind them had to tap Jesse's shoulder to make him move along.

Caleb decided not to acknowledge his brother, just in case they were going to the same movie and Jesse and his date ended up hanging around for the rest of the evening. Jesse might just do that, to be annoying.

"Who's the girl, then?" Bea said. "I thought he was dating that dark-skinned girl... Neysa, was it?"

"Neysa was ages ago. This one starts with N, too... Nina, Nicky... I forget. Hasn't brought her home yet."

Bea wrapped herself around Caleb's arm and lowered her voice. "Can I come home with you tonight? I have a birthday present for you to unwrap. I'm wearing it. Something... silky and lacy."

"Sure."

Bea pouted. "Caleb, that's not the reaction I wanted."

Distracted by seeing Jesse and stowing his credit card and compulsively checking his phone to see if Joy had texted, Caleb had completely missed Bea's suggestive tone. He kissed her by way of an apology. Times like this, when she was able to get away for the night, were very important to her.

"Sorry, hun. I can't wait for my birthday present."

She gave him a taste of his present in the darkness of the theater, raising the seat arm so she could drape herself on him to make out, her hands sliding under his shirt then moving down to do as much damage as she could without actually getting him off. They were in the back row and the relative privacy made him respond more than he'd normally allow himself. He was turning twenty-five years old tomorrow. He'd grown up and learned to behave many years ago, and reverting to juvenile behavior wasn't his style. He let Bea do it because he was about to tell her she had to be out of the house early tomorrow morning. She'd no doubt planned a different way to spend his birthday.

They ate at a favorite Greek place of theirs. It had been easy to become a part of Bea's life — so much so that after only a few months they had favorite eating places. If his life hadn't been upturned over the past week, he'd have welcomed the increasing pace of their relationship. Instead, he had a new set of problems to deal with.

She was talking about Saturday. "Mom asked if you wanted a cake. I've told her you don't eat sweets but she insisted. She's making a banana cake. She thinks it's healthier, even though it has half a pound of brown sugar in it. We need to be there by noon. Can we get going? I'd like an hour or so alone with you before Jesse gets home."

Another suggestive look. Caleb snapped out of his thoughts. "Jesse's going to see a band. He'll be home late."

"So, do you want to go home now?" She smiled and put her hand over his on the table.

"What time did you say tomorrow?"

"At my parents' by noon. For your birthday lunch."

"Oh, hun, I can't do that. I have to leave for Yakima at 9:30."

"What?"

"We're meeting with Wynter and her foster mother."

Bea withdrew her hand. "How could you not tell me this earlier? I told you about the birthday lunch last week."

"I didn't know your plans were final. I'm sorry. I don't have any leeway with Wynter. I'm at the mercy of her caseworker."

"So, you'd have canceled the lunch even if you'd remembered it."

"I guess so." He bit his tongue on what he wanted to say, which was that he needed her support in this. "I assumed we'd do something tomorrow evening."

"My parents aren't available in the evening. They can't babysit. That's why I'm here tonight and that's why we're doing lunch tomorrow."

"How about Sunday?"

"I can't believe I can't spend your birthday with you."

"I've had a tough week, Bea. A really weird week. You're gonna have to roll with this one. I'll be back at five. I can come over then."

She gave a tight smile to show she wasn't rolling with it yet.

He brought her home. He unwrapped her clothing to discover the sexy lingerie underneath, and unwrapped that, and spent a long time trying to make it up to her.

Afterward, he lay awake in the dark hoping they were going to be okay. He heard the front door latch as Jesse came home, and then the sound of the TV. He listened for the girl's voice but it seemed Jesse was alone. Caleb and Jesse had a live-and-let-live understanding about overnight guests, and because of it Caleb had a pretty good idea of who Jesse was seeing and what stage the relationship was at. When Caleb was eighteen he'd been in high school, dating high school girls, and would never have risked bringing them home to meet Harry. Like most teenagers he'd had to get creative to find places to have sex. His little brother had turned eighteen the month he graduated high school. He was already in college, dating girls one and two years older than himself and making the most of living in a tolerant household.

But not tonight, apparently.

Caleb went out to see him. It was almost three in the morning.

"Did you see your mail there?" Caleb asked him.

"Yeah, my background check came through. Yours didn't?"

"No. I guess they're a little quicker for you juveniles."

Jesse scowled. "I'm not a juvenile."

"Close enough." Caleb raised an eyebrow to show he was joking. He'd been trying his best lately not to treat Jesse like a kid.

"Anyway, I've been deemed an upstanding member of society. Good to know."

"We're leaving at 9:30. Get to bed."

"Is Joy coming?"

Caleb fetched his phone from his jacket pocket. He'd forgotten to switch it back on after the movie. Joy had sent a message earlier in the evening. "She says she has a job interview."

"That's good, isn't it?"

"On a Saturday?" Caleb hated doubting her, but it did seem odd and very last-minute.

"Why is she so reluctant to get involved with us and with Wynter? Did they brainwash her?"

"I don't know, Jess. We need to give her some time."

"Time for what? To forget about us again?"

"I hope not. How was your evening?"

"Let's talk about yours. You seemed to be enjoying yourself." Jesse gave him a knowing grin. "Yeah, we were in the same theater, right across the aisle."

"I did enjoy the movie," Caleb said uncomfortably, "but Bea's upset I'm not spending tomorrow with her." He nodded toward his bedroom where Bea was sleeping.

"At least you managed to bring her home. Natalie won't sleep with me."

"Who's...? Oh, Natalie." He mentally filed away the correct name. "How many times have you been out with her?"

"Two, but we hang out all the time with friends and she decided she was my girlfriend before Christmas. I went along with it, expecting a 'Christmas present'. This is the first time I haven't slept with a girl first and *then* decided to date her and put the work in."

"Take it easy. Always best to let the girl set the pace."

"Yeah, you always say that. I never liked someone so much whose pace is so much slower than mine."

"If she's worth it, you'll have to exercise some patience. Get to bed. I'm not gonna let you drive if you're tired in the morning."

One and Only

Jesse was keen to take the wheel for the drive to the restaurant. It would make the social worker anxious — she had to put her life in his eighteen-year-old hands. And in his beat-up 1991 Chevy Caprice wagon, no less. He drove very safely, of course, because Caleb was right there, and talked about the local jazz band he was drumming for. From the back seat Tina queried whether he was old enough to be playing on licensed premises.

Great. One more thing they were doing wrong.

"The law allows underage musicians on stage in bars," he said confidently.

"I do believe you need to be eighteen."

"I *am*—"

"Didn't you say you've been playing with them for a year and a half?" She directed her disapproval at Caleb.

"On and off," Jesse muttered. "Mostly off." He changed the subject to the funky smell coming from the roof in the dining room that Caleb needed to check out.

At noon they arrived at Homestead Hills, a family-style restaurant with bland décor and an inoffensive menu. As they waited to be seated, Jesse saw Wynter get out of a red Audi cabriolet in the parking lot. The small, conservatively dressed woman who got out with her did not look like someone you'd expect would drive a red convertible.

Jesse ran out and gave Wynter a hug. She was so excited she almost dragged him to the ground. Rosa gave him the once-over and he deliberately did the same to her. When Caleb was around he always felt like the little brother. Now he was the big brother, all six feet of him, and he let Rosa know with a glare that he wasn't happy she was looking after his little sister instead of him and Caleb.

Rosa introduced herself and they went inside. Caleb put his hand on Wynter's shoulder and Jesse willed him to hug her, but Caleb wasn't the hugging type. Nor was Wynter, as far as he could tell. He was still in shock over her earlier greeting.

Caleb shook Rosa's hand. This was so wrong, this pinched-faced stranger taking care of their Wynter.

Wynter looked around. "Where's Joy?"

Caleb said, "She couldn't make it. Next time, okay?"

Wynter looked more confused than disappointed. Jesse had been confused all morning. Why did Joy get Wynter out of that place only to ignore her?

They sat at a round table. Rosa was unimpressed with the restaurant but took great care not to show it. Caleb made small talk with the women, displaying those perfect manners that took a man a long way in this world. Jesse had always used his charm in a different way — you could persuade people to do what you wanted by making them like you, which in his case meant making them laugh. Caleb didn't make people laugh — people did what he wanted, even if they didn't like him, because he was polite and firm and trustworthy and expected the best from everyone. As for Indio... Jesse wasn't sure how Indio got what he wanted, but the scruffy good looks and guitar had something to do with it.

Everyone ordered, with Wynter waiting until Jesse ordered and asking for exactly the same. He knew it was because she didn't know how to interpret the menu. Something else to add to the list of things he'd teach her. When she came home.

And she would come home. Jesse had no faith that Joy would come through — he knew nothing about Joy — but he had faith Caleb would *make* her come through.

Jesse found Rosa quite fascinating to watch. She was like a bird, tilting her head to listen, fluttering her hands as she talked. He scrutinized her, deliberately double-dipping his carrot sticks in the hummus because it seemed like exactly the sort of behavior that would piss her off. Caleb pointedly moved the bowl out of his reach.

"You wanna go through that math test?" Jesse asked Wynter as they waited for their desserts. "Show it to me."

She pulled it out of her backpack. It was painful to see the mistakes she'd made. The arithmetic part was perfect, but she had no concept of graphs or algebra, and the worded questions with real-world contexts confused her. She looked at him glumly as he read through it.

"What's this?" He pointed to some squiggles she'd made in the margins.

"I was just trying to figure them out."

He looked carefully at her diagrams and realized she'd made visual representations of the questions. "This is good. I can see what you were trying to do." His mind jumped ahead to how he could teach her using a more creative diagrammatic method.

The desserts arrived. Wynter stirred her ice cream until it was soupy. It was clear she had something else on her mind and she finally spoke up about it.

"I have some questions about this book I brought with me," she told Jesse. "Can we go outside and look at it?"

Jesse looked to Caleb for permission. Caleb nodded before any objections could be raised by the women. He'd passed his background check, after all. Not even a speeding ticket. What more could they want? He abandoned a plate of soggy pancakes drenched in hot fudge and followed Wynter outside to sit on a bench near the entrance.

He'd assumed she meant the Hawking book. What she took out of her backpack was a large, thin, hardback book titled *Your Body Is Amazing!*

"Rosa gave me this to read. It's got cartoons and jokes, so I don't know if it's accurate or just stupid stuff for little kids."

Jesse thumbed through it and quickly discovered it was, in fact, for much younger kids — colorful pages featuring cartoon characters having silly conversations. He laughed outright at the absurdity of an almost fifteen-year-old learning about sex and puberty from a cartoon bee.

"How much of this did you already know?" he said.

"I knew the names of the body parts. I did learn new things about puberty." She turned ahead a few pages, to a spread depicting egg-and-sperm diagrams and surreal illustrations of fetuses. "I liked this chapter. I did not know babies looked like that in the womb."

"Pretty freakish, huh? Like goofy aliens with those huge foreheads and tiny arms."

"I thought you liked science?"

"Uh, I didn't mean freakish. I meant... *interesting*."

"Look at the last chapter."

He flicked to the back of the book. The last chapter was called "Different Kinds of Families" and explained various configurations — mom and dad, single parent, two moms, two dads, grand-parents, foster families, adopted families.

"There's no siblings-only family," she said. "Is that why I can't live with you?"

"No, that's not why. And our family is still a family, Wyn, even if we don't all live together."

Out of curiosity, he turned to the page on conception. His own knowledge had been accumulated from many sources throughout childhood, followed by a sit-down with Caleb when he was about twelve. That had been more about respecting girls than the mechanics of it, which Indio had already explained in meticulous, mostly accurate, detail. He was curious how seven-year-olds were formally introduced to the idea.

"*Mommy and Daddy are cozy in bed,*" he read. "*They cuddle up so tightly that his...*" He stopped, aware of Wynter looking at him. "Uh, did you know this stuff already? The anatomical side of it, I mean."

"Yes, I know which bit goes where during... you know."

"During sex. It's okay, you can say the word. This book is silly, Wyn. Sex isn't much like that. It's okay to explain it this way to little kids, I guess. At your age... Your friends at school would be laughing at this, too."

He could see she didn't understand. She had that edge of panic in her eyes, once again discovering how far behind she was. Then he had another thought about what the panic might mean.

He turned to her on the bench. "Can I ask you something about the ashram?"

Wynter huffed out a breath as if to steel herself. But she didn't say no. She bowed her head.

"Wyn, please look at me. It's important." He waited for her to look up. "Did anyone do this stuff with you? Men or boys asking you, or forcing you, to do things that made you uncomfortable?"

She shook her head, surprised, like she thought he was going to ask something else.

"No? You sure about that?"

"The men and older boys lived on the other side of the compound. We didn't see them much at all. The kids were all in the homestead with the dorm and kitchen and classroom."

"Okay. I just needed to ask. Because the thing about this—" He tapped the page. "—is it's supposed to be between consenting adults. Otherwise it's wrong and illegal."

"How old do you have to be?"

"Well, teenagers do it, so I guess it's not just for adults. You have to be sixteen in the state of Washington."

"What about in Arizona?"

"I don't know. It's different in every state, for some stupid reason."

"So it could be fifteen or fourteen?"

"Pretty sure that's illegal."

She looked down again, sucking on the inside of her cheek.

"Wyn?"

"Okay, I'll remember that," she said flatly.

He desperately wanted to know what she was thinking. He turned through the pages. "This book isn't gonna help you. Give me your phone."

She handed it over and he searched for a website specifically written for teens. He dismissed a couple of them as too clinical or too judgmental before finding one he considered suitable.

"Okay, I've bookmarked this one for you. It talks about—" He read off the menu. "Puberty, Dating, Relationships, Sex, Contraception, STDs, Slang Words. The last one here is Sexual Abuse. That's what I just asked you about. When you get around to reading that, if you do think maybe something like that happened to you, you need to tell someone. Me or Caleb or Bea. A counselor at school. Or Rosa, I guess."

"I don't think anything like that happened to me, but I'll read it tonight."

"And if you have any questions about the rest of it, ask me."

"You won't tell me to ask Rosa, like Caleb did the other night?"

"Nope. You can ask me anything."

She looked very relieved.

"Just bear in mind," he added, "the info you get from kids at school isn't necessarily accurate, even from the ones already having sex. And the teachers are just gonna give the politically correct answers so they don't get fired. I am your one and only source of accurate information."

"Thank you. I do have a question for you. At school the girls wanted to know if my brothers were hot, and I said yes. And they laughed like that was the wrong thing to say. Was I supposed to say I have ugly brothers?"

Jesse chuckled. "The thing is, the question was just a joke. Sisters don't think their brothers are hot. You could've said something like, *My brothers' girlfriends think they're hot.*"

"Do you have a girlfriend?"

"Yes, and she thinks I'm hot." Not hot enough to sleep with, apparently.

"How come I haven't met her?"

"Caleb hasn't met her either. It's not that serious. Mostly we hang out with a bunch of other friends from college. Natalie's pretty cool and open to reason. I convinced her Friday the thirteenth doesn't mean bad luck."

"Why would it mean bad luck?"

"It's a superstition, an emotional crutch. I explained confirmation bias and today she's about seventy percent less superstitious than she was yesterday."

Wynter looked at him, wide-eyed. He'd utterly lost her.

"Never mind. I'm just saying she's receptive to my perspective, for the most part."

"And your perspective is the correct one," she said, mimicking him from a few days ago.

"Exactly. You're a quick learner. And so is she. She listens to me about all kinds of things. I think she might be worth putting a lot of work into."

"Does Indio have a girlfriend?"

"Uh... not really. He likes girls. He *loves* girls. Lots of girls. Has trouble with the girl*friend* side of things."

"What sort of trouble?"

"I just mean... since high school, he's in the habit of moving on as fast as possible."

"What about Jenny?"

"Well, she was different." Jesse snapped the book shut and handed it back as he considered how to explain. "Jenny saw something else inside him. I can see it too, and Caleb would if he'd focus for one second on what goes on inside a person's head instead of only their actions. I think Mom—" A sudden sense of discomfort stopped him. Well, that was new. He never had trouble talking about anything and here he was not knowing how to continue. He had no idea how Wynter would react to a conversation about Miriam.

"What about her?" Wynter asked quietly.

He pressed on. "I have this theory — Caleb thinks it's irrelevant but I *know* it's true. See, I don't remember her at all. I have no emotional stake. And Caleb just got on with what had to be done. But Indio was kind of messed up by it. He once told me he and

Mom had a big fight, right before she left with Joy. That's his last memory of her. Little kids blame themselves for stuff like that and it can follow them for years."

"And that's why he doesn't have a proper girlfriend?"

"It's complicated, but that's the gist of it. He'll get over it eventually."

"I don't have a last memory of her."

"Why not? You were ten, right?"

"I didn't see much of her. I just sort of realized she wasn't there anymore. Joy told me she'd gone to Thailand so I found a map and... it was so far away. It didn't seem real. I tried to think back and find the last memory, the last time I actually talked with her rather than just seeing her around the place. But it was weeks earlier, and I guess not very significant. I never found it."

"Do you want her back?"

"Do you?"

"She's nothing to me."

"I used to." Wynter drew a deep breath and gazed across the parking lot. "At some point I stopped hoping for it."

"What about Joy?"

"She always wanted to join Momma. She lied to me, to make me leave the ashram. She said Momma was flying in from Thailand. I'd tried to stop caring about her, but suddenly I *did* care. Suddenly I wanted to see her. But it was just a trick. And I thought maybe Joy wanted to leave the Light. But she went right back to them. So, now I don't know why she made me leave. I'm glad she did. I'm glad I met you. For a few days I thought I was on the right path, but the universe put me in Richland where everything feels wrong."

"It's just for a little while."

She gave him a tiny smile, more to make him feel better.

He sat up and said brightly, "Did you know today's Caleb's birthday?"

"No. Is that important?"

"Most people think birthdays are important. To be honest we never made a big deal of them in our family. I'm the only one who cares. I got him a gift but I don't want those awful women to be there when I give it to him. When he goes up to pay, we have to whisk him out of the place before they notice. Just for two minutes."

She nodded conspiratorially.

Caleb could see why Dr Rosamund Meyers spent four days a week teaching and only one with clients. She came across as flighty and cold. He couldn't imagine how she put her patients at ease with that demeanor. Not that *he* had the bedside manner to make it as a shrink, either. At least he knew his limitations.

Anyway, he wasn't trying to be at ease. His only concern was Wynter.

"Her blood tests were all clear," Tina was saying, "but she needs to put on some weight."

"That shouldn't be a problem," Rosa said. "She's eating very well. I'll be taking her to the clinic over the next few months for vaccinations—"

"The next few *months?*" Caleb couldn't help interrupting. Surely Wynter would be Joy's responsibility by then. He turned to Tina. "We need to talk about Joy's custody hearing."

"Where *is* Joy today?" Tina said.

"She has a job interview."

"I see. How do you feel about her readiness to accept custody?"

"I've no doubt she's ready." Caleb did have doubts. Of course he did. Joy had clearly told him she didn't want custody. She'd been hard to contact over the past week and she hadn't shown up today...

"Let's be realistic," Tina said, with that *I know best, so please shut up* tone that raised his hackles, just like it raised Indio's when Caleb used it with him. "From everything you've told me, it's going to take a while for Joy to get herself organized. Wynter has a safe, settled place with Rosa. Let's see how she does there."

Caleb gritted his teeth. "The girls can live at home with me. What is unsafe or unsettled about my home?"

Tina and Rosa exchanged a look, and Tina said, "Wynter has unique issues. She'll benefit from being under professional care. We couldn't have hoped for a better home than with Doctor Meyers."

"I'll find her a counselor, if that's what she needs."

Rosa leaned forward. "Let's consider this an assessment period. I'm in a position to observe her every day and decide on what treatment she may need. I understand she hasn't been forthcoming to you about her time in Arizona."

"Has she to you?"

"Not yet. We're making progress but these are sensitive issues. There's the possibility of sexual abuse."

"She hasn't mentioned anything like that."

Rosa gave him a patient smile. "Would she even recognize sexual abuse? Her experience is so limited. I'm sure I'll get it out of her, and then we can start the healing process."

Get it out of her. Her wording made Caleb's skin crawl. "She needs her family. And it's my job, my *duty,* to—" He stopped talking because Jesse and Wynter were heading back to the table.

Wynter said, in an odd tone, "I'm going to the restroom," and walked off again.

"D'you wanna come over and pay?" Jesse said. "I have a coupon. Let's see if they'll take it."

Caleb excused himself and followed Jesse to the cash register at the front. "I *know* you don't have a coupon for this godforsaken place."

"Come outside for a minute?" Jesse took his arm, threw a quick look over his shoulder, and hustled him out.

Wynter was on the bench outside. She jumped up, a gleam in her eye. Jesse guided him across the parking lot at a quick pace, Wynter alongside, and they ducked behind a van.

"Okay, bro, I got you a gift. You need to overreact — squeal with delight, give me a wet kiss, you know the routine." Jesse winked at Wynter. "Them's the rules."

Caleb gave him a warning look.

"Is it a real house rule?" Wynter asked Caleb.

"It's an aspirational family tradition that no one follows," Jesse said. "Me giving thoughtful gifts on special occasions — *that's* a house rule." Jesse pulled out a small flat packet. "Happy birthday."

The simple phrase made Caleb's chest squeeze. Birthdays were a sore spot for all of them. Even when Harry had bothered, he'd do something embarrassing or stupid that always involved alcohol. In recent years Jesse had done his best to create better memories, and Caleb forced himself to go along with it.

He opened the package and tipped four tiny figures into his hand.

Wynter leaned in. "What are those?"

Caleb knew. "It's our family, see?"

"Our family in plastic," Jesse said. "This one's you, Wyn." He picked out the shortest figure, with long light brown hair and blue shorts, holding a tiny mug. "That's the hot chocolate I gave you. These are the Fairn boys. I tried to match our hair. Caleb's got a wrench, see? Indio's got a guitar, and I'm holding *A Brief History of*

Time. It's a tile with a sticker."

"Where did you get these?" Wynter asked, fascinated.

"It's called Lego," Caleb said. "We were desperate for Lego when we were kids. It was too expensive, so we only had a few bits. Thanks, Jess. They're very cute."

"Where's plastic Joy?" Wynter said.

"When I've met her," Jesse said, "I'll make her figure."

They sat together in contented silence, enjoying their moment of freedom.

Caleb's phone rang. Freedom over. "Tina."

"Where on earth are you? Wynter is *not* in the restroom."

"We're right outside."

He ended the call and stood, signaling for Jesse and Wynter to do the same, and they emerged from behind the van. Rosa was in the restaurant doorway, scanning the parking lot. Tina joined her looking flustered. And behind them, the server, even more flustered because it looked like they were all about to do a dine-and-dash.

Caleb, Jesse and Wynter walked over.

"I need to get back to Richland." Rosa was annoyed with all of them. "Say your goodbyes, Wynter."

"I'm going to the restroom first." She stood on tiptoe to put her lips to Caleb's ear. "To make what I said not a lie."

Consequences

Caleb pulled up in the driveway to find Jesse chatting excitedly on his phone as he worked on a small snowman in the middle of the front yard that was otherwise devoid of snow, as was the entire city. The front door stood wide open.

"...I swear I'm not making it up. I'll send you a photo when he's done... No, a tiny one. Two feet tall. I got sick of waiting for snow so I drove up the mountain and fetched some." Jesse patted the snowman's shoulders into shape. "Yes, pretty sure he'll last until you get here. I'll wrap him in a thermal blanket. In any case, we can take you to see the snow *in situ* on Saturday."

Caleb caught his eye as he walked up the path, giving a little shake of his head. They really shouldn't make promises they might not be able to keep. "Let me talk to her."

"She says it's even colder in Richland, but no snow there, either," Jesse said, handing over the phone. "We *have* to take her to the mountain. Where's the harmonica?"

"Do we have one?"

"Yes! I'm sure we do..."

Jesse disappeared into the back of the house. His creation at Caleb's feet sagged lopsidedly, its carrot nose drooping, a woolly hat pulled low over its head. Indio would've sculpted something spectacular just to show him up, and Jesse would've been perfectly okay with being mocked over his objectively poor artistic talent.

"Hey, hun," Caleb said. "Has Rosa talked to you about the visitation schedule?"

"Tina says you're allowed to visit me twice a month," Wynter said, "as long as it doesn't interfere with Rosa's plans, whatever that means. And I can visit Seattle once a month, starting this weekend. She says more than that would be *overdoing it* because I'll be so busy with schoolwork and friends."

"She could be right. Your life is about to get real busy."

"But I don't have any friends. I don't understand anything those kids are talking about."

"It'll get better."

"So the good thing is I can stay the night on Saturday because the evening bus gets in too late. But then I have to catch the bus back at nine on Sunday morning."

"Plenty of time for pancakes first."

"And Tina says you have to pay for the bus!" she said indignantly.

"I know. I already spoke to her this afternoon."

"You have to book the ticket in advance, to get the best price."

"I'll do it tonight."

Tina had made more demands than just paying for the bus. No leaving the state. No unsupervised visits with Joy until she completed her background check. No unsupervised visits with Indio *ever* because of his history. And not just his criminal record. Tina had unearthed other problems that Caleb needed to talk to his brother about, and which he hoped she hadn't mentioned to Wynter.

Wynter said, "She told me Indio's not allowed to stay overnight in Seattle or when he visits here, or drive me around or even leave the house with me. He's not a bad person. Why are they acting like he is?"

"He's not a bad person but he's done some irresponsible things. He had a few rough years, hun. He's away from that crowd now. He'll do great at Portland."

"Please don't make him feel bad about it. He might not want to see me."

"Of course he will."

"Will you bring Joy with you when you visit? She hardly ever replies to my texts and she never picks up when I call her. I sent her photos of my room and my school and I don't know if she got them."

"She's busy sorting things out."

"Have you seen her again?"

"Yes, just once, to give her the background check forms." He'd also given her cash for the fee, instructions on how to get a fingerprint card, and an affidavit form for her statement that she was present at Wynter's birth, which was one of the many necessary steps to getting Wynter a birth certificate. And that had been the only time he'd spoken with her, because she didn't respond to his messages, either.

He said goodbye as Jesse came back with the harmonica and a couple of drumsticks for arms. He'd sacrificed one to the cause — it was broken in half with the pieces taped together at an angle.

"So the little guy can hold the harmonica, see?" Jesse said, holding it up for accolades.

Caleb handed back the phone. "What do you know about the trouble Indio was in at Ohio State?"

A flicker of irritation crossed his youngest brother's face. "Uh, what trouble?"

"Drugs, drinking, fighting. Sound familiar? Tina told me about it today. She must have contacts in Ohio because those were internal sanctions at the university. The police weren't involved."

"Well, I didn't know about it, specifically, but I guess it doesn't surprise me. Is that a good answer?"

"A good answer would be a truthful one."

"That's the truth. I didn't know about the sanctions."

Jesse went outside before Caleb could interrogate him further. Caleb didn't pursue it — it really had nothing to do with Jesse, who hated even thinking about what Indio was up to because it scared him.

Caleb braced himself to call Indio, going into his room so Jesse wouldn't have to hear. Indio sounded like he was in a pretty good mood until Caleb got to the reason for the call.

"Five sanctions — and I'm guessing those were only the times you were caught."

"You already knew I had good reason to transfer to Portland." Indio sounded like he'd rather be having a cavity drilled.

"I'm not calling to chew you out. I'm calling to tell you the consequences. Wynter's caseworker won't let you see her without my supervision. I have to be physically in the same room."

"How the fuck would Social Services know if you were in the same room or not?"

"That's not the point. I'm saying all the shit you pulled is gonna haunt us for a while."

"What can I say to get you off my back? Two weeks ago, we didn't know she existed. I couldn't have predicted this."

"You're telling me it never occurred to you that punching kids on campus could cause problems down the track?"

"I never punched anyone. Jesus. Those were scuffles. One time I only got reported because the kid's dad was a professor at—"

"Indio, I don't care what your excuses are. Excuses don't erase the sanctions." Caleb bit back the next three things he was going to say. Castigation wouldn't help. "On the weekend we'll sit down together and fill out those forms to get your juvenile records sealed."

"Awesome," he said flatly. "I look forward to that."

"And your background check, too. I'll pay for everything."

"What's the point? That caseworker knows about my record. She won't let me see Wynter unsupervised either way."

"You won't be able to see her *at all* if you don't do the background check. Tina's given you two weeks' grace."

Indio sighed. "Fine. But I don't need your help. I'll deal with it."

He never wanted help, no matter how Caleb offered it — except for the financial support that had enabled him to leave home, of course.

A sudden thought occurred to Caleb. "Is there something else a background check is gonna turn up? Something I don't know about?"

"I said I'll deal with it."

"God, please tell me you're gonna do better at Portland," Caleb said, more to himself.

"I've only been here a few weeks. At least give me a fucking chance to screw up before you start, okay?"

Indio hung up, his go-to response once the conversation devolved into cussing. Caleb regretted the entire call. He wouldn't be surprised if his brother refused to take another call from him for the remainder of the semester.

He found Jesse sprawled on the couch reading a book.

"How about you clip those hedges while you're out there?" He'd told Jesse that morning to get it done.

"In the dark? I'll do it first thing tomorrow."

"Fine. Call Indio tomorrow and remind him about Wynter's visit this weekend. I'd like him here by midday."

Jesse turned a page, not looking up. "Is he not talking to you again?"

"I think that's probably the case."

"Well, you had a good run. What was that — ten whole days?"

Fighting with Indio was a very old habit. It was easy to forget how it affected Jesse, who made light of almost everything regardless of his true feelings.

"Sunday after next, you and me are driving to Richland," Caleb said.

"I know. You texted me two hours ago. Is Joy coming?"

"I hope so. She's not very communicative."

"You bust her ass and I'll bust Indio's, and between the two of us maybe we can put the family back together again." Jesse finally looked up. "Whose ass do we bust to bring Wynter home?"

"I know you're upset about this, Jess. We have to make the best of it."

"I always wanted a little brother. A little sister will do. I hated being the baby. *Hated* it. And I feel bad saying that, cuz I know I took advantage of being the baby. I know you went easy on me."

"Are you saying I should go easier on Indio?"

"I'm not gonna get involved with you and Indio. I'm saying you're easy on me. Why didn't you send me into the roof the other day to find that maggoty rat?"

"Why didn't you offer?"

"I'm just saying, that's the perfect job for me. I mean, it's a disgusting job but I could've done it. Since I was a little kid you got me mowing the lawn and taking out the garbage. Lawn, garbage, lawn, garbage. I can do other stuff. If I had a little brother, I'd be sending him into that roof, for sure."

"I'm fairly certain you'd put your foot through the ceiling."

"So, you won't make me do something that's hard for me? How come you're always making Indio do things that are hard for him?"

"Such as?"

"Such as being a mini-you. Punctual and practical and unemotional and duty-bound and dependable and monogamous. Like a freakin' robot. Indio doesn't work that way."

"And you know how Indio works?"

"I got a pretty good idea." Jesse tapped his temple meaningfully.

"Good. Please use that privileged knowledge to make sure he shows up on Saturday. He'll have a gig the night before and it's a three-hour ride, so I know it's gonna be *hard* for him."

Jesse groaned, tipping his head back on the couch. "Everything I said went right over your head."

"I heard you, Jesse. And if he would just *talk* to me, I would hear him, too. He still needs to be here. Not for me. For Wynter. Then he can go back to Portland and be as impractical and unpunctual, and all the rest of it, as he likes, as long as he passes his classes and stays out of trouble." Caleb eased back. This really was nothing to do with Jesse. "You wanna lift weights before we eat?" Caleb had been to the pool after work so he was already in sweatpants.

"I'm doing something else right now."

"I don't see you doing anything."

Jesse waved his book around. "*This* is something."

"Let's lift."

Jesse gave in, put his book down and followed Caleb into the garage.

"Did he really transfer to Portland to play in Turk's band?" Caleb said. "Or was Ohio gonna throw him out?"

Jesse gave him a sidelong look as he loaded the bar with weights. "All I know is they gave him one more chance. I guess he figured he should get out before he was thrown out. Some woman in Admin gave him a little inside help transferring."

"Why would she do that?"

"She was a long-time fan of his music," Jesse said with an eye roll.

Caleb could only assume "fan" was a euphemism. Then again, Indio could be very charming when he needed to be.

"By the way," Caleb said, swinging a leg over the bench and lying down to grab the bar, "what's his sex life or mine got to do with anything? Why'd you even throw that in there earlier?"

"You're right. No reason to think robots would be monogamous."

New and Improved Version

On Saturday morning, Rosa drove Wynter to Pasco for the 8 o'clock bus. Caleb had emailed her a ticket to print off and in her school bag was her homework and a change of clothes. Nothing else, because everything she needed was at Caleb's house — her family, a roomful of guitars, and that small safe bedroom with the gray quilt on the bed.

Joy was going to be there, and Indio was riding his motorcycle up from Portland to arrive around lunch time like her. He could only stay a few hours because he had a gig later. That was okay. It would be the five of them, all together for the first time.

Wynter snapped a photo of her bus before she boarded and texted it to Joy, to show she was on her way. Joy rarely responded to written messages, but a photo sometimes prompted a smiley face. That single emoji couldn't compete with Indio's little cartoons, which he drew just for her, or with Jesse's patient, sometimes hilarious responses when she asked her endless questions, or with Caleb's encouraging words over the phone when she told him about a difficult evening with Rosa. Still, it kept her connected to her sister.

The trip was over four hours, with several stops. Wynter hadn't slept much the night before and she refused to sleep on the bus. She'd trained herself to stay awake and to ignore a rumbling stomach — necessary survival skills in the Light, and today the anticipation made it easy.

Caleb picked her up at the station.

"Jesse's got a few things to do downtown, and then he's fetching Joy." He put her bag on the back seat of the truck and they got in. "Indio can't make it, hun."

Wynter's heart lurched. Not so much because of the news, but because of the way he said it.

"Why not?"

"He texted Jesse half an hour ago. Something came up."

"What does that mean?"

Caleb started the engine and pulled out of the parking lot. His face was set hard, making him look angry even while his voice was calm and his smile in greeting had been real. "He has very busy weekends – gigs, school work. I'm really sorry."

"Is he sorry?"

"Yes, of course."

"Is it because you were mad at him over those sanctions at Ohio?"

"How... Did Jesse tell you about that?"

"He also said you and Indio weren't talking to each other again."

"Regardless of any problems me and Indio are having, that's no excuse for him not to see you."

They stopped at the grocery store to buy what Caleb called "fixin's for lunch." Wynter couldn't stop thinking about Indio being too busy for her. He hadn't even sent her a message about it.

At home she unpacked her bag into Indio's closet even though she didn't have much. They organized the food and waited for Joy and Jesse.

✿

Jesse pulled up in front of the Light's downtown office. He must've passed this building a hundred times, paying no attention because it looked like a New Age bookstore. The lettering said *Healing Center* and there were no signs or logos to associate it with the Light. Since meeting Wynter, his research had revealed the chapter offices across the country were essentially recruiting places for the various retreats and courses run by the Light. You'd never know if you walked in off the street.

The building was set back from the street, squashed between a nail salon and a small general store boasting Chinese herbs and cheap international phone cards. The two off-street parking spaces in front were taken so he parked crosswise behind both cars. He'd only be here a minute. A poster in the window advertised yoga classes on site, and another offered personalized spiritual healing therapy.

Pushing open the door, Jesse was assaulted by the stench of incense. A young man behind the counter, sporting terrible acne and a weird earring, watched him anxiously.

"I'm sorry, you can't park there."

"Is Joy here?"

"Would you mind moving your car, please?"

"Would you mind fetching Joy, please?"

Jesse was enjoying the guy's discomfort at having to deal with a belligerent member of the public. Growing up, he'd never given the Light a second thought even though he knew Joy and his mother were with them in Arizona. Since meeting Wynter he'd decided he hated every person and their dog who'd ever associated with the Light. Spotty here wasn't impressing him with his parking rules and regulations.

Jesse did feel sorry for him, though. Evidently the Light didn't pay well enough for him to buy Clearasil. Or maybe he just wasted all his pay on their stupid courses and crystals.

Spotty's lips tightened and he went out the back. Jesse dug his fingers into a glass bowl of tumbled stones on the counter. The slippery-smooth sensation was almost enough to soothe his soul. According to the card next to the bowl, "Lucky" aventurine, when taped to his cell phone, would protect him against toxic emanations. The blue quartz would vibrate his number four chakra. Astrophyllite — he liked the sound of that one — would help with astral travels. Cool. He considered stealing one while he had the chance, just to deprive the Light of $2.95. The stones really were nice. The explanatory card, on the other hand, turned his stomach. He'd started hating the Light sixteen days ago but he'd hated this sort of crap all his life.

Spotty returned and took his seat behind the counter. "She'll be out in a minute. She said you're her brother?"

Jesse let the stones run through his fingers. "These are fascinating. What does this one do?" At random, he picked out a bright orange stone.

"That's carnelian. It enhances creativity and helps you recall past lives, rejuvenates your cells and aids with pollen allergies." The man spoke earnestly, hopeful Jesse was seriously interested.

"Bit of an all-rounder, this carnelian," Jesse said.

"One of my favorites. It'll help you manifest your desires."

"So, it'll get me laid?"

Before the guy could stammer an answer, the bead curtain behind the counter parted and a young woman emerged. She scanned the store, taking no notice of Jesse.

"Hey, Joy," Jesse said.

Joy looked at him, surprised. "Jesse?"

"I went to your place in Magnolia and your friend said you were here."

"Yes, here I am."

She offered no explanation for the change in pick-up arrangements. She came around the counter and they stood awkwardly for a moment. Then they both went in for a quick hug. She looked as fragile as Wynter, but tall and with his and Caleb's coloring.

"I was expecting Caleb," she said.

"I'm the new and improved version. Come on."

Joy didn't move. "He's not with you?"

"He went to pick up Wynter from the bus station. They'll be home by now. Let's go."

"I was hoping he'd bring Wynter here for the visit. I have a session scheduled this afternoon."

Jesse couldn't believe his ears. "A session of what?"

"A healing and counseling session. They've been very kind to slot me in."

He tried hard not to sneer and wasn't sure he succeeded. "Some people would say spending time with family is like a healing and counseling session."

"That's very sweet, Jesse. I'm sure you're right. It's so lovely to see you again. Look at you — you must be six feet tall. I suppose you don't remember me at all."

"No, sorry. Are we going, then?"

Still she hesitated. What would Caleb do? Well, Caleb had failed to keep her in the house that day she showed up two weeks ago. Maybe he'd have failed here, too. Jesse was determined not to fail. He'd do everything humanly possible to get Joy in the car, and if it didn't work out it would be her fault and her loss.

"Let me fetch my purse." Joy faded away through the bead curtain.

Jesse glared after her, psyching himself up to go on back there and drag her out by the hair if she didn't return very quickly.

"Where were we?" Jesse said pleasantly, picking out another stone. "This is rose quartz, right? The love stone. Will this put my girlfriend in the mood?"

He got a terse smile and silence from Spotty in response. Jesse roamed the store, casually picking up and putting down candles and CDs and boxes of incense, trying to look like he was about to pocket something just to fuck with poor Spotty.

After five minutes he wheeled on his heel and marched through the bead curtain.

Yeah, this is what Caleb would do.

He found himself in a musty corridor with two doors. The first was open — an office with a computer and filing cabinets and not much else. The second door was locked. He walked around the corner.

"Excuse me! Excuse me!" Spotty called after him.

Jesse went through the door at the end of the corridor into a larger room with cushions scattered on the floor and posters all over the walls. Two people sat on cushions in the corner, talking quietly.

"Joy!" Jesse yelled, startling them both. "Where's Joy?"

One of them stood up, an older man who looked like a Jedi master with his ponytail and neat beard and pale baggy clothes. "Can I help you?"

"I'm here to pick up Joy. She has a family engagement."

"And you are...?"

"...here to pick up Joy!" Jesse was not leaving this place without her. He was not coming home to Wynter without her, not after Indio fucked himself up, too fucking wasted to ride.

A door on the far side opened and Joy slipped into the room, fiddling with her purse.

"I'm here, Jesse. I'm coming," she said quietly.

She scurried across the room and followed him out of the store. It was freezing cold outside and she had no coat.

In the car, he half expected her to scold him for making a scene. She was almost four years older than him, after all, and he'd been a bit of a dick. But she sat meekly, clutching her purse, saying nothing. He had to remind her to fasten her seatbelt. He drove through the lunchtime traffic on Rainier Avenue, wondering how to put it right.

"Look, I'm sorry. I thought you backed out. You can't back out. Wynter's counting on you."

"Of course. I understand. I was just fetching my purse and speaking with my healer before I left."

"Okay. Okay." Jesse drew some deep breaths. "Did you change that session thing? Wynter's staying the night. It would be great if you could stay the night."

He glanced at her, pressed against the car door to make herself small. If Wynter had been hit or hurt in the Light, it made sense Joy had been, too. She'd lived with them since she was six years old. Jesse should be gentle and patient. Trouble was, he was too angry at her for failing to be what Wynter needed right now.

When she didn't answer, he said, "One of the venues I play at, they have a notice up for a waitressing job. Five or six nights a week. You could do that, couldn't you? The boss is a great guy and he really likes me. I've put in a good word. I bet you could get the job."

"That's kind of you. Why don't you text me the details. Five nights a week, though... I'm not sure I'm ready for that."

"Anything will help, right? Once you have a job, we can get Wynter away from that awful woman."

"What awful woman?"

"Her foster mother! She's *awful*. She doesn't understand Wynter at all."

"Wynter is a little hard for anyone to understand."

What was wrong with this girl?

"What're you talking about? I understand her. I'm gonna teach her everything. Caleb understands what she needs and Indio connected with her over music. Everything will work out once the court gives her to you."

Joy was staring out the side window, at the frigid gray sky that refused to deliver snow. She must've been thinking along the same lines because she said, "I remember the snow in Montana. That last Christmas, Mom took us to Harry's parents in Anaconda. Harry was only around for a day or two, but we stayed for two weeks. It snowed every single day. Mom taught us how to cut paper snowflakes. Well, not you. You were too little for scissors. Indio made the best snowflakes. Will he be there today?"

"Nope." Jesse didn't elaborate and Joy didn't ask, which was odd.

She said, "Do you remember that house?"

"Of course. We lived there for six years after... after Mom... you know... After she *left* us there with Harry and took you to Arizona."

"I loved that house. Ever since you were a baby, Mom used to take you there to stay with Grandma and Grandpa for days at a time while she worked. You loved it. You loved the snow, too. That Christmas Day you took off all your clothes and tunneled naked through the drifts up against the house, laughing the whole time as you turned blue."

"That doesn't sound like me. It sounds completely irrational."

"You were two-and-a-half."

"Yeah, but I was born rational, so..."

"Never mind. I shouldn't have mentioned it."

"No, no, that's okay. I was joking."

Sort of joking. He was fairly sure he *had* been rational, even at that age, but he felt bad for making her feel bad. Or maybe she was deliberately taking offense just to shut down the conversation. He drove on in silence, not wanting to make things worse. So far, he wasn't as impressed with the older sister as with the younger. Didn't matter. What mattered was that she take responsibility for Wynter. He didn't need to forge a relationship with her if she wasn't willing. He didn't remember his mother and he didn't remember her.

Did she even deserve to be immortalized as a Lego minifigure?

Turning Pages

Jesse was pretty proud of himself. He'd brought home Joy. Plus, Wynter was thrilled with his harmonica-playing snowman out the front.

Over lunch Wynter told Joy about her classes and the cold snap in Richland and her foster mother's allegedly incredible meals. Jesse was fairly sure Wynter would describe any halfway decent home-cooked meal as gourmet. He was forced to concede Rosa's competence in that department was a blessing because Wynter needed to eat well. He kept the concession to himself.

"How was that job interview last week?" Caleb asked Joy.

Joy put down her fork and took a sip of water. "It didn't go anywhere, unfortunately."

"I told Joy about the waitressing job at Sticky's," Jesse said, to get it on the record, in front of Caleb, that she had other options.

"I asked Patricia for help, too," Caleb said. "She's a family friend. She may be able to give you some shifts at the diner. And her friend has a bakery just a few miles from here — he's looking for a sales assistant, if you're an early riser."

"That's very kind of you to ask around for me," Joy said. "I don't think I can do sales or waitressing, but I'm sure something will turn up."

"Well, you think about it. Wynter says you know bookkeeping. That's a useful skill."

"I did think of that. I asked my friend about it and discovered the software I was using is fifteen years out of date. Things move so fast out here."

"The community college will have courses to get you up to speed." Caleb had an edge of nervous desperation to his tone that Jesse had never heard before. "I'll help you. I'll do anything to keep the two of you together and close by."

Joy gave a wan smile but didn't answer.

Jesse went to help Wynter clear up the kitchen.

"Did Indio tell you why he couldn't come?" she asked him.

How much to tell her? He was angry with Joy but he was boiling mad at Indio today. As her one and only source of accurate information, Jesse owed her the unvarnished truth.

"He planned to come. He had a gig last night and got wrecked. You know what that means?"

Her jaw dropped. "He wrecked his bike?"

"No, although he would've if he'd ridden today. He partied too hard and now he has to sleep it off."

"Oh." She was devastated, and trying not to show it because, after all, what right did she have to expect Indio to behave on the one fucking night it mattered?

"This time tomorrow he's gonna be feeling really, really disappointed in himself," Jesse said.

"I don't want him to feel bad. I just want him here! He hasn't even met Joy yet."

Jesse didn't think that was such a big deal, given his own lack of connection with his older sister. Then again, maybe Indio and Joy would get along. They were twins and both kind of pathetic in their own way – on this weekend, anyway.

"We could drive up the mountain," Jesse said. "Let's build a huge snowman in the truck bed and bring it home to keep the little one company."

Wynter brightened at the suggestion. "Can we do that?"

"If we make him, or her, exactly eight times bigger, we can call them Frostbyte and Frostbit."

She had no idea what he was talking about. So much to teach her.

"Joy's not keen on a drive," Caleb said quietly, coming into the kitchen to make coffee. "I already asked her."

Of course she wasn't keen on a drive. God forbid Joy let herself experience the joy of a simple family trip.

"She was telling me about the time I burrowed into the snow stark naked," Jesse said as Joy brought in the last of the dishes to rinse. "I'm hoping you remember the story differently, bro."

"Sounds about right."

"He thought he was an Eskimo, so we made him an igloo," Joy told Wynter. "It was *huge*. Grandma kept bringing out soup and hot chocolate while we worked."

Jesse was astonished by the change in her as she dwelled on the memory — for the first time, her voice was animated.

Caleb did his best to encourage her. "We rolled dozens of snowballs and stacked them in a dome. It held together for days."

"It was so warm inside!" Joy almost laughed. "You and Indio wanted to camp overnight in there."

"I picked up a couple of photo albums from Harry's," Caleb said. "There might be a photo of the igloo."

He went out to the garage to fetch them from the truck. He hadn't told Jesse about the albums, which was kind of neat — he'd planned to show them all together, as a surprise. Instead, Indio hadn't shown up and now Joy was looking nervous. Jesse watched the flicker of life drain from her.

"Jesse, would you mind driving me back?"

"Now?"

"I have things I need to do."

"I thought you'd stay longer," Wynter said, startled. "You can stay the night. I'll sleep on the couch."

"I really can't, darling, I'm so sorry. I have an appointment this afternoon and a meeting tonight."

"Don't you want to see the photos?"

"Of course. Next time."

Jesse watched Wynter shut down, protecting herself from the pain.

"I'm not driving you back right now," Jesse told Joy, offering no excuse. They locked eyes and he watched her come to the realization that his stubborn refusal was final.

She said, "Well, I'm sure Caleb will oblige."

Caleb came back with two photo albums and stacked them on the dining room table. "These are '88 through '03, up until we moved to Seattle. I know there's a later one somewhere — couldn't find it."

"I must get going," Joy said. "Thank you so much for lunch. Can you drive me back, Caleb?"

Caleb glanced at Jesse. He looked down, refusing to engage.

"Let's take a quick look, okay?" Caleb said.

"I'm afraid I don't have time today. You could drop them off at the office, perhaps? I'd love to take a look, but I have a session."

The entire point had been to look at them *together*. Jesse glared at the albums on the table, feeling the air thicken.

"I'll drive you back in a couple hours." Caleb's tone brooked no argument. Joy gave in with a fluttery fake smile.

Caleb took a seat and opened up the first album. He grabbed the edge of Wynter's chair and pulled it closer, right up against his, then put his arm across the back, not touching her but sending a clear signal that he was there for her. Wynter slid him a look of gratitude and leaned forward to see the first page.

"Anaconda, Montana, January 1988," Caleb said. "Yours truly. Age: one day."

Jesse moved his chair around the table and sat on Caleb's other side. "You had more hair at one day old than I do today."

"It all fell out, then came in lighter, then turned dark again."

Wynter stroked baby Caleb's cheek. He was cradled in someone's arms — Miriam's arms, presumably. How was Wynter going to react when a photo of their mother came up?

How was *he* going to react? Harry had never displayed photos of her around the house but Jesse had seen a few pictures. Caleb had sometimes bought disposable cameras with his pocket money when he was eight or nine, and had his own photo album of the family from that era. And Indio used to have a picture of her from before she was married. He'd used it as a bookmark when he was in elementary school. When it had gotten ratty, he'd covered it in sticky tape to try and preserve it. Could be anywhere now. Maybe trashed, or lost in a book in one of the boxes in Indio's closet.

On the opposite page was baby Caleb wrapped in blankets. "They say I came out at four in the morning, and the heater was broken."

"You were born at home?" Jesse said. "I didn't know that."

"This is *the* Anaconda house — Grandpa and Grandma Fairn's house, where Harry grew up. Miriam lived there the last few weeks of her pregnancy, and moved in properly some time after I was born while Harry was stationed in Germany. I was sixteen months old before he met me."

Joy came around to stand behind Caleb. "Indio and me were born there, too. Mom wasn't supposed to have twins at home, but she insisted. By the time you were born, Jesse, we were living in Billings for a while and you were born in the hospital."

"Was I born in the hospital?" Wynter asked her.

"No. Remember, darling, I told you — I was at your birth. They wouldn't have let me be there if Mom went to the hospital. You came a month early, in the end, so it all happened quickly. It was the most incredible thing. I was the first one to hold you."

The sisters exchanged a warm smile and for a moment Jesse thought everything would be okay.

Caleb turned the pages. Now baby Caleb was a curly-headed two-year-old on a trike with Christmas ribbons still attached. Serious-looking even back then. And there was Miriam kneeling beside him, smiling at him like he was her world.

"Jesse, he looks exactly like you," Wynter said.

"Hear that, Jess? She thinks you look two years old."

Caleb's voice was tight, despite the joke, and his hand on the page was curled into a fist. Wynter didn't notice. She was already looking at the photo on the opposite page, Harry and Miriam's wedding picture after Harry left the army.

Joy excused herself and went to the bathroom. Jesse watched his brother's gaze lingering on that first photo of Miriam, the picture-perfect loving mother in acid-wash jeans and cowboy boots, a tasseled suede jacket and knitted scarf. Jesse felt nothing but mild curiosity at seeing his mother and the wedding picture, and Wynter also seemed unfazed. She asked Caleb if he remembered the wedding and it took him a moment to snap out of it and answer her.

"No, I was only just two. I have some memories of the twins when they were little."

He turned a couple more pages with toddler Caleb until he reached a photo of the new babies, blond Indio and brunette Joy. Maybe baby Wynter had looked like a cross between the two of them. Did they even have cameras at the ashram?

Joy came back in the room just then, and Caleb told her, "When one of you cried, the other one started crying just for the hell of it. I used to pile my Matchbox cars in your crib to try and distract you."

"I'm sure it helped," Joy said, patting Caleb's shoulder and leaving her hand there. Jesse held his breath, knowing Caleb was doing the same. The simple gesture became ridiculously significant.

"I remember this toy." Caleb pointed to a Christmas photo when he was almost four.

"Is that a parking garage?" Jesse said.

"Yeah, it had an elevator between floors, a spiral ramp right there, and a car wash at the bottom."

"How come I never inherited that? I'd have loved that."

"I guess it didn't last that long."

"I'm sure you played with it," Joy said. "I'm sure you ate one of the foam rollers from the car wash. Or maybe that was Indio."

"No, that sounds like Jesse." Caleb grinned at him.

Then came the baby Jesse photos. Miriam had thrown Harry out when Jesse was a couple of months old. It wasn't evident from the photos because, as chief photographer, Harry was in hardly any of the shots anyway.

"Jesse, you're the cutest thing ever!" Wynter exclaimed.

It was true, too. Universally accepted family lore was that Jesse had been objectively the cutest child. He stood out, as the only extrovert, pulling faces for the camera before he even turned one. The outrageous curls and chubby cheeks didn't hurt, either. He'd sometimes wondered what being a parent would feel like — he'd be an awesome dad, of course — but seeing page after page of super-cute baby pictures was making him uncomfortable. *This* was what his mother had rejected. Not his current self, the hyperactive, sometimes demanding, often annoying teenager, but this adorable tot.

"There's the pink house in Great Falls." Caleb tapped a photo of the twins playing in the front yard of a narrow two-story clapboard house. "D'you remember it, Joy? We were only there a few months. Indio mixed up a batch of dirt and water and set about repainting it brown so his kindergarten friends wouldn't make fun of him."

"I took the hose and washed it all off," Joy said.

There were several photos of the four kids in both candid and posed shots, the later ones in the Missoula house near the Clark Fork River, with the patio that Caleb sometimes talked about.

As the years turned with the pages, Jesse felt the tension rising again. There it was, his third birthday. He was wearing a dinosaur t-shirt and grinning behind a rocketship cake with lit candles, one big brother on each side of his chair.

"This is back in Anaconda," Caleb said. "Harry returned from god-knows-where to live in his childhood home after Grandma died and Grandpa moved into the community home. We hadn't seen much of him in three years. He was working as a prison guard, twenty-five miles out of town. Mom took us to stay for the summer. Jesse had a stunning tantrum after he blew those candles out. We never figured out why."

Jesse shrugged, mystified.

The doorbell rang.

"That's my taxi," Joy said.

Wynter took a second to catch on. "You called a taxi?"

"I did say I had an appointment." Joy slung her purse over her shoulder.

Caleb hadn't moved or reacted, as if he'd expected it. Even after her hand on his shoulder and her animated reminiscing and smiles, he'd expected it. Jesse had to admit it took some *cojones* for her to sneak out and call a taxi after apparently succumbing to Caleb's family bonding plan.

Joy went to answer the door. "Just a minute," she told the driver. "Caleb, I'm so sorry," she called out. "Can you lend me the fare?"

Caleb pushed back his chair, retrieved his wallet from the table near the front door, and gave her two bills.

"You'll let me know if you want help with those jobs we talked about," he said flatly.

Wynter had followed him, almost hiding behind him as she said, "Thank you for coming."

Caleb put his arm around Wynter, properly this time. "I'm driving up to Richland next Sunday."

"Please come," Wynter said.

"Of course, if I can. Send me the details. Bye for now." Joy leaned around them. "Bye, Jesse."

Jesse stayed where he was, tilting back in the chair, fuming. He was glad when the door closed behind her.

Caleb took the albums and they sat together on the couch to look at the rest of the photos. There were no more pictures of Joy. And the reason there was no Joy in Jesse's third birthday photo was because a few days earlier, after taking the kids to Harry's in Anaconda, Miriam had left with her and they never came back.

Twins

Indio was used to screwing up. He was used to Caleb's recrimina-tions — those times Caleb found out about it. He wasn't used to screwing up, and Caleb knowing about it, and then getting silence. He was sick of the recriminations but the silence was worse.

For the first time in a very long time, he found himself thinking about what Jenny would think of him. Until that evening at Patty's, he hadn't seen her in two-and-a-half years. Jenny would never know what he'd been up to this past weekend but that didn't ease the shame.

By Sunday night he felt ready to contact Wynter. She'd be back in Richland, maybe finishing homework before bed.

A woman answered the phone.

"Hello, this is Rosa."

"Where's Wynter?"

"Indio, is it? I saw your name on the incoming call and thought I'd better answer it. Wynter told me you couldn't make it to Seattle this weekend. She seemed quite upset. I'm just confirming every-thing is okay, so I can tell her, and then I'll hang up."

"Let me talk to her."

"I'm sorry, I don't allow electronic devices after 9PM. But I'll certainly let her know you called, right away, to ease her concerns."

Indio gritted his teeth. "Let me talk to her."

"I have rules, and Wynter knows the rules. It's a pity you didn't call earlier. She's been home since three."

Indio pressed his fingers against his temples to massage a tension headache. He felt like crap and he needed a shower and he had two tests next week and a project due in twelve hours that he'd forgotten about until two minutes ago. And Piper was tangled up in it all somehow. Friday night was very unclear, Saturday night not much better. Turk was going to kill him.

"It's important I talk to Wynter," Indio said slowly. "I need to apologize. Can you please let me do that?"

"No, I can't do that. Perhaps next time you'll be a bit more responsible and think before you disappoint—"

Indio hung up. Jesus, with that cultured accent and holier-than-thou attitude she was worse than Caleb at his worst.

He debated whether to call Piper. Piper wasn't a groupie, she'd just behaved like one for some reason that involved an undisclosed A-bomb cigarette, tequila shots, and a private lap dance culminating in the weirdest blow job of his life. Crazy bitch. Turk was better off without her.

He scrolled through his contacts and reached Joy's name. Jesse had sent her number a few days ago.

His sisters had been out of that place for almost three weeks and he'd seen Wynter once, and Joy never. When was the last time he saw Joy? The entire family had been together for a week or so at Harry's house that summer in Anaconda. On the day Miriam left, that morning Harry had promised to take them all to the new Discovery Center in Yellowstone if they got up early enough the next day for the long drive. Little Jesse was excited about seeing bears. Indio wanted to see the wolves. Miriam warned that three hours was too long to sit in the car, especially as the four kids would be squashed in the back with Jesse's car seat.

Indio *had* gotten up early enough the next day, pleased there would be only three of them in the back after all, two if Caleb sat up front, because Miriam and Joy had left the previous afternoon on an unspecified vacation of their own. He packed snacks and colored pencils and sketch paper. He even got Jesse's breakfast organized and helped him hunt around the yard for a missing sneaker.

They never did go, though, because Harry wasn't in a fit state to drive.

In retrospect, Indio realized Harry probably drank himself stupid the previous night because his ex-wife had just taken off with his daughter and no clear indication she intended to ever return. Or maybe he was just a drunk regardless of the circumstances. At the time, this was Indio and his brothers' first direct experience of what they soon learned was their father's standard behavior. Indio's anger at not seeing the wolves had mellowed over the months and years into the sickening ache of constant disappointment punctuated by random bouts of rage.

"Don't hope for anything and you'll never be disappointed!"

Harry would say, like he'd uncovered the secret of life.

It was good advice. Indio had slowly learned to trust a small number of people but he knew better than to ever hope for anything from his father or from the universe in general. Or from himself. This evening's sickening ache was directed inward and wallowing in past disappointments wasn't helping. Nor had it succeeded in calling forth his last memory of Joy.

Didn't really matter. She was back in their lives — reluctantly, according to Jesse — so he'd make a small effort and be done with her.

He tapped her name, expecting to get voicemail. He'd leave a message, she'd never call back, and that would be that.

"Hello?"

"Joy, it's Indio."

"Oh, Indio! How wonderful. I can't talk just now."

Well, that was short and sweet.

Something made him persist. "Sorry I didn't make it to Seattle yesterday. I want to meet up with you — maybe Tuesday or Wednesday night?"

"I'm rather busy during the week. I've signed up for an evening class."

"That's great. What's the class?"

"It's a lecture series, actually. The Seattle chapter is running it from a community center near the office."

So, just stupid Light crap.

"I'll come along one night, and we can talk after." He could hardly believe the words coming out of his mouth. "Tuesday?"

"Really? You'll come to a lecture with me?"

Great. Now she thought he was interested in the Light.

"Sure." *Whatever.*

"It would be best to come tomorrow, for the very first lecture. If you like it, you can finish the series in Portland at a later date."

"Okay, Monday it is." So much for studying for Tuesday's test.

"That's wonderful. I'm so pleased you called. I'll text you the address and meet you there. It starts at seven. And it's $19.95 for the one lecture."

Of course it was. He wasn't above paying for spiritual enlightenment if it gave him the chance to see his long-lost twin. That would fix one-third of the mess he'd made of this weekend. He'd have to find another way to make it up to Wynter and to Turk.

✿

At the community center, Joy introduced Indio around to her Light friends, clinging to his arm like she needed the support. He wanted to get her alone to talk, to make up for screwing up. First, he had to sit through an hour of Light nonsense with other members of the gullible public at various stages of their spiritual journey.

Ten minutes into the lecture, his phone buzzed and he checked it, anticipating a message from one of his other siblings. Something from any of them would've been nice, even Caleb. It was Piper, of all people.

> Hunny were did u go
> u know were to find me

He winced at her spelling and the lack of punctuation and the eggplant emoji. He blocked her number. He should text Wynter or Jesse. He'd been thinking about it all day and done nothing. While Joy made copious notes beside him, he spent the rest of the lecture slouched in the chair with his arms crossed, trying to remember which Disney princess had been her favorite and which one Wynter would've liked at age six, if she'd had a normal life. He was fairly sure there were no Disney princesses in the Light.

"Let's go for a coffee," Indio said when it was finally over.

"I'm just going to chat with the presenter." Joy was already making her way over there.

"I don't have long. I have a two-hour ride back and a test tomorrow."

"Two hours to Portland? That doesn't sound right."

"I ride fast."

She laughed, following him outside. "Oh, Indio, you shouldn't do that."

They walked a few blocks and talked about the city, which she hadn't yet had time to explore.

"You haven't been up the Space Needle? Come on," he said. "We'll get an Uber and I'll buy us tickets. I've never been, either, and it's open 'til midnight."

"I'm sure I'd be scared of heights."

He couldn't persuade her.

"Why didn't you come on Sunday?" she asked.

"Rough weekend." He wondered what she'd been told and whether she disapproved, like Caleb, or was merely angry, like Jesse. "So, what d'you think of the great big world?"

"I'm bewildered, to be honest."

"We'll help — you know that. Just ask." He didn't sound like himself, saying those words. He would help her, of course, but why was he giving advice he'd failed to follow himself? He'd never asked Caleb to help him.

She didn't ask, either.

"So, Harry moved you all here ten years ago?" Joy said.

"He was heading into a good patch — took a managerial job with a cleaning company, started taking responsibility. Three years later Caleb joined the Coast Guard and basically vanished for four years, so I guess he thought Harry was doing okay with the dad thing."

"Was he?"

"For a while. But, no, not really. We survived." He decided not to tell her about things falling apart and the assault charge, and the other things even Jesse didn't know about.

"Caleb said you're playing in a college band—?"

He had to grab her arm suddenly, because she'd been about to cross the street without checking for traffic. Growing up in a fenced compound had left her with no road sense.

"You should come see us," he said, guiding her safely across. "Ask Jesse to drive you — he won't need much of an excuse."

"Jesse is... quite determined, isn't he."

"You mean opinionated? He's eighteen, only just out of high school. The world'll knock him into shape soon enough. He had an easy time of it. An *easier* time of it."

"You mean with Caleb?"

"With things in general. Jesse takes everything in his stride or finds a way around it."

"That's what tonight's lecture was about, I suppose. Tapping into your inner light to navigate the bumps and scrapes of life. Keeping the source of your spiritual food close, and the rest of the world at arm's length."

"Honestly, I wasn't listening to it, Joy. Keeping the world at arm's length — that's fine, I guess, but I think you've lumped Wynter into that category. She's the one you should be keeping close."

"Wynter isn't in the Light. She never truly was and never will be. Has she told you the things she did? She was quite obstinate. Quite wild."

"Lived up to her name, then," he joked, uninterested in hearing criticisms of Wynter. They'd stopped outside an espresso café and he held her arm again, this time to make her face him. "Tell me what they did to her when she was wild."

"What do you mean?"

"How was she punished for being *quite wild?*" He kept his tone conversational, while his stomach twisted into knots.

"All children need discipline."

"Tell me what they did."

"Nothing, Indio. Nothing out of the ordinary. All the children were a bit feral. When I was younger it wasn't like that. You want me to stay close to her, and of course I'll do that, as her sister, but she isn't spiritual food. Can you understand that? She played those beautiful songs, she had that beautiful voice, but she wouldn't open herself to the Light. We always feared there was something wrong with her. A dark heart, they call it."

Indio didn't know what to say. He sure as hell didn't like what *she* was saying. He managed to say, in Wynter's defense, "She was a child."

"There are no children in the Light, in a spiritual sense. The Light speaks to the soul, and all souls are ancient. She's cut off from the universe somehow. It doesn't speak to her. She walked the dark path many times and glimpsed the Light — as we all do, even if our hearts are closed. She glimpsed the Light and still she rejected it."

Indio pushed his hand into his hair and looked to the night sky, not knowing whether to laugh or cry. "What the *fuck* are you talking about?"

"I'm sorry, I'm using unfamiliar terminology." Joy recovered quickly from his outburst and pressed on. "I looked up the lecture schedule in Portland. There's a wonderful series starting in March that serves as a sort of primer for those interested in opening their hearts to the Light. You'll find it really helpful. I'll call ahead and you'll get a discount. You were always so creative, Indy. I used to call you Indy, remember?" She spoke so fast there was nowhere for him to interrupt. "You and me and Momma — we have that creative streak that makes us perfect vessels for the Light. The Light has used Miriam for a wonderful purpose abroad. And us being twins, that's a special bond. I sense the Light is going to use me, and I sense it will use you, too."

He shook his head to stop her. "Please, no more about that. I don't care. I never will. If that means I have a dark heart, too, I'm fine with it."

His words offended her. She blinked back sudden tears, tracking the movement of passers-by to cover for it. He tried to drum up some sympathy, knowing a good deal of his resentment toward her should actually be directed toward their mother.

They went into the cafe and she said she didn't drink coffee. She ordered a lactose-free chai-something that came in a glass tumbler.

"Have you spoken with Miriam yet?" he said.

"No." Her mouth twisted, her tongue pushing against her cheek like she was still trying not to cry. "If she can't forgive me, I don't know what I'll do."

"What does the Light say about forgiveness?"

The question seemed to give her hope. "Oh, it's necessary. It's absolutely necessary."

"You got nothing to worry about, then."

"It may take her a while to purge those unhealthy emotions. And I have work to do, as well. My new friends at the Seattle office have been so nice to me, giving me a place to stay and allowing me to attend lectures and healing sessions for free."

"Did it occur to you they're being nice because of who your mother is? Miriam's a hotshot guru now, right?"

She frowned at his cynicism. "They're helping me retune myself to the universe. I made a mistake. Next time, I'll listen more carefully and make the right choice."

"Getting Wynter out of there wasn't the right choice?"

"Miriam doesn't think so."

"Think for yourself, Joy." He couldn't help himself from pushing her, even though she clearly hated it.

"The healers are helping me find my way back to the Light, so I won't lose everything I've worked for. Maybe I'll never be accepted as a devotee at the ashram again, but I can at least try to make things right with Miriam by forging a path to atonement."

"Sounds like fun," he said dryly, picturing her in a hairshirt. "You did nothing wrong in getting Wynter out, and they don't want her back. What's the problem?"

"I went about it the wrong way. Miriam has a great deal of power among the leadership. To defy her wishes was... very foolish of me. I panicked. I wasn't thinking straight."

"What made you panic?"

"I already explained."

"Her dark heart? Maybe she was due for a bit of *atonement* herself?"

"Atonement doesn't cure a dark heart. It's intractable. Those souls don't belong in the Light. Bad things can happen."

She wouldn't meet his eye and he felt, unexpectedly, disgusted with her. They both had the same blood relationship to their younger sister — yet, whereas he'd felt an immediate and instinctive bond with Wynter, the sister who'd known her all her life seemed ready to discard her over some ridiculous religious belief.

Joy gave a quick shake of her head. "Let's not talk about this. It won't help with my spiritual journey. Wynter is where she needs to be."

"Not quite. She needs to be with you." Even as he said it, he was no longer sure it was true. "With family, anyway. If you don't take her in, Caleb may have to curtail or end his career to take custody of her."

"No... would he do that?"

"I don't think he's thought that far ahead." *Because he still has faith in you.* Hopeless faith. Not that it was Indio's job to persuade Joy to step up. "He'll do whatever it takes to get her out of foster care. He'll put a lot of pressure on you to file for custody."

"I really don't need any kind of pressure."

"Just telling it like it is."

"I see." After an awkward silence, she made a deliberate effort to change the subject. "Caleb showed us an old photo album. Do you remember that parking garage he had? I loved that thing. I used it as a riding school for my plastic ponies."

Indio decided to play along. "I remember those ponies. I stole a pink one from your room and redecorated it with a Sharpie. Made you cry." He forced a grin. "Sorry about that."

"Caleb helped me color the entire thing black, and we dipped her mane and tail in glitter and renamed her Beauty."

Yay, Caleb. Fixing things, even back then.

"Mom threw my ukulele in the trash as punishment."

"Oh! Now *I'm* sorry."

"It all worked out fine. I fished it out, hid it under the bed and played it when she was away. I even smuggled it to Harry's that summer she took us to Anaconda. A couple years later, he took pity and bought me a real guitar." Indio felt a flicker of happiness. "Wow. Haven't thought about any of that in years."

"Momma let me name her. Did she tell you that?"

"Wynter?"

"I didn't get Christmas that year she was born, you see. I missed

Christmas. I missed the snow and the snowmen we used to build, and that amazing igloo. The snowball fights and the frost patterns on the window panes. It was fifty, sixty degrees all through the winter in Arizona, and not even a frost in the mornings. I missed that untouched pure white blanket the morning after a heavy snowfall. Those freezing mornings when the four of us would pile into Momma's bed and play footsie under the blankets with our ice-block toes."

"We used to cut paper snowflakes from old magazines."

She smiled at the memory. "Yours were always the best. Better than Momma's. I couldn't comprehend how a six-year-old could do *anything* better than a grown-up. At the ashram, I cut out paper snowflakes for Wynter's crib. Not as nice as yours were, but I did try. Miriam put a stop to it. So I'd sneak out and pin them to the chain-link fence, in the corner of the compound where no one went. But you could see them from the road. At least, I hoped you'd see them."

"You hoped *we'd* see them?"

"I thought Harry might drive past with you boys in the back, on your way somewhere. The Grand Canyon, maybe. My sense of geography wasn't the best. I thought you'd see the snowflakes and know I was there, and..."

"And rescue you?"

"Just a silly childish fantasy. Once I understood the Light, I realized the outside world was in darkness."

Indio folded a cheap white napkin. Half, half, thirds. "Do you still think that?"

She gave him a tolerant smile and didn't answer. As Indio began to tear pieces out, she avoided watching his fingers. He realized she regretted talking about their childhoods — maybe that was a Light thing. Maybe her childhood wasn't spiritual food. He had plenty of awful, disappointing childhood memories, but maybe he shouldn't have discarded the good ones along with the bad.

"Can I ask you about that summer?" he ventured. "When Momma left with you for Arizona, what did she tell you? Did you know you weren't coming back?"

"I don't think *she* knew, to be honest. We went there with one small suitcase. I left all my toys behind. We arrived at the ashram and Miriam loved it — the intensity of it, the fellowship. She threw herself into it. And we just... never left."

"But for a while, you wanted to leave."

"No, I shouldn't have said that. I was happy to be spending so much time with her. She always found time for me."

Her words dragged on Indio's heart and his chest tightened. It was as incomprehensible to him now as it had been then — why their mother would choose one child to take with her and abandon the others.

"Did you miss us?"

"Oh, Indio, I don't know."

"Caleb tells me we were close. I gotta admit I don't have a lot of memories of us — of you and me."

"Well, we were very young."

Yet he had plenty of memories of his brothers from that time, and even earlier.

"There's no point agonizing over this. Do you understand?" Joy touched his hand as he unfolded the snowflake, gently teasing apart each of the six points. "What happened was for the best. Miriam knew what she was doing."

"You truly believe that?"

"Of course. It's clear to me she chose the right path because her life has been filled with blessings. For myself, I haven't figured out my path yet. I've made missteps. I've made poor decisions — the universe has made that quite clear. But I'll get there in the end."

She allowed him to smooth out the paper snowflake, with its soft ragged edges, on the dark wood table in front of her. She traced her finger over it.

When they left the cafe, she left the snowflake behind.

Emoji Hell

Wynter clicked *Send* and waited.

Her inbox was filled with eight pages of *Address not found* bounced emails. And now, one more. Seconds later, an email from Jesse arrived with links to his new YouTube video and articles about scientific methodology, strawberries, and Kepler 20f — a recently discovered Earth-sized planet in the constellation Lyra with a surface temperature of...

Wynter closed the article with a lump in her throat. Why was a planet too hot to live on and too far away to reach of any interest to anyone? Yet if Jesse were here she'd have listened to him talk about it just for the pleasure of basking in his enthusiasm.

Her phone rang. Seeing the name on the screen, she answered in a hurry.

"Indio!"

"I'm sorry about Saturday. Rosa wouldn't let me talk to you on Sunday." He sounded subdued, weary. "I called too late."

"She told me."

"I understand if you're mad at me."

"I'm not. I just wanted a text message or... something." *So I know you haven't forgotten about me already.*

"I didn't know what to say. I won't fail you again, I promise."

"Okay."

"Hey, I saw Joy in Seattle last night."

"Was she okay? On Saturday she left abruptly and Caleb was..."

"He was what?"

"I don't know how to explain it. He was... nothing. He didn't show it, but he was really upset. I could tell. I heard him punching that big red bag in the garage, late at night."

"Don't read anything into it. The big red bag can take it."

Wynter couldn't help but read something into it. She'd gone out there and watched him, from the shadows, watched the sweat flying off his face, the way the bag swung in a heavy arc, the way he clung to it, exhausted, to catch his breath before starting up again. He'd seen her, at last, his expression melting to concern upon registering her shock. *Back to bed,* he'd said. *Early start tomorrow.* He'd hardly sounded like himself.

"Joy's like the opposite of you, baby," Indio was saying. "Maybe he thought she'd be the same, wanting to be out in the world, to be part of the family. We all hoped that."

"Are you giving up on her?"

"There's only so much any of us can do. We had a pretty nice chat, for the most part. She told me about the photo album and it brought back good memories."

"Did she talk about me?"

Indio hesitated. "A little bit. She has an odd way of looking at things, but I know she wants the best for you. So, what are you up to?"

"Um, homework." She didn't want to admit to sending two hundred emails to Xay, each with a slightly different number or letter combination. "I have to write a poem."

"Awesome. Send it to me. I'll turn it into a song."

"It has to be a poem about flowers, in the style of Wordsworth."

"Uh-huh." He sounded a good deal less enthusiastic about it now.

Rosa called from the hallway. "Two minutes, Wynter. Take your phone downstairs to charge."

Wynter sighed. "I have to go." She kept talking as she went downstairs. "Will you tell me why you didn't come on Saturday?"

"I'm sorry. Really sorry."

"You don't have to keep saying that. Just tell me why."

"I did something dumb. Nothing to do with you. I wanted to be there."

"Jesse said you partied too hard."

"Uh-huh."

"Does that mean you took drugs and couldn't get up the next morning?"

He was silent for too long.

"Indio?"

"Something like that. It was stupid and kind of accidental."

Rosa was in the shadows of the kitchen, filling the kettle at the sink. She made a little hand motion to tell Wynter to hang up.

"Send me some more photos, okay?" Wynter said. She wanted to ask him about the sketchbook Rosa had censored, but not with Rosa standing there. In any case, maybe Rosa was right about the sketches. She was allowed to keep six of them and she didn't want to fight with Rosa over the rest.

She hung up and plugged the phone into the charger.

"What photos does he send you?" Rosa asked.

"Just stuff from his life."

"By the sound of it, his life is not suitable for a fourteen-year-old girl to be involved in."

"I'm not involved. He sends me photos from his gigs and selfies with his friends."

"Do you send him photos?"

"Sometimes."

"Does he *ask* you to?"

"I guess so. Sometimes."

"Does he ask for selfies of you?"

"Not specifically. I don't know. I don't think so."

"You need to tell me if he asks for anything inappropriate."

Wynter felt the conversation turning into one of Rosa's weird Q&A sessions. Rosa had figured out she couldn't extract information by interrogation, so she'd work up to it. An innocent question about Wynter's classmates turned into a discussion about friends in general, then about boys, then about what boys liked to do with girls. Wynter had read most of the website Jesse gave her and learned more about contraception and sexual positions and the meaning of various slang words than she'd surely ever need to know. She read the pages on sexual abuse. No matter how often she told Rosa nobody had hurt her that way, Rosa found a new angle of attack.

The idea that Indio could be used as another angle of attack infuriated Wynter.

"He's done nothing wrong. Stop asking about him."

"Nothing wrong? He just confirmed he was so high on drugs he wasn't able to go to Seattle to see you." Rosa backed down, calming herself. "This isn't your fault, Wynter. I know it's difficult for you. I know you wanted to see him. I'm going to have to ask to look through your phone."

"What? Why?"

"As your foster parent, I have to be very careful about the people you're associating with. Especially the adults in your life. You understand that, don't you? Is there anything you want to tell me before I look? Anything that anyone has told you to keep secret?"

"I don't know what you're talking about. Take a look. I don't care."

Wynter went upstairs, flushed with anger she dared not express. Caleb would say her phone was a *privacy issue*, she was sure about that.

✿

"Car, house, clock, thumbs up," Stacey read from Wynter's screen — an incomprehensible message from Jesse that consisted of nothing but two dozen emojis. They were puzzling it out together before the first bell.

Wynter hadn't yet told Jesse that Rosa had looked through her phone and returned it the next morning, without comment. Several of his bookmarks were gone. She wanted to ask him about it, but what if Rosa was right? What if those sites were inappropriate?

"And then a calendar and a sun," Stacey went on. "I guess it means he's driving up to visit, at midday on Sunday. Then a bunch of music notes and three guitars. You're going to a concert?"

"I think that means we're gonna jam."

"The magnifying glass and six kinds of books and papers mean he's going to help with your homework. That's nice of him. Then he's asking if you want to play video games or watch movies, something like that."

"How do you know?"

"See? Gaming console, TV, alien monster, question mark. And then about ten party poppers — those speak for themselves."

Wynter clamped her lips together to stop herself asking what a party popper was. Rosa wouldn't want Jesse throwing a party at her house, if that was his intention.

"The surgeon's mask and the knife... Not sure what that means," Stacey mused. "Is someone having surgery?"

"No."

"Okay, it gets weird at the end. A shrug and a rainbow, a bunny rabbit and a cookie and a cherry blossom... I don't know about those. And some X's and O's. He seems sweet, other than the knife. Is this the rockstar brother? Are you ever gonna show me a picture? Can I come to your house on Sunday?"

"My aunt says I can't have friends over until I clean my room." Wynter had overheard someone giving a similar excuse in the cafeteria a few days ago.

"Clean your room on Saturday."

"I have horse riding and a piano lesson on Saturday. Then I have to take my cat to the vet, and after that—"

"You have a cat? Me too! What's its name?"

"Her name is Strat. Anyway, after that, in the evening, my aunt's taking me to the ballet." Wynter surprised herself with how easily the lies rolled off her tongue.

"I didn't know you liked ballet."

"I hate ballet. It's her birthday, so I suppose I have to go. It's so boring. *She's* so boring." Wynter had observed you were supposed to speak badly of your parents as often as possible. Parents were boring, unreasonable, and never stopped nagging.

"I *love* the ballet! I've been four times."

You were supposed to like the things your friends liked. Wynter backtracked. "I guess ballet's okay. I like dancing..."

Stacey's friend Keira was marching over with a determined look that startled Wynter — not so much the look, but the fact it was on Keira's face. Keira was notoriously sulky and disinterested in everything.

"My mom's friend Lavinia goes to your aunt's church," Keira told Wynter in an accusatory tone. "Or should I say, your *foster mother's* church. You never lived in Montana. You grew up with hippies in Arizona. You never even met your real family until a few weeks ago."

Stacey's jaw dropped.

"That's... not true," Wynter said. The last part certainly wasn't true. Joy was part of her real family. So was Miriam.

"Are you saying I'm lying?" Keira said.

"Maybe Lavinia is lying."

"*Maybe?*" Keira gave a derisory laugh. "Did you grow up in Montana, or didn't you?"

"I did."

"Where in Montana?"

"The west."

"Which town?"

Wynter hesitated, trying to recall the name of the town where Caleb was born. Some kind of snake...

"Name one city or town in west Montana," Keira challenged her. "*Anywhere* in Montana."

"Go on, name one," Stacey said. She looked shocked, and very disappointed.

Wynter closed her locker and headed to class.

"Do you even have a cat?" Stacey screamed after her.

By lunch, the word was out. Wynter escaped the stares and jeers by hiding between the bookcases in the library. She crouched on the floor and typed hundreds of random emojis to Jesse to punish him for his earlier message and for not being available to talk during the day. It gave her no satisfaction to imagine him tying his brain in knots figuring them out.

For the rest of the day Stacey refused to sit by her in their shared classes, and whoever did sit by her, because they didn't know better, was quickly informed she was a liar. It was definitely the worst day of her life on the outside.

During last period, the school counselor fetched her from class and talked to her for half an hour. He'd been told by a teacher, who'd been told by some of the kids, that she was being teased and ostracized. He wanted to know why. She told him why, because she was done with the lies. She couldn't bear to imagine Caleb's face when he discovered what she'd done.

Maybe Caleb didn't have to find out. She could just... *not* tell him. Or Jesse. She needed them to like her, but she no longer cared whether or not the kids at school liked her. She had nothing in common with them. She didn't understand three-quarters of anything they said, and before she came up with her interesting past they'd laughed at most of what she said.

On the bus ride home, she found Jesse had responded to her nonsense messages with a single text:

> XOXO was all you needed to send

So, he hadn't tied his brain in knots after all. She sent him hugs and kisses.

When Rosa came home, she already knew what had happened. Wynter had hoped to at least get through the weekend without having to admit anything, but the counselor had called Rosa that afternoon. Rosa was surprisingly sympathetic. Wynter knew she deserved to be punished. Instead, Rosa made her sit on the couch and asked questions that all started with *Why?*

"Why did you feel the need to make up stories about your past? You have nothing to be ashamed of. Why did you tell them Caleb was married? Why did you make Joy a successful businesswoman? Why did you say your parents were dead?"

Wasn't it obvious why she'd said those things? Rosa wanted those questions answered so she could use the answers as springboards to probe deeper, ever deeper. And Wynter didn't want to go deeper. Rosa could barely hide her frustration.

After a while, Rosa talked herself into deciding it was a minor incident and not worth fussing over. She was more concerned with Wynter regaining the friendships she'd lost.

"Are you gonna tell Caleb?" Wynter said.

"There's no need to involve him. Now it's all out in the open, we've dealt with it, and it's over. We can keep it a secret from Caleb."

Wynter didn't like that word — *secret* — when it came to Caleb. *No secrets or lies in this house*, he'd told her. And now Rosa was asking her to keep a secret from him, which could also involve telling lies if he asked her about school.

She lay awake half the night weighing the humiliation of disappointing him against the shame of disobeying him.

A Philosophical Discussion

Jesse texted Wynter for the third time in two hours with an ever more precise arrival time. Rosa had invited him and Caleb to Sunday lunch, asking them to arrive at noon because that's when she got home from church. Jesse had persuaded Caleb to leave an hour early "in case of traffic", and so at eleven o'clock they were on Rosa's porch ringing the bell.

Wynter opened the door a second later, as if she'd been waiting on the other side. She threw herself at Jesse, catching him by surprise, and accepted a kiss on the top of her head from Caleb.

"Did you bring your guitars? Where are they? We have one hour alone! We have to play."

They fetched two guitars from the back of the Caprice and went upstairs to her room. Jesse and Wynter sat cross-legged on the floor, and Caleb sat on the little vanity stool, and they jammed for a while. Jesse couldn't compete with either of them for chops but he played well enough to have some fun. Mostly he sang, which he didn't get much chance to do behind the drum kit.

"This room is pretty neat," Jesse said during a pause in playing. "Not too girly."

"Is girly bad?" Wynter asked.

"For a teenager, yeah. I mean, *I* think so. At least it's not pink and purple."

"I like Indio's room better."

"That's nuts. This room is great. This house is a mansion. It's *huge*. She has Zulu masks in the dining room, and a didgeridoo. Did you see that, Caleb? I'm dying to play it. You have to breathe in through your nose while you blow out with your mouth. It's called circular breathing."

"I like your house better," Wynter said.

Jesse grunted at her contrariness, though she was telling the truth, at least from her perspective.

"She keeps asking me if the boys and the men at the ashram touched me," she said, out of the blue. "Why does she keep asking me?"

Caleb flicked Jesse a look before telling her, "She wants to be sure you weren't hurt. When children are hurt that way, it can cause other problems as they grow up."

"It's because she deals with sexual abuse cases," Jesse said. "She sees it everywhere. She even thinks we'd hurt you."

"She doesn't think that," Caleb said.

"Then why won't they let her stay with us more than one night a month?"

"How's school going?" Caleb asked Wynter, frowning at Jesse's negativity.

Wynter drew breath to speak but said nothing. Jesse sensed his brother's radar ping.

"I was gonna say everything's fine," Wynter said at last. "But it's not."

"What happened?"

"Rosa said not to tell you. I don't want to keep secrets from you." She fiddled with her guitar strings, very uncomfortable.

"I'm not a fan of secrets, either," Caleb said carefully. "You know you can tell me anything."

Before she could speak, they heard the front door open and Rosa called out her name. They sat in silence, listening to Rosa checking the front rooms and then mount the stairs. She would've seen the car, of course, and was on the hunt to find them.

"Ah, there you are." Rosa paused in the doorway and surveyed the scene. "You brought guitars. What a good idea. Perhaps next time you could use one of the rooms downstairs?"

"It's more comfortable here," Wynter said, which was true. From what Jesse had seen of the other rooms, they were all rather formal.

"Still, it's not appropriate to have people in your bedroom, Wynter."

Jesse felt a flash of anger. Caleb warned him with a look not to speak his mind.

"They're not *people*." Wynter already sounded like she wasn't going to argue the point.

Rosa gave a bright smile. "Let's eat lunch, shall we? I left a casserole on all morning."

The food was incredible — some sort of pork that melted in the mouth, with bits of bacon and apple in it. Jesse tried to mind his manners while gobbling down as much as the other three put together. He scooped out a fourth helping onto his plate.

Caleb said, "Upstairs just now, Wynter was about to tell me something about school."

Rosa put down her fork and looked at Wynter. "Oh? If it's what I think, there's no need. You're not in any trouble — we already talked about this, dear."

Jesse ground his teeth at the endearment.

Wynter went ahead anyway. "I made up some stories about my past. I didn't want to tell my friends about the Light, so I said the five of us were orphans who grew up together in Montana with horses. I said you were married with a baby, and that Indio and Jesse were rockstars." Her words tumbled out as she looked directly at Caleb, transfixed by his gaze — as if that gaze compelled the truth from her. "I said Rosa was my aunt and I only lived here during the semester to attend that school. I didn't want them to know I'm in foster care, that I don't even have a birth certificate. But they found out on Friday it was all lies."

Jesse felt instantly defensive on her behalf. His life had been a dream compared to hers. In her shoes, he'd have done the same thing — wiped the cult and Miriam and all those bad memories, whatever they were, from existence.

Caleb leaned his elbows on the table, his fingers steepled against his lips. Had Jesse told whoppers like that, Caleb would've chewed him out for sure. But this was Wynter, and from day one he'd been gentler with her.

"You don't have to tell the kids at school anything you don't want them to know," Caleb said. "That's your life, your past, and you can keep it private."

"But I didn't know what to say. They kept asking questions."

"We can figure that out together. Something that's not a lie, but maintains your privacy. Okay?"

She nodded gratefully.

Caleb reached across the table and slapped his hand down on Jesse's wrist because he'd been unwittingly tapping his knife handle on the table as he contemplated her situation. Beside him, Wynter ducked for cover, an instinctive reaction to Caleb's sudden movement. Her hands went up as her butt slid back in the seat.

"It's okay," Caleb told her, realizing what had happened. "Jesse, you're being annoying."

Wynter inched forward again and moved food around on her plate with her fork.

"How did the kids find out the truth?" Jesse asked.

Wynter's gaze shifted to Rosa. Jesse met Caleb's eye and saw his brother figure it out the same moment he did.

"Did *you* talk about her?" Jesse told Rosa. "You can't go telling people about Wynter's private stuff."

"It wasn't at all like that." Rosa's tone suggested that having to explain anything to Jesse was beneath her. "I'm friendly with someone associated with the school, who said a few things that made me realize she had incorrect information. So, I corrected her information and I suppose it got back to Wynter's classmates."

"You admit it, then. You violated Wynter's privacy. You told her to keep a secret because of *your* guilty conscience."

"Nonsense. In any case, it's more important to establish *why* Wynter felt the need to make up the stories. We can learn a lot about a person's issues from the stories they choose to tell, or not tell."

"She had a shitty childhood and she doesn't want people to know," Jesse said. Caleb glared at him for the cuss word. Jesse wasn't done. "She doesn't want to talk to them *or you* about it."

Rosa said, very calmly, "If you would kindly respect my professional expertise in this matter? Wynter needs to talk these things through with someone who can help. This is a textbook example of suppressing the—"

"She's not your fucking research project!"

"Jesse!"

Caleb's voice cut between them. Wynter hunched her shoulders and stared at her plate. Caleb put his hand over hers on the table, but he was looking at Jesse, waiting.

Jesse mumbled the required apology. Caleb jerked his thumb at the doorway.

"Excuse me," Jesse said, very politely. He took care not to clatter his fork against the plate as he put it down. He pushed back his chair. "I liked the part about being a rockstar."

He got a tiny smile out of his sister.

There was no door to slam on his way out — not that he would have because Caleb had a house rule about that, too, and it probably applied to any house. There was just a ridiculously tall archway with carved columns. He hunkered down against the wall, out of view. He'd seen apple pie on the kitchen counter and wondered if he'd be getting any. Oh well. Small price to pay for the privilege of putting Dr Rosamund Meyers in her place.

"Well," he heard Rosa say, "what a shame to spoil our nice lunch like that."

Another chair scraped back. "Excuse me," Wynter murmured.

She came out of the room, saw Jesse on the floor and sat with him, her shoulder pressed against his. He squeezed her hand.

"Don't ask her again to keep secrets from me," Caleb said from the dining room.

"We simply didn't want to bother you with it," Rosa replied coolly.

"We? You mean you. Wynter volunteered to tell me. You should know, better than anyone, that teaching kids the habit of keeping secrets doesn't end well."

"She was embarrassed when a few tall tales came out. You can hardly draw a parallel between keeping that from you, and someone telling a child to keep abuse secret."

"I don't care. No secrets. I won't compromise on that."

"I hardly think you have the authority to dictate any terms."

"Would you like to argue that secrets are a good thing?"

"Of course not. But—"

"Then don't make an argument out of nothing."

Jesse had to smile at that. He'd given up having rhetorical or philosophical arguments with Caleb a long time ago, much as he enjoyed those discussions with his friends. If you wanted to engage in an argument with Caleb, you'd better start out on solid ground.

Wynter stood, tugging at Jesse's hand, and they went out the back. The yard was tiny, entirely paved over in different shades of gray, with an array of cast figurines and a bird bath. Other than a couple of hanging plants, there was nothing green. No doubt it was supposed to look modern and serene. To Jesse, it looked like a miniature prison exercise yard.

They sat on a wooden bench under the roof overhang, watching rain drip on the gray stone.

"What am I gonna do?" Wynter said. "I don't ever want to go back to that school. They all think I'm crazy."

"It'll blow over."

She shrugged. "I don't care. I don't need friends."

"Friends are important, Wyn."

"I know they're important to you. You have eight hundred and twelve friends on Facebook. Should I go on Facebook?"

"No, that's not gonna help — you have to start with real-life friends for that. Maybe you could join a discussion board and make some online friends."

"What do they discuss?"

"There's a million different ones. Find one that sounds interesting. Don't give out identifying info — we went through that, right?" He sighed. "Why didn't you tell me about this when it happened? You can tell me anything, and ask me anything."

"I didn't want you to know. Or... I didn't want Caleb to know."

"Well, now he knows and it wasn't so bad, was it?"

She gave a rueful smile. "Not for me, but he's mad at Rosa."

"Well, he's never gonna be mad at you."

"How do you know that?"

"I just know. He's different with you — compared to how he was with me and especially with Indio. You saw what he did because I cussed at Madame Headshrink. He'd never throw you out of the room or raise his voice. I bet he'd never punish you at all. When we were kids, if we did something wrong it was *Drop for twenty!*"

Wynter gasped and pressed both hands over her mouth, cowering against the bench. Jesse remembered the way Joy had done that, in the car after he'd pretty much demanded she come home with him. And the way Wynter had flinched earlier. She stared at him, wide-eyed.

"What? What's the matter?"

"Twenty what?" she mumbled from behind her hands.

Jesse suddenly realized how she'd misinterpreted him. "Push-ups, Wyn. Twenty push-ups."

"Oh." Her hands lowered. She was very pale and breathing fast from an adrenaline surge.

Jesse slid across the bench and put his arm around her. "He never hit us. Never."

She nodded, head bowed, hands twisting in her lap. "I thought for a second you meant... something like *six of the best*, when they... Do you know what that means?"

"That British school thing with a cane? Did you ever get six of the best?"

"I panicked for a second, thinking he... I know he wouldn't do that. I *know* he wouldn't. But just for a second..."

"Wyn, please, answer my question." But Jesse knew she wouldn't. The moment had passed and he was left not knowing how angry to feel.

She drew a deep breath and exhaled slowly, carefully. "Why push-ups?"

"It's just a harmless punishment." Jesse picked up a handful of gravel under his feet and threw the pieces one by one at the back fence, aiming at a knot in the wood. "It's no fun but it's good for you, makes you stop whatever dumb thing you're doing that got you in trouble. Actually, it *was* fun, sometimes — if we both had to do it, we'd race to see who could get it done fastest. Indio usually won cuz he'd only dip halfway when Caleb wasn't looking."

"Isn't that cheating?"

"Yes. And he didn't have to cheat — he'd have beaten me anyway. He's four years stronger than me. The only thing I can beat Indio at is an argument."

"Not even karate?"

"He's probably the better fighter. He hasn't committed to the testing. No, I would not fight Indio. Wanna learn a game?"

Jesse crossed the yard in the rain and squatted at the fence to select a few flat pebbles from around the base of Rosa's rockery.

"Is it tic-tac-toe?"

"That's lame." Jesse laid out the pebbles on a paver in front of the bench, in two rows of six. "This is an ancient game called mancala. These stones are supposed to be little pits, so we'll have to pretend. We need four chips of gravel on each one."

She sat on the ground opposite him and helped set up the board. He went through the rules and they played a couple of practice rounds.

"Let's play for real," Jesse said. "You're picking it up fast."

"You explain things well. I'm gonna lose, aren't I?"

"Most likely."

"Don't let me win just to be nice."

"I won't. Told you, I've never beaten Caleb at chess — he didn't let me win, just to be nice, even when I was four years old."

She giggled. "I'm imagining that and it's very cute — four-year-old Jesse and ten-year-old Caleb playing chess. What are Indio and Joy doing in that picture?"

"If I'm four, then Joy's gone."

"Oh. I forgot."

"Eight-year-old Indio is defacing Caleb's homework with cartoons."

"I wish Joy was in that picture, growing up with all of you, and with two parents."

"Our lives would all be a lot different."

"There would be no me at all."

"True." He grinned at her. "Don't worry, I wouldn't know there was supposed to be, so I wouldn't be cut up about it."

She threw a chip of gravel at him. "That's mean. I'd be cut up if there was no you."

"But you don't exist in this scenario. *I think, therefore I am.* Conversely, if you *are not*, there is no *you* to be thinking about being cut up about anything."

"Are we having a philosophical discussion?"

"Yes. Is it fun?"

"It's more fun than the previous subject." Wynter picked up the chips for her turn. "Did your dad hit you?"

"I have to answer that, when you wouldn't answer my question?"

"You don't *have* to."

Jesse did anyway, although he gave her the sanitized version. "He would lash out in frustration, push us around. There were scuffles and black eyes. After Caleb had a growth spurt at thirteen years old and pushed back, things got better. Harry was mostly just lazy and uninvolved. He's the opposite of Caleb, the anti-Caleb — no guidance, random with the discipline, almost never right. Caleb's always right, as you know. It was a relief to have someone you could count on."

"How come Indio doesn't see it that way?"

"Indio doesn't like being told what to do."

"Do you?"

"Caleb's very conventional and a bit unimaginative, but we don't get in each other's way. He deals in facts, which I respect. In some other family, Indio would've been fine. In this family, somehow it brings out his worst. He resents Caleb too much to appreciate him. He does beat himself up about it. Harry never beat himself up about anything, even a seven-day bender."

"What's a bender?"

"A drinking spree."

"Is Indio gonna turn out like Harry in the end?"

"No, because he has us to keep him in line."

"How do we do that?"

"We don't have to *do* anything. Just be there for him."

"But I'm not there."

"You talk to him, right?"

"Not really. He called to apologize about the weekend. I've called him a couple times. I always felt like I was interrupting. And I don't know what to say, anyway. I've only spent two days with him."

"I've spent about six days with you — feel like I've known you forever."

She smiled at that.

"Does he text you?" Jesse said.

"Yes. Pictures, mostly. Maybe he doesn't know what to say, either. Yesterday he sent me a photo of his gig from the night before. Before that, he sent a comic strip he drew."

"For a class project?"

"No, just for fun."

"Ah, was it Dimiti Dime, by any chance?"

"Yes! A talking dime making funny comments about his adventures in people's pockets and in cash registers and vending machines."

"He invented that character when he was ten. Dimiti Dime has traveled all over the country. He once spent a decade accidentally stuck with gum to the bottom of a church offering box in New Orleans, listening to all the coins inside the box boast about how they were gonna be spent on charitable works. He would say silly things from underneath the box, and his voice echoed around inside the box so the other coins thought it was the voice of God. Anyway, that's great, that he sends you stuff. He sends me stuff like that, too." Jesse reconsidered, given the last thing Indio sent him was a link to a weird '80s porn flick dubbed from French into hilariously posh British English. "Well, not quite like that. Anyway, it means he's thinking of us, an improvement over when he was in Ohio. You just made an illegal move."

Wynter picked up the gravel and redid her move. "I wish we were at home right now, playing this silly game, and I'd ask you questions and you'd give me your long-winded answers — my only source of accurate information. You'd help me with my homework and we'd get takeout. We'd play music with Caleb and Indio in the jamroom for six hours every night. No, not takeout — I wish I was a brilliant cook!"

"I wish I was a famous TV star. We can't have everything we want."

"That's really what you want?"

"Specifically, I want to be a cool science educator. I want to tell people about science and space and robots. I also want to be that rockstar in your fabricated backstory, so at some point I'll have to choose. You gonna explain to me these emojis?" He showed her the message she'd sent on Friday.

"I was responding to *your* emojis. They made no sense."

He scrolled up to the message he'd sent her. "What's not making sense? It's all perfectly clear."

"The surgeon and the knife?"

"That's a doctor, meaning Rosa. They don't have a headshrink emoji. The shrug is me asking if you want me to murder her with the knife while I'm here."

"That's not respectful and it wouldn't solve any of my problems."

"I like that, Wyn. I like that you're so rational. Together we'll think of a more creative solution for dealing with Rosa."

"What about the rabbit and things at the end?"

"That's me sending you nice thoughts. Rainbows and stuff."

"What's nice about rabbits? We ate rabbits at the ashram and they don't taste good."

He pulled a face. "It's a cute fluffy bunny. No one eats *bunnies*. That's insane."

"But murdering my foster mother isn't insane?"

The sliding door opened and Rosa peered out. Jesse could only hope she hadn't heard the last comment.

"It's very cold out here. Come inside, please, Wynter." Rosa stepped out to see what they were doing. "I do hope you'll put those river stones back exactly as you found them."

Jesse and Wynter exchanged a look, two scolded children who didn't give a fuck. They brushed the gravel from the pavers and scooped up the pebbles.

"Don't go out in the rain, dear," Rosa said. "I'm sure Jesse can manage."

Jesse took the stones from Wynter and braved the light drizzle to return them. As Rosa and Wynter went inside, he replaced the stones and rearranged a resin fairy and a small concrete garden gnome into the missionary position.

Shiver

Wynter put her phone on speaker and listened patiently to Jesse's informative lecture on *Animal Farm* and the Russian Revolution.

"I just needed to know what the sheep and the crow mean," she said when she could get a word in.

"You need the background to understand the novel in context," Jesse insisted.

"Are you sure about that? Because for the last ten minutes you've been mostly talking about American politics."

"Sorry, the topic did morph a bit. I voted for the first time last year and I'm still bummed that my best friend didn't bother."

"What difference does one vote make?"

"*What difference...?*" His voice rose in horror. "Okay, I'll save that rant for another time. Do you have what you need?"

"Yes, thank you. I was taking notes whenever you said something relevant."

"Awesome. We'll watch the movie next time you're here, the original 'fifties one."

"Would Rosa approve of the movie?"

"What's she got to do with it?"

"She didn't approve of that website on sex. I didn't tell you this on Sunday because your visit was already going off the rails, but she took my phone to look through it and deleted that bookmark and a few others."

"Why did she want to look through your phone?"

"Something about Indio's text messages. Is she allowed to do that?"

"No. It's an invasion of privacy." After a pause, he added, "What's wrong with Indio's messages? Didn't we already talk about this?"

"She asked if I sent selfies to him. Why does she care?"

"Nothing wrong with selfies, but that's not what she meant."

"Well, that's what she said — *selfies.*"

"She assumes Indio's a pervert because he's not a saint like Caleb. Well, she doesn't like Caleb either, but for different reasons. Shit, I wonder what she thinks about me?"

"She asked me if I moved her garden statues. I didn't, so now she knows you did."

"Did she tell you *how* I moved them?"

"No."

"Hmm. Do you wanna know?"

"I think you probably made them have sex."

"I'm an open book to you."

"So now she thinks you're a pervert, too."

"Jeez, it's just sex. That fairy was already half naked and busting out of her bodice, giving the gnome come-hither looks... I'll stop there, cuz I'm sure I'm being inappropriate. I'll talk you through how to lock your phone with a password, and then I have to go. I've got a gig tonight."

His excitement made her wistful. "I wish I could come see you play. What's the band?"

"We're called the Slip Sliders. And it's a bar, so you can't come. I'll get a buddy to video it for YouTube. Don't talk to Indio about jazz, by the way. He'll give you wrong information. I'm your man for fusion jazz, rap, EDM, classic pop. Caleb for old timey blues and for free jazz, which normal people gotta be stoned to enjoy. Indio for classic rock and blues, and indie rock, and pretty much anything from the 'eighties."

"Hang on. I have to write it down."

"There's some overlap in our expertise, obviously."

"What's EDM?"

"That's dance music. I'm gonna teach you to dance."

"Caleb already did."

"In a manner of speaking. We'll go clubbing when you're a bit older."

"Will you teach me to hit a bong?"

After a brief hesitation, he said, "D'you know what that means?"

"Something to do with drugs. I know it's supposed to be fun but I don't want to get high if it's scary."

"No reason it should be scary. We'll talk about this again when you're a *lot* older. It's now legal in Washington, no thanks to my buddy who failed to vote in the referendum. Well, not quite legal until we're twenty-one but even Caleb would rather you had a blunt between your fingers than a tequila shot. *Do not* tell Rosa or your social worker I said any of that."

After Jesse hung up, Wynter still had social studies and science homework to complete. She looked up a few things online but there was so much information it was impossible to filter. She needed Jesse's help just to figure out how to get the internet's help. After an hour she was ready to give up.

Help me with my homework! she typed into her browser in frustration.

She scrolled down the page of hits and clicked a link at random. She found herself on a discussion board for kids with homework questions. Perfect. Jesse would certainly approve, because he'd told her to find online friends with common interests. She signed up.

She spent the rest of the evening looking up questions on the eighth-grade forum, posting her own, and sifting through the answers that other users produced for her. After a while she found herself on the general discussion forum, which was even more interesting. Kids posted about their lives, their families and friends, their hobbies and favorite TV shows, their problems on everything from pocket money to pregnancy. She found sad tales of foster kids and added her own woes, careful to follow Jesse's guidelines about not giving out identifying information. She found music lovers and would-be philosophers, and kids with awful parents and bullying siblings and cute pets.

It was so much easier to chat when she could think about her written answers and choose who to respond to and who to ignore.

In the morning, when she logged on to see if anyone had responded to her post about behavior contracts, a tiny green flag was flashing at the top of her screen. She'd received a private message.

✿

Wynter's stomach grumbled for lunch. She'd been studying in her room all morning — it was Monday, a week since her brothers' disastrous visit, and today was a student-free day so she was catching up on her English reading. Later, Tina was coming to Richland to check up on how her placement with Rosa was going. And after that, Caleb and Joy were visiting to talk about Joy's custody plans.

Rosa had left sandwiches in the refrigerator before heading to the office. Wynter didn't know what she was going to tell Tina about the placement but if she needed to come up with something positive she'd mention the food, which was always good and plentiful.

Joy called as she was heading downstairs. Joy never called. Stunned, Wynter answered her phone.

"Change of plans," Joy said. "I'm on the bus to Pasco. Let's spend the afternoon together!"

"I thought Caleb was driving you over for six o'clock?"

"I didn't like the idea of spending four hours in the car with him. He's been pressuring me ever since I arrived in Seattle and I just can't take it. Can you get to Pasco for two o'clock when my bus gets in?"

"I can take the local bus. But we have to be back here in time for the meeting with my caseworker."

"We'll find a nice place to have lunch and talk about things. I have a surprise for you – don't tell Caleb. He'll spoil everything."

"But he's going to the Light office at 2PM, to pick you up."

"I'll text him right now and tell him not to bother about me."

Wynter was uneasy keeping a secret from Caleb, but she hadn't spent time alone with Joy since they left the ashram. In fact, she hadn't spent much time alone with Joy *at* the ashram, either. Not for years.

She checked the bus schedule and walked down to the bus stop. On the ride, she took out her phone to continue writing back and forth with the friend she'd made on the homework forum. She and Felicity had been chatting for days and had lots in common, from favorite music to a love of ice cream. When Wynter lamented being in foster care, Felicity revealed she'd been a foster kid for a few years. She was back with her family in Oregon now. Wynter wasn't supposed to give out personal information so she wrote nothing about her own family, but Felicity's story gave her hope.

> Hi again, littlesistersong.
> Have you decided yet if
> you're going out with
> those girls at school?

Stacey, who was being warily friendly again, had organized a movie outing on Friday with friends and invited Wynter along. Stacey's mother or the school counselor were probably making her be nice.

> My foster mother is making
> me go. I'm sure it's good for
> me. I need to make friends
> at school but it's hard.

> I know what that's like when you're new and feel like you don't belong. So glad you and me can be friends!

> I did have two good friends in Arizona. I lost touch with them when one moved away and the other one ran away.

Talking about people from her past wasn't really giving anything away, was it?

> That's a shame. Did I tell you my uncle's a private detective? I wonder if he could find them for you.

> Does that cost a lot of money?

> I bet he'd help you cheap, maybe even for free. I'm his favorite niece. I'll ask him!

> But don't tell anyone, okay? He'll get into trouble with his boss if he works for free.

Wynter could hardly believe her luck. Could this be her chance to find Xay and Roman? She'd never told anyone about them — not even Joy. Especially not Joy.

> I won't tell anyone. I really want to find them.

> Awesome. Just give me their names and birthdates. My uncle has access to all kinds of databases.

> They were born in 1995. Their names are Xay and Roman. Xay's mother is Ember. I don't know their second names.

> They lived in Byron Bay in
> Australia until 2011, and then
> in Arizona for about a year.

> They might be in Nevada
> or they might've gone
> back to Australia.

> Unusual names —
> easier to trace! I'll call
> my uncle tonight.

Wynter fiddled with her phone. Did she really want to bring back those boys from the Light? Caleb was working hard to help Joy with custody. In a few weeks she might be living in Seattle in his house, or nearby, jamming in the basement, attending Jesse's old school and sitting with him every night with her homework. That was the future she wanted.

But there was no harm in seeing if Felicity's uncle could find Xay and Roman. They were probably back in Australia anyway. If he could track them down she'd decide then what to do about it.

Joy met Wynter off the bus. She had a smile on her face that made Wynter's heart leap. She couldn't remember the last time she'd seen Joy smile properly.

"We're going to the Franklin County Clerk," Joy said as they walked through town. "You'll never guess my exciting news."

"Is it something wonderful?" Wynter said dubiously. Joy's last *something wonderful* had been a lie.

"Wynter, you know why I had to say that. This time it's real." They were passing a spacious park. "Let's take a nice photo here."

She grabbed Wynter's hand and they walked a short way across a lawn dotted with trees. Joy took a selfie of the two of them and sent it to someone. She was acting nervous, although not scared like the night they left the ashram.

"We have some paperwork to deal with at the County Clerk's office," Joy said, watching her phone, "and then we'll have something to eat."

"What paperwork?"

Joy patted her tote and said nothing. Her phone rang. She held it out, triumphantly, glowing with excitement. The screen said *Miriam.*

Joy put the phone to her ear. "Momma! Is that you?"

Wynter's skin prickled as a shiver went through her. She hadn't spoken to her mother since she was ten years old, had never received a letter or even a personal message. The trees spun around her as she adjusted her world, a world where Momma... cared again?

She focused on what Joy was saying — something about filling out forms and getting cash. Joy put the phone on speaker and tilted it toward Wynter.

"She wants to talk to you, Wynter. Say something!"

"Hello? Wynter?"

It *was* Momma.

"Hello, darling," Momma said. "Isn't this exciting? I can't wait to see you again."

"We're going to Thailand!" Joy said.

Wynter stared at the phone, unable to speak. Her hands were shaking, and her knees too, and it spread through her body until she was trembling all over — a deep, stark panic as her instinctive yearning warred with memories of all those times she'd needed attention or reassurance or affection and gotten so very little, and then nothing at all, ever again.

"She's overcome," Joy said into the phone. "Maybe we could call you back after we've finished the passport applications, and I'm sure she'll talk to you then."

"No, no, don't do that. It's early in the morning here and I have a class in half an hour." Momma's tone had turned snappy and impatient, which was more like the voice Wynter remembered. She must not realize she was still on speaker. "You get everything sorted, and I'll organize the visas and plane tickets from this end. Don't you dare tell your brother or the authorities. I don't want anyone else involved."

Joy gave dutiful answers and hung up.

"Can you believe it? Momma wants us to join her at last. I've waited so long for this."

"She really wants us?"

"Of course she wants us. She loves us. She took me with her when I was six years old. That has to mean something, doesn't it?"

Wynter didn't know what it meant, except it had been very unfair to their brothers. But Joy didn't see things in terms of fairness. The Light taught that everything happened the way it was supposed to, in the end. Momma was supposed to follow her own path to spiritual enlightenment. Caleb and Indio and Jesse were supposed to grow up on a different path, a path with no mother. Wynter had joined her brothers' path one month ago and from that first step it had felt exactly right.

But the universe had other plans. And she was deaf and blind to the universe, always had been. She was the last person to dispute the way things were supposed to be.

Joy took Wynter's hand again and together they crossed the street.

"We're going to get passports," Joy said.

"Why couldn't you get them in Seattle?"

"Because you won't be coming to Seattle during business hours." Joy's hand was painfully tight on Wynter's. "It's because of Social Services," she said abruptly. "Momma found out you're in foster care and that just can't be. Caleb thinks he can sort it all out. I thought he could. I trusted him when I sent you there. Instead he's trying to force me onto a different path, tying me down for three more years. How does that help? He's an idiot, floundering in darkness like all these idiots." Joy waved an arm toward a cafe where people ate their lunch at tables under heaters.

Wynter held her breath and dared not interrupt. Those people were giving Joy strange looks as she went on and on.

"The authorities will never let you go. They had no right to take you. Someone at the office told her. Some *bitch* at the office," Joy spat.

Wynter kept her mouth shut on more questions. Joy must've kept the information secret as long as she could, knowing Momma would blame her for creating the situation. Joy had no reason to be upset *now*, surely. She was going to get what she wanted.

"You belong with Momma," Joy muttered as they entered the building. "*We* belong with our mother. There are so many forms to deal with, especially as you don't have a birth certificate, but everything will fall into place. It has to."

They waited their turn. Inside Joy's tote was a stack of paperwork for the two of them — from the ashram and from Miriam, who had sent it by courier — neatly filled-out forms and signed statements that Wynter couldn't even begin to comprehend.

The young man behind the counter wanted Wynter's birth certificate, asked three times if she was Native American, and then had to consult his supervisor to figure out what to do. The supervisor asked the same questions all over again.

"This is an affidavit from our mother," Joy said. "The checklist says we can use this." She was starting to look panicked as she argued with the men for an hour. The clerks had to stop now and then to deal with someone else. Joy's earlier elation turned to anxiety as she tried to convince these people, the *authorities* as Miriam had always disparagingly called them, that Wynter was a real person. They had to consult a special list on their computer to make sure the information provided was good enough to prove she was real without a birth certificate.

Wynter felt herself floating away because she really *didn't* exist without that one piece of paper.

I'm right here! I exist!

"You need a certified copy of the mother's passport," the supervisor was saying. "You need a signed statement from her, as the guardian, to authorize the child to apply for a passport and leave the country."

"I'll get it. I'll get everything you need and bring it in a few days," Joy said, breathless with fear. Wynter knew that fear — Joy was terrified she would fail and then Momma would stop talking to her again. Maybe even stop loving her.

Wynter's phone rang — Caleb.

Joy saw his name on her screen and said, "Don't answer that. We need to get this finished."

A minute later, her voicemail flashed. Wynter stepped away to listen to it. Caleb sounded stressed and upset. He said he couldn't make the meeting at six. He didn't say why. Why would he skip such an important meeting?

"It doesn't matter," Joy snapped when Wynter told her. "We don't need a custody hearing. Do you understand? Miriam is your mother, your guardian, and she's bringing us to Thailand. We'll all be together again."

Joy set Wynter in a corner against a white screen to have her photo taken by the younger man. Joy was hopeful again, and Wynter caught her mood. They were going to Momma. Everything would work out. She smiled for the camera.

"No smiling," the man said.

After the photos, there was trouble again — something to do with money.

"I have forty dollars," Wynter said, in case it would help. Half of that was her allowance from Rosa, which she was supposed to use when she went out Friday, and half was a gift from Caleb when he was here last week. Using Caleb's money to remove herself from his life brought on a pang of guilt.

But the problem wasn't lack of money. Joy had a lot of cash with her but the office would only accept a money order or check for the passport fees. They walked down the street to the post office, passing a museum on the way that Joy agreed they could visit after they were done. Then back to the clerk's office with several hundred dollars' worth of money orders. The office would not lodge the application until they had those extra bits of paperwork, so Joy put everything back into her tote and they left at last.

"Can we visit that museum?" Wynter asked her sister.

"I didn't realize this would be so exhausting." Joy did look exhausted. "You mustn't tell anyone, understand? Social Services will kick up a fuss, now they've got their claws into you. Once the passports come in a few weeks, and the visas and tickets are sorted out, then of course we'll explain everything to them. And to Caleb."

"Caleb doesn't like secrets."

Joy stopped walking and shook Wynter's arm. "You will not tell him. We can't take any chances. Don't cause trouble, Wynter."

Joy wouldn't take her to the museum and ignored Wynter's suggestion about food, even though Wynter offered to pay.

"Are you coming back with me to stay the night?" Wynter asked. There were no buses to Seattle until the morning.

"Didn't you listen to a word I said? No one must know about this. Don't you dare tell anyone I was here, or what we did. I'll stay in a motel." She stopped and took Wynter's shoulders, her expression turning gentle. "Everything will work out. We've waited so long for this, haven't we, darling? And now we get everything we've always wanted. Ko Samui is the most beautiful place on Earth. It's a tropical island — imagine that! I'll email you pictures. I know you'll find the Light there. I know you will. It'll be a fresh start." She hugged Wynter. "You're shaking so hard. It's the Light, filling you up!"

Wynter couldn't feel the Light filling her up, but she did feel the lightness of hope. No teachers. No warehouse. No living in fear all day, every day, that pain was coming. Or worse — the pain of indifference as she faded into nonexistence, where even Joy didn't see her.

Momma would see her at last.

In a daze, she got on the bus to Richland. A few weeks ago she'd knocked on a stranger's door and Jesse had looked at her like he was seeing a ghost. But Caleb had seen her clearly, as a solid real person with a story to tell. The bitter tinge of doubt crept in. She was leaving Caleb. And Jesse, too — he saw her now. He was filling her mind with all the true things she needed to know to survive in the world. And there must be a reason Indio had told her, *I won't fail you again.* She'd made a small impact on her brothers' lives. She existed for them.

Was Momma going to fail her? Wynter drew deep on childhood memories, searching for something to cling to, something that would reconstruct her trust in a mother whose every decision was based on messages from the universe yet not once had the universe reminded her that her own child needed her.

Pointless to look backward. Momma wanted her daughters at her side in paradise. She'd filled out all that paperwork, sent Joy the money to make it happen. As the bus rumbled on, Wynter scrolled through the pictures Joy had sent. Rainbows of tropical flowers and birds, shallow blue waters, serene buildings with clean lines and peaceful people. In every way, it was the opposite of the ashram in the desert.

Jesse would be very, very upset about this. Indio would understand.

Caleb's reaction she found impossible to imagine.

No Choice

Caleb was on the road by fourteen hundred hours. Earlier, he'd gotten a text from Joy saying she wasn't coming to the meeting in Richland. He'd tried, really tried, to avoid analyzing the true meaning of those words. But it was clear now that Joy didn't intend to step up as Wynter's guardian.

So, he would do it.

He'd figure out a way to make it work. He was fairly sure his EO would be sympathetic. Since Wynter's arrival he'd certainly made the effort to be flexible with Caleb needing days off or leaving early, like today.

Tina did not like him, but that was her problem. A judge would decide where Wynter lived, not Tina.

Rosa didn't like him either. He could attribute half the viper's pit in his gut to Joy. The rest came from the thought of seeing Rosa again. He was more than a little annoyed with himself, both for his behavior at her house and for being worried about it now, more than a week later. He'd handled personalities of every stripe and it was disconcerting to find someone who could rile him so easily. It wasn't Rosa's fault. She was the wrong person to be taking care of Wynter, and he resented her for that, and that was unfair of him.

Just get through this. If they could get a swift hearing, if he could sort out the Family Care Plan that the military required of single parents, Wynter would be back in Seattle soon.

He was forty-five minutes along I-90 when his phone rang — a number he didn't recognize. He answered on speaker.

"Caleb? This is Anže Turk... um, Turk. Indio's friend. We've met a couple of—"

"Turk. What's up?" Caleb's heart had already dropped through the floor because he *knew* this wasn't good. Especially as Indio and Turk were barely on speaking terms since Indio's stunt in January.

"So, Indy didn't want me to call you but I sorta have to. He was arrested Saturday night after our gig in Lake Oswego."

Caleb swallowed a curse word and pulled over on the freeway. "Is he hurt?"

"He's fine. He's been sitting in jail for two nights. We need $750 to bail him out. I'd do anything for him, you know that, but I can't raise that kind of cash."

"Where is he?"

"Clackamas County Jail, about half an hour south of the university. I can text you the address—"

"I'll find it. Are you there now?"

"No, man, I gotta get to class. He made me swear not to call you but I couldn't just—"

"I'll deal with it. Thanks for calling."

Caleb hung up and realized he hadn't even asked why Indio had been arrested. Not relevant at this moment. He was supposed to be in Richland at six. Wynter was depending on him.

He had no choice. *No choice.*

Still, he sat there clutching the steering wheel, forehead pressed to his knuckles, pushing down his anger at Indio. At *Harry*.

Five years ago, Caleb hadn't been there for his brother. That April he'd returned from a four-month deployment on an ice-breaker in Antarctica. Harry was no better or worse than usual and Caleb was more interested in spending time with a black-haired red-belted spitfire of a young woman at his dojo than with his family. Four weeks later he was sent out again. Days after he left, Indio was in juvenile court on felony assault charges.

Five years ago, Harry hadn't been there for his son. Harry had refused to take Indio home after the initial arrest, so he'd remained in detention. The judge had ordered Harry to attend future hearings and slapped him with contempt when he again failed to show at the arraignment. And made him do an online parenting class, which Caleb was pretty sure thirteen-year-old Jesse had completed for him.

Caleb had done what he could from the other side of the world, and maybe half as much as he should — bullying Harry into visiting Indio in juvie and to take part in their family counseling programs to make sure they'd discharge Indio into his father's care when the sentence was served. The alternative was foster care or some other facility until Indio turned eighteen. They might even take Jesse away. Caleb used the one thing that meant a damn to his father —

he threatened to request a hardship discharge from the Coast Guard and come home to take custody of the boys if Harry didn't buck up. He was twenty years old but he was prepared to do it, to fight for them, to throw away his career and force Harry to accept what a lousy job he'd done.

Harry had never been prouder than the day Caleb put on his dress blues for the first time — and so the threat worked, because Harry did still have some pride. He made the effort and played by the rules just long enough to bring Indio home.

Caleb put down the truck window and filled his lungs with sun-warmed, fume-laden air. It was a beautiful day, unseasonably warm. Jesse was welcome to his mountain snow. Caleb loved the sun, and this afternoon's spring-like weather had filled him with hope for the meeting ahead, once he'd made the decision to fight for Wynter. Turk's call left him feeling utterly powerless and that wasn't even the worst of it. Had Indio called for help thirty-six hours ago, he'd be out of jail and Caleb would be halfway to Richland by now.

Wynter didn't answer her phone so he left a message. *Something came up... very important... so sorry...* He hardly knew what he was saying. *Can't be there.*

Can't be there for you.

Tina's phone went to voicemail as well. He left a slightly less garbled message for her, something about a family emergency and a request to reschedule. He left a message for Jesse. He called the lawyer on the base who'd been advising him on Wynter, got a recommendation for a criminal lawyer in Portland, and left a message with the firm's receptionist.

He pulled back into the traffic, took the next off ramp, turned around and backtracked thirty minutes toward Tiger Mountain before turning south. A few miles farther, his GPS directed him to a local branch of his bank and he withdrew $750 cash before continuing on the four-hour trip to Clackamas County Jail.

✿

"We've talked about this. I need to know where you are, every minute of the day."

Rosa's voice was making Wynter's ears buzz. She moved the phone a few inches away from her ear.

"I'm already on the bus back," she said.

"But where have you *been*? I get home to an empty house, not so much as a note or a text message."

Wynter reeled off the first lie that came to her. "I took the bus to school and met up with three friends. We went to that pizza place and studied."

"Which friends? Do I know their parents?"

"I don't know who their parents are. It was a last-minute thing." Was there even one kid at school who would back up her lie if she asked them to? Let alone three. She should've said something simpler that didn't involve anyone else.

Rosa let it drop — for now, at least. "Tina's already here for your meeting. What time does your bus get in?"

"About twenty minutes. I didn't do anything wrong." Well, she was telling lies, which was wrong, but the passports were nothing wrong. She had every right to a passport, didn't she? And Momma certainly had the right to have her own daughter live with her.

When she got off the bus, she was surprised to see Rosa waiting there in her car.

"It's only a ten-minute walk," Wynter said, slouching in the passenger seat.

Rosa said nothing until they were at the house, where Tina waited in the front room.

"You need to tell us what happened this afternoon," Rosa said. "The truth, please."

"I told you already. I went to school and came back."

"I know that's not true."

"You saw me get off the bus!"

"Yes, Wynter, it was the right bus but it came from the opposite direction."

Think fast. "I went... to Pasco. To the museum."

"Which museum?"

"Um, the one with the steps and the red roof." The one she'd *wanted* to go to.

"You mean the Franklin County Historical Museum? Did you go inside?"

"Yes." Wynter was emboldened by the questions. "It was very interesting."

"You went *inside*?"

Wynter nodded. Rosa's brow went down and Wynter's mind raced ahead. What if she asked about the exhibits? Wynter had no clue what was in that museum. Jesse wanted to take her to the science museum in Seattle to see dinosaurs. Would a dinosaur fit inside that building in Pasco?

Rosa leaned forward. "Wynter, you signed a behavior contract that says you'll always be exactly where you're supposed to be."

"Why should I not be in a museum? Museums are educational. Jesse says—"

"That museum is closed on Mondays."

Wynter's stomach dropped. "Are you sure?"

"I know the place very well. I'm a member of the Franklin County Historical Society."

"The thing is..." Wynter floundered. "I *wanted* to go inside. I thought they might have dinosaurs."

"Of course they don't have dinosaurs! Now, why did you lie? People don't lie except to cover something up."

Wynter couldn't think of anything else to say.

Tina said, "Caleb left me a message earlier to say he couldn't come this evening and that Joy had canceled. Were you upset about that? Is that why you went out today?"

Wynter grasped at the excuse. "Yes. I was disappointed so I got on the bus to Pasco and sort of wandered around for a while."

"I'm going to ground you for the rest of the week," Rosa said.

"What about the movies on Friday?"

"I will allow that because it's important for your social development. Hand over your phone, please. You can have it back Friday."

"You won't be able to look through it this time. It's locked."

Rosa glanced at Tina. "That's not acceptable. Tell me the password."

"It's private."

"Rosa," Tina said, her lips stretching in to a smile, "why don't you get that casserole on the table while Wynter and I have our little chat."

Rosa left the room and Wynter sat for half an hour with Tina giving monosyllabic answers to questions about how she was settling in. It was easy to blur her way through — what did it matter? She was leaving the country soon and she'd never see Tina or Rosa again.

Lecture

At a gas station in Oregon, Caleb tried calling Wynter again. Moments later, Rosa texted him three times in quick succession.

> Please do not contact Wynter. I've confiscated her phone and banned email until Friday because she left the house this afternoon without permission and lied about where she went.

> She and Tina have completed their meeting this evening.

> What a shame you and Joy didn't show up.

Caleb didn't trust himself to have a civil conversation with Rosa, so he called Tina who told him bluntly that she wasn't seeing the required level of commitment from either him or Joy.

"I *am* committed to Wynter. I also have a life to deal with and this was unavoidable. We can reschedule."

"Yes, we can reschedule," Tina said, confident she had the upper hand, "but I'm not due to visit Wynter for another month."

"We'll meet up next time she's in Seattle. That's... Saturday the eighteenth, right?"

"I have a life as well, Caleb. I prefer to work during normal office hours—"

"Don't make this harder than it has to be. Wynter doesn't even have to be there. *You* don't have to be there. Joy can go to court without you. And if she can't get custody, or won't, then I will."

"I see. That brings up a whole new set of issues, especially in the case of a high-risk child. In unusual circumstances such as these, you will need my recommendation in court. Given she has a stable home in foster care, it's very unlikely a judge would award you custody as a single parent in the military. What happens if you're deployed?"

"I'll name someone as her temporary guardian."

"Someone? Who?"

"I'll find someone."

"The fact is, while you're on active duty you cannot take sole responsibility for a dependent. The department would certainly recommend against it. In addition, you have no history with her. I can't help noticing that you've demonstrated no particular affection for her. Rosa has observed the same thing."

"What the hell are you talking about?"

"On every parameter, Rosa's home is the best place for Wynter."

For two sickening heartbeats Caleb wondered if she was right. His duty was to Wynter, yet he had another duty to his country and he couldn't throw away his career. Jesse would be a phenomenal influence on her but he was years away from being ready to take sole responsibility for her during a deployment. And if Caleb took credit for that kid, he must also take credit for the criminal drug abuser currently sitting in jail.

On the third heartbeat, Caleb discarded his self-doubt. Tina was one misaligned cog in the machine — a machine he'd always believed in. He would bring Wynter home, somehow, and he'd do it by the book.

He hung up and drove on, with music blaring too loudly for him to hear his thoughts.

⚙

Hours later, Caleb was on the road back to Portland, sitting in the center lane on cruise control, which on principle he rarely used, with Indio beside him. Indio had nothing to say except that he wasn't hungry, which couldn't be true. Caleb contemplated stopping for food anyway — it was nine o'clock and *he* was starving — then found himself begrudging his brother a ten-dollar meal after forking over half the contents of his bank account to get him out of jail. Shame or resentment held Indio's tongue, and Caleb wasn't yet in the mood to prompt him.

Instead, he drove straight to Indio's apartment where half a dozen people were playing cards and video games and guitars amid empty pizza boxes. Turk hustled everyone out, turned off the music, whipped up quesadillas and beans and unobtrusively cleaned up the kitchen while they ate. Indio held his fork awkwardly because of a bruised right hand that he hadn't offered to explain. Then Turk quietly left to spend the night at a friend's place, telling Caleb he could crash for the night on his bed.

Caleb stacked the dishes. "I talked to a lawyer while I was waiting for them to process you. We're seeing her tomorrow at ten."

"We?"

"She's hopeful the charges can be reduced or dismissed at the pre-trial meeting." Caleb leaned on the sink as his gut clenched. "What the hell's going on, Indio? Why didn't you call me Saturday night? Why don't you ask for help when you need it?"

"Your help always comes with a lecture."

"Have I lectured you tonight? Have I said one word?"

"I feel it coming on."

"I just want to know what you were thinking."

"I was high. I wasn't thinking."

"Why were you high?"

"What kind of question is that? It's something I do sometimes." Indio scrunched a napkin in his fist, working it into a tight ball as he stared at the streetlight outside the window. "Jesse told me Wynter's foster mother looked through her phone the other day because she thought I was... doing something wrong. Sending stuff to her. Asking her for... I would never do that."

"I know."

Indio gave him a sharp look. "How do you know? How do you know what I would or wouldn't do? Look how I spent my weekend. Maybe I'm exactly the screw-up that woman thinks I am."

"I know you'd never hurt Wynter. I trust you on that. The rest of it..." Caleb shook his head, unable to contain his dismay any longer. "Okay, you made a mistake that night. Lots of mistakes. But resisting arrest? What the hell was that about? I've told you and Jesse, a hundred times, you do what the cops say. Don't resist, don't joke around, don't talk. If they're wrong, you sort it out later. Instead, you compounded the problem."

Indio didn't react because, of course, this was the lecture he'd predicted.

Caleb calmed himself. "Okay, no more. We'll talk about it tomorrow with the lawyer."

Indio hauled himself out of the chair. "I'm gonna take a shower."

"Does that hand need attention?"

Indio rolled his wrist, assessing the damage. "Wonder what happened there. Pretty sure I didn't punch anyone this time." There was the hint of a sly smile on his lips that irked Caleb more than it should because he was only joking. Assault was nothing to joke about. Then again, assault wasn't among the charges for this arrest.

Indio disappeared into the bathroom. Caleb was desperate to call Wynter to explain himself, but once again Rosa had taken control of their communications. He was about to call Jesse when Jesse called him, returning his earlier voicemail. He denied knowing anything about the arrest. He sounded offended that Caleb would think he wouldn't tell him. Of course Jesse would tell him. Why was Caleb second-guessing himself again?

"Do I have a problem showing affection?" Caleb said, opening an overhead cabinet to find coffee mugs. "Tina says there's a problem."

"You're kinda closed up, I guess."

"What does that even mean? Bea tells me I don't pay her enough attention. Is that why she keeps..." He stopped himself, awkward about discussing this with Jesse.

"Keeps feeling you up in public places? Forcing the issue, so to speak?" Jesse chuckled to himself, but it was a strained sound because he was clearly worried about Indio. "I think it has more to do with things like that one-terabyte portable hard drive."

"She had two crashes this past year. That was a perfectly practical gift."

"Oh, sure, I agree it was *practical*. I'm not the most romantic guy on the planet either, but even I know not to give a girl a backup drive for Christmas. As for Wynter, a hug now and then wouldn't kill you. Although..."

"Although what?"

"C'mon. You know what Rosa would say if she saw you hugging Wynter for one second too long."

"I haven't hugged Wynter."

"—because you have issues with affection. I know that. I'm just saying, if you *did*, Rosa would freak out. She's a prude. Which is funny given her career choice. Also, not funny at all because she's gonna get the wrong impression. She has affection issues of her own. She has issues with sex."

"So, I can't win with her."

"Probably not. Forget about her."

Jesse was right. They both had to work around Rosa. He needed to concentrate on Wynter.

Caleb switched on the coffee machine. "Did you see how Wynter flinched at the table when we were at Rosa's? You used to do that, when Harry made any kind of sudden movement."

"I had to reassure her you never hit us."

"I hate to think she's scared of me."

"She's not. It was just instinct. They hit her at the ashram."

"She told you that?"

"No. She keeps deflecting questions about it, and Joy deflected Indio's questions about it, which is how I know it's true."

Caleb pushed past the helpless anger. "I was going there today to tell Wynter I'll seek custody."

"Yes! You should've done that a month ago."

He was right, of course. Caleb had been resisting all this time because he'd believed Tina and his own lawyer who kept telling him Joy was the better option. He'd second-guessed his own ability to take care of another sibling despite having raised a kid as awesome as Jesse.

"Tina's going to fight me, so don't tell Wynter — not yet. Actually, you can't tell Wynter anything because she's grounded until Friday."

"We have homework dates lined up!"

Caleb paced the kitchen, exhausted. "You could drive down on Saturday."

"Isn't that illegal or something? We're not supposed to see her until the week after. Why is she grounded?"

"She went AWOL for a few hours today. Let's get through the week and on Friday you can ask her what happened." Caleb toed the pedal on the trash to lift the lid, and dropped in the used coffee filter. "She opens up to you, doesn't she?"

"If changing the subject is *opening up* — sure."

"You'll get there. We'll all get there. I'll talk to Rosa for you about Saturday."

On top of the trash was a cereal box. Out of habit, Caleb moved it to the adjacent recycle bin. Underneath was more stuff in the wrong bin — handwritten lecture notes, paper guitar string packets, forwarded mail with Indio's Portland address scribbled over the Ohio one...

Caleb stopped with the envelope in his hand.

"I don't know if Saturday's good for me," Jesse was saying. "I need to sort something out with Natalie."

"Okay. I gotta go."

Caleb hung up, turned around, and there was Indio in sweatpants and t-shirt, hair dripping on his shoulders, eyes fixed on that envelope.

"Erie County Court, Buffalo, New York," Caleb read off the return address. "Something else you need to tell me?"

The Only Lie

In Ohio, Indio had fallen into the habit of getting wasted every weekend. Every. Single. Weekend. His record over the past couple of months in Portland was actually a great improvement. Not that he was congratulating himself. He had a long way to go.

Last weekend was Blunderbelly's drummer's cousin's birthday. Indio didn't even know the guy but he had nothing better to do after Saturday's gig than hang out in a park in Lake Oswego with his bandmates and a dozen others, including a girl from out of town he'd met the night before.

Indio hadn't been in a party mood. What Jesse told him about Rosa would normally have rolled off his back because Rosa didn't mean a thing to him — he'd never met her and never wanted to. So he was caught by surprise when her implied accusations left him infuriated. He worked it off by partying. There was a lot of alcohol available. He'd always hated excessive drinking, although that didn't always stop him. That night he took a tab of acid instead because... Well, why not? Wasn't just Caleb's expectations he was living down to now, but Rosa's, too.

When the cops showed up, he was sitting in the driver seat of someone else's coupe, messing around with the laser pointer key-chain. Pointing a laser at a cop was a Class A misdemeanor. Who knew? The drunk eighteen-year-old with him, who'd been trying to persuade him into the backseat where he was frankly never going to fit for the purpose she had in mind, had a Smirnoff Ice that she decided to tell the officer he'd given her. He probably had. He didn't recall in this instance but it wouldn't be the first time he'd furnished a minor with alcohol. He wasn't usually stupid enough to do it in a public place. Another misdemeanor. Resisting arrest, which was presumably the cause of his hand injury, added one more. The cops weren't done. There was Disorderly Conduct and a couple lesser misdemeanor charges on his ticket because, among other things, a local reported a group of them had wandered into a nearby parking lot at three in the morning and relieved themselves against the wall of a building that turned out to be a church. Indio accidentally admitted he was among that group. And just because the arresting officer was a dick, he added a citation for possession thanks to the joint in Indio's pocket.

All in all, the unopened letter in Caleb's hand was starting to look a lot less dramatic by comparison.

"Open it," Caleb said.

Indio had reached his limit. He could tell Caleb to fuck off out of his home or he could get it over and done with tonight. At some point he was going to have to get that background check and everything would come out anyway. Even if he got his juvenile record sealed, nothing was going to make the Buffalo thing vanish.

"You open it," he said, a final, pointless act of belligerence.

Caleb slapped the envelope on the counter. "Open it."

Indio ripped it open and handed Caleb the letter without looking at it.

Caleb's brow went up as he took it. "You already know what it says?"

Yes, he knew what it said, more or less. "I owe the state of New York nine hundred dollars."

It could've been worse — so much worse. A sick feeling came over him as he recalled that Christmas vacation in Buffalo. Another party, another arrest, only this time it was a felony possession charge and he'd faced prison time. He pleaded it down, which was the way these things usually went for polite white boys — and he *had* been polite that time — but he hadn't known it would be that easy. He'd spent the night before in a cell, shaking in fear yet unable to call Caleb or Harry for help.

Indio flopped onto the recliner in the living room, mentally steeling himself.

"This was two years ago," Caleb said, incredulous as he glanced over the letter. "You haven't told me in two years? Does Harry know? Does Jesse?"

"No one knows. You'd just been stationed at the base in Seattle, just kicked Harry out. Didn't want to ruin your homecoming or burden Jesse with a 'secret'." He air-quoted the word as a nod to Caleb's stupid house rule. Well, not stupid, but highly inconvenient and often unrealistic.

"What was the conviction for?"

"In the end, a Class A misdemeanor for possession — a few PCP tablets. Weren't even mine. I was literally just counting them out on the table when—"

"Jesus Christ, Indio, I don't care about the details. Is this why you never filed the paperwork to get your juvenile records sealed?"

"The conviction made me ineligible for two years."

"And now, just when the two years are up, you've managed to screw up again." Caleb breathed deep, that self-control thing he did when he was pushing it all down. He came into the living room and set down the coffees. "Do you have any intention of paying the fine?"

"It's New York. I figured they wouldn't chase me across the country for it."

"Clearly they are chasing you. You could be arrested for this."

"For nine hundred bucks? Not likely."

"Interest makes it almost eleven hundred dollars now."

"May as well be eleven thousand. I can't pay it."

"Here's what's going to happen." Caleb sat heavily on the couch. "*I'll* pay it and—"

"I don't want your money."

"You'll pay me back."

"Or what?"

"There is no *or what*. That's what you'll do. You'll probably owe the state of Oregon as well, after last weekend. Sell some of those damn guitars or the bike."

"I'm not selling my guitars."

Caleb gave a slow shake of his head. There was no way past him. "Listen to me. You fucked up. You pay the consequences, you clean up your mess, and you move on."

Indio thought of all the things he could say to prolong the fight. He was good with words that way. He used to talk circles around Harry, poking the hornet's nest for fun when he could be bothered. Other times he just walked away. Choosing between the options gave him some control over what happened next, where ultimately the aim was to deflect violence. And it actually left Harry with a smidgen of respect for his middle son. It was different with Caleb, though. Whereas Harry was always wrong, Caleb was usually right and in any case violence was off the table. No fun battering Caleb with words and cleverly twisted logic when it wasn't going to make Caleb respect him or diminish his own shame.

So he simply said, "Is the lecture over?"

Caleb tipped back his head as he rubbed his hands over his face. "Lecture over. Oh, and you owe me a hundred for the bail because they never return it all. Administrative charges or something. I'll pay for the lawyer, so count your blessings. Jesse and me can eat instant noodles for a few months." He took one last look at the letter on the coffee table. "That isn't you, Indio. You're a musician, an artist. You have an incredible future. You could be someone Wynter looks up to."

The only people who looked up to Indio were the girls in the front row.

He frowned at his bruised knuckles. Caleb could be right. *Something* had happened in that basement a few weeks ago. A connection was made, not only with a fellow musician but with a girl who was going to be a part of his life for the rest of his life. He could nurture it, if he made the effort.

Which was ridiculous. Being a role model for Wynter was a whole heap of pressure he didn't need.

"Isn't that your job?" he said lightly.

"Here's my job." Caleb leaned forward, elbows on knees. "Given Joy skipped the meeting today, given she's shown no interest in taking Wynter in, I'm going to seek custody."

"How's that gonna work?"

"I don't know yet. I have to try."

"You took care of Jesse since he was three years old. You've done your duty to this family."

"This family just got bigger, and so did my responsibility. I have exactly the same duty to Wynter — and to Joy, for that matter — as I had to the two of you."

Indio wasn't going to argue the point. He wanted Wynter out of foster care as much as Caleb did. "Don't you ever get tired of being perfect?"

"You know, better than anyone, that I'm not perfect." Caleb tipped forward to take something from the rack under the coffee table — a photo album. "I was looking for this at Harry's. Didn't know you had it."

"Don't know why I have it. You can take it."

Caleb gave him a look as he settled back to open it, a look that said he understood it was no accident the album was here. Indio had taken it years ago, hauled it around with the rest of his stuff from Washington to Ohio to Oregon. It was the only one without *her* in it.

"Christ, Harry was right. I really did dress like an accountant."
Caleb tilted the first page in Indio's direction — a photo of him
dressed in a suit, a cute blonde on his arm. "That was the school
Winterfest dance, my sophomore year. Anita Green — still the
sweetest girl I ever met."

"Doesn't everyone say that about their first?"

"How d'you know she was my first?"

"Wasn't she?"

Caleb set his jaw, like he was going to refuse to answer. "Yes,
although I wasn't hers," he admitted, turning the page. "No Christmas photos that year. Did we even celebrate it?"

"Not really. Harry was doing *great*, though," Indio said sarcas-
tically. "We'd been in Seattle half a year, he had a good job —
bragging cuz he was middle management. *I don't work for the man,
the man works for me!* As if he owned the company. But he was a
weekend drunk, all the same. You came home from that dance and
got into a fight with him cuz he insulted your date. Not in front of
her, so you really should've let it drop. He walked out with a shiner
and didn't come back for a week, and you had to call the cleaning
company every morning to tell them he was still bedridden with
the flu."

Indio relished the story, and relished telling it, to remind himself
as well as his brother that Caleb was no stranger to pre-emptive
violence. Not that Indio could think of a single time *after* that
incident where Caleb and Harry had come to blows.

"And then Harry waltzes home like he's been on vacation,"
Indio continued, enjoying Caleb's discomfort, "a crate of beer,
smiles all around, and it was never spoken of again. We all sort of
forgot it was Christmas morning."

"I think the neighbor dropped in an apple pie and leftover ham."

"I remember that. Great ham. Jesse wouldn't eat the pie cuz
there was no ice cream. He was almost as picky about his own food
as he'd been about that—" Indio stopped himself and swallowed.
Caleb looked up, waiting for the rest. "—that dog's food." Indio
hadn't meant to bring up the damn dog. Now he'd done it, he
found he needed to finish the thought. "Remember that time in
Anaconda — two years earlier, I guess — you sent me and Jesse to
the store with a few bucks to buy groceries and we spent it all on
dog food?"

"The expensive stuff, too."

"Exactly. Jesse was — what, seven years old? Standing there in the aisle reading labels on the cans. Had to be high protein." And Caleb had yelled at *him*, not Jesse, when they came home with three cans of premium dog food and nothing else.

"I think that dog was..." Caleb frowned, getting his words in line. "That dog was when things started going wrong between us."

"You mean when he *ran away*?" Indio leaned on the words. He and Jesse had gone camping for a week in July with a family from school, and Skar was gone when they got home. "Jesse used to agonize over the odds he could survive in the wild, and Harry laughed about it when he was drunk. *Maybe he was hit by a truck. That dog had the worst road sense.* Well, he was a stray. I was still teaching him to stop at the curb." Indio grabbed a deep breath to quell the hot pressure behind his eyes. "I told Jesse some other family probably took him in."

Caleb flicked over the pages in silence. At last he said, "That was the only lie I ever told you."

"Harry took him to the pound, didn't he?" A twitch in Caleb's jaw told Indio he was right. "That's what I thought. Was it on that first day we left for camp? Or did he wait a while, maybe until Skar chewed through something or dug another hole in the yard so he could justify it? Did he tell you what he was gonna do, or did you get the same lie?"

Caleb closed the album. "Harry made *me* take him. I refused to do it until he threatened to drive him out to the mountain with his shotgun. Maybe that would've been okay — Skar wouldn't know the difference. I walked him forty-five minutes to the rescue place on the edge of town."

A calmness came over Indio. The truth, at last. And now he wanted every last detail. "Why all the way out there? The city pound was just around the corner."

"I'm gonna guess he didn't want the neighbors to know."

"Everyone on our street loved that dog."

"*I* loved him. It was the toughest forty-five minutes of my fourteen-year-old life. On the way there I was furious. Grieving, too." Caleb cleared his throat. "The girl who processed him, a high school volunteer, I guess, not much older than me, she couldn't hide her contempt when I explained it to her. *We can't keep him. He's too much trouble.* On the way back, I thought about how to fix things. *Let's tell them he ran away*, I told Harry, and he was good with that. Wasn't his fault if the dog ran away."

Nothing was ever Harry's fault.

"I'll bet he was put down," Indio said. "He wasn't exactly a puppy."

"Seems likely."

"Why didn't you tell us the truth?"

Caleb shrugged. "Didn't want you to know Harry could do something like that."

"A wasted lie. Of course I knew Harry could do something like that."

"For Jesse's sake, then. Jesse got his first drum kit out of the deal."

"He did?"

"We were all astounded by Harry's generosity, remember? Weeks after Jesse's eighth birthday had come and gone, and suddenly the drum kit appears. I always thought that kit was a guilt offering."

"Huh. Might be the only nice thing Harry ever did for Jesse. How did that kid turn out so great? There's Wynter's role model, right there, if he doesn't screw it up."

"He's been taking it very seriously."

"Too seriously. That's my point. I hope he gives her space to breathe."

"I made a conscious decision to do the best I could for you and Jesse," Caleb said. "You could make that decision, too. Wynter wants to learn from you. She admires you. And you both..." Caleb gave a quick shake of his head.

"Both what?"

"Suffered the same loss. You know what I mean. I thought maybe I could help her because we were about the same age when Miriam left. But our situations were so different. I don't know how to talk about it with her. You two... I think you both feel it in the same way. You could help her get past it."

Indio silently congratulated his brother on perhaps the most insightful thing he'd ever said. Other than the last part, anyway. How could Indio help Wynter get past it when he himself wasn't past it?

"I've just been charged with peeing in a churchyard," Indio said, standing to stretch. "She was better off getting guidance from the Light. I'm going to bed."

Perfect Son

Wynter had no phone or computer at home, but she could still log on to the homework forum in the school library. On Tuesday she told Felicity about moving to Thailand in a few weeks to live with her mother. In writing the words, she managed to make herself excited about it again. She hoped Felicity would be excited, too — Felicity had been reunited with her own family after several years in foster care, so she'd surely understand this nervous hope Wynter was feeling.

On Wednesday Wynter wrote again, with links to photos of the beautiful scenery of Ko Samui.

> It looks like a place where
> nothing bad could happen

The act of writing the words made them seem true.

By Thursday there was still no response from Felicity although she was active on the forum itself, commenting to other kids about Rihanna's latest album and the best lip gloss flavors and her Ragdoll cats. She hadn't mentioned cats before, but there she was on the Pets forum posting cute photos of Dollie and Smooch. Wynter couldn't help feeling disappointed at being ignored. They could've stayed friends after she moved to another country. Had Felicity even asked her uncle about finding Xay and Roman?

It didn't matter. Soon she'd be in paradise with Momma. Joy would be happy, filled with the Light. Wynter might have a harder time with the Light but she'd give it a shot. She'd have to forget a lot of what Jesse had taught her, but Jesse wouldn't be there to scowl at her for being illogical.

She looked at the pictures again. So much easier to think about everything she hoped to gain instead of everything she was about to lose. No one at school would miss her and Rosa would probably be glad to get rid of her. Her brothers would return to the lives they'd had before, where they didn't even know she existed.

Rosa handed back her phone on Friday morning so she'd have it this evening when she went out with Stacey's group. Jesse had sent her a dozen messages during the week, knowing she wouldn't see them at the time. She read them on the way to school, smiling and then laughing at his jokes. On Tuesday he'd written he might come up on the weekend, although he didn't mention it again. He could still send her messages when she was in Thailand, couldn't he? Or would Momma not let her have a cell phone? No one at the ashram had a cell phone, but Momma lived at a meditation retreat that served the public and Wynter knew how attached people were to their phones. Perhaps she could stay in touch with her brothers after all. Would Momma approve of that sex website? Of Dimiti Dime? Of rock music?

Joy had texted, too — she'd received the missing documents for the passports via Express mail from Thailand and was coming to Pasco today to lodge them in person rather than starting all over again in Seattle.

> Let's do something together. Rosa won't mind, will she? We don't have to sneak around this time.

> I'm seeing a movie with my friends after school. You could come with us!

To Wynter's surprise, Joy agreed. She texted her the address of the theater. Then she called Jesse to confirm his visit on Saturday.

✿

Jesse was walking to his first class of the day when Wynter called. All week he'd been agonizing over how to tell her about Indio's arrest, knowing Caleb wouldn't want her to worry about it and Indio would just keep it to himself if he could. *Someone* had to tell her. She was part of their family. But now he was actually talking to her, he found himself putting it off. Indio's pre-trial hearing was Monday and his lawyer was confident. Made sense to wait until that was over before stressing her out over the whole thing.

She wanted to know what time he was coming up tomorrow, which reminded him he'd rashly promised to visit.

"I can't come up. I'm sorry."

"Did Rosa say you couldn't?"

"No — although she probably would've because it's not *authorized*. I'm spending Saturday with Natalie for Valentine's."

"What does that mean?"

"Valentine's Day. The day for lovers. Not that Natalie and me... Well, I can hope, can't I. It's on Thursday, but I play a regular gig on Thursdays so we're going out all day Saturday instead."

"You could come over tonight. I'm seeing a movie with the girls from school."

"Thought those girls weren't talking to you."

"They've been told to be nice to me, to include me so I don't feel the need to make stuff up. My online friends are better."

"What online friends?"

"I've been writing to students on a homework forum. All kinds of interesting people. Please come? We're seeing something called *Star Wars 3D*."

"That's the reissue of *Phantom Menace* from 1999. You have to wear funny glasses."

"Why?"

"You'll see why."

"Why did they reissue an old movie? Am I supposed to know what Star Wars is? What is the Force?" She sounded a little desperate. "Stacey laughed at me when I didn't understand what she was talking about."

"Everyone under the age of sixty is expected to know the basics of Star Wars. I'll go through it with you."

"So, you'll come?"

"I'm not driving over there for a movie. We won't even be able to talk."

"Joy's going to be here!"

What on earth was Joy doing there? "That's not like a huge incentive."

"What does that mean?"

"We haven't... you know, clicked."

"She's your sister." Now she sounded truly peeved. "She's more your sister than I am."

"Don't say that. It's not true. It doesn't feel true."

"I want us all to go out together, all five of us, just one time."

"One time? We'll have loads of chances to do that." He was itching to tell her about Caleb's plans for custody, but Caleb had told him not to say anything until he'd sorted things out with his EO.

"We won't have loads of chances, Jesse. We won't... I'm not..."

Her stammering set off an alarm in his head. He lingered outside the lecture room. "Why not? What's going on?"

"We're leaving. We're going to Thailand. I'm not supposed to tell you. We went to get passports on Monday and we're leaving when they come through."

"*What?*"

"Miriam wants us to live with her."

"She doesn't want you, Wyn. How can you think that?"

"How can you *say* that?"

"Because she left you five years ago without a word! She left *us* in the same way. Maybe she wants Joy, I don't know. She doesn't want you."

"But we're getting passports," Wynter said indignantly.

"Tell her you don't want to go."

"I *do* want to go!"

"You belong here. I've only just started showing you... There's so much..." He swallowed the lump in his throat. "Please don't go back to the Light."

"This is nothing to do with the Light. I don't care about that. I want to be with Momma. Aren't I allowed to want that?"

She sounded so plaintive, Jesse couldn't bite back. Something was wrong, though. Something *must* be wrong. Why would their mother change her mind after all these years? Just because the ashram didn't want Wynter, suddenly she did?

"Did I push you too hard?" he said. "Is that why you don't want to stay?"

"I want to stay, Jesse. But I want to go."

"I should've let you find your own interests and developed your own worldview. I know that. I'm sorry."

"That doesn't matter now. Star Wars doesn't matter. Homework doesn't matter. None of this matters anymore."

"I can't believe this is happening. I was gonna show you everything. Please don't get brainwashed. Remember what I told you about scientific methodology, okay? *Ubi dubium, ibi libertas.* Tattoo that on your brain. And the kids in Thailand know about Star Wars, by the way, so you still need a primer."

"We can still talk on the phone, can't we? You can still help me with homework. Or is that too expensive?"

"We could do video calls if they let you use the internet — essentially free."

"Oh! Let's do that!"

"But you'll be half a day ahead, which means your evening will be, like, 5AM for me."

"Oh." After a long pause, she said, "Can you please be happy for me?"

"I'm not happy for *me*. And don't ask me to keep it secret. I'm telling Caleb and Indio."

"That'll get me in trouble."

"I'm telling them, Wyn. Why would you get in trouble? Miriam loves you so much, evidently. I'm sure she'll forgive you."

"She *does* love me. Joy said so."

"Oh, okay, then. If *Joy* says so." He regretted the sarcasm creeping into his tone. Maybe she wouldn't notice, over the phone.

"I don't ever want to hurt you," she said quietly. "I wish she'd come and live here."

"Then I'd have to visit her."

"Don't you want to see her?"

"No. If she didn't want me at my three-year-old cutest, why would she want me now?"

"Maybe she just doesn't like little kids. She and Joy got along well once Joy was grown up."

"She might not like the grownup I've become. I mean I've tried, but..."

"Tried what?"

Jesse sagged against the wall. "Tried to live up to my potential. That's the important thing, isn't it? To reach your potential in life. I've tried to feed my brain only the good stuff. Tried to be the perfect son, so she can never say... never say..." His throat closed up.

"Never say it was your fault she left you?"

"Yeah."

"You are perfect, Jesse."

"Thanks," he grumbled.

"You're my only friend on the outside."

"Then why are you...? No, it's okay. You get your mother back. That's a chance we never had."

"Will you visit me in Thailand?"

"When I get my hands on fifteen hundred dollars or so. I'll ask Indio for a loan." He chuckled bitterly to himself. Indio had to find a fortune to sort out his own life first.

"Why are you making me feel bad about this?" Wynter's voice was shaking, and Jesse's hand holding the phone was shaking in sympathy. "She's my mom and she wants me back. You don't understand. You don't even remember her."

That cut so deep, Jesse could hardly draw breath to speak. Wynter wasn't being deliberately hurtful, he knew that. And on a fundamental level she was right. She'd known a mother's love, such as it was, and lost it, and now had the chance to regain it.

He'd never felt the need for it. *Never.* Never needed Harry, either. His brothers loved him. Pretty much everyone he'd ever met loved him, from the kind ladies on the street back in Anaconda who'd give him home-baked treats if he hung around their yard, to his friends at college he could laugh with, to the girls sexting him in the hope of being his next project. That had always been enough.

"No, I don't understand."

Floating Away

Stacey and her friends were making a pretty good effort to be nice to Wynter. Before the movie they went for pizza and no one made fun of her again for not knowing anything about Star Wars. Sharmila asked if she wanted to split a dessert and they bought a chocolate sundae between them. Keira, who had never paid her much attention before, knew more about early pop and punk music than Wynter did so they talked about The Cure and Green Day.

"I'm going to Sri Lanka over spring break," Sharmila told the group. "I can't wait! My uncle lives in a mansion — seven bedrooms. My cousin's taking me to a cricket match."

"What's *cricket*?" Keira said in that croaky monotone she used to express disdain.

"I know about cricket," Wynter said. Xay had explained the game to her. "It's a bit like baseball, but a match lasts five days."

"Don't be stupid," Stacey said.

"She's right, though," Sharmila said. "I'm just going the first day. I'm not wasting my entire vacation at a sports stadium. They don't even have cheerleaders."

"Do you know anything about baseball?" Stacey asked Wynter, without acknowledging she'd been right about cricket. "Football?"

"My brother Jesse likes ice hockey."

"Ugh. Hockey is *horrible*. You missed the entire football season. Which high school are you going to? We'll try out for the cheerleading squad together in September. Sharmila's mom won't let her and Keira's not interested so I'll need someone to come along with me."

"I'm not going to high school here." The way Stacey had dismissed her, *and* Jesse, made her defensive. "I'm going to live with my mom in Thailand."

The girls stared at her.

"Your mom's dead," Keira said bluntly.

"She's not dead."

"I'm sure my mom said she's dead or something and that's why you're in foster care."

"She lives in Thailand, on a tropical island called Ko Samui."

"You're lying," Stacey said, rolling her eyes at her friends. "*Thailand?* Where did you dream that up? Where is Thailand, anyway? Is that in China?"

Wynter pressed her lips together. *This doesn't matter.* Cricket and ice cream sundaes and Stacey's creative geography... none of it mattered. In a few weeks she'd never need to talk to these girls again.

They bought their movie tickets. Wynter had almost given up on Joy, but she appeared as they left the concessions stand.

"Did you buy a ticket?" Wynter asked her.

"Not yet. I'm late — I'm so sorry." Joy nodded to the other girls as Wynter introduced them. "Wait here for me? I'll buy my ticket and come right back."

The girls didn't want to wait, so they went to find seats. A few minutes later Joy returned and she and Wynter went into the theater. Wynter thought about making Joy tell the girls they really were going to Thailand but she wasn't supposed to have told anyone. The girls were halfway down the auditorium, which was quickly filling up, and they hadn't saved seats. Wynter and Joy sat in the row behind them.

"Isn't this exciting?" Joy said, settling into the seat.

Her excitement was fake. Joy was excited about Thailand but she had no interest in Star Wars. Neither did Wynter, but Jesse was going to love talking to her about it. Not that it mattered. Jesse didn't matter.

"I sent you a link — did you see it?" Joy said under her breath. "It's the school Miriam's chosen for you. She's already downloaded the application form. A wonderful international school. You'll meet kids from all over the world."

Wynter checked her phone as the theater lights dimmed. The link took her to a website full of pictures of clean neatly dressed happy children in blue uniforms and smiling teachers. Everyone looked like they wanted to be there. Wynter wanted to be there. She glanced over the introductory text, which talked about *developing a lifelong passion for learning* and the school's exceptional senior academic results. Jesse would definitely be impressed. She sent him the link with a quick message.

> I'm going to this school in Thailand.
> It looks amazing, doesn't it?

Instead of the promised 3D movie, the huge screen started show-ing advertisements. After the fourth one, Joy began to fidget.

Wynter's phone rang — Jesse.

Stacey turned around in her seat and hissed, "Turn it off!"

As her phone rang out, the very next ad showed some cartoon characters telling the audience to switch off their phones. Wynter wasn't sure how to do that. Moments later it pinged and Stacey glared at her again. She looked at Jesse's message.

> That school is in Pattaya City
> on the Gulf of Thailand

So what? The retreat was on an island in the Gulf of Thailand. She could take a ferry to school every day like people in New York. She didn't like the idea of floating on water but she'd get used to it. A ferry to school might be fun, although probably slow. She could catch up on homework or listen to music—

Her phone pinged again. Jesse had sent a map, a screenshot showing the locations of Pattaya City and Ko Samui on opposite sides of the Gulf. And between them, going all the way around the gulf, was a blue line. There was no ferry. The blue line was the route by road.

There would be a bus, probably, like here in the Tri-Cities.

> 560 miles

Wynter stared at Jesse's words in the little gray bubble.

> It's a boarding school

But Momma wanted her close by, didn't she?

Ping. Ping. Ping. All three girls in front of her were shushing her now.

> 13 hours by road

> Great program though

> You can take French just like
> you always wanted LOL

> Award-winning music teachers

> You could learn to play
> one of those Thai lutes

> I'm feeling jealous already

> Students from all over the world

> Nothing like it in boring
> old Washington

> Only 2 hours from the
> bright lights of Bangkok

Wynter pushed her way out of the seats and stumbled up the aisle, out the door, down the corridor and into the foyer. Jesse's messages came every few seconds.

> Awesome extracurricular activities

> Beach and art gallery
> trips on weekends

> Last year the kids visited
> a turtle sanctuary!

> Did I ever tell you I'm
> partial to turtles?

> Or if turtles aren't your thing,
> choose from ice skating, kayaking,
> zip-lining in the rainforest

> The beds in those dorms
> look real comfy

> I bet you'll get extra credit
> for your hospital corners

Outside, Wynter drew in lungfuls of cold wet air and wished those gray bubbles would stop rolling up her screen.

"Wynter? Wynter!" Joy was right behind her.

> $29,000 fees per year

> Our mother wants only
> the very best for you

His words drove icicles into her chest. Was this what brutal honesty felt like?

> She must love you so much.

✿

Wynter found herself in the parking lot, weaving aimlessly around cars. She couldn't hear Joy calling her anymore. Must've lost her in the dark.

She'd had one clear path ahead, the path to Momma. Now that path led somewhere she didn't want to be. She didn't exist on that path. She would not take it.

Which left her standing still, nowhere to go.

She needed to talk to someone. Felicity had been so understanding in the past and certainly more genuine and helpful than the girls at school. Surely she'd be there when Wynter needed her most? She sat on the hood of a car, found the homework forum on her phone, and jabbed at the tiny keyboard to tell Felicity she wasn't going to Thailand after all. She didn't elaborate. No point wasting energy if Felicity really wasn't her friend anymore.

Seconds after sending the message, Felicity wrote back.

> Hi littlesistersong. What happened to your sister and your mom?

> I found out they don't really want me.

> That's too bad.

> Guess what?

> I think my uncle found Roman! This afternoon he told me there's a Roman living in Reno NV, born in Australia. He's exactly the right age. Could it be him?

> Do you want his number?

Wynter's breath caught on a surge of hope. The first thing Roman would've done, after running away from the ashram, was try to find Xay. Maybe he had found him. Or if not, they could search for him together.

She ran her fingers over her braided bracelet. It was already frayed in places and repaired with tiny knots from where she'd broken it earlier. Pushing the bracelet up revealed the tiny cogwheel tattoo on her wrist. She'd thought it meant she belonged with Caleb because he had a matching symbol on his t-shirt.

The universe doesn't speak to you, Joy had said.

If she couldn't interpret signs, maybe she'd gotten that sign wrong. The tattoo was the only part of her that belonged to Xay. Not Caleb. No interpretation necessary. Xay had put this mark on her skin because he'd loved her and wanted to stay with her.

She'd tried to leave everything about that place behind, washed it away, even the good parts. But the fear she'd lived with much of her life was threatening to resurface — those terrifying pieces pushing their way up from her stomach to her chest and heart, to her throat. Here on the outside, where she wasn't allowed to be where she needed to be, where Joy didn't want her and Indio was too busy for her and Momma wanted to shut her away again, she had to reassess her priorities.

Make one promise to yourself and keep it.

She whispered, "I promise myself I will find Xay."

She wrote back.

> I want his number

The number came through, and more messages from Felicity.

> Text him your pic. If he recognizes you, you'll know it's him!

> Again, don't tell anyone, okay? This is our secret. My uncle could get into major trouble and he's been so nice about helping out.

"Do you mind?"

Wynter raised her eyes from the screen to see a woman standing right in front of her. She had plastic shopping bags bunched in each hand. Her three young children were staring at Wynter like she'd done something unforgivable.

"This is my car. You can't just sit on someone's vehicle."

Wynter slid off the hood as Joy's voice echoed across the lot.

"Wynter!" Joy hurried over. "I'm so sorry," she said to the woman, gripping Wynter's arm and pulling her away.

"Did you know?" Wynter said. "Did you know she doesn't really want me?"

"What are you talking about?"

"That school is hundreds of miles away. I'm not going with you if Momma doesn't want me."

"Wynter, that's a very good school. Very expensive."

"I'll be all alone. I won't exist!" She wrapped her arms around her head and yelled, "You *did* know, and you kept it secret just so you could get what you want."

The woman was coming over and now she looked concerned. "You alright there? Do you need help?" She gave Joy a suspicious look. How could a total stranger see her and want to help her when Joy had tried to trick her and her own mother couldn't see her at all?

Never would.

"She's perfectly fine. She's my sister," Joy said, taking Wynter's arm again and marching her through the parking lot. "Calm down, Wynter. Miriam knows what's best. She finally wants us to join her — what more could we want?"

"I thought we were going to be together," Wynter choked out, "like a real family. Five hundred and sixty miles... That's too far."

"Miriam has a busy life. I suppose she thinks the retreat is no place for children."

"I don't want to go. I won't go!"

"Don't talk nonsense. This is the path we're supposed to be on."

Out of habit, Wynter looked around for a sign. She couldn't think straight. She'd invented signs to make Joy send her to Caleb, but now she couldn't come up with anything to let her stay. And what use was a sign, anyway? She might convince Joy, but it was Momma's decision that mattered.

She stopped dead. "I'll tell Caleb everything. He'll call the police. They'll go to the ashram and find out the truth."

Joy paled. "What on earth do you mean?"

"You know what I mean. If Miriam doesn't leave me alone, I'll tell them what happened there. Someone will pay."

"You'll ruin everything," Joy said in a breathy voice full of fear. "You can't betray us. You can't make trouble."

"Tell Momma to let me stay here. You can stay or go — I don't care anymore. But I'm not going if I won't exist for her."

Joy looked so very frail and scared as she stood at the edge of the parking lot, clutching her purse.

"I don't blame you, Joy. I know you just wanted her to love you again."

"She does love me. She *chose* me. She left the boys behind and chose *me*."

"Then go!"

"Why are you always so much trouble?" Joy said, pleading now.

"I won't be trouble for *you*. You don't have to worry about me anymore."

Wynter walked away and around the corner, crossed the street and waited at the bus stop. Joy didn't follow. Wynter was supposed to call Rosa to pick her up but Rosa wasn't expecting the call for another two hours.

The bus carried her toward "home" — that place that would never be home. Could she follow through on her threat if Miriam didn't change her mind? She imagined being interrogated by severe detectives in a small airless room like she'd seen on TV. She tried to put together the words she'd have to say and found it impossible to form the sentences, even in her head, just as she'd been unable to tell Caleb or Jesse.

But the way Joy had looked at her... *Joy* believed she'd do it, and that was what mattered. Joy would tell Miriam, and Miriam would back down because nothing must *ever* tarnish the reputation of the Light.

Wynter got off the bus and instead of going up the hill to Rosa's, turned in the other direction, down to the river. There was a track to the river bank and from there she walked along the muddy shore in the dark. Rosa had told her this place was beautiful in the spring, when the grass turned green and the birds returned.

Maybe she wouldn't be here long enough to see it. She had another option now. She had Roman's number — she should've acknowledged the sign days ago when Felicity first offered to help. She sat on a rock and looked up Reno on the map. More than six hundred miles away. About the same distance as that boarding school from Miriam — certainly not a place she could visit in a day and come back. She needed to run away. She'd need money and a plan.

She found a selfie on her phone, taken during her second week of school — she was holding up the project she'd made in art class that day, where they had to sculpt something from wire. Wynter had first tried to make a miniature guitar with six wire strings and tiny tuning pegs, but it was a crooked, tangled disaster. So she'd started again with something she knew she could do well. She'd twisted the wire into a dreamcatcher, complete with dangling feathers. She could weave dreamcatchers in her sleep, although using wire had been a minor challenge. The art teacher had given her the Student of the Week award, which was surely only because she was the new kid. The selfie was intended for Indio but in the end she'd never sent it.

If she'd made a successful wire guitar, she would've sent it.

She cropped out the dreamcatcher, because Roman would prob-ably make some snide comment about it, and attached just her face to a new message.

> Hi Roman. Is that you? I hope
> so. I got out, too. I'm living in
> Washington. Do you know
> where Xay is? If it's really you,
> please write back.
> Wynter XOXO

Her phone rang. She drew a deep breath, her mind filling with all the questions she needed to ask. But the screen said *Caleb*.

Jesse would've told him by now about Thailand and about the school. The thrill of finding Roman had made her forget what Caleb would think about her leaving. She let the call go to voice-mail.

Moments later, a new message arrived.

> Wynter! I can't believe it.
> Yes, it's me. How are you?
> You look just the same!

Wynter read the message through twice. She'd found him. She'd found Roman. At last the universe was making sense.

> Did you find Xay?

> I don't know exactly where
> he is but I have some clues
> I need to follow. We could
> do it together!

> I want to meet you in Reno.
> Are you doing okay? Send
> photos! Can I call you?

> I'm out with friends so
> don't call just yet. They'll
> get all nosy about it. Let's
> keep this between the two
> of us until we find Xay.

> Let's meet halfway, that's
> fair. How about Eugene,
> Oregon? I have a friend
> there I can stay with.

Wynter's bus from LA had stopped in Eugene, a couple of hours south of Portland. Not too far away.

> I need to get some
> money. I'll let you know.

> I start a new job Monday
> after next, so we have to
> meet up this coming week.

> I understand. I'll figure out a
> way. Can we talk tomorrow?

> I'm camping this weekend
> and my phone's almost
> dead. I'll talk to you Sunday.
> I'm so glad you found me!

Wynter headed toward Rosa's house, brainstorming ideas for getting money. Her allowance wasn't going to help much and she'd spent this week's on food and a movie she hadn't watched. What could she sell? The only thing she had of value was Indio's guitar. Maybe she could sell it to someone at school. It was, after all, Indio who'd told her to make a promise to herself. Selling the guitar would help her keep that promise.

As she walked up the hill, Caleb called again. She wasn't going to Thailand but he didn't know that yet. Would he encourage her to go? Or would he fight to keep her? Curiosity made her answer the call.

"Jesse just told me about the school. He thought you seemed upset." His voice anchored her, as always, and she was struck by a desperate desire to stay right here until she could be with him, to defy the universe after all, to forget about Xay and Roman, to endure Rosa's cold unwelcoming house for as long as it took to be where she belonged.

"I thought Momma wanted me," she stammered, "but I was wrong."

"That's not necessarily true."

"I don't know if I should go." Go to Roman, she meant, not to Miriam. But she needed to see if he believed there was an alternative, a path where he chose her. If he could do that, if he wanted her despite the trouble it would cause him, maybe she didn't need Xay.

"That has to be your decision."

Wrong answer. He wasn't going to fight for her.

"She's your mother," Caleb went on in a resigned way. "After everything she's done, I didn't believe she could be an adequate parent but that's not my call. I understand if you want to go to her. You'll see her several times a year. You'll be at a great school. You won't be in the Light. It won't be like before, hun. You'll be safe."

Everything he said was true, and yet she couldn't go. That decision was already made. She would not go to the other side of the world only to be ignored. Now she needed him to give her a reason to stay *here*, to give her hope he would take care of her.

She said, "If I stayed, would you help me?"

"Always. That's my duty."

"Your duty..."

She could barely speak, anguish driving the air from her lungs. Until this moment she hadn't realized she needed to hear him speak about love. Speak those words that no one but Joy had ever said to her, and when Joy said them it never sounded true. To Joy, love was something to be given and snatched away on a whim, something you had to win back through atonement.

Did Caleb know what love was?

If he knew, and if he said the words, she'd believe him.

He didn't say what she needed to hear. He said, "Girls need their mothers."

She thought of teenaged Caleb taking on all the responsibility, of Jesse insisting it didn't matter because he didn't remember her, and of six-year-old Indio waiting for her to come back, day after day, year after year, until he stopped hoping.

"So do boys," she said.

"That ship's sailed," Caleb said heavily. "But you have the chance to start again with her, even if it's not exactly the way you wanted. Maybe you should take what she's offering, what she couldn't give us."

"When I was little," Wynter said, drawing on painful memories, "I felt like I deserved more. Maybe I wanted too much from her. Maybe I was greedy. Joy was so much easier, always compliant. I think I was a burden. I think you and Indio and Jesse were burdens and that's why she left you behind."

Caleb hesitated, taking it in. "I can't explain what she did. Things are a lot simpler from where I sit. You have to decide, Wynter. But if you do stay, I want to be the one taking care of you."

Her throat ached as hope surfaced again, and that same terrible fear that hope always brought with it. "Are you saying you'll try for custody?"

Silence. She counted her heartbeats. One, two, three...

"That's what I want," he said at last. "But right now I have another duty. This afternoon I got orders to deploy. I ship out of Key West in Florida for two months in April. When I get back, I'll work with Tina. I'll work with my executive officer to come up with a family plan the Coast Guard is happy with."

Her mind felt hollow, her body light. She was floating away. She sat on the step of Rosa's porch, hugging her knees. "You're talking about... June? I can't wait that long."

"We have to work with what we've got."

Behind her, Rosa opened the door. "Why are you back so soon?"

"Goodbye, Caleb," Wynter said, and hung up.

She went in, ignoring Rosa's questions. The path to Caleb had been an option, but his deployment was a roadblock. The path to Roman was the clear way ahead. She'd found him so fast and it would cost her no more than a bus ticket to meet him.

This was the way the universe wanted her to go.

Pretty Desperate

> I'm figuring out how to get the money for the ticket. Tell me all about your new job. Send me a picture!

No response. Wynter tried calling Roman but it rang out. On Sunday he wrote back.

> Sorry I missed your call. Let's stick to text because I'm on the road with friends all weekend and I haven't told them about you yet.

As they texted back and forth all day, Wynter was becoming increasingly apprehensive about seeing him again. While she was thrilled to have found him, this was colored by the disappointment that it was Roman who'd been found, and not Xay. Roman was Xay's friend — in fact they'd grown up together, as close as brothers when she first met them two years ago — but her relationship with him had always been cautious. He seemed different now, friendlier and more open. Roman could be a lot of fun but at times he'd not been particularly nice to her. He'd been jealous that Xay liked her so much. The way he talked about the two of them searching for Xay convinced her he was over that now.

Jesse called to help with homework on Monday night. She told him she didn't need help, and he didn't push. Neither of them mentioned Thailand or the school or all those messages he'd sent on Friday night. That subject was a gaping chasm between them. They must either shout at each other across the chasm or not talk at all. It was easier not to talk.

She thought about asking Caleb or Jesse for money, about the lies she could tell. Caleb didn't have a lot of money. Jesse had his YouTube money but she had no idea how to access it. And the idea of stealing from either of them made her feel sick.

"This is the remainder of your school fees for the term," Rosa said at breakfast on Tuesday, handing Wynter a blue form. "Don't forget to hand it in."

Wynter glanced over the form. The fees amounted to $45 — a good start. It might even be enough, if she booked her ticket a few days in advance. She didn't mind so much about stealing from Rosa. The universe was on her side.

"Where's the money?" she asked Rosa.

"Right there." Rosa pointed to the credit card details and her signature at the bottom of the page.

"Oh. We don't have to give them cash?"

"Goodness, no. I've paid with my card, and Social Services will reimburse me. You be sure to collect a receipt, please."

Wynter's heart sank but she wasn't deterred. The universe would give her what she needed, one way or another.

✿

Wynter was on the bus on Wednesday morning when Roman wrote again.

> I'm sorry I can't send a pic!!!
> My stupid phone camera broke.
> My buddy says he'll take some
> pics later in the week and I'll
> send you a bunch.

> Okay

> Let me know as soon as you
> book your ticket. I'll drop
> everything and drive to Eugene.
> It's 7 hours away and I've got a
> packed bag in the trunk.

She smiled at that word, *trunk*. The boys had always called it the boot, and the front of the car the bonnet instead of the hood. Roman was learning to speak American at last.

At school, Wynter pinned a flyer to sell her guitar on the noticeboard. It must be worth at least one hundred dollars because Indio did not play it on stage. Or perhaps it was worth so little it wasn't good enough to play on stage. She split the difference and put fifty dollars on the flyer.

A niggle of doubt stirred her conscience. This was Indio's guitar, not hers to sell. But he'd given it to her. He hadn't said he ever wanted it back. *It's just gonna lie around here doing nothing.*

Stacey and Keira came over and Wynter tensed for a difficult conversation. She'd walked out on them at the movie theater five days ago and hadn't spoken to them since.

"Can one of your so-called hot brothers be my Valentine?" Stacey said sweetly. "Or do they all live in Thailand like your mom?" She gave Wynter a withering look to show she still believed the Thailand story was another figment of Wynter's imagination. "Got pictures? I'll pick one for myself, and Keira and Sharmila can have the rejects."

"I don't think they date eighth graders," Wynter muttered, straightening the flyer. She knew *that* much about dating.

"I like older guys," Keira said, snapping her gum. "Zac Efron and Robert Pattinson are *ancient* but still hot. The Harry Potter guy is cute. Kit Harington — oh my god, yes please. And that Aussie guy in *The Hunger Games.*"

"Hey, let's get together and watch *The Hunger Games* at Keira's house," Stacey said, like it was the most incredible idea anyone had ever had. "She's got an entertainment room with theater seats and everything. Wynter, maybe you'll actually make it to the opening credits this time."

"I'm banned from the entertainment room until Easter, remember?" Keira told Stacey. "Cuz of those videos Marshall's cousin sent me." She turned to Wynter. "So, who's your Valentine?"

"She'll just make someone up," Stacey said.

Wynter kept quiet. It wasn't at all clear to her how important it was to have a Valentine. Jesse had called it the day for lovers. Wynter didn't understand the first thing about love.

"We'll find you someone!" Stacey said. "Who d'you think is hot? Do you like boys?"

"Boys are fine." Boys were certainly better than girls, in her experience so far.

"Yeah, but which boy?" Keira persisted. "Tomorrow you have to leave candy on the desk of the boy you secretly love."

Wynter said, "It wouldn't be a secret if I told you."

The girls gave up and left her alone, giggling to each other.

✾

Jesse had been waiting all afternoon for Indio's call. He was suffering from an acute case of survivor guilt — Indio had wanted him to go to that gig and to the party afterward. Jesse hadn't gone because Natalie hadn't wanted to. He was being *very* attentive to Natalie and she was setting the pace in every aspect of their relationship. When she wanted him to watch a *Twilight* movie marathon with her, he did that. When she wanted him to write her practical reasoning paper for philosophy class, he did that. When she wanted to make out, fully clothed, in the back of the Caprice on the lake instead of driving to Oregon to see his brother's band, he did that. He told himself it all amounted to extended foreplay.

If he'd gone to the party, maybe he'd have been among the four kids arrested that night on a bunch of random trumped-up charges. And trumped-up they were, as it turned out.

"They dropped everything but Disorderly Conduct as soon as we walked in the room," Indio told him when he finally called that evening, following his plea negotiations. "I plead that down to a Class C misdemeanor — Abuse of a Venerated Object."

"God, that's an impressive thing to plead guilty to. That's *majestic*. Did you pee in the baptismal font or something?"

"Just the church wall."

"What denomination?"

"Uh, Lutheran, I think."

"Lutherans bug me."

"All denominations bug you. Including non-denominational."

"Yeah, but Lutherans are all about God's grace. Like, there's nothing you can do to influence his decision, no good works or anything. You just have to cross your fingers and hope he's in a good mood on Judgment Day. And the big guy's not exactly known for his equanimity."

"I'm not gonna put much stock in an atheist's opinion of God."

"It's all in the Good Book."

"Well, someone was watching out for me, cuz all I got was a two-thousand-dollar fine."

"A two-hundred-dollar-an-hour lawyer on Caleb's dime was watching out for you, bro. How are you gonna pay?"

"Pray for a miracle."

"God's not gonna put much stock in an atheist's prayers."

"I'm a *heathen*, not an atheist."

"I doubt God discriminates between the two." Jesse needed to start calling himself a heathen. Not as subversive as the A word. Less threatening to girls. Romantic, even.

"What's going on with Wynter?" Indio asked.

"We're sort of not talking. That's okay. She can sulk for a week. She didn't even ask about my marathon Valentine's date last Saturday."

"Maybe that's because, like me, she thinks you should dump that girl. Is she going to Thailand or not?"

"I've been instructed not to ask her. Not to talk about it in case she feels pressured. And Joy's not answering Caleb's messages, as usual. When Wynter visits this weekend I'm gonna pressure her *a great deal*."

"Does she know about my arrest?"

"No. Caleb thinks it'll stress her out. We have a few weeks to change her mind. We have to do something."

"Change *her* mind? Miriam's her mother. Last I checked, parents have the right to decide where their own children live."

"Are you siding with Miriam?"

"No. It sucks. And there's nothing we can do about it."

✿

Wynter brought Indio's guitar to school on Thursday because Giselle from her music class had seen the notice and shown some interest. They met up in the music room. Giselle spent ten minutes strumming away, looking unimpressed. Wynter took over and played two classical pieces and a blues riff Indio had shown her, and Giselle said she would bring the money tomorrow.

Light-headed with success, Wynter put the guitar away with the other instruments and walked to her homeroom as the bell went.

As soon as she went in, she knew something was wrong. Everyone stared at her. Half of them sneered and giggled.

"You're pretty desperate for attention, Wynter Wild," someone said.

Mrs Ling arrived.

"Miss, she's put love notes and chocolate on every single boy's desk."

"Settle down, please," Mrs Ling said.

Wynter felt her face heat. "I didn't do it. I only just got here."

Mrs Ling gave her a sympathetic look. Her classmates weren't nearly so sympathetic. Wynter found herself back in the library, hiding between the bookcases, skipping social studies which had gotten too complicated for her to follow in any case. She texted Jesse a dozen times in a row until her phone finally vibrated as he called her back.

"They played a trick on me."

"Who?"

"I don't know. Maybe Stacey. I hate Valentine's Day."

"Join the club."

"But I thought you had a date on Saturday?"

"The date was great. Didn't have a happy ending, if you know what I mean. I guess maybe you don't know what I mean."

"Did you have a fight with Natalie?"

"Not exactly. I'm being mega patient with her."

A teacher stormed toward her. "Put that phone in your locker, now!"

"Gotta go," she whispered, and hung up.

She sat in a restroom stall to check the bus schedules on her phone. A bus from Pasco left at 2:10PM, and this one went direct to Portland where she'd transfer, rather than through Seattle. Portland was little too close for comfort to Indio but no one would know she was missing for a few hours. She was already hatching a plan.

She went to the front office.

"I handed in a form yesterday and my foster mom says there's something wrong with it," she told Myra behind the counter. "Can I check something?"

Myra looked through three different inboxes to find the form, and gave it back. Around the corner, Wynter copied the credit card details into her phone before returning the form.

She sat at a computer in the library and booked a one-way ticket to Eugene with Rosa's credit card. The same-day purchase cost almost twice as much as she anticipated. That was okay. The universe had put that credit card number into her hands and she was supposed to use it.

She printed out the e-ticket. Then she texted Roman.

> I'm doing it! I booked my ticket for TODAY. I'll be at the Eugene bus station at 8:50PM.

> Can you meet me there? Can we stay with your friend?

She was giving him almost ten hours' notice and he'd said his bag was already packed. The bell went for class.

Wynter walked slowly down the hallway. Waiting...

The little *ping* made her jump.

> I'll be there!!!

Chemistry of Love

Wynter sat quietly through her classes, her toes drumming the floor.

Fifteen minutes before the last morning class ended, she told her teacher she felt sick and got a hall pass and a note for the nurse's office. She went to her locker to retrieve her wallet, leaving her backpack behind. She walked off the school grounds without a permit, which was entirely against the rules, and caught the bus. This was the same route she took every day to and from school, and she held her breath as the bus sailed past her usual stop. Rosa wouldn't be home anyway – she was working from her office. The bus took her to Pasco.

Xay had told her that when you stole something it was best to buy something cheap at the same time, to avoid suspicion. She'd rather not have stolen anything, but three dollars was all she had in her wallet and she used it to buy a lipstick from the drugstore. At the checkout, she had one hand in her coat pocket fingering the scarf she'd slid off the rack before choosing the lipstick. It was silky and patterned like the ones Rosa often wore, except this one was made from a cheap shiny fabric.

The entire front part of the store was a display of chocolates, sparkly heart-shaped balloons, and teddy bears atop big baskets of pink and red frosted cookies and mugs. She wondered who had bought candy for all the boys in her homeroom and who had written the silly notes. Then she remembered she didn't care. She didn't ever want to go back. If she found Roman, and together they found Xay, why would she ever need to go back?

On the way to the bus terminal in the rain, buttoning up her expensive camel coat to stay warm, she walked by the historical museum she'd wanted Joy to take her to. It was open and she'd have liked to take a look inside. No time today, and she wasn't ever coming back to Pasco.

In the restroom she twisted her hair up and wrapped the scarf around her neck. She spent a long time applying the lipstick — she'd never done it before and it took a few tries to make it look neat. Four weeks ago she'd sat waiting in this bus terminal with Rosa, on her way to visit Caleb, and Rosa had filled out an Unaccompanied Minor form. She didn't have a form today so she needed to look sixteen years old.

The lunch break at school was over by now. It was unlikely they'd report her missing yet. Rosa would get an email first thing tomorrow saying she'd been absent without a note for the afternoon. Rosa, of course, would discover she was missing when she got home some time after 6PM.

Wynter showed her e-ticket to the driver, staring boldly at him like an adult would. He waved her on board, uninterested even in meeting her eye. She was taking a long bus ride to another state with nothing but the clothes on her back — well, she'd done that before.

The bus set out toward Portland.

She loosened her hair. She unwound the scarf and used it to scrub off the lipstick so Roman wouldn't make fun of her for being inauthentic.

She plugged in her earbuds and listened to one of Indio's playlists. Jesse would tell her disparagingly that half the songs on it were "three-chord rock", and they were, but she knew why Indio liked them, and why Xay liked them. The beat suffused her body and overwrote her heartbeat. Closing her eyes, she returned to her sanctuary and her fingers blindly worked a dozen tiny, familiar braids into her hair so that Roman would recognize her.

As the bus pulled into Portland, hours later, Wynter jolted upright from sleep, the music still blaring in her ears. She got off to find her connecting bus. Instinctively she looked around for Indio, just in case they'd figured out what she'd done. But how could they know? And what would they do, anyway, when they learned she'd vanished? Caleb *wanted* her to choose Thailand, and Jesse was mad at her for even thinking about leaving, which was very unfair of him. Indio's music called to her but he'd rather get high than make the effort to get to know her.

It felt wrong to think badly of them. They owed her nothing. She had no right to blame them for anything.

Yet as she sat on the metal bench waiting for the boarding call, she couldn't stop thinking about her brothers. From the moment she'd seen Caleb walk up to her in darkness, she knew she belonged with him in that house. She belonged in the jamroom playing nine guitars with Indio. She belonged with Jesse, who had so much to teach her even though half the time she didn't understand what he was saying.

She'd thought she belonged with Joy, but all Joy wanted was Momma's forgiveness and acceptance. Joy was entitled to that. One of them, surely, was entitled to that. And there was one other thing Joy had wanted. Wynter still didn't understand exactly why Joy acted on that January night, but it was clear she wanted her little sister out of the Light. No matter what happened next, Wynter was grateful to her for that.

Of all these nameless things she felt, was any part of it *love*?

She took out her phone and sent a message to her four siblings.

> **What is love?**

She sat very still, watching her screen, waiting for those little gray bubbles. She gasped as a new message appeared. Caleb.

> **Love is doing what needs to be done for the people who depend on you**

He was speaking of duty again. He'd raised his brothers and he served his country — it was all the same to him. *Nobody* depended on Wynter. How could she love if no one needed her?

Her hand shook as she gripped the phone, desperate for answers. Jesse had a gig later tonight. He might not see the message for hours. Joy rarely answered texts or calls, and Indio's life was a complete mystery to her.

A minute later, another gray bubble, from Jesse this time. Nothing but a link. Wynter tapped it — an article titled *The Love Molecule* with a lot of long words in the first paragraph. She pressed her fingers against her lips to suppress the scream in her throat.

"You're wrong, Jesse. You have to be wrong," she whispered. Love wasn't candy and balloons, and it wasn't science, either.

> **Here's another interesting one**

Jesse had sent a second link that informed her love was a chemical reaction in the brain that could be controlled like any other emotion—

She flipped the screen face down on her thigh and waited, waited, waited for more. For fifteen minutes she waited. The boarding call came but she couldn't move. Nothing from Joy — after their last encounter that wasn't surprising, but the Light had a good deal to say about love and even a meaningless platitude would indicate Joy had thought about it for a few seconds.

Nothing from Indio, who had promised to never fail her again.

As she got up from the bench to head for the bay door, her phone rang.

"Are you okay?" Indio said, before she'd even spoken. She *couldn't* speak. "I just saw your text. Baby, what's going on?"

He was somewhere very noisy, with voices and traffic soaking through the line. He was probably only a mile or two away. She had the sudden urge to ask him to hide her in his apartment. She could live there in secret. She'd weave friendship bracelets and mandalas and sell them online to help pay her way. She was very good at it. When she was a bit older and the *authorities* had forgotten she existed, she'd get a job flipping burgers and eventually she'd buy him that eight-thousand-dollar guitar. Every Friday and Saturday she'd go to his gigs, and every other night they'd play music together, just the two of them in their sanctuary. Maybe Jesse, if he promised to keep the secret.

Caleb, of course, did not like secrets — he played by the rules. But Indio did not.

Would Indio break a few rules for her?

Outside, the last person in line was getting on the bus.

Indio wasn't going to let her hide out. She didn't know much about this world, but she knew it didn't work that way.

Make one promise, he'd said. *Something that keeps you true.*

In both this world and the one she'd left behind, nothing was truer than the cogwheel tattoo on her wrist and what it meant. Xay had never said he loved her, but he had loved her. Roman would help her find him and these strange, painful weeks would become a few more dark pieces she could leave behind.

She hung up on Indio and boarded the bus. Rosa would be home from work by now. Wynter texted her to say she was spending the evening studying with a friend.

> Which friend? I need his or her parents' number.

> You may not organize a study date without my permission and knowledge.

> Where are you?

> Call me immediately.

Wynter finally figured out how to switch off her phone.

Unbreakable

Caleb was a little late getting away from work. He had a 7PM dinner date with Bea, and he was going to ask her to marry him.

Earlier, as he was leaving his desk for the day, he'd gotten a strange brief text from Wynter who must have agonized for days over Miriam's decision to bring her to Thailand and then put her in boarding school on the other side of the country. He had no clue whether Wynter still wanted to go. Today, his lawyer had told him she pretty much had no option. So now, really, the only thing he could do was be supportive and positive about it.

What is love?

Wynter might be confused about love, but Caleb knew his mother well enough to know that an expensive school counted for something. It was, to her mind, an act of love.

Grieving over his lost opportunity to take in Wynter was a waste of energy. He had Bea, who he definitely loved no matter how you defined it. He would marry her, and he would do his duty by loving Jilly as his own.

Harry called as he reached his truck.

"Son! Whatcha up to on this fine night?" It was *technically* a fine night, overcast, cold and damp but not raining. Harry sounded halfway to drunk and in a very good mood.

"Heading out with Bea for dinner," Caleb said.

"I'm sitting here with my lady having pre-dinner drinks. How fancy is that! We're in a sports bar on Lake Union. Let's double-date."

"I'm off to Renton, just as soon as I get home and take a shower."

"Bring Bea to the lake! Already booked a table for four. Wasn't too hard in the end, with everyone wanting a table for two tonight."

"There's a reason for that." Caleb gritted his teeth and got into the truck. While he appreciated his father making a rare overture, no way was he going to propose to Bea in front of Harry. Or in any sports bar. "We could all meet up for lunch on Sunday." Lunch was safe. He could tell Harry the good news in person, and by then Bea would have a ring on her finger to show off.

"I've got shifts all weekend. What a shame. I wish you'd join us. Charmaine's been dying to meet you both."

"I made my plans a while ago."

"How about I text you the address, in case you change your mind? Or just join us for coffee after."

That edge of hurt in Harry's tone meant it would be Caleb's fault when he failed to show tonight, and then Harry would casually berate him for it for the next six months.

"Can't be there," Caleb said firmly. "Sorry, Harry. You and Charmaine have a pleasant evening."

A few seconds after he hung up, Harry did text the address along with a photo of him and his date — an overly made-up woman in her forties with an ash-blonde bob, wearing a plunging hot pink dress, a tacky heart brooch, and way too much eye makeup. She was holding up a margarita with a wide grin. If this was the woman he'd mentioned from AA, it would appear the twelve steps weren't working out too well for either of them.

There was another reason Caleb didn't want to see Harry yet. Harry didn't know about Indio's arrest and he couldn't tell him tonight, the night he proposed to Bea. Nor could he sit through a meal with his father *without* telling him. So the meal would have to wait.

Caleb set off for home, the traffic slowing him down after a couple of miles when he hit Beacon Avenue. Tonight wasn't the night to be thinking about his father or his brother. Bea was his chance to start again and build a new family. His imminent deployment, and any future ones that would have made single parenthood impossible, weren't an impediment to Bea. Her dad was retired army. She understood that life. They would set a date after Caleb returned home in June. Jesse was turning nineteen that same month and he really should leave home. Jilly would be almost two, still young enough to attach to him as a parent.

Marriage hadn't been on his mind when he booked the seafood grill place in Renton two weeks ago. He'd made the booking because taking out his girl on Valentine's Day was the right thing to do. And he wasn't one for big romantic gestures. He hadn't pre-emptively bought a ring that she might not like. He wouldn't be getting down on one knee. They'd discuss it like rational people. She wouldn't be expecting it, given their recent conversations, but he already knew she'd say yes. She'd burst into tears and hug him and he'd *feel*... anticipation, happiness, love.

The time was right. It would make up for losing Joy. It would almost make up for losing Wynter.

Rosa called while he was stopped at lights. He put her on speaker.

"What's up, Rosa?" At the back of his mind was the constant worry she'd find a reason to cancel Wynter's visit this coming weekend, or take her phone again.

"Have you spoken to Wynter today?"

He felt a flicker of unease. "Not spoken, no. Where is she?"

"She texted that she's at an unnamed friend's house for the evening. This was not pre-arranged. I just spoke with her best friend Stacey, who says she wasn't at school this afternoon."

"Let me call Jesse. I'll get back to you."

Caleb pulled over and collected himself. He called Wynter first — it went straight to voicemail. He texted her a quick message, asking her to call. He called Jesse, who was at a jazz club in Wall-ingford preparing for a gig.

"She had a bad day at school," Jesse told him. "She called me this morning and said the kids played a prank. She was pretty miserable. And I got this question from her about half an hour ago, for a homework assignment, I guess. Something about love? Sent her some links but she didn't thank me for helping. We've been having a difficult few days ever since—"

"Never mind about that," Caleb cut in. "She's vanished into thin air."

"Maybe she took the bus to Seattle and made her own way to the house. She could be waiting on the porch right now."

Caleb had intimate knowledge of the bus schedule between Pasco and Seattle. "The evening bus doesn't get in until 6:40." No need to panic yet. Surely Wynter would come to him if she was in trouble. Wouldn't she? "Can you get to the bus station and see if she's on that bus?"

"We're not going on until 7:30. I can be there just in time."

"Thanks."

"But d'you think..." Jesse hesitated. "Could they already be gone?"

"Those passports were supposed to take weeks. I guess it's possible Joy paid to expedite them."

"If Joy fetched her from school, and if they flew out of Seattle, they'll already be at LAX. They might already be on a plane to Thailand. She wouldn't just leave without saying goodbye, would she?"

But she *had* said goodbye. *Goodbye, Caleb.* That was the last time Caleb had spoken to her.

He was thinking about that dog again. About eight-year-old Jesse, learning Skar was gone.

He wouldn't just leave us, would he?

Thinking about six-year-old Indio, learning she was gone.

She wouldn't just leave us, would she?

The same question at seven years old. At eight. *I can't fix this one, little buddy.*

Somewhere around age nine he stopped asking. That camping trip to Lost Creek State Park — he'd stopped asking by then, hadn't he? He seemed happy on that trip. He looked happy in that photo.

Wynter... you wouldn't just leave us, would you?

"Let's do what we can from this end," Caleb told Jesse. "I'll drop in at the Light office. Then I'll go home and make some calls."

✿

The Light office storefront was closed. A sign directed people around to the back entrance where there was a yoga class on.

Caleb heard the commotion before he saw it. The loudest voice was — impossibly — his father's.

"She's my daughter! I just wanna take her out for dinner. Let me talk to her!"

Caleb ran around the building. A man in loose clothing — the so-called Jedi master, per Jesse's description — clasped Harry's arm and struggled to get him out the door. His lady friend hovered nearby, bobbing up and down on her stilettos.

"Harry!" Caleb barked as he approached.

"She's in there. I saw her!" Harry said, breaking free. The Jedi had his phone out, ready to call the cops by the look on his face. "Why won't they let her come out? This place is a cult, a fucking cult. Get her out of there!"

Caleb put his hand on Harry's shoulder and directed him away from the door.

"Thought we'd take her out, me and Charmaine," Harry said in his most aggrieved tone. Charmaine came to clutch his arm, hanging off him for moral support. "Why not? Haven't seen her in years and we were only five miles away. You backed out on me, so why not?"

"I didn't *back out*." Caleb shook his head. Arguing semantics wasn't going to fix a thing. "Go back to your bar, Harry. There's something else I need to deal with here."

"Something else? That's my little girl in there. I got every right to talk to her."

"Wynter's missing. I need to ask Joy about it."

Harry did shut up then. Caleb turned for the door, where the Jedi master blocked the way, one arm extended.

"I need to see her," Caleb said. "Nothing to do with *him*."

"I'm sorry, but she doesn't want—"

Caleb deflected the arm and slid past him. Joy was right there, in the narrow corridor, flattened against the wall behind another staff member, an older woman in exercise gear.

"Do you know where Wynter is?" he demanded.

Joy slunk back a couple of steps.

Caleb reconsidered his attitude. He stopped his advance and lowered his voice. "Have you heard from her? Is she here?"

"I don't know what you mean. Of course she's not here," Joy said, near tears. "I can't see Harry. I can't deal with that negativity."

"You don't have to see him." Caleb put a hand on her arm and encouraged her to move down the corridor, away from everyone else. "Wynter's been missing since this afternoon. Any idea what's going on?"

"What's going on," Joy stammered, "is that she's ruined everything. She won't go to Thailand, and Miriam won't let *me* go without her."

"What d'you mean, she *won't* go?"

"She'll do something terrible if we make her go."

"Such as?"

"It's not your concern, Caleb. You need to stay out of it. I've taken care of her for almost fifteen years. It was my turn to get what I want. Why won't Momma forgive me?" Her expression distorted and her voice wobbled. "I don't know what I'm doing. I don't know where I am..."

Caleb led her through the bead curtain, into the dark store and away from the perplexed staff as he adjusted his mindset. Wynter was *not* going to Thailand. She was staying right here in Seattle and that meant she was still his responsibility.

"It's my turn to take care of Wynter now," he told Joy. "I'm going to get custody, one way or another."

"Miriam won't allow that. She thinks you'll poison Wynter against her. She won't allow it."

"Then don't tell her, and in a few months the Washington family court will decide where she lives."

"You only just met her — you can't possibly love her."

"Does Miriam love her?"

"How can you ask that? She's her mother."

"I'm doing everything I can for Wynter. That's love."

"That's duty. It's not love if you don't *feel* it."

He had never honestly considered the difference, and now was not the time for it. Duty had served him well, his entire life.

"You are both part of this family," he said. "We'll put everything back together the way it was supposed to be."

Joy pressed her face into her hands. "You don't understand. I was supposed to be with Momma again. She loves me. Doesn't she? She chose me over all of you. What happened to her love? I did everything right. I saved Wynter that night."

Her anguish tore at him. This was the pain Miriam had inflicted on him and his brothers, and on Wynter, and Joy was finally feeling it in full force.

"I need your help to save her *tonight*, Joy. Has she ever talked about running away? Where would she go?"

But Joy had nothing to add. Caleb left her being comforted by the woman he'd seen earlier. He checked his phone. No further news from Rosa. Jesse had written that Wynter wasn't on the bus from Pasco.

Caleb needed to get home and figure out what to do next. And he needed to cancel on Bea. There would be no marriage proposal tonight. His confidence that Bea would accept had been predicated on Wynter being on the other side of the planet.

Outside, Harry paced back and forth while Charmaine fussed over him to no effect. He stopped when he saw Caleb.

"I should've made that woman leave this nonsense before it got out of hand," he opined. "She was pregnant with the twins and she had to find the *meaning* of it. As if it was a remarkable situation."

"I don't have time for this, Harry. I have to get home."

"Well, I'm not gonna talk about the ex in front of my fiancée, but three percent of pregnancies are twins, I told her. Look it up. Happens all the time. And I dabbled a bit myself, I admit it. Tried to be supportive. Went with her to those lectures and retreats and shit. And for all that, she throws me out for one little mistake. Hardly saw my own kids for years, and suddenly she's at my door that summer, acting like we can be one big happy family again. I would've taken her back. We talked about reconciliation. But she had conditions. I had to be in the Light. I wasn't gonna stand for that. A bit of yoga, a bit of crystal magic, sure, but I wasn't gonna lose myself like she had."

"You're doing a great job not talking about your ex," Caleb said, with uncharacteristic meanness that shamed him. And he hadn't missed that word, *fiancée*. It meant nothing. Harry asked for a woman's hand in marriage every couple of years and he'd never married one yet. Tonight, of all nights, the word had a bitter after-taste.

"Didn't realize she'd punish me and vanish with my Joy, that's all I'm saying."

"Regardless, you need to respect Joy's wishes."

"I'm sure your mother turned her against me."

"Joy planned to come to you when she left the ashram, so that can't be true."

"Why didn't she, then? Why won't she see me now?"

Because you're a drunk. No one wants you in this state.

No one but Charmaine, apparently. Caleb didn't say the words but his father could probably read them in his expression.

"Look at this, then." Harry brightened and lifted Charmaine's left hand to flash the ring on her finger. "We're getting married! Myself and the lovely Charmaine. We were gonna make the big announcement, champagne and everything, if you'd joined us for dinner."

Caleb made himself pause and react appropriately, more or less. "That's great news. Congratulations. You be sure to let me know the date."

"Goodness, we don't have a date yet," Charmaine said, bubbling over. "I'm staying with my folks in West Seattle until the big day, so we'll make it sooner rather than later."

"Best of luck to you," Caleb said to his future stepmother. Or probably not. "Please walk it off before you drive, okay?"

"Don't worry about it. We're not rushing back," Harry said. "We'll eat somewhere a bit cheaper in this neighborhood, won't we, Charms? You fancy Chinese?"

"Those cocktails were ridiculous," Charmaine said. "Twelve dollars! I'm sure they put the prices up because it's Valentine's."

Caleb had the niggling feeling he'd been invited to the sports bar only because they'd run out of money for the meal and had hoped or even expected him to pay. As they walked off he kept his eye on them to make sure they went past Harry's truck, parked crookedly on the side of the road, and kept going.

"Is it true, what he said?" Joy was standing behind him, speaking softly. Very calm. Serene.

"Which part?"

"Did Momma take me to punish him?"

"That's how he sees it."

Together they watched their father walking away.

She said, "He bought me a different pony every time he visited. Never the same one twice. He sat on the floor and played with me, making the ponies sing to each other in funny voices. Momma never did that."

"She was not a playful person."

"He cheated on her."

The revelation didn't surprise him. Still, it was hard to hear. "That's why she threw him out?"

Joy nodded. "He did a terrible thing to her. Shattered her world. He's not a good person. So why are all my memories good?"

"I remember those visits were good, too. He didn't cope well with raising three boys full-time, but before that, as a part-time dad, he did okay. Taught me to shoot a rifle when I was seven years old, and how to clean it afterward. He was meticulous about gun safety and so proud of me."

"Does that wipe out the bad things he's done?"

"No. The bad things make it hard to trust him. Doesn't mean we can't remember the good."

Caleb put his arm around his sister's shoulders in a gesture that felt both awkward, because he was unused to physical affection within the family, and also necessary. He'd played with those ponies, too. He'd made stables for her from cardboard boxes because not even Harry was going to buy her the pink-and-white plastic playset from the store. Despite the pall of neglect and violence over their collective childhood, there were hundreds of little moments like these, the shared memories unique to their family that bound them together and made his duty to her unbreakable.

"I know you're disappointed right now," he said, "If you want to be in the Light, that's okay. If you need to find a way back to

Miriam, that's okay. But please don't turn away from us. Don't let anyone make you turn away."

Their father disappeared around the corner, staggering on Charmaine's arm. Joy leaned into Caleb's embrace — not quite a hug, but close enough.

✿❁

Not until Caleb was back in the truck did he realize he was well and truly overdue for his date with Bea. She hadn't left a message — another aspect of his job she understood was that sometimes he was unavoidably detained. She never hassled him over being a little late.

He called to apologize and to cancel. She was anxious about Wynter, of course, and completely forgiving because she was a wonderful woman and one day he *would* marry her. When he was in a position to put her and Jilly first.

Home was dark, cold, empty. As he walked in the door, Rosa called, frazzled.

"I've checked my credit card statement online. There's a ninety-three-dollar charge to the bus company but no information about the ticket itself. Their customer service people wouldn't tell me a thing without the booking number."

"That's too much for a one-way ticket to Seattle, and not enough for a return."

"Where did she go?"

"I don't know, Rosa. The ticket might not even be for today. She wasn't on the evening bus to Seattle. I need to think about this. Jesse said the kids played a prank on her at school. Talk to Stacey again and find out what happened."

Caleb hung up and thought about his next move. If Wynter wasn't coming to him, was she going to Indio? No point calling him — he wouldn't pick up, given the current state of their relationship. Caleb texted him instead.

Worthy

Indio pushed his hands into his pockets, moved to the edge of the crowded sidewalk to keep out of the way, and wondered if he was about to be made a fool of.

The text from Wynter must've come while he was in the shower. He hadn't seen it until a few minutes ago.

What is love?

What the hell did that mean?

No, he knew what it meant. He didn't know the answer to the question, but he knew what it meant. She was drowning. She was asking for help. So he'd called, and she was speechless, which left him feeling inadequate, and she'd hung up.

He'd call her tomorrow after school to check up on her. He'd avoided making contact since the arrest and he didn't know what to say about Thailand. Thinking about it opened old wounds, pains he wasn't willing to suffer. It seemed likely she was going back to Miriam — even if it meant boarding school. He didn't blame her for that. Must be hard for her to leave Caleb and Jesse. Maybe not so hard to leave him, the one who wasn't even allowed to be alone in a room with her. He was going to miss the opportunity to make music with her, assuming she ever would've spoken to him again after his latest misadventure.

He'd shown her the blues turnaround, so that was something.

Earlier in the day, he'd been thinking of riding up to Seattle for Jesse's gig tonight but there was the pesky issue of his suspended license. His brothers didn't know it, but the least serious charge from last weekend — a citation for that half-smoked joint in his pocket — was going to cause him the most grief.

Just as he'd decided to risk the trip to Seattle anyway, to debrief with his little bro, Jenny had called. Despite taking his number weeks ago she had not kept in touch and he hadn't expected her to. Tonight she was visiting friends in Portland and wanted to meet him for a drink.

On Valentine's Day.

So here he was, standing outside an Irish pub a short walk from his apartment, waiting for her, his heart light with anticipation yet not truly believing she'd show. But this was Jenny, who never played games — unless you counted slow-dancing with him while dating an actor. Of course she would show.

At 6:30 on the dot, she walked up to him with that smile that made him *want* her in a way that had nothing to do with the reasons he wanted all the girls he'd ever been with. She tilted her face to kiss him on the cheek with a touch of shyness that convinced him she was still with Stefan.

"So, why are we here?" he said pleasantly. "Did Stefan cancel on you?"

"He's in rehearsal. I was sort of relieved he was busy tonight, of all nights. A Valentine's date puts a lot of pressure on a fledgling relationship."

"What's this, then?" He indicated the two of them.

"Let's call it catching up with an old friend on a regular Thursday night." She reached for the door handle. "Shall we?"

He held the door closed with his foot, making a show of it. "Are you old enough to come inside?" he quipped.

"I came of age last month."

He should know that. He used to know that. January nineteenth, which was Martin Luther King Day that year, his senior year. The week before, he'd overheard Kevin Tsang telling her he'd take her to see some R-rated horror flick on her birthday, which Indio was pretty sure she'd hate. She'd told Kevin she was born at four minutes to midnight so she would still be sixteen while watching the movie, and they'd have to bring her mom with them to make everything legal. They'd laughed about her breaking her first law. Even though she really wasn't.

Indio and Jenny stood inside the doorway with half a dozen other couples hopeful of getting a table on this busiest of nights.

"You left a gift taped to my locker for my seventeenth birthday," Jenny recalled, reading his thoughts. "Sheet music for *The Devil Went Down to Georgia*, rolled into a scroll with a wax seal."

"You never thanked me for it."

"There was no card. No one to thank."

"Did you ever learn to play it?"

"I did. Grandpa loved it, as you'd expect, but it freaked out my parents. They pretty much forbade anything but classical music at home." She smiled. Damn, she was so beautiful and he still couldn't have her. "I knew it was from you, of course, but I couldn't say anything. Kevin was so jealous. I almost left you a gift on Valentine's Day, as a sort of thank you. But that would've been..." Her mouth twisted with what he hoped was regret.

"Fucking cruel," he finished for her.

"Kevin's gift to me was a Mozart Pez dispenser. I hate Pez."

"That makes me feel better."

"When's your birthday?"

"September fourth, the day I met you."

"Really?"

"I'm gonna get corny for a second," he said, keeping his tone playful. "The sight of you, that first day of school when you opened your locker two doors down from mine, was the best birthday present I ever had. That's what I thought at the time." Meeting Jenny had been his *only* birthday present that year, other than the Pop Rocks that Jesse snuck into his lunch box, purely an in-joke. Nothing from Harry, who was still not talking to him since his release from juvie two weeks earlier. Nothing from Caleb, either, who was on his way home from a four-month deployment in Alaska.

Jenny looked like she was going to say something. She was distracted by the hostess announcing there was a one-hour wait for a table.

"Let's go to the bar," Jenny said, indicating a couple of stools that had just been vacated.

Her Sidecar and his bourbon straight were served with superfluous heart-shaped swizzle sticks and a wink. The bartender thought they were a couple. Jenny's smile saved it from being awkward.

"How's your sister?" Jenny asked. She must mean Wynter, because he'd never told her about Joy.

"She's going to live in Thailand with our mom. Last I heard, anyway."

"That's good news, isn't it?"

He struggled to explain. "Our mother is... She isn't... She's not great. I think maybe Wynter can't resist the chance. She's been giving us the silent treatment for the past few days, so I don't know if she still wants to go."

"What would you do, in her shoes?"

Indio stared into his drink, swirling it around the glass. He was six years old, hiding out in the back alley with the Super Soaker he stole from Caleb's suitcase while Caleb and Jesse were at the park. They were living out of suitcases, staying at Harry's for the summer. Most of his toys were back in Missoula. Even if he'd brought all his toys to Anaconda, he'd still have taken the Super Soaker that afternoon — the most coveted toy in the family. Indio would've traded all four of his Teenage Mutant Ninja Turtles for it — a trade Caleb had no interest in making.

Indio had about two glorious hours with that gun, all to himself. He was shooting his turtles off the wall when Momma came to say goodbye because she was going out with Joy. All he remembered about it, that last time he saw her, was that he'd accidentally blasted her skirt with water. On another day she might've laughed about it. Her reactions were often unpredictable. That day, she yelled at him and he squirted her again, deliberately this time, and she went away.

What kind of kid turns a Super Soaker on his mother for no reason? Evidently, the kind of kid who grows up to become the kind of man who pees on a church wall.

She never said goodbye to Caleb or Jesse. She didn't say goodbye to him, either, and yet something had made her seek him out before she left. He'd always held on to that, hoping it meant something. Hoping he was important to her in the smallest way.

Indio cleared his throat and said, "At Wynter's age, I think I would've gone to her."

He'd still loved her at fourteen, long after the hope faded. He'd been looking for a mother in every friendly neighbor, every kind teacher, every girlfriend Harry brought home. Just once he thought he'd found her, that summer they moved to Seattle.

As Jenny stroked his hand on the bar counter, he opened his mouth to talk about that one, about how it turned sour, and found he couldn't burden her with it. Not when the odds were high this evening was going to end in disappointment.

Jenny's phone buzzed and she checked it. "Hmm. Stefan's bought tickets for Benaroya Hall next week. Best seats in the house, he says."

"Yay, Stefan."

"We're keeping it casual, but this was a big deal to him."

"Looks to me like he's taking it to the next level."

Jenny turned her phone face-down without answering Stefan. "There's a Jackie Prouser gig tonight, just down the street. I saw a poster earlier. She was one of the supporting acts at that outdoor concert — our second date, remember? Would you like to go?"

"Uh, sure. I'm sure Stefan won't mind," he said with gentle sarcasm.

"No more Stefan. You're the one I've been thinking of, ever since that dance at Patty's. And plenty of times before that, if I'm honest."

She was always honest. And kind. And sweet. And genuine.

Perfect.

He needed to be honest in return.

"I made this promise to myself," he said, slipping his hand out of reach of hers, and leaning his elbow on the counter. "I keep breaking it. I think maybe you asked me here tonight to see if I'm ready yet. Ready for you. I'm not." He was in danger of talking himself out of it. A chance with Jenny, and he was blowing it all by himself.

"It's just a gig, Indio. Can we go, and see what happens?"

He should tell her about the arrests. That would surely put her off. Or would it? Jenny had always seen the person he wanted to be more clearly than the person he was, or had been. Maybe she wouldn't care about his latest troubles, and that was unsettling. If she accepted the worst part of him, it would somehow sully her. He wouldn't do that to her.

"I'm not quite as keen on Stefan's concert at Benaroya Hall as he is," she prompted.

Indio's phone pinged on the bar counter. At the sight of Caleb's name on the screen, his stomach clenched — an almost imperceptible yet familiar, instinctive reaction. The guy's timing could not be worse. Then he read the message.

> Wynter's missing since noon today. Have you heard from her?

"Shit!"

He grabbed the phone and called Caleb, remembering to throw an apologetic look in Jenny's direction. Caleb answered on the first ring.

"How the hell can she be missing?"

"Listen up. She bought a bus ticket but not to Seattle. There's a chance she's on her way to Portland or traveling through there. I'm firing up my laptop to check the schedule."

Indio was already on his feet. Jenny was already handing him his jacket, catching his alarm. "Does Joy know where she might go?"

"No. Somehow, the whole Thailand thing is off. Can you get to the station?"

"On my way."

"The bus from Pasco got in an hour ago. Please get over there."

Indio rang off and shrugged into his jacket. He slipped his hand around the nape of Jenny's neck, under her sleek warm hair, and kissed her very softly at the corner of her mouth. Then, reluctantly, he let her go.

He was not, by any measure, good enough for Jenny. Most likely never would be. But there was a slim chance he could be good enough for Wynter.

Indio called up a photo of Wynter on his phone, one of those cute selfies Rosa had demonized him for, and showed it to every single person at the Portland bus station, on the benches and in the lines and behind the counters.

At last he found someone who recognized her, a middle-aged woman waiting with her husband. "She was here. No luggage or anything. Got on the southbound bus about half an hour ago."

"The bus to LA?"

"That's the one."

Indio called Caleb to tell him.

"I'm reading off the board," Indio said. "It stops in Salem, Eugene, Redding, Sacramento, and a bunch of curbside stops in between. I'll get on I-5 and catch up to the bus, and follow it until she gets off."

"Wait one second. I'm checking to see which fare matches Rosa's credit card statement... Got it. Ninety-three dollars — that's the one-way fare from Pasco to Eugene for a same-day booking."

"One-way? Why?"

"Get to Eugene, Indio. I'm gonna call the sheriff's office down there."

"You really want to involve the cops? I can beat that bus to Eugene. It's an hour and a half, at the most. I'll make sure nothing happens to her."

Caleb sighed. "Okay. You're right. We shouldn't blow this out of proportion."

Impossible not to wonder what Wynter was up to. Indio had met her once and exchanged a few ultimately meaningless texts and cartoons. He didn't know what went on in her head and he didn't know the intricacies of her life. He felt connected to her but she wasn't as similar to him as he'd first imagined. She wanted to be with her family — she *wanted* Caleb's rules and expectations. She wouldn't run from that.

Yet she had run. Something had pulled her in the opposite direction.

✿

More than an hour later, doing eighty most of the way, Indio overtook the bus on the dark highway ten miles out of Eugene and arrived at the station ahead of it. He parked the bike and walked around the entire block, not quite sure what he was looking for. He checked inside the building, where a few people waited.

As the bus arrived, he crossed to the opposite side of the street and watched from the shadows of a parking garage stairwell. Wynter was the first one off the bus. A dizzying wave of relief crashed through him at the sight of her. She was okay. He resisted the urge to call out. Caleb would call out and rush over and force her to come back, without even finding out first why she'd run. Indio wasn't going to do that. As long as she was in his sight, she was safe. He was going to find out what the hell she was up to *before* he brought her home.

Wynter put her head around the door of the bus station on the street corner but didn't go inside. She tapped on her phone with a confused, desperate air.

A few yards down the street from Indio, a man in his forties got out of a parked sedan, pushing his phone into the jacket pocket of his cheap suit. He crossed the street and approached Wynter.

Indio's heart raced as he realized what might have been.

As the man and Wynter talked, Indio drew up his sweatshirt hood, put his head down and crossed the street, unnoticed by the two of them. He kept walking a few paces, going around the side of the building. The man's back was turned and he blocked Wynter's line of sight, so Indio was able to watch as well as hear them, unseen from just around the corner.

"...and he's waiting for you," the man was saying. "He's so excited you found him. Come on, I'll drive you straight to him."

"Why didn't he come with you?"

"He went to the store to buy you a gift. He'll be back by the time we get home."

"Home?"

"My place. He told you, right? He and my son Corey are good friends. He drove up this afternoon, all the way from Reno, and he's staying with us. You can stay with us, too, if you like. With me and my wife."

"I wish he'd answer his phone." Wynter's voice quivered as doubt set in. Indio's heart ached for her. She'd come here full of innocent hope, with no clue she'd been manipulated.

"He went out to the store, like I said."

"You met him, then?"

"I did. Just met him briefly for the first time today, when he arrived. He knows my son. Come along. It's getting cold."

"I don't mind the cold."

"Still, we can't just stand here all night. Roman's waiting for you."

Wynter gave a little nod, like she'd made her decision. She spent a moment fiddling with her phone, folding it back into her wallet, while the man walked a few paces to the street corner to cross. He waited for her.

"Is his hair still really long?" she called out. "He never did send me a photo. I'll be so disappointed if he cut it."

"It's long, sure. Not girlie or anything. Good looking guy, your Roman. He's gonna be so—"

"Really? It's all the way down his back?"

The man turned and looked at her, very carefully. Now he knew it was a test and he had no idea what to say. "Didn't really notice, love," he said tersely. "He was wearing a beanie."

"I think I'm gonna call someone to fetch me." Wynter retrieved her phone.

"What're you talking about? What's Roman gonna think? He's driven all the way up here from Reno. He hopped in his car just as soon as you bought your ticket. He drove seven hours to be with you."

"I'm calling my brother."

"Your *brother*? Thought you said... Thought you told Roman you were a foster kid living with some woman in Washington."

Wynter put the phone to her ear. While her hand shook, her defiant eyes stared the man down.

The man took a couple of steps toward her, and Indio tensed. "This is a fucking waste of time. Come with me right now or I'll—"

A harmonica riff erupted, startling all three of them. It took Indio a moment to realize it was his phone.

He fumbled for it in his back pocket. Wynter's name was on the screen.

She'd called *him*. Not Caleb. Him.

He stepped into view as the man turned toward him. Wynter ran to Indio with a cry. The grinding beat of *When the Levee Breaks* played on as his arms went around her. His gaze fixed on the man in the cheap suit, and in his mind he was punching him into the asphalt.

"What the fuck is this?" the man cried, skittering backward. He spun and took off across the street.

Indio took Wynter's shoulders and set her firmly away from him. "Do. Not. Move."

He crossed the street and caught the man by the scruff of the neck as he was getting into his car. He yanked him out and slammed his face against the edge of the roof.

Once, twice.

He threw him headfirst into the vehicle and left him sprawled across both seats, moaning. Indio snapped a picture of the license plate as he walked off to the sound of the guy retching all over his upholstery.

He returned to Wynter, grabbed her hand, and led her quickly around the building, to his Moto Guzzi in the parking lot.

"I've never ridden a motorcycle before," Wynter whispered, pale with shock.

"You're gonna love it."

Indio strapped the spare helmet on her head and fixed his own. Across the back of his hand was a spray of that sick fuck's blood. He toed down the passenger pegs, mounted the bike and flipped up the kickstand.

"A mile or two out of town, I'll pull over and call Caleb, okay? Hop on. Hold tight."

She got on behind him and slid her arms around his waist. Her body trembled violently against his. Indio's mind raged with blind, unprocessed fury, but he was rock steady.

Rant

Wedged between the spare drumsticks sticking out of the holder attached to his cymbal stand was Jesse's phone. He glanced at it every thirty seconds during the first set. Every fifteen seconds during the second. Right before the gig, Caleb had called to quickly fill him in. Thailand was off. Joy was devastated. Wynter might be in Eugene. Indio was riding down to check. Jesse's head was spinning and then he had to hang up because it was time to go on.

At 9:04, the screen lit up.

> Indio has Wynter. She's
> safe. Call me ASAP.

They were a few bars into their penultimate number, Herbie Hancock's *Watermelon Man*, with six bloody minutes to go. Jesse managed another two minutes before forcing it to a close, pulling his confused bandmates along with him. He stumbled off the drum throne, grabbed his phone, and stuck his drumsticks into his waistband.

"Sorry guys. Sorry. Gotta go. Sorry..."

He jumped off the low stage and pushed through the tables, past startled patrons. He dashed out the front door of the club, punching his phone, and talked with Caleb while unlocking and getting into the Caprice, starting the engine, and backing out.

"Where is she? Is she okay?"

"She's okay. Indio picked her up in Eugene and he's taking her back to Portland on his bike. I'm gonna drive down there and meet them."

"No, no, no. Are you at home? Wait for me. I'm leaving Wallingford. I'll pick you up on my way through."

"You're done for the night?"

"Yes. Done. Great timing, dude. We just finished." He wasn't going to tell Caleb he'd fled the place — Caleb would make him return and complete the set like a professional and drive to Portland without him.

Jesse rushed home to find Caleb waiting on the street.

Caleb opened the car door and said, "I'll drive."

"I gotta pee."

"I locked up the house. Pee in the yard."

Jesse dashed into the far corner of the front yard and did as instructed. He got back in the car and Caleb drove off.

"So, she's out of the state on the back of a motorcycle in Indio's unsupervised company," Jesse mused, beating his drumsticks on his thigh. "Tina's gonna have a conniption."

Caleb said nothing.

"What did Indio say?"

"Not a lot."

"You didn't talk to Wynter?"

"No. She didn't want to. I'm thinking she's feeling a bit ashamed of herself."

"*Ashamed* of herself? You're confusing her with brother number two. That's not it."

"What, then? Why would she run? We never blamed her for the lies at school, did we? I was trying to be supportive about Thailand."

"Why would you do that, anyway? Why the hell would you encourage her to leave?"

Caleb flinched to hear Jesse cursing him. "That's not accurate. I didn't want to influence her either way, especially after she found out she'd be living on the other side of the country. She told me she thought she'd been greedy, all her life. Greedy for her mother, for attention. For love."

"She deserves to be greedy, after what she suffered." Jesse made up his mind, there and then, to spoil Wynter rotten once they got her back.

"I thought..." Caleb shook his head sharply. "I thought we'd all have time to come to terms with this, and instead she just ran away from it."

"She didn't run away. No matter what's going on at school or with Joy, she wouldn't run away from us." He'd been an idiot earlier, to allow himself to believe, in a panic, that Wynter would leave them. Leave him. "No. She was running *to* something."

"To... the Light?"

"Never."

"Well, I'm all out of ideas. *Stop that.*"

Caleb whacked Jesse's forearm and he tossed the sticks on the back seat, irritated he wasn't allowed to work off some nervous energy. Caleb had been punching that bag in the garage a lot more than usual lately, a sign he had some frustrations of his own.

Jesse scratched at his curls and stared out the window for a while. He couldn't shake the feeling that he was somehow part of this. Had he pushed her too hard? Did she hate him for those texts about Thailand? Was he supposed to *not* tell her about her impending exile at the amazing international school? Mostly what he felt was raw frustration that Wynter had been taken from them, forced to deal with everything alone. Compelled to keep secrets, apparently, and plot another escape.

"You should've never told Social Services about her," he blurted out.

Caleb watched the road with a hard, uncompromising gaze.

"The ashram never even reported her missing," Jesse persisted. "We could've just kept her. Who would've questioned it? We'd send her to school and just act like it was legit. I lived with you for eighteen months as a minor. You weren't my legal guardian. No one ever questioned it. She'd be living with us if you hadn't brought in Social Services."

"The clinic called Social Services. Should I not have taken her for a check-up?"

"She wasn't sick!" Jesse's throat closed up as tears threatened. He was going to die of humiliation if he cried in front of Caleb. "Everything was fine. That first weekend... She was learning to be happy, she felt safe, and they took it all away and you *let* them."

"It's pointless to think that way now. We have to look ahead and figure out what to do next."

"She should've been with us. She's had no one—"

"Okay, I'll let you rant," Caleb muttered.

"—her entire life. Not even Joy, evidently. You should've made sure she could stay with us. You're supposed to fix everything. You're supposed to make people do what you want. I could've helped her find real friends instead of fake ones. I could've—"

"Wait, what? Fake friends?"

"She said she made some online friends." Jesse's sense of unease grew.

"Can you log into her email account and see if there are any clues in there?"

"Uh, isn't that a violation of her privacy?"

"Do it."

Jesse tried logging into her account on his phone. "She's changed her password. Which I did tell her to do."

"I should've told her I wanted her to stay because of..." Caleb flinched again. "Love, not duty. I should've said that. Didn't want to put pressure on her. Miriam has a duty, too. I've no right to take away her mother's opportunity to have her. That's what I was thinking. We will bring her home, Jesse. But we have to play by the rules."

"That's bullshit. The rules say she can't even have a permanent custody hearing for six months. You think Tina's gonna just hand her over?"

Caleb swerved sharply onto an exit ramp.

"Are you pulling in to give me a lecture?" Jesse said, ready to stand his ground.

"I'm pulling in to get gas." Caleb threw him a sympathetic look to show he understood, even if he didn't agree.

They went into the store for a sandwich because Caleb hadn't eaten since lunch. In front of the counter were discounted long-stem roses in a bucket, chocolate hearts wrapped in pink foil, and fluffy white teddy bears holding love notes.

"I'm gonna buy her a Valentine's gift," Jesse said.

"Those little bears are cute."

"You're crap at gifts, you know that? She's not a teddy bear sort of girl."

Jesse went to the back of the store and found what he was looking for.

Valentine's Gift

Indio parked outside an all-night pancake diner in Portland.

"Hope you're hungry," he said, strapping down the helmets.

Wynter remained utterly bewildered by his sudden appearance at the bus station. "How did you find me?"

"We figured it out."

She waited while he messaged Caleb the address. The rattle of the motorcycle had knocked the trembling out of her, leaving numbness and confusion over the incomprehensible rules of the outside world.

"But how?" she persisted.

"We can thank Rosa, actually. She thought to check her credit card transactions. Caleb will be here in about an hour. Let's eat."

"Can't we wait in your apartment?"

He gave a crooked smile. "I don't think so."

"Is it not an appropriate place for me?"

"Probably not. I couldn't tell you from one minute to the next who's there or what they're doing. Come on. I'm starving."

They found a booth and dumped their jackets on the seat between them. They ordered pancakes from a server who knew Indio by name.

"This is the sister you told me about?"

"Yup, this is Wynter."

"What a cutie. You both get extra ice cream."

"You told her about me?" Wynter said when the server had left.

"Of course. I've told everyone."

"What did you tell them?"

"That I have a cool little sister I only just found out about, and she's a musician."

"I'm not cool. Nobody would say that."

"I just said that. You rock the guitar, so you're cool."

"Is that why you play guitar? To be cool?" She tried to sound interested — she *was* interested — but her voice came out flat and quiet.

"I wanted to play piano. Not keyboards. A real grand piano in a concert hall. Caleb had free lessons in elementary school for years but they didn't have space for me. I taught myself from his books, using Harry's old piano."

Wynter was hypnotized by his voice, the intense wistfulness so different from Jesse's earnest, animated explanations.

"Pretty soon I was better than Caleb," Indio continued, "and more interested in playing rock n' roll. Harry was always promising to pay for lessons. His promises weren't worth shit, of course. One day, he won big at the races and I thought it was finally gonna happen. He spent most of his winnings on liquor and a new scope for his rifle — he'd just lost his job so he probably should've put it to better use. He bought me a guitar with the last few bucks. I was disappointed at first. Turns out, he knew what he was doing. That's the guitar I gave you."

"Oh." A flush of despair heated her face. "I sold it this morning."

"Hmm. How much for?"

"Fifty dollars."

He scowled, sucking in air through his teeth. "That's a Fender Montara cutaway from the early 'nineties. Strat neck, convex back. Very rare."

"Very expensive?"

"Harry got a bargain. They go for four or five hundred bucks these days."

"Then why did you give it to me?" she cried.

"Why would I give you a crappy guitar?"

"And I stole money from Rosa, too. I'll have to repay her." Wynter pressed her hands over her face as the reality set in. "How am I gonna get ninety-three dollars?"

"Rosa can spare ninety-three dollars."

"Maybe she won't want to foster me anymore." Wait, that was a *good* thing. A sliver of hope made its way to the surface. "Maybe Tina will find me a new home, closer to Seattle."

"I don't think that's gonna happen. You have to accept living with Rosa until Caleb can get custody."

"What if he fails?"

"Caleb never, ever fails. I told you that already."

"What about Joy?"

"She's not gonna take care of you, baby. You have to accept that, too. Caleb used to say, people can only give as much as they're capable of, and it won't always be as much as you need. He was talking about Harry and Miriam, and maybe even himself."

And now Joy.

The food came. Indio showed her how to make pancake tacos stuffed with ice cream and strawberry "salsa" and drizzled with syrup.

"These are good," she proclaimed. "Not as good as Caleb's. Where do they get strawberries in February? Oh!" She clapped her hand over her mouth. "Jesse was looking forward to giving me my first strawberries in the summer. I've spoiled it for him."

"I won't tell him."

"*No secrets, no lies.*" She bit her lip, remembering all the secrets she'd kept and the lies she'd told.

"Not everything Caleb says is the law," Indio said. "Not everything Jesse says is the truth."

"That's the best I've got, though, isn't it? Out here where I don't understand anything. Caleb said I was strong enough — but I'm not."

"You were strong enough to reject Momma once you found out the truth. What she was offering, that was never gonna be enough for you. Nowhere near what you deserve." Pain hardened his expression and his voice went very quiet. "I understand why you were tempted to go to her. I would've gone, too. I don't think *they* would — Caleb's tied to his life here, and Jesse doesn't care about her at all — but I would go."

She pictured the six-year-old boy in the photo album, the one who didn't know yet that his mother wasn't coming back. How long had he held out hope? When did he realize he'd become nothing to her?

"She never said your name, or theirs. Not once," Wynter said. "She'll never ask you."

He touched her hand on the table, smiling grimly. "You understand plenty out here. You gotta trust yourself. You trusted yourself tonight. I watched you figure that guy out."

"Who was he?"

"He was nobody."

"Why did you hurt him like that?"

Indio exhaled heavily. "He wasn't quite nobody. He was somebody who was gonna hurt you."

She didn't want to think about that, about the hope that had buoyed her up for the past few days, and the disappointment that followed.

"Did you know…" She stopped, swallowed, and tried again. "At the ashram, there were somebodies who hurt me."

He squeezed her fingers. "I know you'll tell us when you're ready."

Now, more than ever, she expected questions. He waited, ready to listen, but she felt under no pressure to reveal more.

She said, "I've been trying to remember one moment of physical pain here on the outside. One tiny hurt. Anything at all. But there's been nothing. Even the cold doesn't hurt. But there's another kind of pain — this fear inside that I might sink to the bottom and drown. That I don't exist. I thought I left all that behind. Caleb made me feel like I exist. But it's still painful. They won't let me live at his house. The kids at school don't like me. I can't talk to Rosa. You and Caleb are fighting because of me. I felt like I was drowning. I thought I found a lifeboat — I thought I found my friend who escaped the Light."

She handed Indio her phone and showed him the messages on the homework forum and Roman's texts. He read through them in silence.

"Is this my friend Roman, or was it all a trick? The girl I met online, her uncle who's a private detective, Roman's friend Corey, and Corey's dad — was it all a trick?"

"I think so. It was all that one man. He figured out what you wanted and made you think it was real."

"The last time I saw Roman, they'd shaved his head. That was a few months ago, right before he escaped. So I knew the long hair was a lie. Roman wasn't waiting for me with a gift. There's no way Roman would think to get me a gift, anyway."

"D'you want to talk about him?"

"I want to forget all of it. The Light and everyone I knew there." *Even you, Xay.* "I want to forget what happened today, what I did and… what you did to that man. I shouldn't have run away. It just seemed like the simplest option. The right path."

"I understand that."

"Because you ran away, too. You ran to Ohio."

"I came back."

"If you're not talking to Caleb, then you haven't come back."

He tilted an eyebrow at her stubbornness. "I came most of the way back."

"I should've asked Jesse about it before I believed. He would've guessed it was a trick right from the start."

Indio directed her attention out the window, where the Caprice had pulled up.

"The first time I saw Caleb walking toward me in the dark, I was so scared," she said. "For a split second I thought he didn't see me. I wasn't even there. I was invisible or I was back at the ashram locked in a room and forgotten, having a strange dream. I'd dreamed up Jesse and the taste of hot chocolate and that wet cold air, and now I'd dreamed up Caleb. He was gonna walk right through me. So I stood very still and I *made* myself solid. I looked in his eyes and I *made* him see me. And he did. I was really there. And he was real. He was really there."

Indio was fiddling with the silverware. He flicked her a look and said, reluctantly, "He'll always be there. For all of us."

Caleb and Jesse came into the diner. Wynter got up and melted into Caleb's warm embrace. He'd never hugged her before and it felt exactly right. How could she ever have believed she didn't belong right here in his arms? She let Jesse give her a bear hug and, for now, avoided the confusion in his eyes. As she sat, she watched Caleb reach across the table to shake Indio's hand, knowing it would take more than a ride down I-5, more than her desperate desire for unity, to patch up their differences. The handshake was a start, or at the very least a temporary truce.

"Pancakes!" Jesse slid into the seat next to Wynter, eyeing what was left of the food. The server approached and he ordered more ice cream. "I'll show you how to make pancake tacos."

"Indio already showed me."

"Cool. You've done the country swing, you've made pancake tacos, you've played music with the Fairn Boys. There's one more thing you need to become a certified member of the family. Here."

He handed her a metal ring with two things hanging from it — a silver key and a charm in the shape of a space alien.

"It's a keychain, and that's a door key," he explained, like he thought maybe she didn't know. Tonight, perhaps he was right to suspect her ignorance of everything.

"What door does it open?"

"*Our* door, Wyn. Our front door in Columbia City. Jeez. Why would I give you a key to some other door?"

Wynter gave him a sheepish look. "Thank you, Jesse."

"And the alien is because... well, there wasn't much choice. I picked that because you and me are gonna work our way through four hundred and sixteen sci-fi movies over the next few years, starting with *Forbidden Planet*. I made the list weeks ago. Okay, on to the pancake tacos," he declared as the ice cream arrived. "Caleb invented these on June 27th, 1999."

"You remember the exact date?"

"My fifth birthday, a Sunday. We ate pancake tacos for lunch at Hotcakes Heaven. I was disappointed cuz they were all out of chocolate chip pancakes, so Caleb made the plain ones fun to eat. At five, I was easy to please. Then he took us to see a movie — don't remember what. We snuck into the theater for free."

"It was that animated version of *Tarzan*," Indio said. "Afterward, you made me tie a rope to the tree in the yard so you could swing on the jungle vines."

Jesse grinned. "I remember that. The knot slipped and I fell flat on my back. Winded myself. Caleb fixed it."

"Caleb knows his knots."

Wynter met Caleb's eye as their brothers reminisced. He'd been watching her and probably had a million questions. For now he didn't ask them, or say anything at all. The corners of his eyes crinkled as he smiled at her.

She turned back to Jesse, her one and only source of accurate information.

"What's a tarzan?"

THE END

More about the Wynter Wild series

books2read.com/saracreasy

Sign up to my newsletter for updates
saracreasy.com

(Note: Mild spoilers in the following descriptions)

LITTLE SISTER SONG (Book 1)

She's about to turn their lives upside down...

On a freezing Seattle night, teenager Wynter shows up on Caleb's doorstep in shorts and sandals, seeking help. Seeking sanctuary. Claiming to be his sister.

Caleb — Coast Guard hero with the perfect girlfriend — practically raised his two younger brothers. He always plays by the rules. He always wins. His duty is clear: give his little sister a home.

Pancakes for breakfast, rock music in the basement... Wynter knows she belongs here.

But when the authorities step in, will Caleb realize he needs to bend the rules?

OUT OF TUNE (Book 2)

Family is forever.

Wynter is struggling to find her place in the world. Now in foster care, all she wants is to move home with her brothers. Music rocks her world but she fails at the social rules required to befriend her peers.

Jesse and Indio find themselves competing for the title of Best Big Brother, while Caleb has a plan to gain custody.

When Wynter discovers the world won't bend to her will, she takes matters into her own hands.

RHYTHM AND RHYME (Book 3)

Gone in a heartbeat...

After 8 months on the outside, Wynter is gaining confidence as she opens up to her brothers about her childhood, and even manipulates their useless father into stepping up at last.

Yet her sister Joy finds life away from the cult increasingly difficult. She reveals a secret about someone from Wynter's past, forever altering the family dynamics.

When a horrific accident threatens to tear everything apart, will Wynter's dreams of a happy family be destroyed?

LOST MELODIES (Book 4)

No secrets, no lies.

Wynter finally has the home she always dreamed of when Caleb buys a ramshackle farmhouse on the mountain. With Jesse to guide her at every step (even when she'd rather he didn't), she has her first boyfriend, her first job, and a new band at school.

But one of her brothers is hiding a shameful secret. Just when her hopes of a united family seem possible... he's gone. And one by one, her successes are falling apart.

Wynter feels strong enough to handle anything. So why is she retreating into fantasy?

DISTORTION (Book 5)

The past taints everything.

Wynter has a safe home with her family. Her music career is taking off with an overseas recording opportunity and a new all-girl rock band. Her brothers could use some help.

Indio returns from London and there's a room waiting for him if he'll take it, as well as an old flame in the wings. Caleb has a new chance at love, and Jesse continues his search for the perfect girl.

Out of the blue, their mother Miriam returns seeking reconciliation. Her years of neglect have distorted her children's chances for love and happiness. Do they want closure on the past... or revenge?

NATURAL HARMONICS (Book 6)

When love makes sense...

Wynter and her brothers are ready to rock venues all over Seattle. No one can deny the natural chemistry Rule212 has on stage.

Behind the scenes there's tension brewing.

It's not easy to work, play, *and* live together. Family means everything to Wynter and she'll do whatever it takes to protect hers.

But something at the very heart of this family is ripping it apart.

No secrets or lies — it's one of Caleb's house rules. So why does everyone keep breaking it?

DUET (Book 7)

Two hearts yearning...

As Wynter and Jesse set out on an adventure-filled road trip to rescue Indio from drugs and despair, Caleb resolves to take control of his family as relationships deteriorate.

Meanwhile in Sacramento, Xay Morant lives with his ailing mother and a whole heap of bitterness over his year spent in the Light. He's doing okay, all things considered.

But he's never forgotten the girl from the ashram who used to climb through a hole in the fence in the dead of night to listen to rock songs on the radio with him...

MINOR KEY (Book 8)

A bittersweet tune...

Three years ago, Xay left Wynter to face the nightmare alone. She's been searching for him ever since — and now he's found her first.

Can he pick up the pieces of a past she's trying to forget?

As Wynter and her brothers prepare to head off on tour with their band Rule212, tragedy strikes this already wounded family.

Where will they find healing?

BROKEN STRINGS (Book 9)

Where does forgiveness begin?

A newcomer forces Wynter and her family to reassess their priorities. Meanwhile, her new bestie could be perfect for Jesse, and Xay has an opportunity to chase his rockstar dreams.

What could break the strings binding this family together?

Caleb, rock-solid, has never faltered... until now. To help him, Indio must find a way through his resentment. With Jesse hiding an impossible secret and Wynter forced into silent anguish, can they all pull together despite the pain?

THE BEAT GOES ON (Book 10)

Strong enough?

A mountain hideaway, an eccentric medieval tower, farm animals, homegrown veggies, and music all day long... Wynter's appearance in her brothers' lives rocked their world.

But something is holding them all back from the bright future they've worked so hard for.

The secret to unraveling the past lies in that off-the-grid commune in southern Arizona where, in her fourteenth year, Wynter met a free-spirited Aussie boy and his best friend who together changed her view of the world forever...

ECHOES (Book 11)

Sunshine and shadows

Wynter and her family have the chance of a lifetime to tour Australia. Every night they step on stage to make music, but offstage they're each dealing with their own challenges. As pressures build and nerves unravel, one of them suddenly vanishes without a trace.

As Wynter struggles to maintain faith in her family and in herself, a heartbreaking secret is sending echoes from the past...

TWELVE DAYS OF JESSEMAS (short story)

Christmas is Jesse's thing. Over the past four years it's become Wynter's thing, too. But these two siblings are growing up and growing apart. What happens when Jesse gets a better offer and decides not to come home for Christmas this year?

Short story sequel to the Wynter Wild series. Available at Amazon in Kindle Unlimited or ebook.

Short stories

WAITING FOR HER (a Fairn boys story)

Caleb is nine years old when Momma leaves him and his brothers at their estranged father's house for the summer. Dad doesn't have a clue how to care for three boys, and nor is he motivated to try. Navigating his moods and covering for his neglect are more than any child should have to face, but as the oldest brother, Caleb knows it's his responsibility to step up and grow up.

With his mother gone, taking his twin sister with her, Indio is battling anger and grief as well as the nagging guilt it's all his fault. Resisting Caleb's newfound authority, struggling to keep little Jesse out of trouble, he never gives up hope. Momma will be home for his seventh birthday, won't she? All he has to do is wait for her.

*Prequel to the Wynter Wild series. FREE when you sign up to my newsletter at **saracreasy.com***

THE FEAST THAT WASN'T (a Fairn boys story)

It's the Fairn boys' third Christmas alone with their father. The last two were miserable, but this year will be different—Harry's girlfriend has invited them to her family's Christmas Day feast! Jesse (5) anticipates gravy and pie, while Indio (9) is reluctant to get into the holiday spirit.

And Caleb (11) is learning that Harry's apathy could ruin everything. Can he inspire his brothers to make the most of the season and give them all a Christmas to remember?

Sequel to Waiting For Her. *Available at Amazon in Kindle Unlimited or ebook.*

About the Author

Sara Creasy grew up in a tumbling-down Victorian house in the Midlands, UK, tapping out her first stories on a tiny blue typewriter. After moving to Melbourne as a teenager, her love of all things fantastical hooked her on escapist drama. Then she grew up—but she still plays with words.

Her debut novel *Song of Scarabaeus* (Harper Voyager, 2010) was nominated for the Philip K. Dick Award and the Aurealis Award. The sequel is *Children of Scarabaeus*.

The Wynter Wild series, starting with *Little Sister Song* (2019), is a contemporary drama featuring musical siblings from bad beginnings who are navigating together through unanticipated life changes, revived family secrets, and the many meanings of love.

Visit her website at saracreasy.com where you can sign up to her newsletter WildWord and stay informed about what she's writing next.

Follow Sara on Facebook:

facebook.com/saracreasywrites

✿

Note from Sara: Honest reviews and word-of-mouth help indie authors like me get our books to readers who'll love our stories. If you'd like to leave a rating or review for my books on Amazon or Goodreads, scan these QR codes — and thank you!

Out of Tune (Wynter Wild book 2)
sample chapters

Re-education

In Wynter's pocket was the key to Caleb's house in Columbia City, Seattle. The key was attached to the space alien keychain Jesse had given her. But she was sitting in the truck with two of her brothers traveling in the opposite direction. To her foster mother's house in Richland.

"I can't believe they canceled your visit this weekend," Jesse said for the fourth time. He was skipping classes to join them — three hours each way — as a show of support.

"They" were Social Services — specifically, Tina, Wynter's social worker, who had dropped in that morning to find out why Wynter had run away the day before and taken a bus to Oregon. Wynter had told the truth, because Caleb was right there, although not the whole truth. She'd told them she didn't fit into this world. The girls at school didn't like her, which she admitted was partly her fault for lying to them. Their mother in Thailand didn't want her. Their sister Joy wouldn't take steps to file for custody. Caleb had said he would, but he was about to be deployed so it would be months before that happened.

So, she'd run. She'd thought she was running to Roman, her friend from the ashram in Arizona.

She told them all this, but she kept Xay to herself.

"I'll visit the first weekend in March," Caleb said. "And you'll be in Seattle for your birthday. After that, I'm pretty sure I can fit in one more visit before I leave."

"You don't have to," Wynter said quietly. "You have to teach your karate class on Saturdays."

"I can run that class," Jesse said.

"But then *you* won't be able to visit."

"We'll alternate." Jesse thumped his fist on the side window. "She can't just cancel your visit, though. That's gotta be illegal."

Wynter stopped herself whining aloud about it. Indio had told her to accept the way things were, and she was trying to do that. He'd also told her to make one promise to herself — and she had.

She'd promised herself to find Xay. Now, she set the promise aside. The universe had put up a clear roadblock on that path. When she could think straight again, she'd find some other promise.

"Let's deal with what we've got," Caleb said. "Wynter, I'll be home in June. I'll petition for permanent custody when you've been here six months. That's when you become a Washington resident."

Wynter did a quick calculation in her head. Six weeks ago, in early January, she'd arrived on Caleb's doorstep. Six months was early July, and until then...

"One hundred forty days." She sighed, wondering how many of those days it would take to make the girls at school like her again. After that, it wouldn't matter. In September she'd be going to her brothers' old high school in Seattle.

And how many days until Joy forgave her?

"Let's stop for lunch." Caleb took the off-ramp.

"Tina said we had to go straight to Rosa's. We're not even halfway back."

Caleb threw her a look in the rear view mirror. "Tina also said you need to put on ten pounds. There's an Italian steakhouse down the street here."

"The one with the carpeted floor?" Jesse said. "I don't trust a restaurant with carpet."

"Are you seriously saying no to spaghetti?" Caleb said.

"I'm saying no to eating on carpet. Who thought that was a good idea?"

Wynter smiled to herself at Jesse's habit of being contrary for the sake of logic, which didn't bother her at all because it was usually good-natured. She made the effort to put herself in a better mood, too. She had the key to Caleb's house in her pocket and in one hundred forty days she'd be going home forever.

✿

Jesse hadn't corrected Wynter, but it was one hundred *thirty-nine* days. She must've rounded up or made a mistake somewhere. Every day counted, of course, but today wasn't the day to criticize his little sister, whose mental arithmetic was generally pretty good.

He ordered a sixteen-dollar spaghetti entree. The carpet looked surprisingly clean, its bright detailed pattern presumably hiding the stains from a decade of spaghetti sauce accidents. He showed Wynter how to wind the noodles neatly on her fork.

He had to rethink her education. Table manners weren't high on *his* list, but Caleb considered them important and Wynter's skill in that area could use some work. Right at the top of his list, as of yesterday, was the dangers of the internet. He'd been taught about it since second grade but Wynter had never been to school until last month. Jesse had begun to fill her mind with the things he thought were important, but he'd gone about it the wrong way.

"We're going to start at the beginning again," he told her now.

"The Big Bang wasn't the beginning?" Wynter said through a mouthful of bread.

"The beginning of humanity," Jesse said. "Human nature. Emotions, friendships, social norms. Stuff the rest of us learn as kids. Winding spaghetti and *not* talking with your mouth full — I never thought those mattered at all, but..." He gave Caleb a nod. "Social acceptance, getting along with your peers, those things are pretty important."

"Thought that's why you were teaching me video games."

"There's more to it than that."

Jesse had never had trouble making friends, had never had to think twice about it. Wynter was from another planet, for all intents and purposes, and she needed to start with friendship cliques and school politics, popular culture, memes, all those cartoons he and his friends watched as kids that put their shared sense of humor into context...

"Is that why we're going to watch science fiction movies?" she said.

"Well, not really. We're watching those because you're gonna love them."

"I think you mean *you* love them," Caleb pointed out. "Maybe Wynter would prefer something else."

"I want to watch what Jesse loves," Wynter said.

"Those movies are good for the imagination," Jesse said, "and imagination is a very human thing. To fit in with your peers you need to broaden your musical tastes, too. We'll start there. I'll send you some playlists. Don't rely on Indio — we talked about that, right? No one at school listens to the Stones or Pink Floyd. And I'll find you some psychology websites. I need to do some research first, figure out a good starting point."

Wynter nodded, hanging on his every word as she sucked in a strand of spaghetti. The weight of his monumental responsibility settled on his shoulders.

"So you know," she said, winding another forkful, "Indio told me not everything you say is true."

Okay, perhaps not hanging on his every word.

A couple of hours later he sat in the truck on the street outside Rosa's house and watched Caleb walk Wynter to the front door and talk with her for a minute. When Caleb gave her a long hug, Jesse exhaled in relief and realized he'd been silently willing it to happen. Caleb had a few things to learn about social norms, too. Hugging your little sister goodbye when you weren't going to see her again for two-and-a-half weeks, which Jesse had done in the truck to avoid facing Rosa, didn't come naturally to Caleb.

The door opened and Wynter vanished inside. The small scowling woman who was pretending to be Wynter's mother talked briefly to Caleb on the porch. Jesse idly spun a plastic straw from the steakhouse through his fingers, glaring at Rosa. That beautiful house with its carved mantelpieces and marble countertops and didgeridoos would never be *home* for Wynter. She didn't even like her huge blue-and-white bedroom or the bathroom with the double shower all to herself. Caleb had told Jesse he had to be positive about it, to help her get through it. He could do that, but he would never warm to that woman.

Caleb jerked his thumb as he walked to the truck, indicating Jesse should take the wheel for the ride home. Jesse slid across to the driver's seat and Caleb got in beside him. They drove in silence for a while.

"Rosa seems pretty sympathetic," Caleb said at last. "She has some sort of... uh, therapy weekend planned for Wynter."

"It's a long weekend, too. Awesome! Wynter's one lucky gal." Jesse was careful to sound super-mega-hyper cheerful. "She's gonna enjoy that. We all know how much Wynter loves to *talk* about stuff—"

"Cut it out." Caleb had his elbow propped on the window, his hand rubbing his lower face as he stared out the windshield.

"You're getting the hugging thing down, so congrats on that."

Caleb gave him a sour look.

"What were you talking to her about just now?" Jesse asked.

"Joy told me Wynter threatened to do something terrible if Miriam made her go to Thailand. I was concerned what that might be. So I asked her if she'd threatened to kill herself."

Jesse's heart stuttered. "And?"

"She said no, nothing like that. She won't say what it was. But I couldn't get that idea out of my head. I had to check."

"She would never do that," Jesse said. "I mean, she might've threatened to do it, I guess, but she wouldn't do it. She loves learning. She's excited about the world. She wouldn't do it."

"Listen, I appreciate you taking her under your wing but go easy on the re-education camp, okay? She has enough to worry about with catching up on school work."

True enough. They'd put Wynter in middle school and Jesse wasn't happy about it. She should be in ninth grade.

"Figuring out how to make friends is important in eighth grade," Jesse said, playing devil's advocate.

"Getting up to speed for the high school curriculum is more important."

"It's *equally* important," Jesse conceded, eliciting a grimace of appreciation from his older brother. Regardless, Jesse ruined the moment with his next remark. "None of this is anywhere near as important as what she really needs, which is *you*. You should quit the Coast Guard and get custody now."

"Christ, Jesse, you don't quit the military. I signed on for three more years."

"If I was a few years older, I'd try for custody. If Indio wasn't such a fuck-up, he'd do it."

"How is this helping?"

Jesse clenched his jaw and sulked. Also, he wasn't entirely sure Indio *would* do it. Indio couldn't even keep his own life under control.

"Have you told her about Indio's arrest?" Caleb said.

"Would that be the possession of PCP tablets in Buffalo that wasn't his fault arrest, or the peeing in a churchyard arrest?"

"Either."

"No. I'll bet Tina can't wait to tell her when she finds out."

"She's about to find out about Buffalo because his background check came through. Fortunately, the more recent arrest isn't on it. I think Wynter should hear about all of it from Indio."

"Is that what you've told him?"

"He'll figure it out."

Jesse smothered a laugh. Caleb's high expectations alone weren't likely to make Indio do a damn thing. "Give me some good news," Jesse said, "cuz I'm about done with all this family drama."

"Our father claims he's getting married."

"*Claims?*"

"I've seen the ring on the lady's finger. We'll see what happens."

The obvious response was, *Why would anyone want to marry Harry?* Jesse bit down on it and turned up his '90s punk/dance CD loud. *Just* loud enough to fall under Caleb's threshold for retribution.

Spiritual Awakening

"I've had an idea for our special weekend together," Rosa said at breakfast on Saturday. "I notice you've pinned up that sketch your brother did. Why don't we go to the mall and find a frame for it?"

Wynter sipped her mug of milky tea. "I only have my twenty dollars allowance."

"And you'll have fifty dollars from selling that guitar."

Wynter scowled. Before getting the idea to steal Rosa's credit card number, she'd sold Indio's guitar to Giselle from her music class in order to fund her escape. She hadn't even received the money yet, but Rosa had already rung Giselle's mother to ensure the deal went ahead.

That guitar was worth hundreds of dollars and Wynter felt sick about it.

"I want to frame all his sketches," Wynter said. The sketches Rosa had deemed *appropriate*.

"I see." Rosa gave a brittle smile, like she thought Wynter was being deliberately difficult. "That will be expensive. You should save some of your money for later."

"You told me I could spend it."

"That's not exactly what I said." Rosa gave a deep, patient sigh. "I suggest you pick one sketch and get a large frame with a nice mat. Bring the sketch with you and we'll get advice about the color."

"I want to buy some Lego, too."

"Whatever for?"

"Jesse made these little Lego people to represent our family, but he didn't make Joy. I need to make a Joy figure. I don't want her to see the others in Caleb's house and wonder why Jesse left her out."

Antagonizing her sister was something Wynter was desperate to avoid. One week ago she'd threatened to bring the authorities knocking on the Light's door unless their mother let her stay in Washington. Joy hadn't spoken to her since, no doubt furious Momma was making Joy stay here as well. Wynter hadn't anticipated that response from Momma. And even though Joy preferred to spend her time with her new friends in the Light than with her family, she was still part of this family.

"I'm sure I have some Lego in the playroom," Rosa said. "We'll take a look when we get home from the mall."

Wynter wanted to take a look *now*. Lego was more important than picture frames. But she'd make the effort to get along with Rosa. She had to accept living here for the next few months. She would play by the rules.

She took Indio's sketch to the mall — the arched black cat prowling on moonlit rooftops — and they found a matted frame. Rosa took her to the food court for lunch and they talked about the girls at school whose friendships she needed to win back. Or if not those girls, some others.

Wynter gave the answers she thought Rosa wanted to hear. She'd be seeing those girls again on Tuesday, after the mid-winter break. Rosa assured her they knew nothing about her escape to Oregon or the man who'd tricked her into going there. All they knew was that she'd skipped school that Thursday afternoon. She planned to tell them she was upset about the prank they'd played that day, and that she'd met up with her brothers for dinner. All true.

Still, she had to agree with Rosa that her evasiveness wasn't going to help repair the friendships. The food court chat was turning into a therapy session. Wynter knew the signs.

"I have homework," she said when Rosa asked about her friends at the ashram and how she'd nurtured those relationships. No nurturing had taken place at the ashram.

Wynter found a hammer in the garage and escaped to her room to hang the picture. Then she snuck into the playroom — a room for younger children with a couch and TV and picture books — to look for Lego. She found a large tub at the bottom of the closet and dragged it out.

Eventually, Rosa found her. "There you are!"

"Why are there no pieces to make little people?" Wynter had been sorting through hundreds of tiny colored bricks for some time.

"That's all I have, I'm afraid. Would you like to make something else with it?" Rosa sat on the floor beside her, tucking her feet awkwardly under her body like someone who'd never sat on a floor in her life. "You can make anything you like."

Wynter had every intention of doing just that.

"And then we'll talk about it," Rosa added.

Great.

Wynter started building, hoping Rosa would leave. Instead, Rosa moved to sit on the couch and watched her.

"My church has a very friendly youth group on Sunday evenings.

They do all sorts of activities — dances, bowling, scavenger hunts, movie nights. I think it'll provide excellent social opportunities. Would you like to come to church with me tomorrow morning to meet the youth leader?"

"I'm not religious."

"You don't have to be."

"Jesse says religion is a crutch, generally patriarchal, and demonstrably untrue."

"He's certainly entitled to his opinion. Don't you want to make up your own mind?"

Wynter pressed bricks onto a small baseboard. She had friendships at school to fix before she could start on new ones at a youth group.

"I'll think about it." What she meant was, *I'll ask Jesse about it.*

"Do you believe in God?" she asked Jesse on Sunday morning, after telling him Rosa wanted her to come to church.

Her call had woken him up and he sounded distracted. "I don't believe in magic," he said.

"But what about God?"

"Same thing, Wyn."

"Does Caleb?"

"Is his belief gonna sway you, one way or the other?"

"Maybe."

Jesse yawned loudly. "He doesn't talk about it. I think he has some nebulous concept of God but he's not religious. You could call him."

"Can't you ask him? Is he awake?"

"I'm in Portland. Gotta call him, though, cuz my dirt bike's making odd noises. I'm going on a ride this afternoon when I get back."

"Rosa says I can explore my spirituality at church. Is that something I should be doing? What does that mean?"

"Let's define our terms." The opportunity to lecture her woke him up a bit. "Spirituality means finding meaning in something bigger than ourselves, something that inspires awe. Think about the universe and how amazing it is — the size of it, for starters. The structure of it, from nebulae and stars and galaxies and supergalaxies, and down to atoms and quarks. The way it formed and the things it's produced, like volcanoes and human intelligence and dirt bikes and endless beetles, and all the things we don't even know about yet. I'm *awestruck* by the universe."

"But what does it all *mean?*"

"Nothing at all. It exists because of physics. I can create meaning, though. I can study physics and create new knowledge. That's a spiritual experience for me."

Head or heart? Head, all the way, Jesse had told her when they first met. But physics couldn't explain everything, and Jesse *did* have a heart — his drum beat and his laugh, his ability to make her laugh. And the simple fact he cared about her journey in this world. If Wynter pointed all that out, he'd probably dismiss it with perfect logic.

Instead, she rephrased his own words. "You're saying that being creative is your spirituality?"

"Never thought of it that way before, but it sounds about right."

"Is Caleb spiritual?"

"Sure, when he's drinking single malt whiskey and listening to John Lee Hooker." Jesse chuckled to himself. "Actually, fixing my dirt bike will be like a religious experience for him. He makes things better than they were before, so in that sense he's being creative. Mechanics is his spirituality." He made a thoughtful sound. "I need to tell him that."

"What about Indio?"

"He's a little sidetracked right now, but he's obviously a creative person. Plus, he ponders the big questions like I do. Doesn't have my philosophical rigor, but he gives it a shot when he's sto... uh, when he's in the right mood."

A few minutes before they were due to leave for church, Wynter went downstairs to explain to Rosa why she didn't want to go.

"I've decided to explore my spirituality by being creative. Don't need church for that."

Rosa looked up from the paperwork she was sorting on the kitchen table. Her eyes narrowed suspiciously. "Did your brother influence your decision?"

"What if he did?" Jesse already had a few black marks against his name in Rosa's book, but Wynter would rather be influenced by him than by Rosa. "I don't *have* to go, do I? It's not in my behavior contract."

Rosa had to admit that it was not.

Wynter went to her room and sat on her bed with a guitar. Not Indio's beloved Fender acoustic-electric cutaway, which was locked up in the music room at school awaiting its new owner. Still, this guitar had its own unique feel and tone. The strings dug into her fingertips in that familiar way.

She was listening for the sound of the front door closing, indicating Rosa had left. She strummed through some chords, gazing at Indio's sketch on the wall, wondering how he wrote his songs and whether it made him feel spiritual. A new progression emerged. The beginning of a new song, perhaps. Something fifteen-year-old Indio might play, sitting up on a rooftop under the night sky, watching a bright-eyed cat stalk the moon—

Rosa burst into her room.

"Whose number is this?" Rosa's face was red, her entire body trembling with fury as she crossed the room with determined strides. She held up her phone, blocking the screen with her other hand — all but the number at the top. "This is absolutely unacceptable! *Do you recognize this number?*"

The tiny digits swam before Wynter's eyes. She didn't know anyone's phone number by heart. Why would Rosa think she'd know some random person sending her a message?

Wynter shook her head, not trusting her voice because her throat had closed up.

"Get your phone and check. Now!" Rosa hissed.

Wynter fumbled for her phone on the nightstand and opened the contact list. It couldn't be Caleb or Tina because those names would be in Rosa's phone. One by one, Wynter tapped the other names. Stacey Adams and Keira Grantwell from school. The clinic where she got her shots. The dentist. On the fifth tap, she found a number that matched.

"It's Indio."

Pink-haired Photographer

Indio emerged from his bedroom to find Jesse making coffee, badly, in the kitchen.

"You look surprised," Jesse said. "Anyone would think you forgot I drove down last night to see you play."

"I do remember." In fact, Indio's memories were quite clear because he'd drunk a couple of Jim Beams and that was *all*. Some kind of post-gig record. Still, he and Jesse had hardly spoken and he wasn't even sure how Jesse had made it to the apartment. "Did Turk bring you back?"

"Yup. Are you guys friends again yet? I couldn't tell."

"We're halfway there."

He and Turk were all the way there twice a week on stage and any time they jammed, but off-stage things remained subdued. Half Indio's fault — and he'd admitted to it — and half Turk's girlfriend's fault. *Ex*-girlfriend, following that weird night in January when they'd shared a joint that she somehow forgot to tell him was laced with opium. She'd tried for hours to get him off while he was barely conscious — enjoying it, but frustrated nevertheless at the discovery that opium's tendency to prevent orgasm was one of its two lesser charms.

Jesse said, "He took me to this lame rave first — only stayed twenty minutes. You would've hated it."

"I hate all raves, lame or not."

"Yeah, well, this one was particularly lame, and then Wynter called at some godforsaken hour this morning and I couldn't get back to sleep. Gotta say, I wasn't expecting to see you before noon. And you look stone cold sober."

"Trying to be good. Set an example."

"For Wynter?"

"Sure. Whatever."

"So you *don't* have a pink-haired girl with a New Jersey accent in your bed right now? The one sitting in your lap backstage?"

Indio scowled at his nosy little brother, elbowing him out of the way to open the refrigerator. "I'm cutting back on my vices one at a time."

"How come you never worried about setting an example for *me?*"

"You were never in danger of getting into trouble."

"What're you talking about? I've taken drugs. I got stoned last weekend for the fourteenth time. You never once told me not to take drugs."

"I figured you'd learn from my poor example. Ever peed in a churchyard?"

"No."

"There you go, then." Indio scraped old bacon grease into the trash before setting the pan on the stove to heat.

"I took LSD at that New Year's after-party thing you made me go to." Jesse was getting defensive, which meant he was going to ramble on for a while. "That's what they told me it was. It's supposed to expand your mind or whatever, but I couldn't get one thought straight in my head. Had a lengthy philosophical discussion with... someone, a male human, I think, and I'm sure it was brilliant but I don't remember a word of it. What's the point of that? I'd rather be clear-headed when I'm being brilliant. What is that — bacon?"

"Hickory smoked." Indio dropped slices of bacon into the pan. "My go-to hangover cure, not that either of us needs it this morning, apparently."

"If you're spontaneously cooking me bacon, you're gonna ask me for a favor."

"I need to sell a couple of my guitars. Can you deal with that in Seattle? Or bring them down here if someone in Portland shows an interest?"

"Sure, for a twenty percent commission."

"I'll give you a list and prices. Don't sell anything that's not on the list or I will break your fingers, drummer boy. I'll write an ad, too, so you may get strangers calling."

"That's fine. Sad, but okay."

"And no commission. I need three thousand dollars yesterday."

"Why would I do it for zero commission? I'm not stupid."

"Yeah, I know. You're *brilliant*. You'll do it cuz I told you to."

"This is bullying."

"I'm making up for all those times I never bullied you as a bratty know-it-all kid."

Jesse's look was calculating as he took a seat at the table, knife and fork in hand. "You're not gonna give me a list. You're gonna procrastinate. Caleb already paid those fines. And our dishwasher died on Friday and we can't afford to fix it. So, thanks for that."

Indio's phone rang, saving him from addressing the issue. He checked the screen. "What the...? It's Wynter's foster mother."

"Rosa has your number?"

"No. I have *hers* — Caleb made me put it in my phone." Indio answered the call warily.

"Indio? This is Dr Rosamund Meyers. I'd like to discuss the—"

"Where's Wynter? Is she okay?" Indio said, unnerved at hearing that woman's voice for only the second time ever. She sounded even more pissed off than last time, too.

"Wynter is fine. I'm sitting in the church parking lot right now..." Rosa's voice shook. "I'm sitting here attempting to calm myself down after that message you sent."

"Uh, I've never texted you anything."

"Half an hour ago! You sent a very inappropriate photograph. To *my* phone! This is not acceptable. I intend to report it to Wynter's caseworker. If you *ever*—"

"Hang on." Indio muted the call and gave Jesse a bemused look as he checked his sent messages. "Maybe I bum-dialed her or something. Oh... okay..."

He *had* sent Rosa a photo earlier — or rather, someone had. A photo of him sprawled in bed with the sheet pulled all the way down to his ankles. Fully naked, on his back, leaving nothing but his toes to the imagination. The message with the photo said, *Look who's a big boy now!*

Jesse choked with laughter as he took a peek. "Oh man, that's not good."

Indio glared at his bedroom door. "D'you remember her name?"

"Why would I know her name?"

Indio wracked his brain. "I think it's... Alannah? Ailene?"

Jesse gave an elaborate shrug. Indio unmuted the phone.

"Rosa, I didn't send it, obviously. I was asleep. Just someone messing around. I guess they sent it to a random name in my contacts list."

"I see. And what if this person had sent it *randomly* to Wynter? I haven't shown her, of course, or even described the nature of it. Still—"

"It won't happen again."

"That's simply not good enough. On Friday, I learned you have a criminal record in addition to the juvenile offense—"

"That's not relevant," Indio broke in.

"—and now... and now... *this.*"

Indio gritted his teeth as he forked bacon on to a plate and carried it to Jesse. "What d'you want me to say, Rosa? It's a picture of me doing nothing. I apologize if it traumatized you."

He hung up and tossed the phone on the table. Probably not the best way to end the conversation.

"Doing *nothing?*" Jesse grabbed the phone and tapped his way to the photo. "One particular part of you is doing *something*, bro. That's not PG-13. That's a little bit o' morning wood. That's a sexually explicit image, a sext, a dick pic, a moderately pornographic—"

Indio clipped his ear to shut him up. "You're lucky I didn't blame it on you."

"Thanks for nothing." Jesse crunched on a piece of bacon. "And if an apology includes the word *if*, it's not an apology."

"Why would I apologize for something that's not my fault!"

"I wonder if she ever drives with the top down," Jesse mused, tapping his fork against his greasy lips.

"What?"

"She drives a convertible. Totally the wrong look for her but, y'know, maybe not. Maybe she's a tight ball of pent-up sexual frustration underneath that frigid exterior, yearning to break free and express her sensual nature. That picture could be, like, *therapy* for her. You could be her sex therapist."

"What the fuck are you talking ab—?"

The bedroom door opened and the girl from last night sauntered out wearing her bra and panties and nothing else, her hair a pink cloud around her face.

"Oh! Didn't realize you had company." She grinned at Jesse.

"Morning, Alannah," Jesse said breezily.

"Close." The girl sneered at Indio, blaming him for Jesse's error, but she was still smiling. "It's Eleanor." She wrapped her arms around Indio's waist from behind.

"Did you take a photo on my phone?" Indio said, unwinding her arms before sliding onto a chair. He dragged it close to the table in case she had any ideas about sitting in his lap again.

"I did! You looked so cute, like a little boy. I sent it to your mom. Couldn't help myself. She didn't mind, did she?"

"That wasn't my mom. That was my sister's foster mom and she minded very much."

Eleanor clamped her hand over her mouth to suppress her giggles. "Oh my god, I'm so sorry. I saw *Mom* on the list and just went for it."

"It says *W Foster Mom*," Jesse pointed out, showing her Indio's contacts list.

Eleanor simpered. "I was half asleep. Am I in trouble?"

"Could you get dressed?" Indio said. "I have to be somewhere in fifteen minutes."

She looked at him shrewdly, assessing whether he was being truthful. He was not.

"You want me to call you an Uber?" he added, to hurry her along.

Eleanor's lips twisted into a pout. "I can walk home from here."

"Awesome." It was forty degrees with rain threatening, but that wasn't Indio's fault either.

Her eyes flicked to the phone. "Um... So, I had a nice time. I'm a huge fan and... Can I give you my number?"

"I think you've done enough damage," Indio said with a tight smile.

"You're supposed to offer to walk her home," Jesse said when Eleanor had disappeared into the bathroom.

"What century are you from? *You* walk her home."

"For twenty percent commission on those guitars, I will."

An Inconvenient Friendship

"I've decided to forgive you for the lies about your family in Montana, and moving to Thailand, and your nonexistent cat, and for running out on us at the movies when we were trying to be nice, and for being a bad friend," Stacey said at the lockers.

She and her friends had barely acknowledged Wynter in the two weeks since she ran away. This was progress.

"I've decided to forgive you for that Valentine's Day prank," Wynter said, mimicking Stacey's tone.

"Oh, you should be grateful for that. One of those boys might've asked you out. Two of them think you're cute." She looked Wynter up and down as if trying to figure out why. "Aren't you going to ask which two?"

"No." Wynter grabbed her books and reconsidered her attitude. "But thanks, anyway, for forgiving me."

"You're welcome. I forgive you out of Christian love."

"How is that different from regular love?"

"We're all children of God. So, no matter what you do, I have to love you like a sister."

"You *have* to?"

"Yes, even though you're not a Christian. I have Christian sisterly love for you."

"I'd rather you forgave me out of regular love."

Stacey tossed her head impatiently. "Anyway. We're friends again, so invite me to your house tomorrow for a study night and sleepover. I'd ask you over but my grandma lives with us. She has her Bridge ladies over on Fridays and we'd have to talk to all the boring old people. I wouldn't put you through that."

A sleepover might be a decent way to repair the friendship. Although Wynter didn't mind eating lunch alone with a book every day, she was supposed to be making an effort with the girls at school. She did need Stacey to be gone by noon Saturday because Caleb was visiting.

Rosa was pleased about the sleepover and made a big fuss of Stacey when her mom drove her over after school on Friday. The study session lasted about an hour, after which Stacey wanted to gossip about kids at school Wynter didn't care about and Hollywood celebrities Wynter had never heard of.

"I have something in my bag you're gonna love," Stacey said, sitting with Wynter on the floor of her room. Stacey's fancy floral overnight bag was huge — Wynter couldn't possibly imagine what was in it. What could anyone need other than a toothbrush, PJs, and a change of underwear?

Stacey retrieved a zip-up pencil case from the bag and spilled its contents onto the rug between them — a dozen skeins of embroidery thread in various colors and a handful of wooden beads. Wynter's stomach dropped when she realized what it was all for.

"See? We can make each other friendship bracelets, like that one you always wear. Who made yours? It looks really old."

"A friend in Arizona."

"A hippie friend on the commune?" She giggled.

"Yes."

In fact, Wynter had made it herself, one of thousands, and it had no sentimental value. They weren't called friendship bracelets in the Light. They were called meditation bands and often had metal protection and healing charms woven into them that cost three cents each from a factory in China. The Light sold the finished bands online for twenty-five dollars.

She felt bad about the lie for three seconds before deciding it was what Caleb would call a privacy issue.

"I've made bracelets before — narrow ones," Stacey said. "Can you make me a wide one like that? You're supposed to wear them until they fall off, right? So a wide one will last for ages. I'm sorry about making fun of you, Wynter. The school counselor called my mom and explained why you lied and that we should be nicer to you. I mean, you seem nice enough and I do feel bad for you, growing up without TV."

Wynter sorted through the irrelevancies in Stacey's natter to focus on one point. "What did the counselor tell your mom?"

"That you were a foster kid and made up stuff as a sort of wish fulfilment thing."

Foster kid. She hated the sound of that. She wasn't supposed to be in foster care at all.

She wove a wide cuff for Stacey, letting her pick the colors and beads, while Stacey made her an unevenly braided narrow one and forgot to add beads until it was finished and it was too late.

Stacey was happy with the result anyway. "I'll dangle some beads off the ends after I've tied it on you."

If Wynter had forgotten to add the required charms and beads as she wove bands for the Light, she'd have stayed up all night redoing it with hands sore from a caning. She told Stacey the bracelet was pretty and they tied the finished bands on each other's wrists. They watched an episode of Stacey's favorite TV show about a girl in high school and Stacey spent the entire hour explaining the backstory of every character. Wynter found it hard to concentrate on the storyline. The girl's main concerns were whether to cheat on an upcoming test (she didn't) and whether to use tongue when kissing her boyfriend (she did).

Wynter was ready for Stacey to go home by ten, but this was a sleepover. Wynter's bed had another bed underneath it, which she hadn't realized until Rosa showed her how to pull it out. There were several other bedrooms in Rosa's house and Wynter would rather Stacey slept in one of those.

"Let's go to the mall tomorrow," Stacey said as they finished up in the bathroom. "Rosa can drop us off and my mom says she'll pick us up at two and bring you home."

"My brother Caleb's visiting tomorrow, so you have to leave at midday."

"Is that one of the rockstar brothers? Oh, wait, was that a lie? I can't keep track." Stacey giggled, like she thought the whole thing was trivial. It hadn't been trivial to Wynter, at the time.

"Two of my brothers do play in bands." Wynter stuck to the facts this time. "Caleb used to. He's in the Coast Guard."

"Is he old?"

"He's twenty-five."

"Ugh, that's old. But my mom loves a man in uniform."

Wynter wrinkled her nose, heading for the bedroom and wondering how Stacey's mother was relevant to anything. "He won't be wearing his uniform."

"What about the other two?" Stacey asked, arranging three pillows and a stuffed bunny on her bed.

"They're in college. Jesse's going to be an electrical engineer and Ind—"

"Ooh, is he really smart?"

"Yes. He knows all about physics and computers, and he's teaching me philosophy."

Stacey's face dropped. "A nerd, then. I bet he's a *real* interesting conversationalist."

Wynter was about to confirm this when she realized Stacey was being sarcastic. She pressed her lips shut and slid into bed with mounting trepidation. There was a fifty percent chance she'd have a nightmare and give Stacey fodder for teasing and gossip. She wasn't entirely sure Stacey even liked her.

She woke suddenly in the night, not remembering whether she'd had a bad dream, but her heart was racing. She breathed quietly, carefully, until she calmed down. As she drifted back to sleep she fingered her new friendship bracelet, hoping it would fall off soon.

✿

"You should absolutely go to the mall with Stacey," Rosa said over breakfast. "What a good idea. I'll give you money for two more school shirts, to save me doing laundry in the middle of the week."

Stacey gave a silent *harrumph*, which told Wynter she didn't want to shop for school clothes.

"I need to be here when Caleb arrives, otherwise it's a waste of his time," Wynter said.

Stacey was horrified. "I can't get through the entire mall in one hour!"

"What do you need to buy?"

"Nothing. That's not the point."

Wasn't that exactly the point?

"I'll get the shirts," she said, "and you can go to the store you want, and we're done."

"I need to teach you how to shop," Stacey grumbled. It sounded like something Jesse would say, not that Wynter knew if Jesse knew how to shop. Even if he didn't, she'd rather learn shopping from Jesse than from Stacey.

Rosa dropped them off. Stacey insisted they go to a fashion store first and then three jewelry stores, two of which had nothing under two hundred dollars. In the third store, Stacey spent fifteen minutes trying on rings. She already had lots of thin rings stacked on her fingers and was adamant she needed another. Wynter watched the clock and calculated when they needed to call Rosa so she still had time to get the shirts and be home on time.

At twenty minutes to noon, Wynter called Rosa to pick them up. If Rosa left the house immediately, they should be back in time.

"Are you gonna call your mom to have her pick you up?" Wynter asked Stacey in the department store.

"I already texted her. She says I can stay for lunch."

That wasn't part of the plan. Wynter grabbed two shirts that were identical to the ones she already had and they met Rosa in the parking lot.

"I've let Caleb know he may have to wait outside the house a few minutes if he's early," Rosa said.

"You could drop Stacey off home on the way," Wynter said.

"Don't be silly," Stacey scoffed. "All my stuff is at your house.

Mom says I can stay until four as long as we do two more hours of study."

So, "lunch" had turned into *four more hours.* Friendships were altogether too inconvenient.

"Oh my god, who's *that?*" Stacey cried as they pulled into the driveway.

Wynter leaned over to look out of Stacey's window. Instead of Caleb's Silverado truck, it was Jesse's Caprice in the driveway. Caleb and Jesse were up on the porch. Wynter opened her door before the car had even stopped, ignoring Rosa's exclamations, and raced up the driveway to fling herself on Jesse.

"What are you doing here? You didn't tell me!"

Jesse laughed. "Surprise?"

"What about karate?"

"We sorted something out," Caleb said.

She gave him a hug too, and then she was forced to deal with Stacey who had made her way to the porch. She introduced them while Rosa unlocked the house.

Stacey ignored Caleb and stepped up close to Jesse, tilting her face to examine him. "Wynter's talked about you a bit. I thought you'd be a super-nerd, but you don't look like one."

Jesse feigned indignation. "I sure am a super-nerd. Left my coke-bottle glasses at home."

Out of Tune (Wynter Wild book 2)

books2read.com/saracreasy